A CHRISTOPHER ELIOPO

COLORED BY REBECCA NALTY

MONSTER MAYHEM

DIAL BOOKS FOR YOUNG READERS

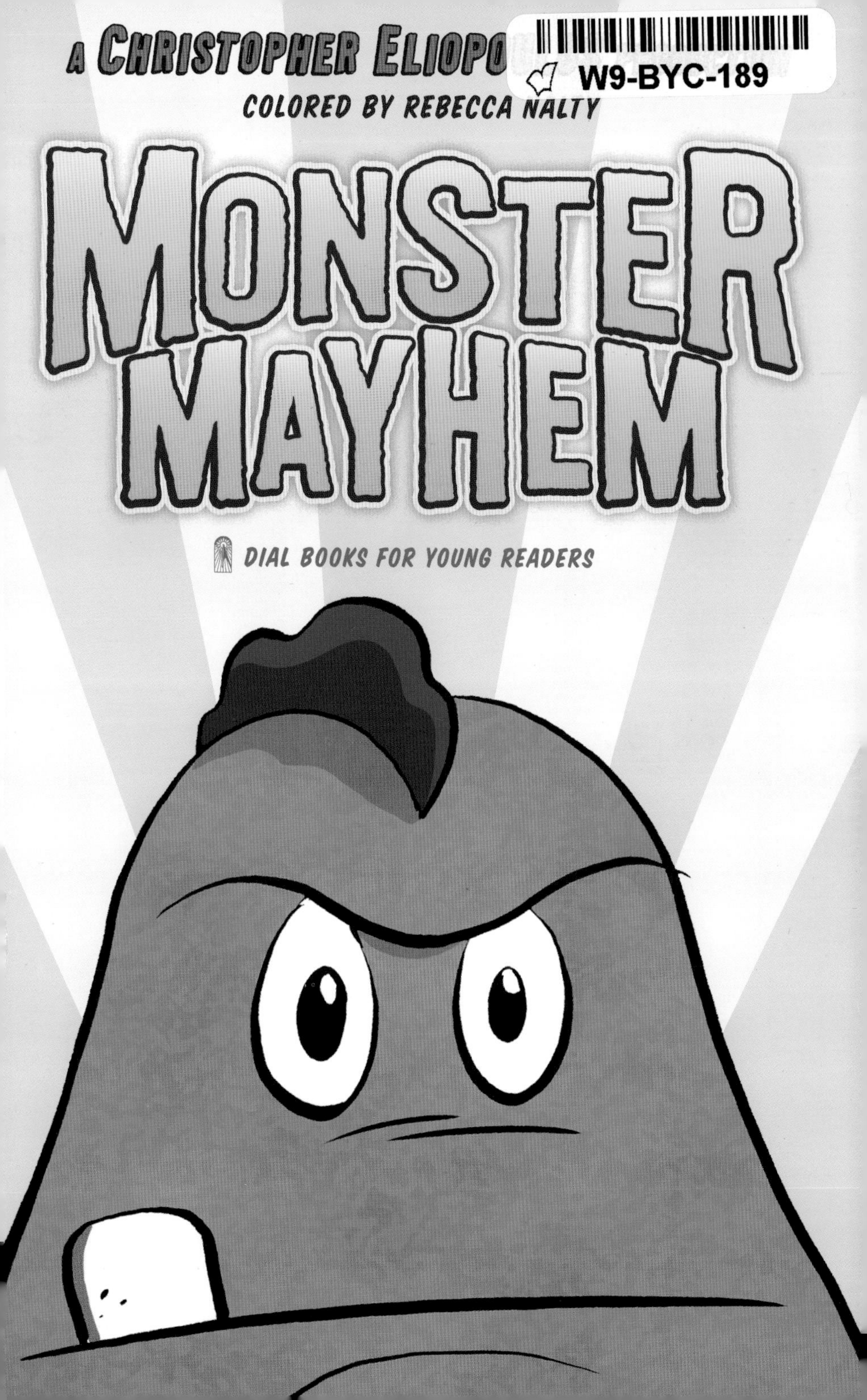

For Jeff, Tommy, Xan, Matt, Nick, Mike, Joey,
Brendan, Eva, Chloe, Lucine, Anna, Kelsey,
Caroline, and Susy. Jeremy and Justin are
lucky to have you as friends.

DIAL BOOKS FOR YOUNG READERS
An imprint of Penguin Random House LLC, New York

Copyright © 2018 by Christopher Eliopoulos
First paperback edition, 2020

Visit us online at penguinrandomhouse.com

THE LIBRARY OF CONGRESS HAS CATALOGED THE DIAL HARDCOVER EDITION AS FOLLOWS:
Names: Eliopoulos, Chris, date, author, illustrator. | Title: Monster mayhem / Christopher Eliopoulos. | Description: New York, NY : Dial Books for Young Readers, [2018] | Summary: "Science-obsessed Zoe finds herself trapped in one of her favorite monster movies and needs to invent her way out of a disaster while also saving the monster who has become her friend"—Provided by publisher. | Identifiers: LCCN 2017059554 | ISBN 9780735231245 | Subjects: LCSH: Graphic novels. | CYAC: Graphic novels. | African Americans—Fiction. | Monsters—Fiction. | BISAC: JUVENILE FICTION / Science & Technology. | JUVENILE FICTION / People & Places / United States / African American. | Classification: LCC PZ7.7.E44 Mon 2018 | DDC 741.5/973—dc23 | LC record available at https://lccn.loc.gov/2017059554

ISBN 9780593110034
Printed in China • 10 9 8 7 6 5 4 3 2

Design by Jason Henry • The artwork for this book was created digitally.

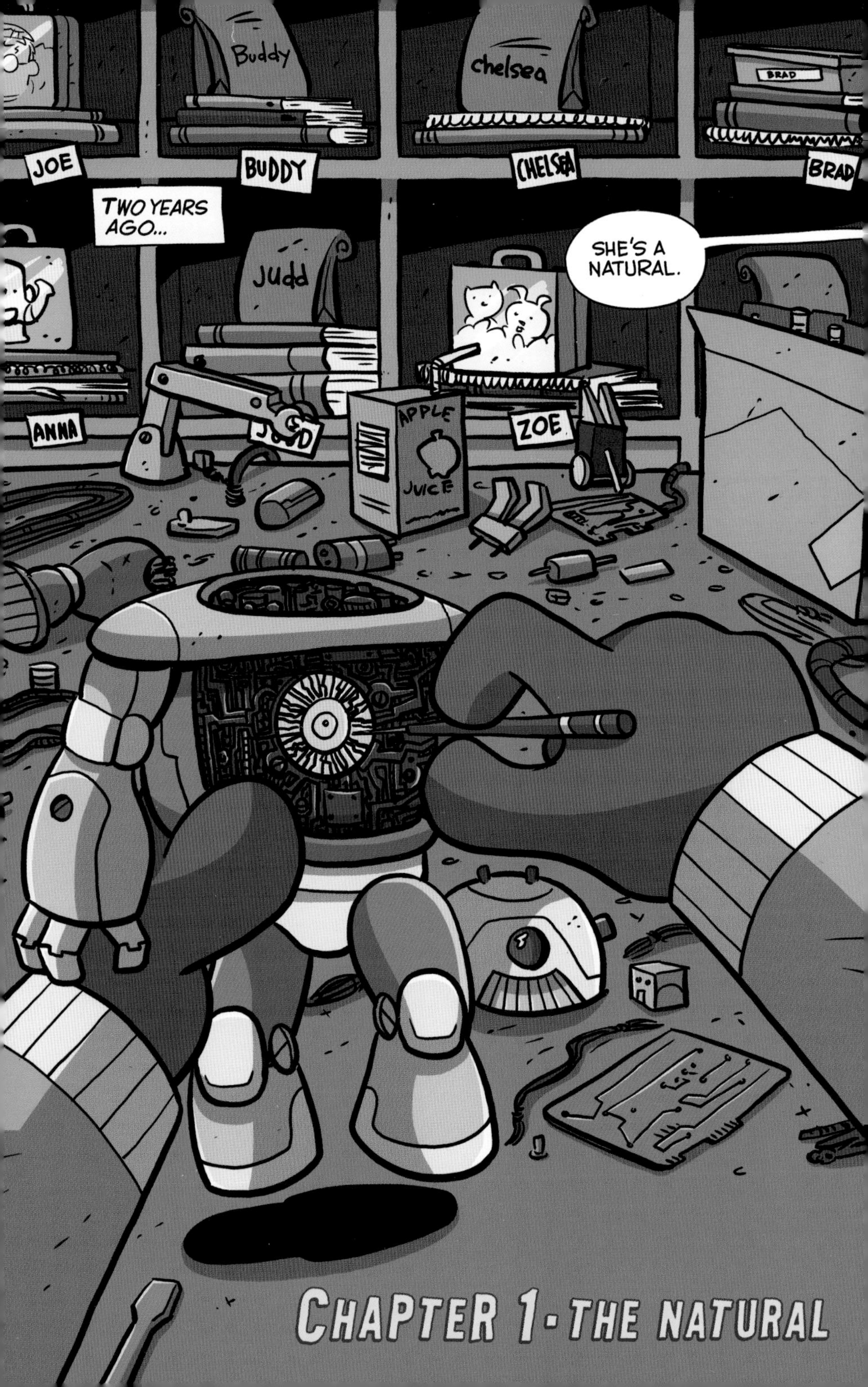
Buddy
chelsea
BRAD
JOE
BUDDY
CHELSEA
BRAD
TWO YEARS AGO...
SHE'S A NATURAL.
Judd
ANNA
JUDD
ZOE
APPLE JUICE
CHAPTER 1 - THE NATURAL

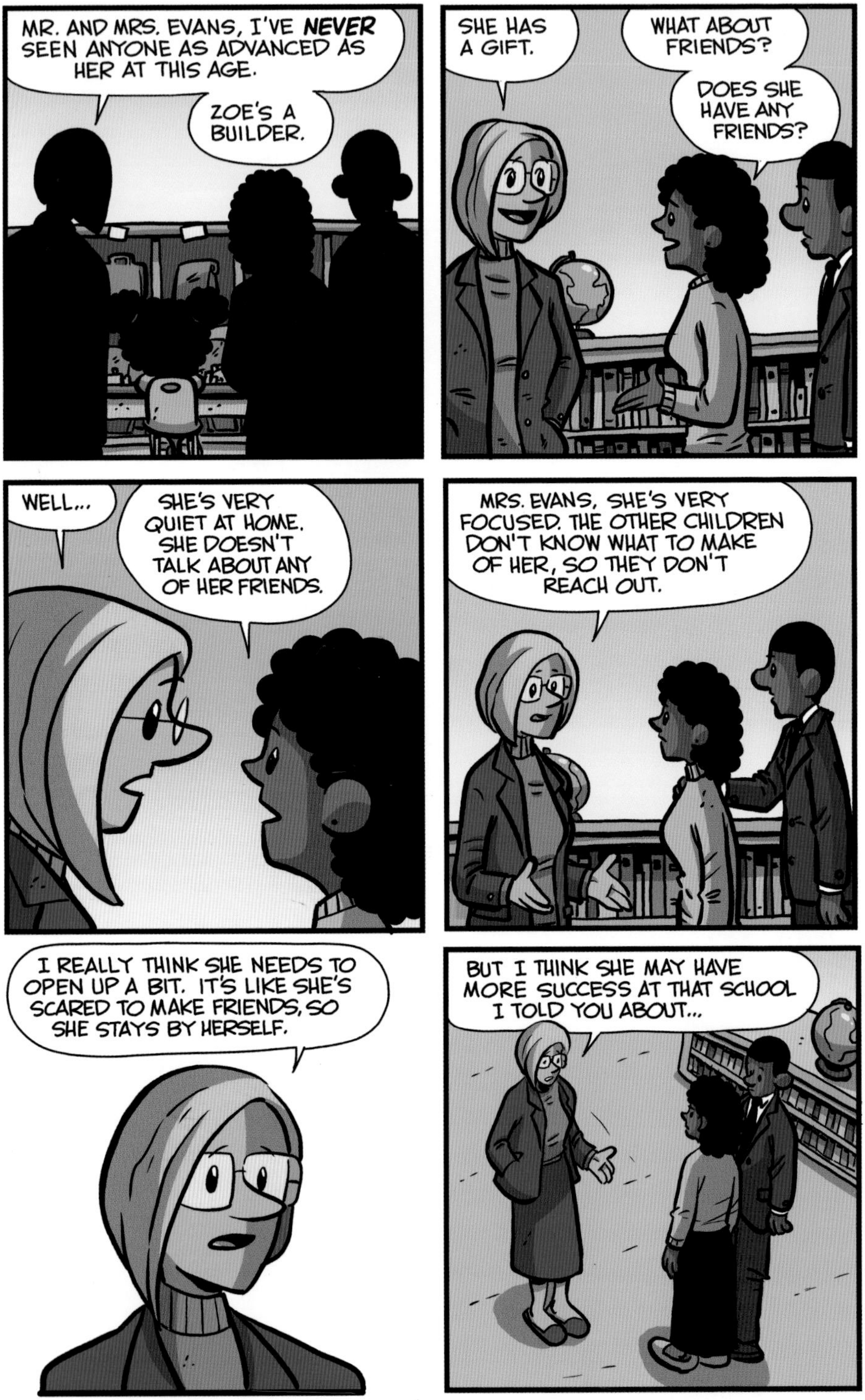
MR. AND MRS. EVANS, I'VE NEVER SEEN ANYONE AS ADVANCED AS HER AT THIS AGE.
ZOE'S A BUILDER.
SHE HAS A GIFT.
WHAT ABOUT FRIENDS?
DOES SHE HAVE ANY FRIENDS?
WELL...
SHE'S VERY QUIET AT HOME. SHE DOESN'T TALK ABOUT ANY OF HER FRIENDS.
MRS. EVANS, SHE'S VERY FOCUSED. THE OTHER CHILDREN DON'T KNOW WHAT TO MAKE OF HER, SO THEY DON'T REACH OUT.
I REALLY THINK SHE NEEDS TO OPEN UP A BIT. IT'S LIKE SHE'S SCARED TO MAKE FRIENDS, SO SHE STAYS BY HERSELF.
BUT I THINK SHE MAY HAVE MORE SUCCESS AT THAT SCHOOL I TOLD YOU ABOUT...

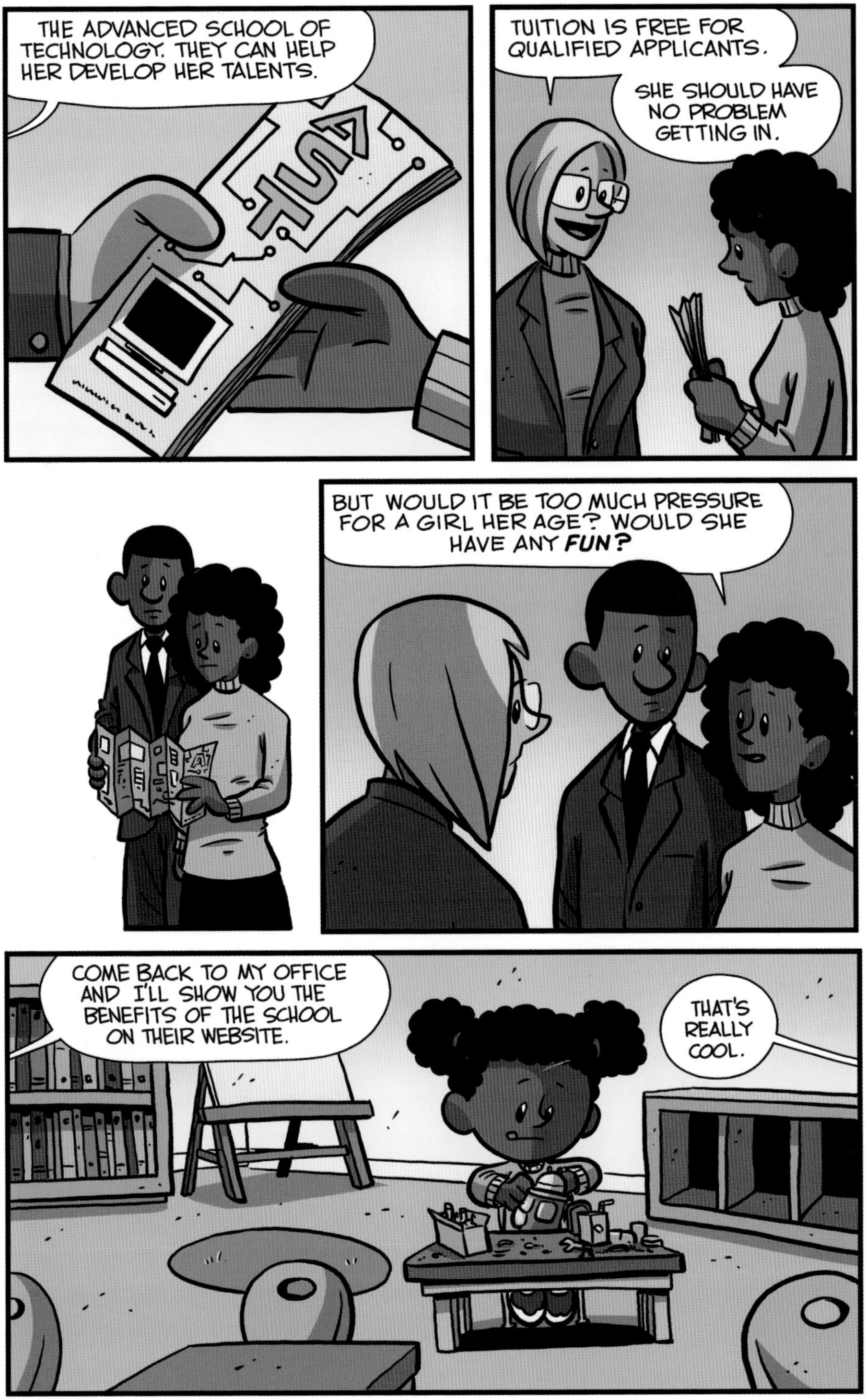
THE ADVANCED SCHOOL OF TECHNOLOGY. THEY CAN HELP HER DEVELOP HER TALENTS.
AST
TUITION IS FREE FOR QUALIFIED APPLICANTS.
SHE SHOULD HAVE NO PROBLEM GETTING IN.
BUT WOULD IT BE TOO MUCH PRESSURE FOR A GIRL HER AGE? WOULD SHE HAVE ANY FUN?
COME BACK TO MY OFFICE AND I'LL SHOW YOU THE BENEFITS OF THE SCHOOL ON THEIR WEBSITE.
THAT'S REALLY COOL.

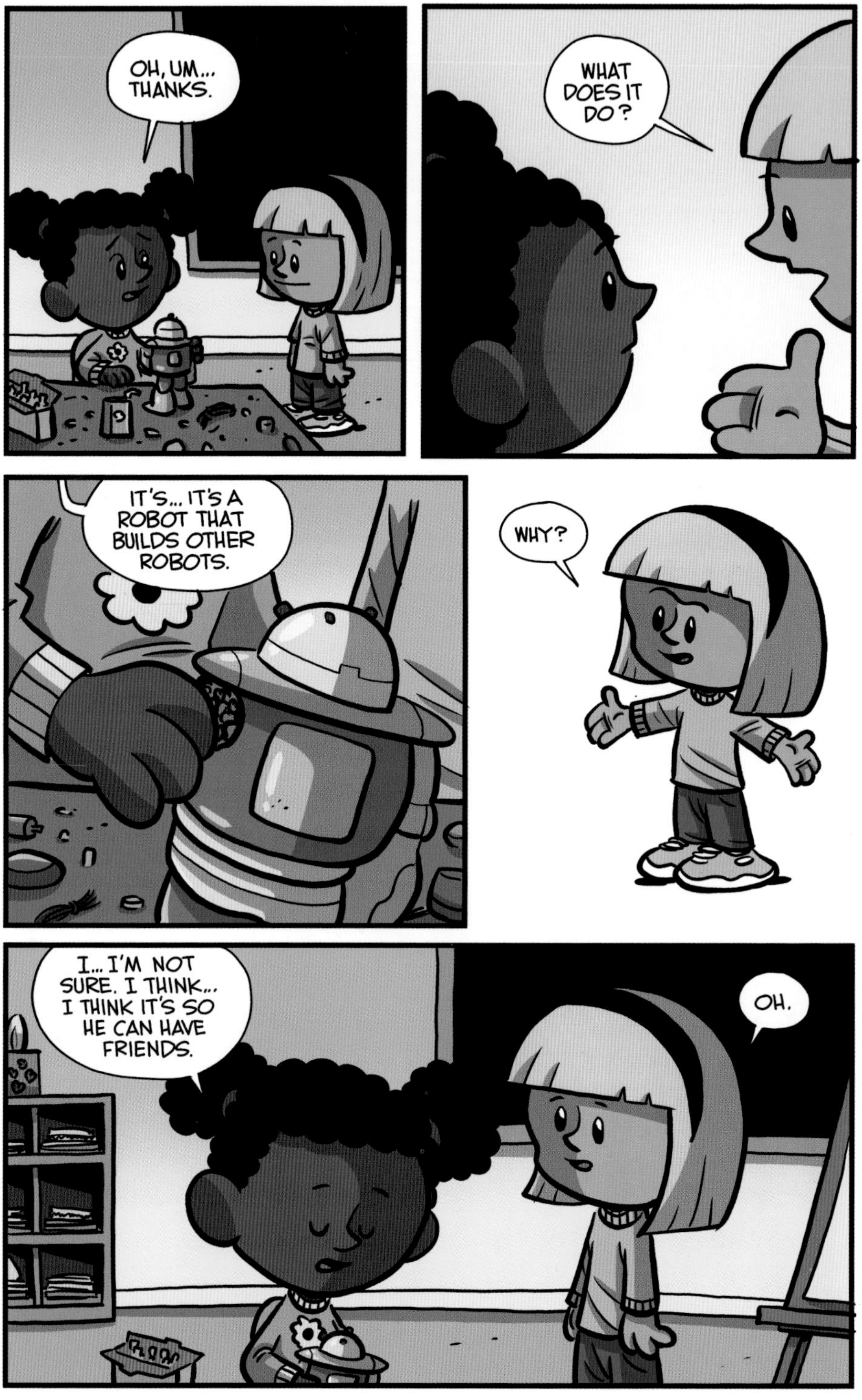
OH, UM... THANKS.
WHAT DOES IT DO?
IT'S... IT'S A ROBOT THAT BUILDS OTHER ROBOTS.
WHY?
I... I'M NOT SURE. I THINK... I THINK IT'S SO HE CAN HAVE FRIENDS.
OH.

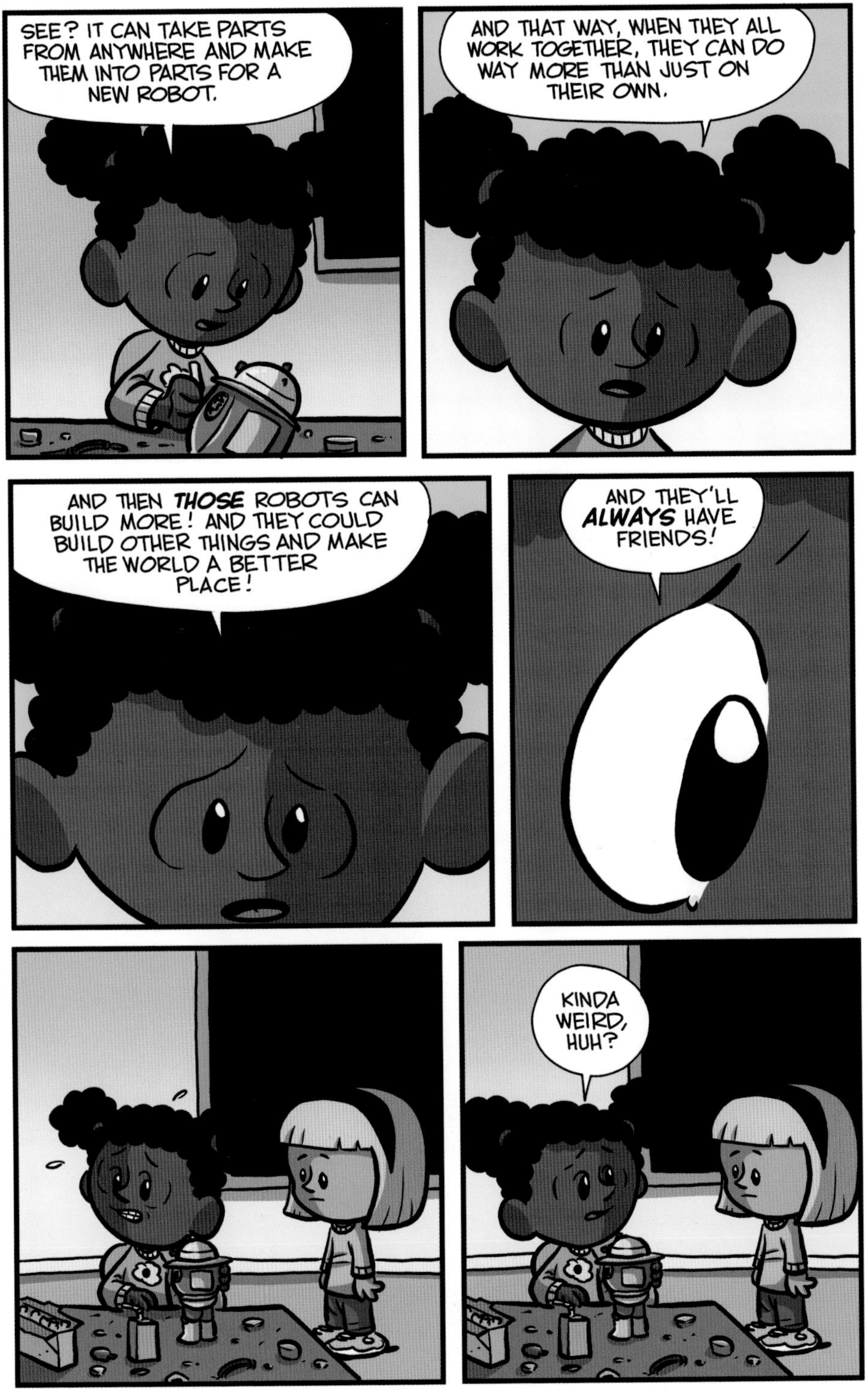
SEE? IT CAN TAKE PARTS FROM ANYWHERE AND MAKE THEM INTO PARTS FOR A NEW ROBOT.
AND THAT WAY, WHEN THEY ALL WORK TOGETHER, THEY CAN DO WAY MORE THAN JUST ON THEIR OWN.
AND THEN ***THOSE*** ROBOTS CAN BUILD MORE! AND THEY COULD BUILD OTHER THINGS AND MAKE THE WORLD A BETTER PLACE!
AND THEY'LL ***ALWAYS*** HAVE FRIENDS!
KINDA WEIRD, HUH?

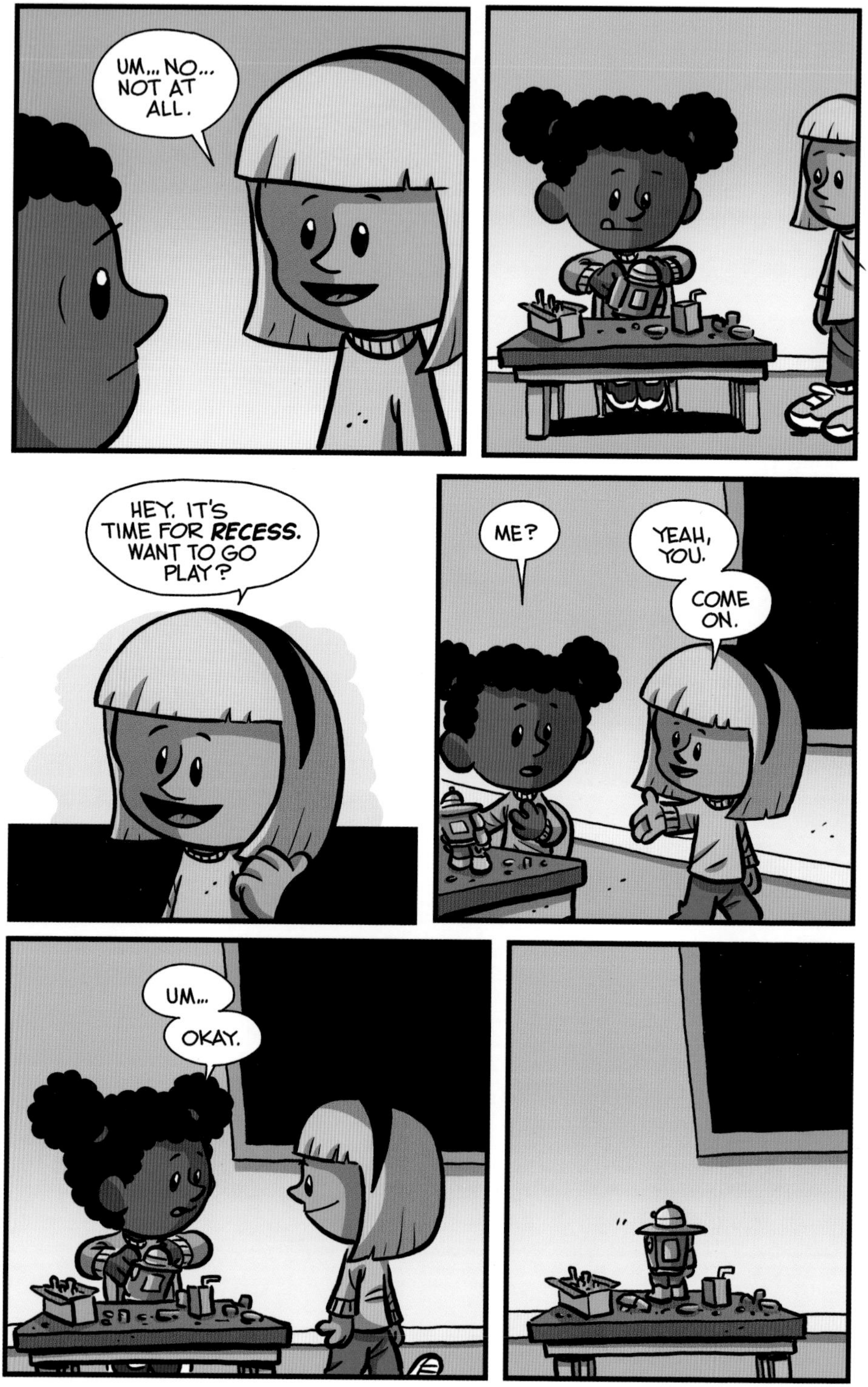
UM... NO... NOT AT ALL.
HEY. IT'S TIME FOR **RECESS.** WANT TO GO PLAY?
ME?
YEAH, YOU.
COME ON.
UM...
OKAY.

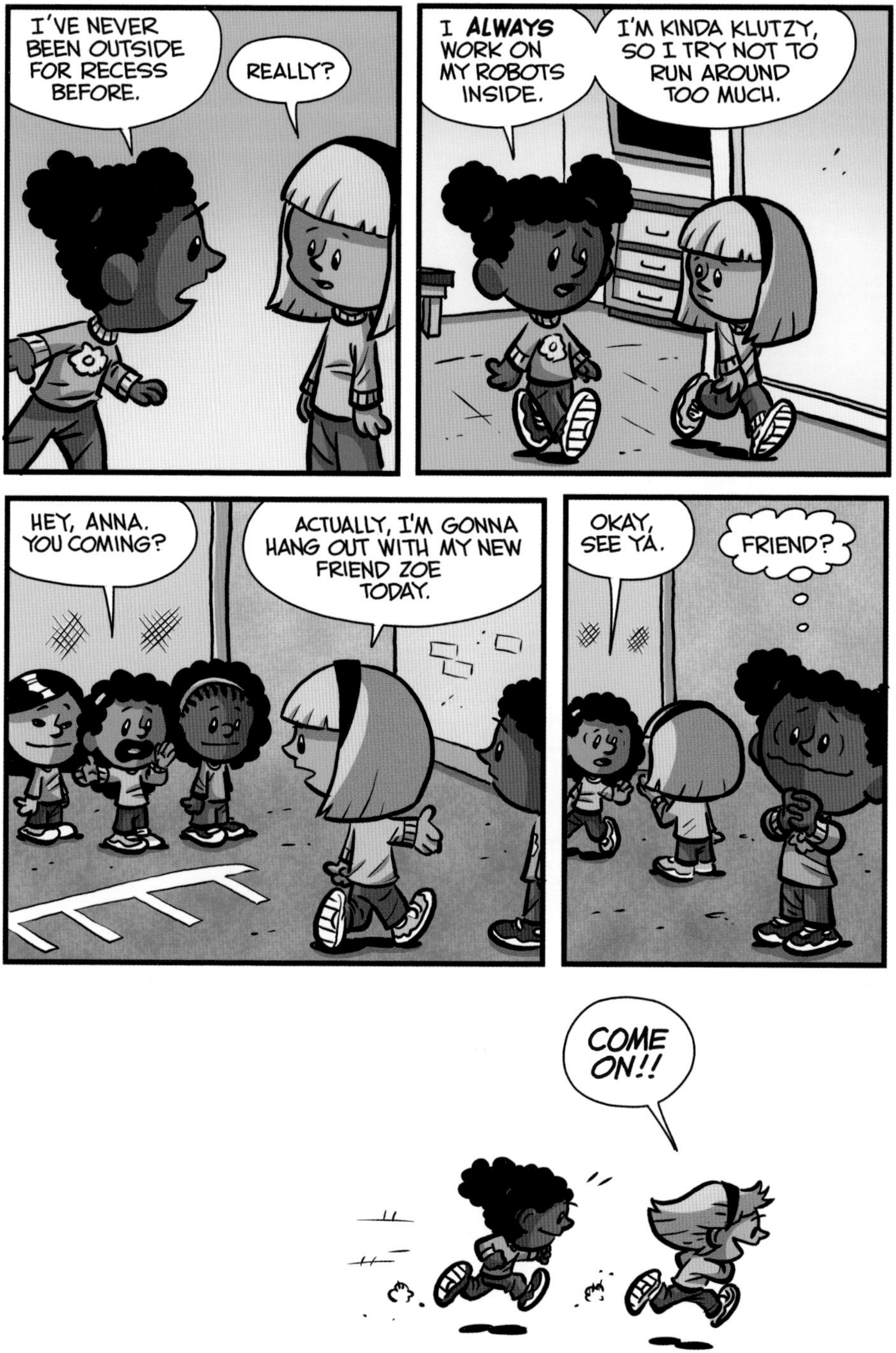
I'VE NEVER BEEN OUTSIDE FOR RECESS BEFORE.
REALLY?
I ALWAYS WORK ON MY ROBOTS INSIDE.
I'M KINDA KLUTZY, SO I TRY NOT TO RUN AROUND TOO MUCH.
HEY, ANNA. YOU COMING?
ACTUALLY, I'M GONNA HANG OUT WITH MY NEW FRIEND ZOE TODAY.
OKAY, SEE YA.
FRIEND?
COME ON!!

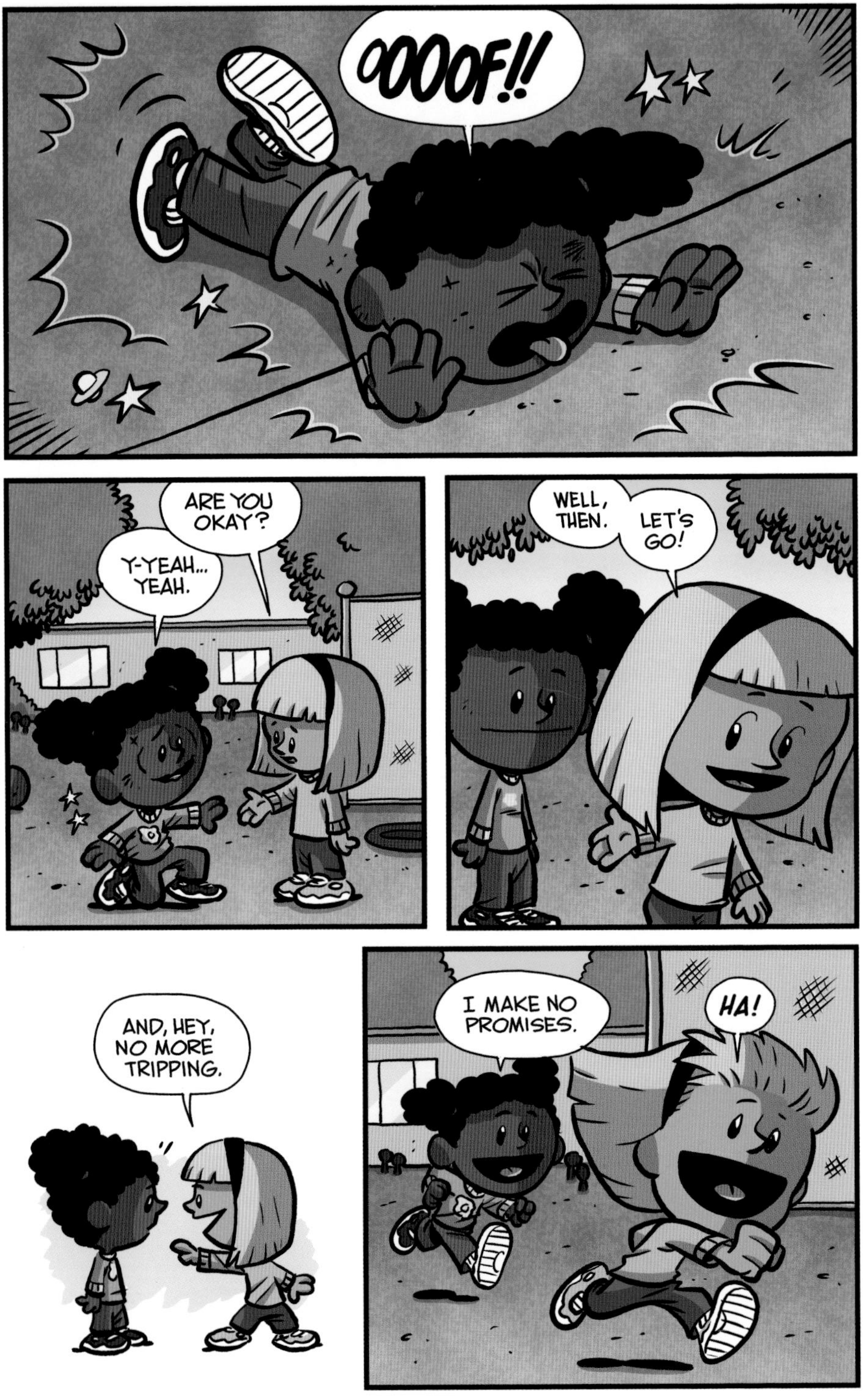
OOOOF!!
ARE YOU OKAY?
Y-YEAH... YEAH.
WELL, THEN.
LET'S GO!
AND, HEY, NO MORE TRIPPING.
I MAKE NO PROMISES.
HA!

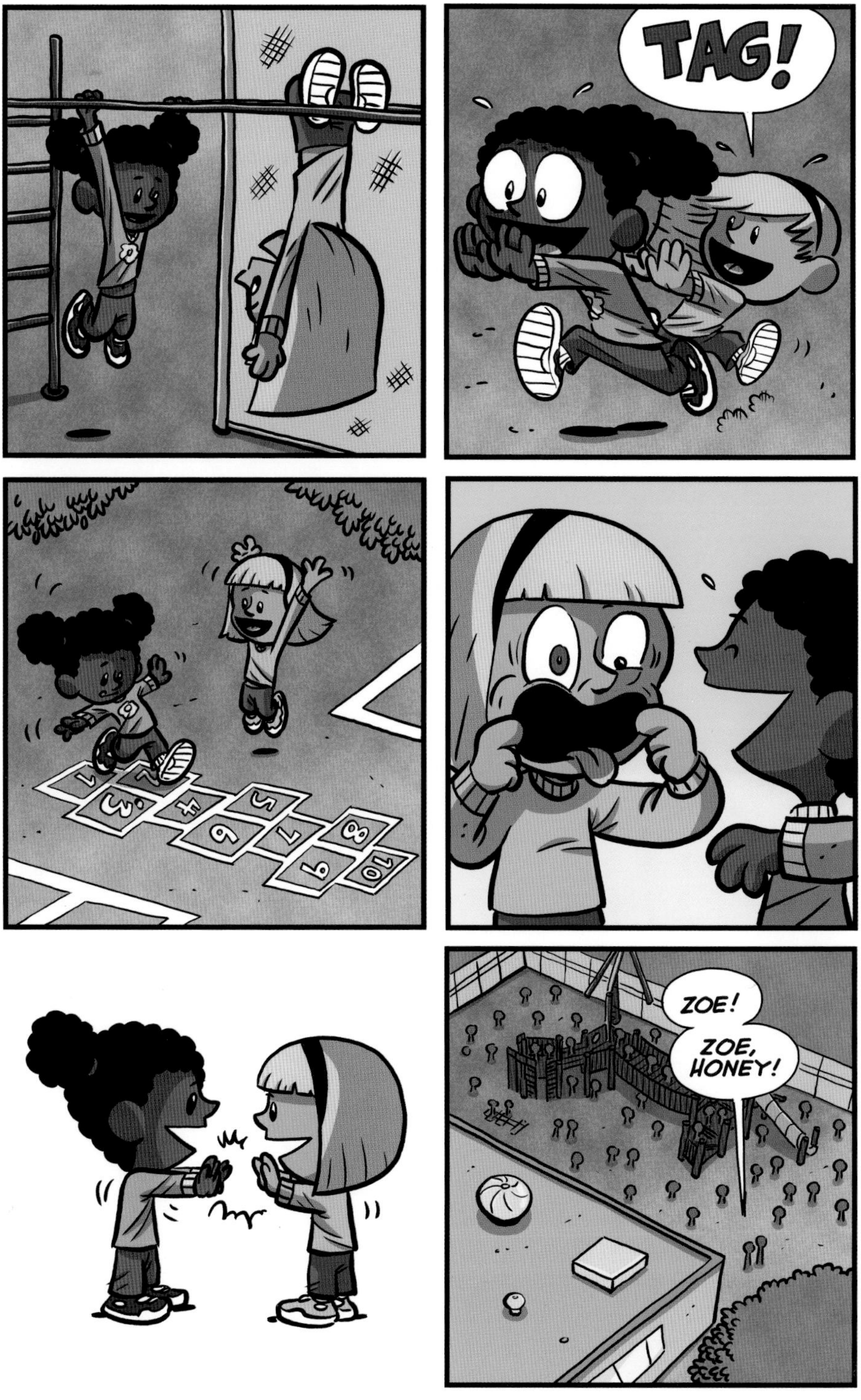
TAG!
ZOE!
ZOE, HONEY!

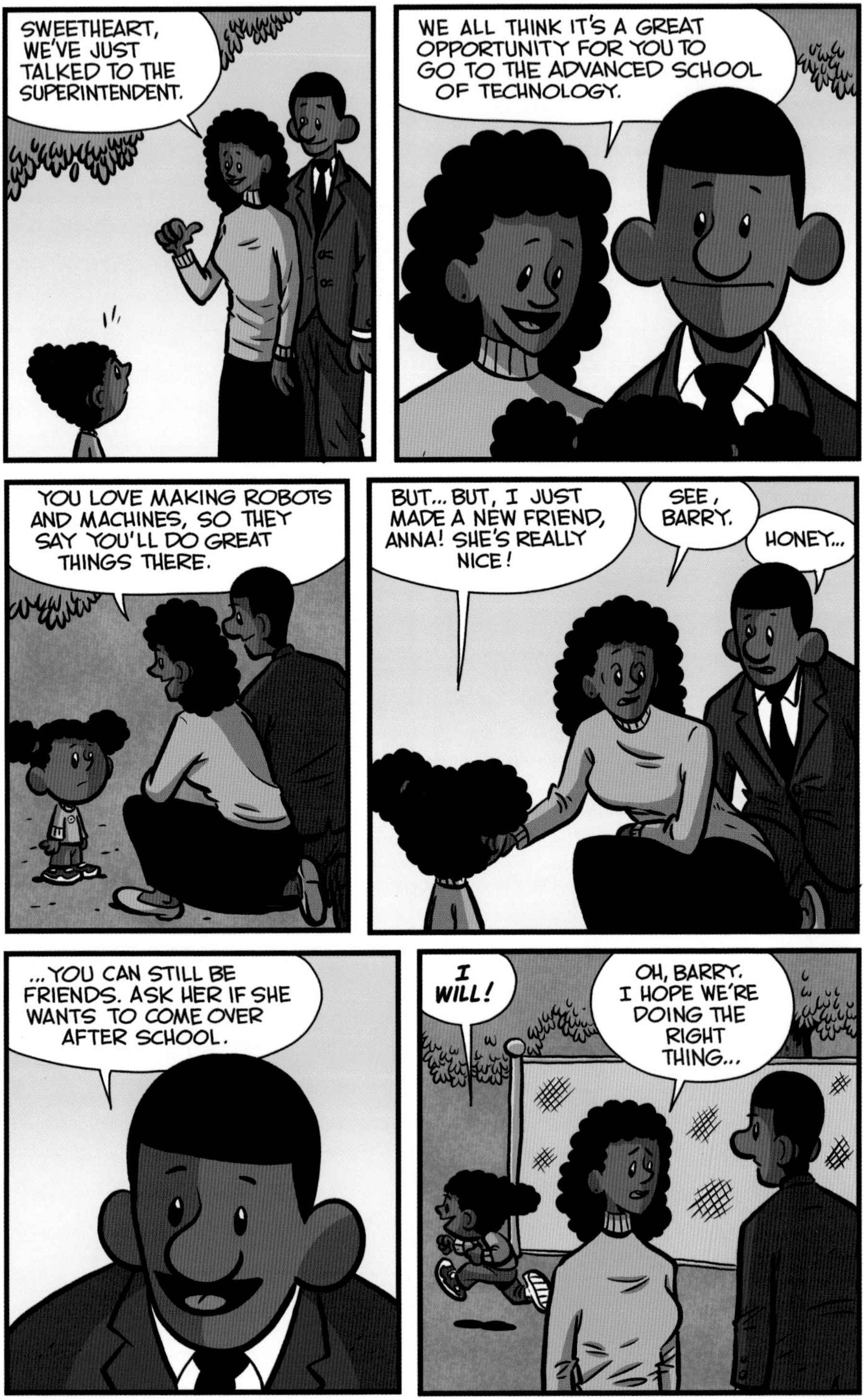
SWEETHEART, WE'VE JUST TALKED TO THE SUPERINTENDENT.
WE ALL THINK IT'S A GREAT OPPORTUNITY FOR YOU TO GO TO THE ADVANCED SCHOOL OF TECHNOLOGY.
YOU LOVE MAKING ROBOTS AND MACHINES, SO THEY SAY YOU'LL DO GREAT THINGS THERE.
BUT... BUT, I JUST MADE A NEW FRIEND, ANNA! SHE'S REALLY NICE!
SEE, BARRY.
HONEY...
...YOU CAN STILL BE FRIENDS. ASK HER IF SHE WANTS TO COME OVER AFTER SCHOOL.
I WILL!
OH, BARRY. I HOPE WE'RE DOING THE RIGHT THING...

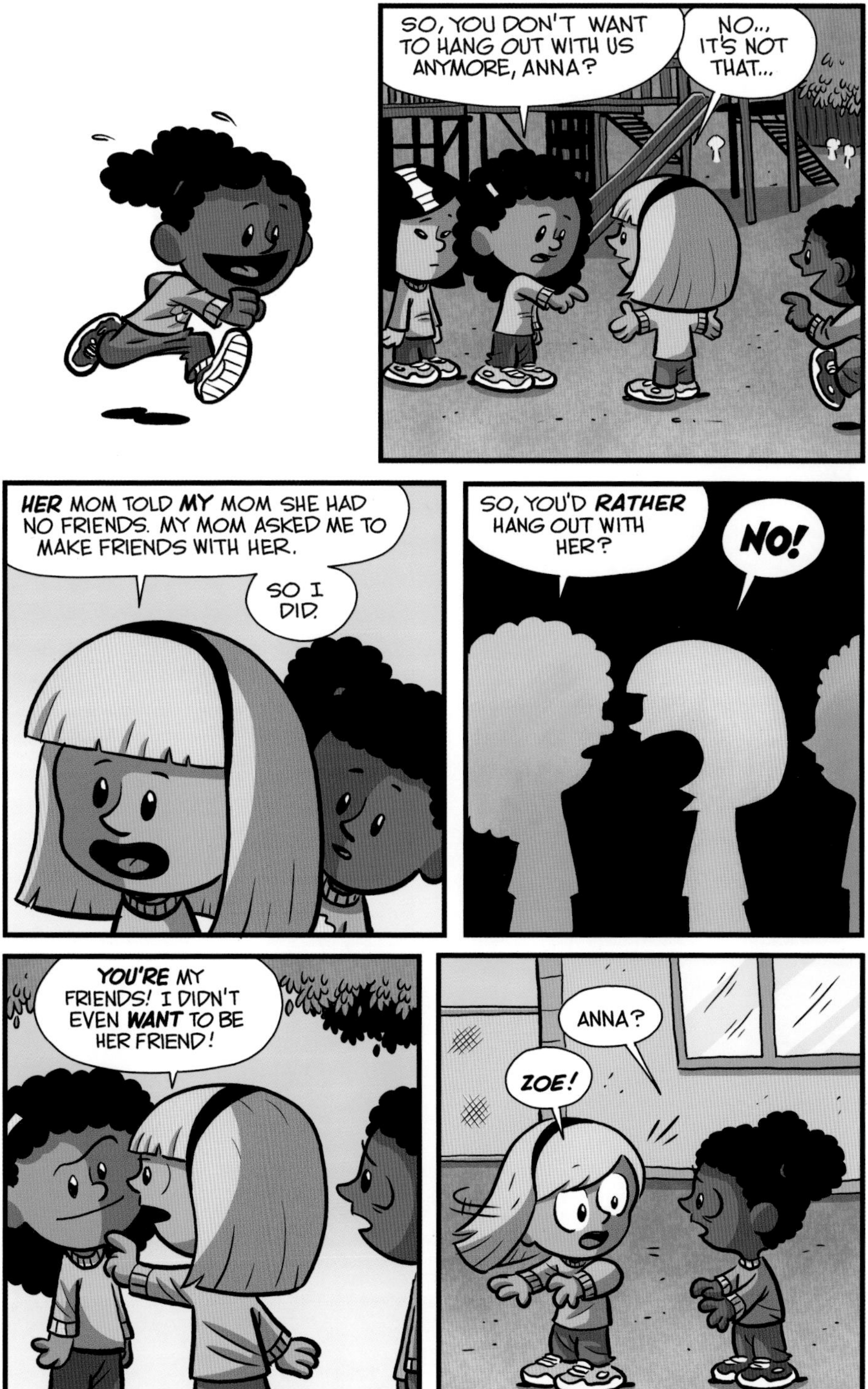
SO, YOU DON'T WANT TO HANG OUT WITH US ANYMORE, ANNA?
NO..., IT'S NOT THAT...
HER MOM TOLD MY MOM SHE HAD NO FRIENDS. MY MOM ASKED ME TO MAKE FRIENDS WITH HER.
SO I DID.
SO, YOU'D RATHER HANG OUT WITH HER?
NO!
YOU'RE MY FRIENDS! I DIDN'T EVEN WANT TO BE HER FRIEND!
ANNA?
ZOE!

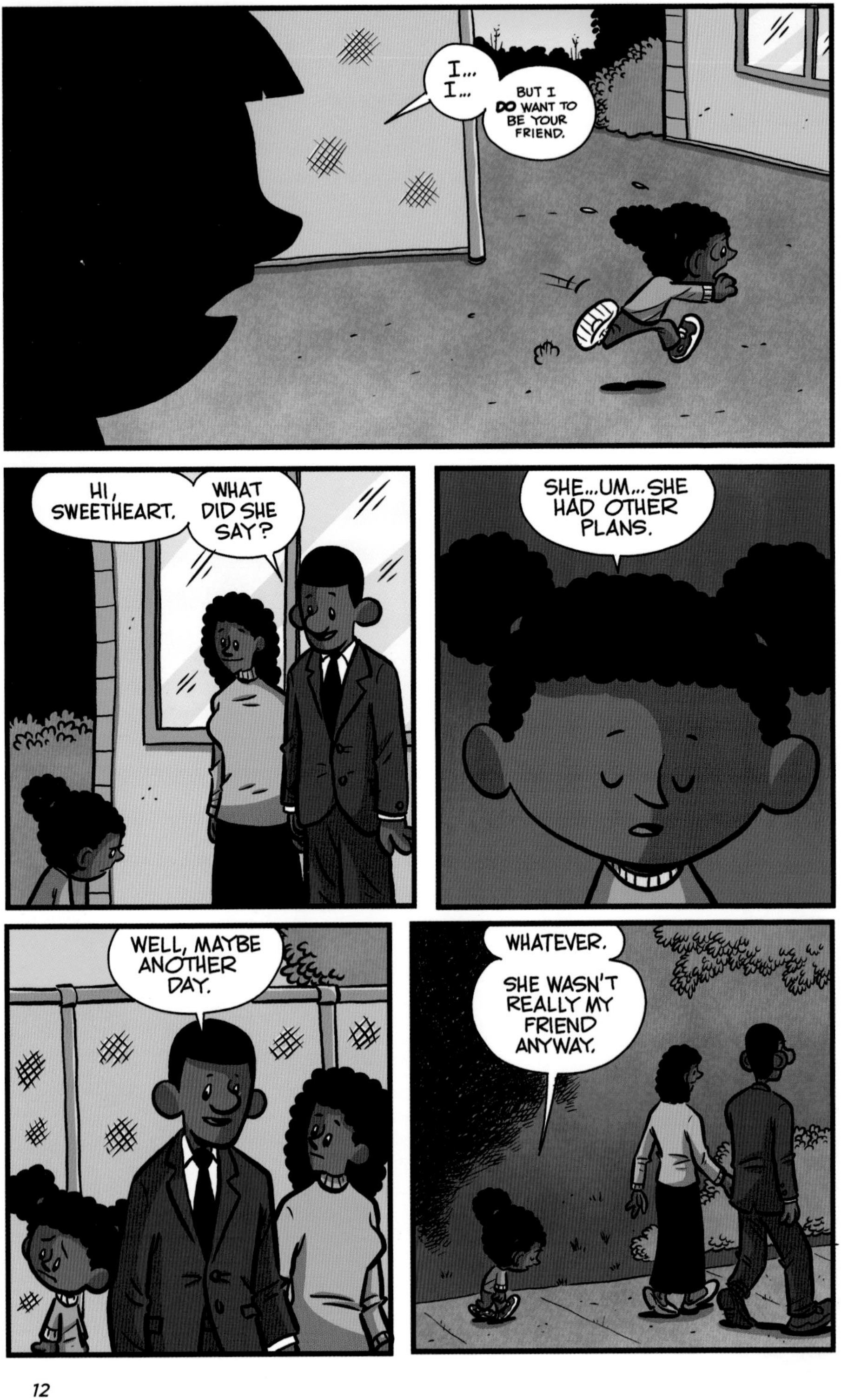
I... I...
BUT I DO WANT TO BE YOUR FRIEND.
HI, SWEETHEART.
WHAT DID SHE SAY?
SHE...UM...SHE HAD OTHER PLANS.
WELL, MAYBE ANOTHER DAY.
WHATEVER.
SHE WASN'T REALLY MY FRIEND ANYWAY.

CHAPTER 2 - KAIJU

NOW...

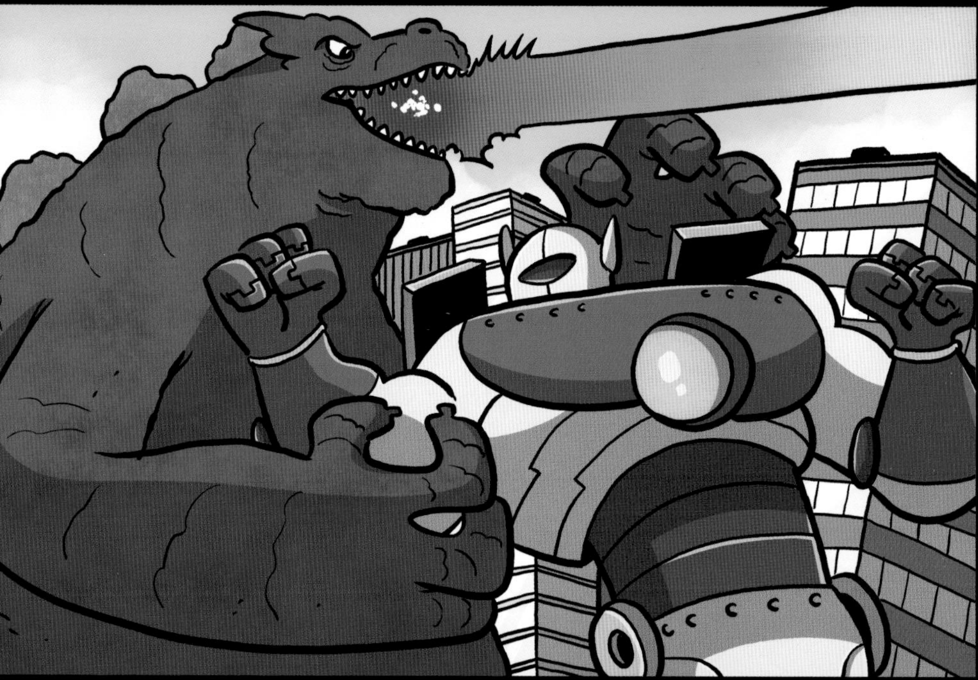

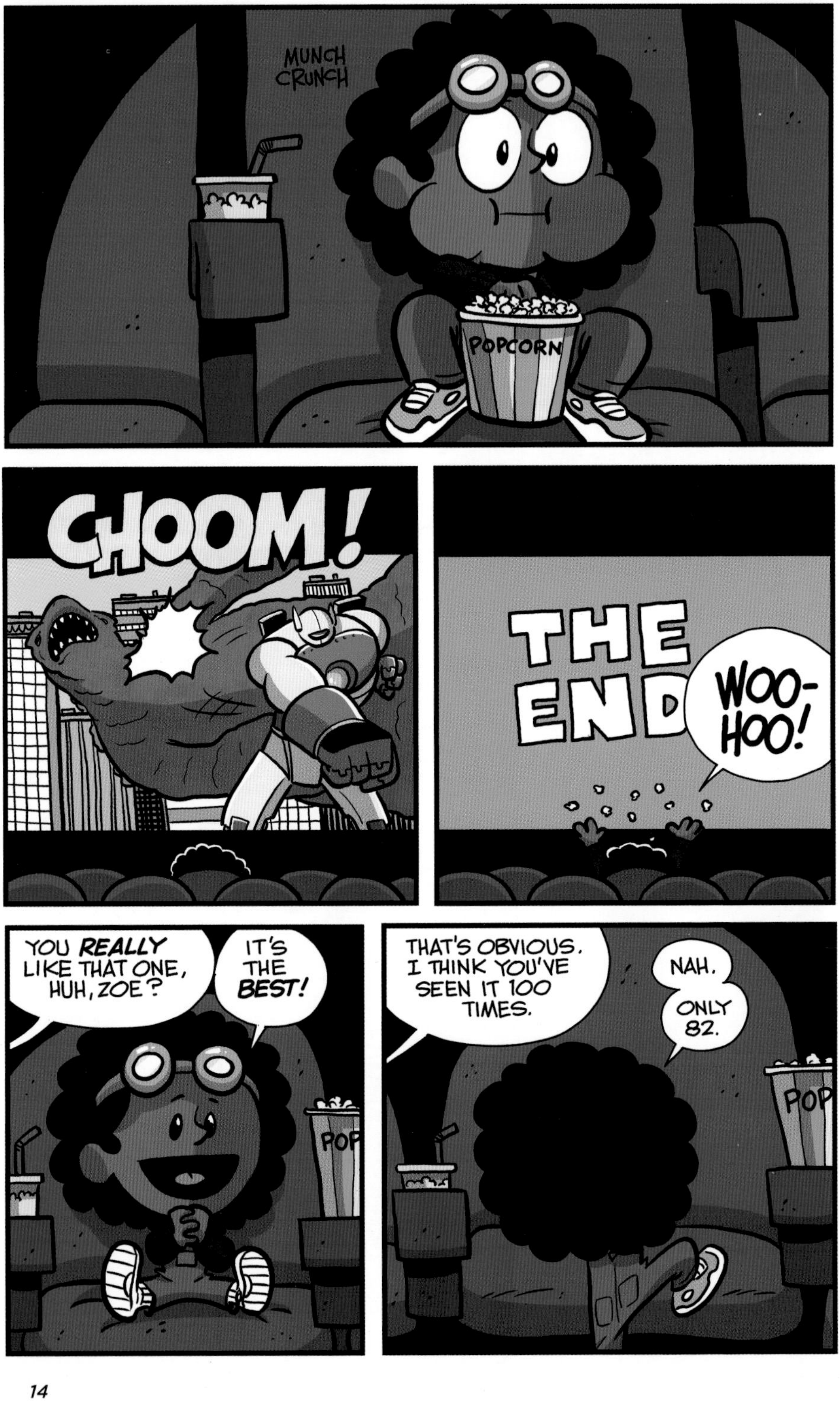

MUNCH
CRUNCH
POPCORN
CHOOM!
THE END
WOO-HOO!
YOU REALLY LIKE THAT ONE, HUH, ZOE?
IT'S THE BEST!
POP
THAT'S OBVIOUS. I THINK YOU'VE SEEN IT 100 TIMES.
NAH.
ONLY 82.
POP

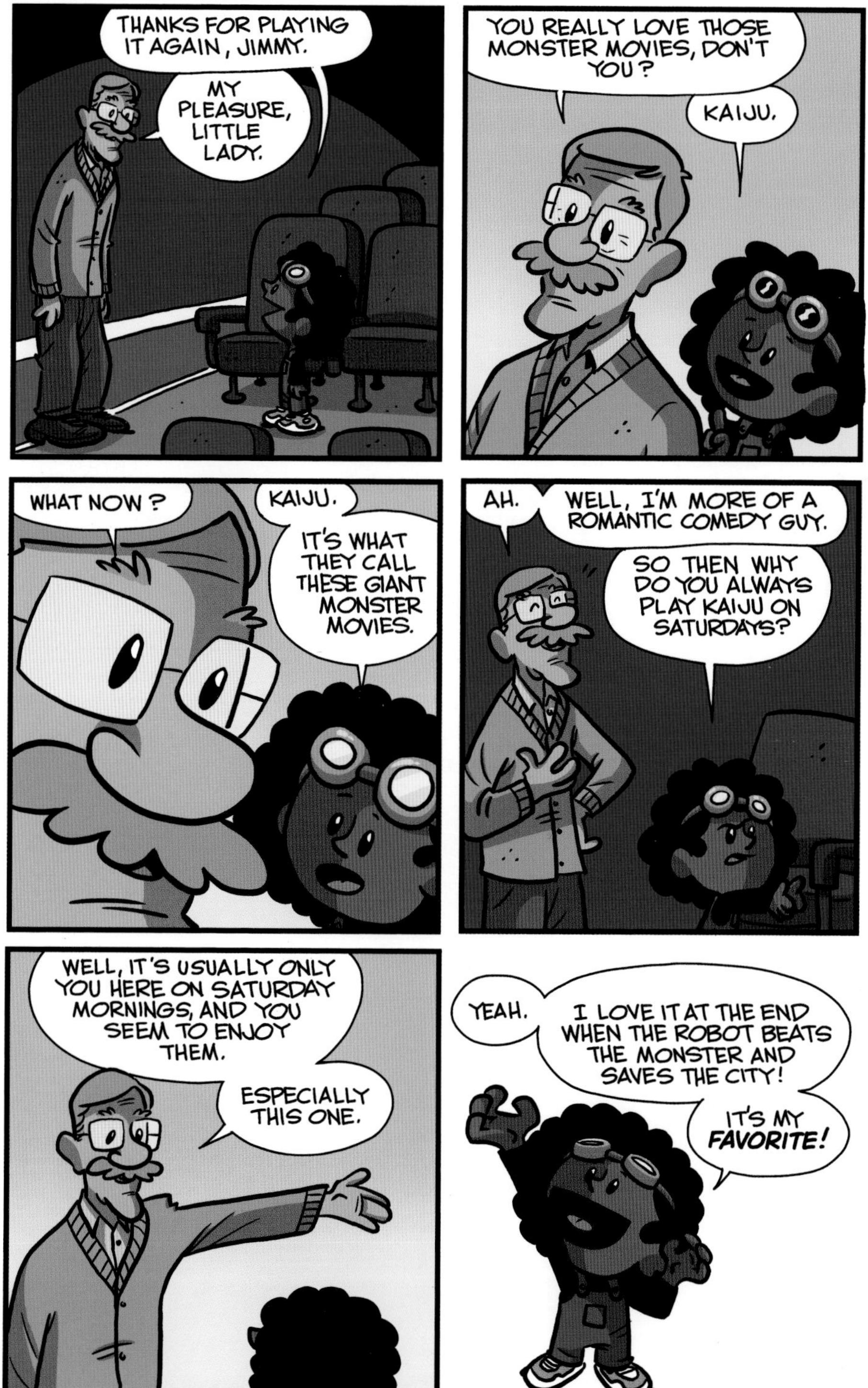
THANKS FOR PLAYING IT AGAIN, JIMMY.
MY PLEASURE, LITTLE LADY.
YOU REALLY LOVE THOSE MONSTER MOVIES, DON'T YOU?
KAIJU.
WHAT NOW?
KAIJU.
IT'S WHAT THEY CALL THESE GIANT MONSTER MOVIES.
AH.
WELL, I'M MORE OF A ROMANTIC COMEDY GUY.
SO THEN WHY DO YOU ALWAYS PLAY KAIJU ON SATURDAYS?
WELL, IT'S USUALLY ONLY YOU HERE ON SATURDAY MORNINGS, AND YOU SEEM TO ENJOY THEM.
ESPECIALLY THIS ONE.
YEAH.
I LOVE IT AT THE END WHEN THE ROBOT BEATS THE MONSTER AND SAVES THE CITY!
IT'S MY *FAVORITE!*

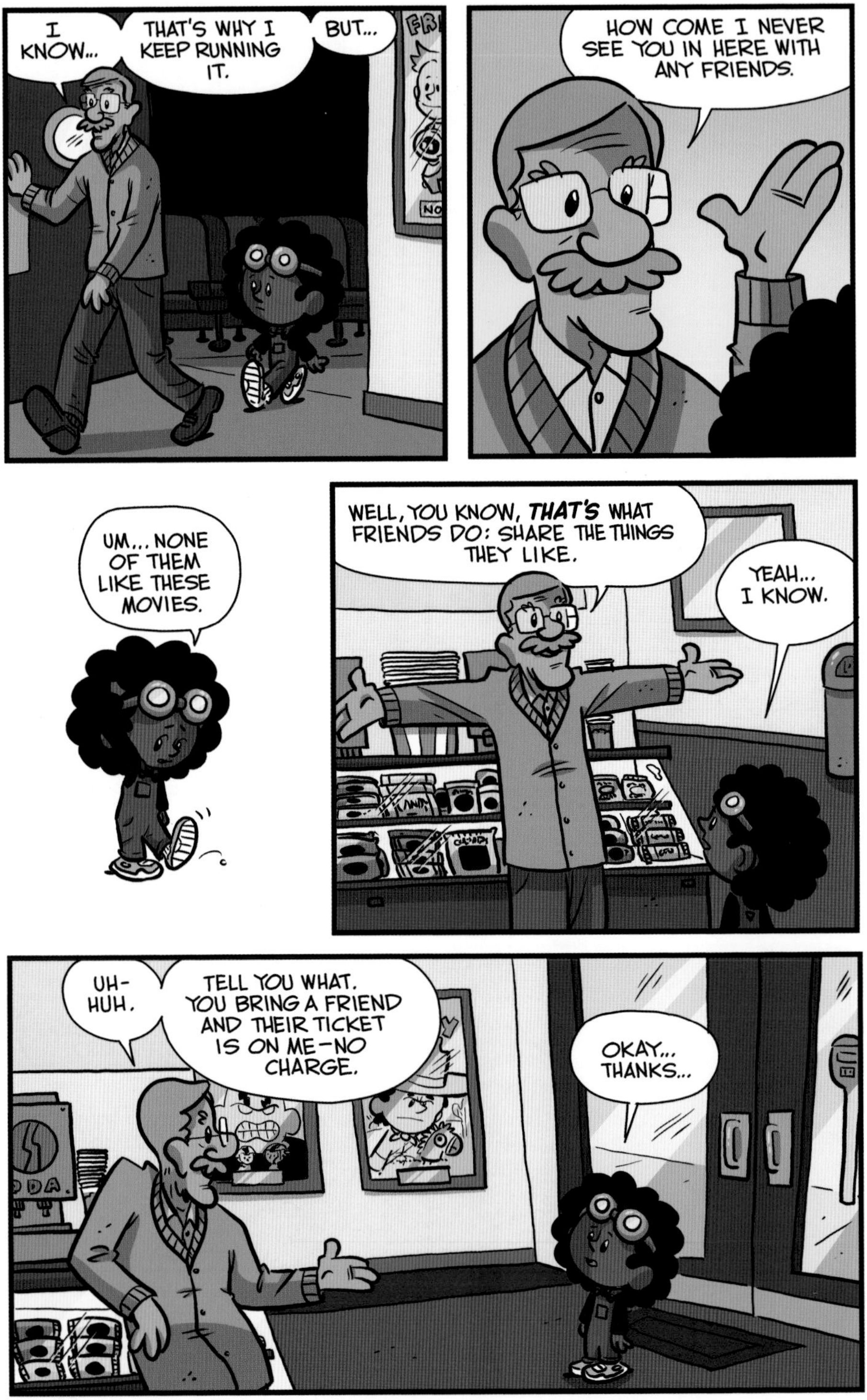
I KNOW...
THAT'S WHY I KEEP RUNNING IT.
BUT...
HOW COME I NEVER SEE YOU IN HERE WITH ANY FRIENDS.
UM... NONE OF THEM LIKE THESE MOVIES.
WELL, YOU KNOW, ***THAT'S*** WHAT FRIENDS DO: SHARE THE THINGS THEY LIKE.
YEAH... I KNOW.
UH-HUH.
TELL YOU WHAT. YOU BRING A FRIEND AND THEIR TICKET IS ON ME—NO CHARGE.
OKAY... THANKS...

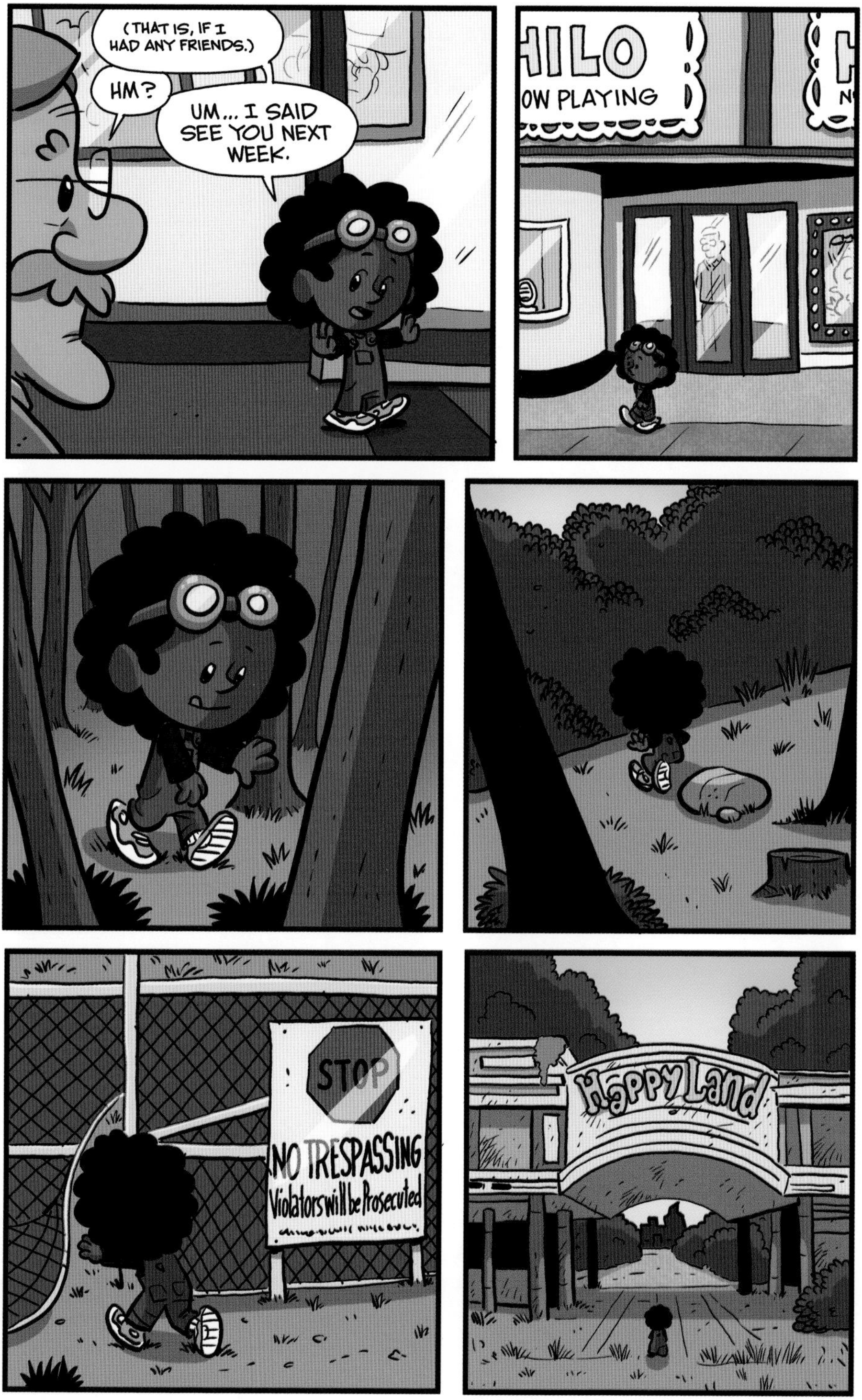
(THAT IS, IF I HAD ANY FRIENDS.)
HM?
UM... I SAID SEE YOU NEXT WEEK.
HILO
OW PLAYING
STOP
NO TRESPASSING
Violators will be Prosecuted
Happy Land

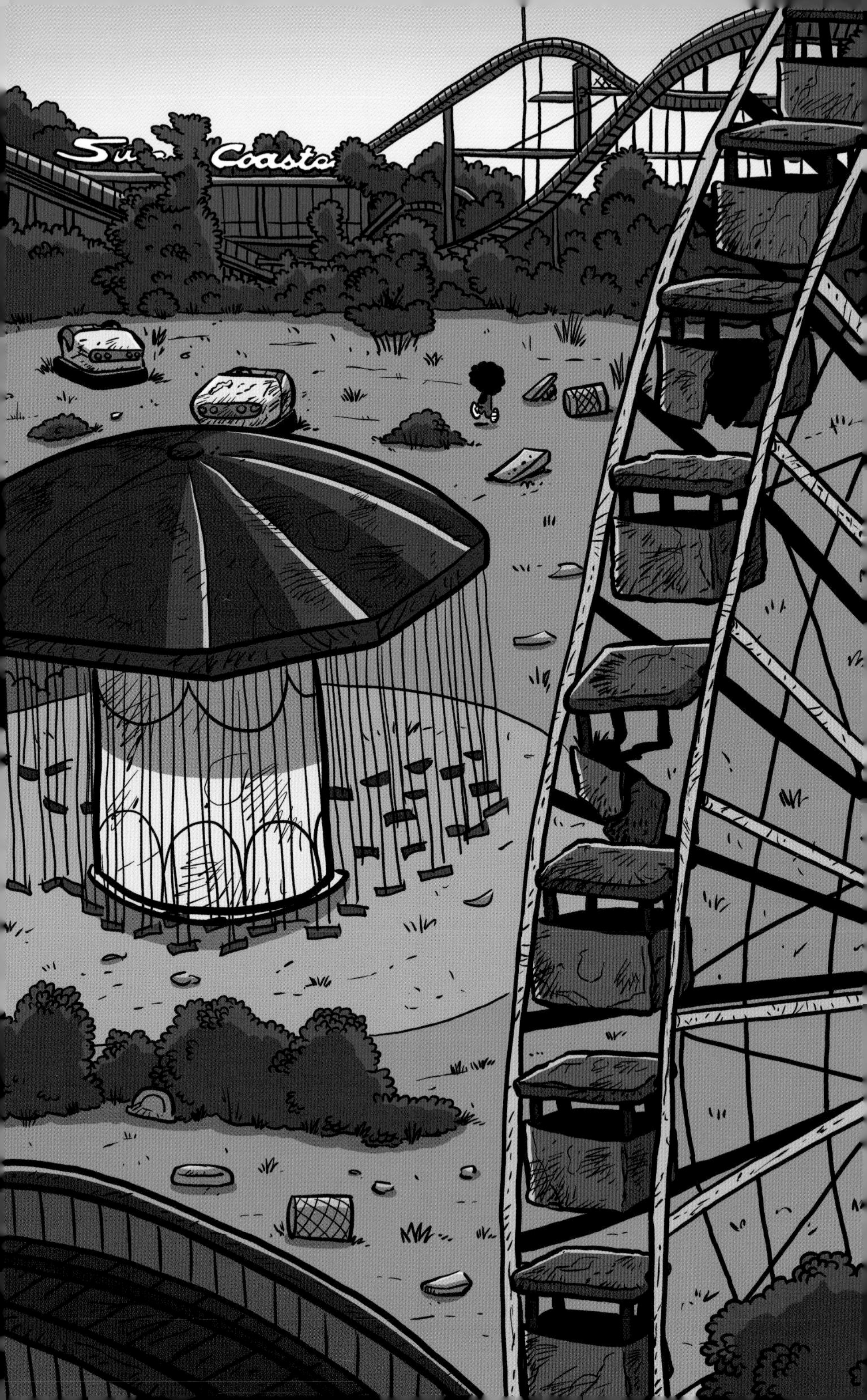
Su
Coaste

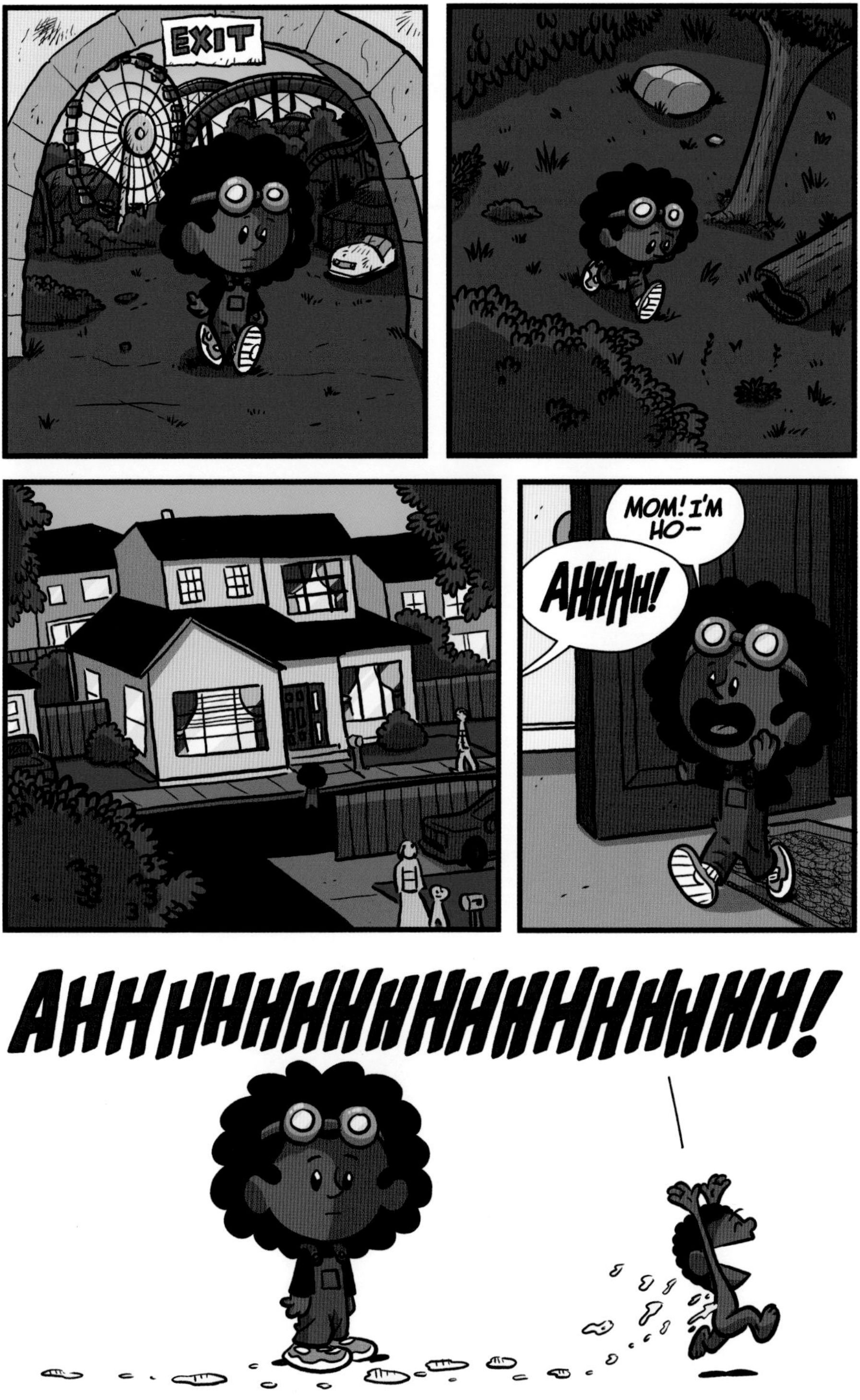
EXIT
MOM! I'M HO-
AHHHH!
AHHHHHHHHHHHHHHHHHHHH!

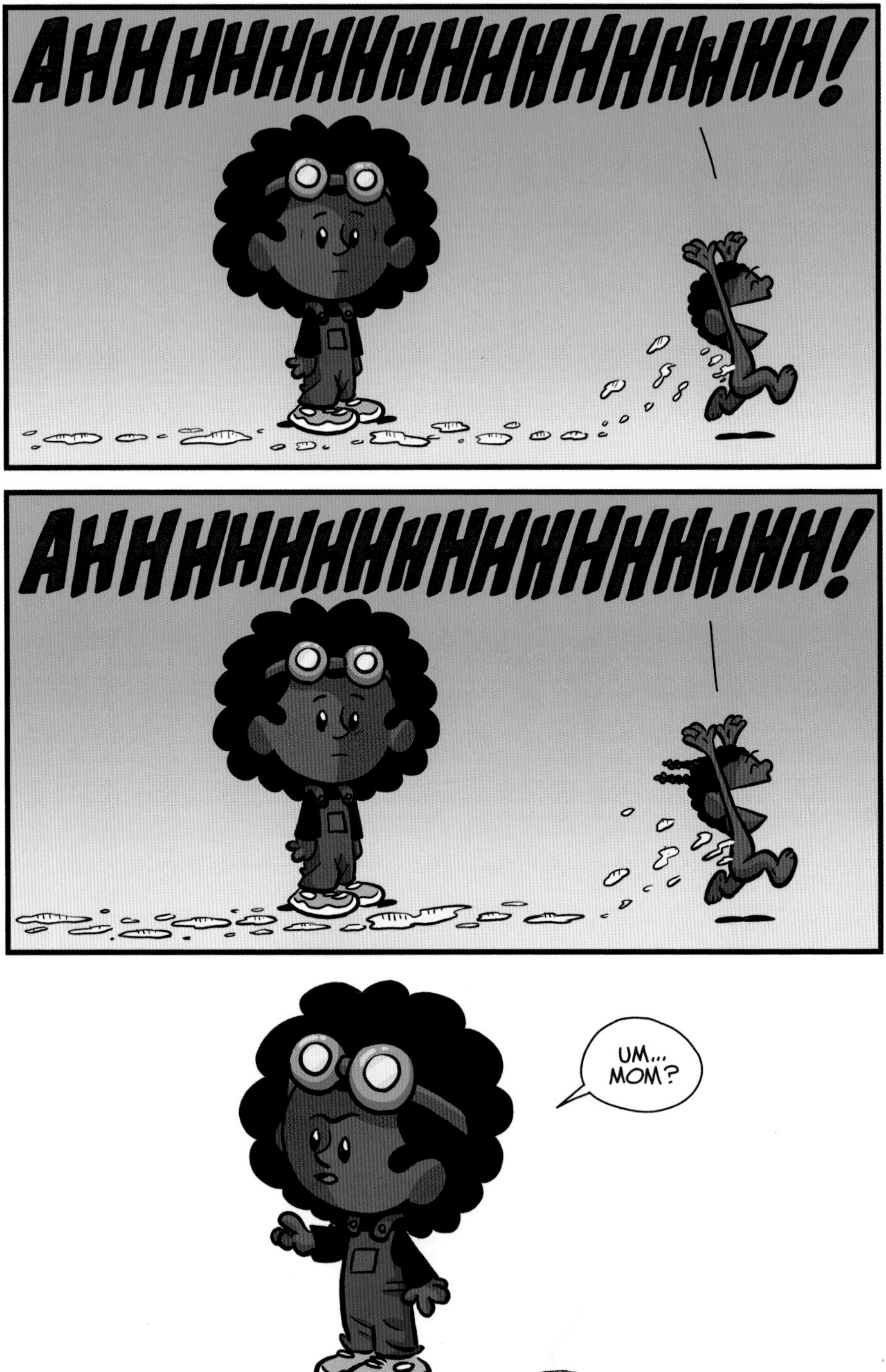
AHHHHHHHHHHHHHHHHHHH!
AHHHHHHHHHHHHHHHHHHH!
UM... MOM?

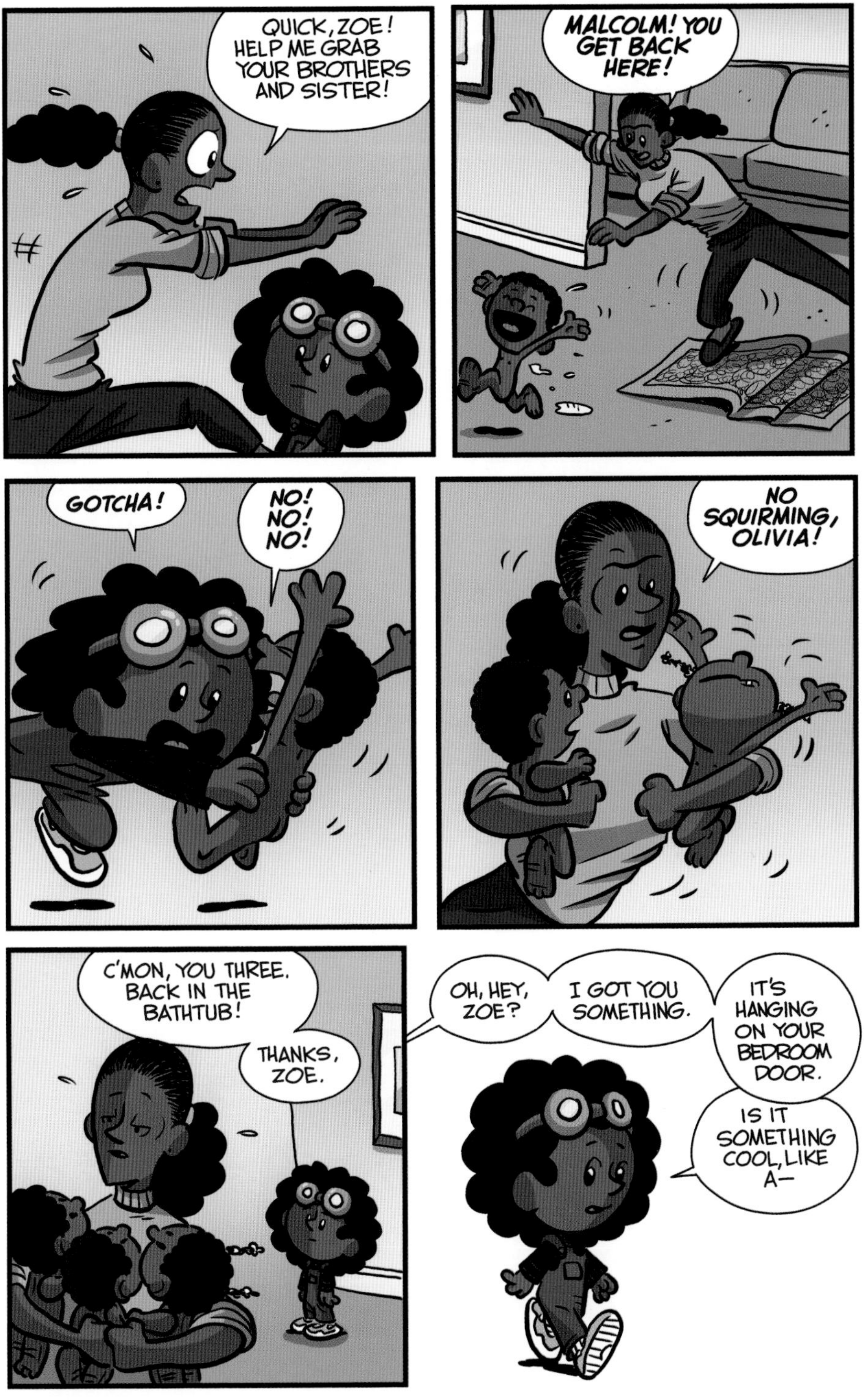
QUICK, ZOE! HELP ME GRAB YOUR BROTHERS AND SISTER!
MALCOLM! YOU GET BACK HERE!
GOTCHA!
NO! NO! NO!
NO SQUIRMING, OLIVIA!
C'MON, YOU THREE. BACK IN THE BATHTUB!
THANKS, ZOE.
OH, HEY, ZOE?
I GOT YOU SOMETHING.
IT'S HANGING ON YOUR BEDROOM DOOR.
IS IT SOMETHING COOL, LIKE A—

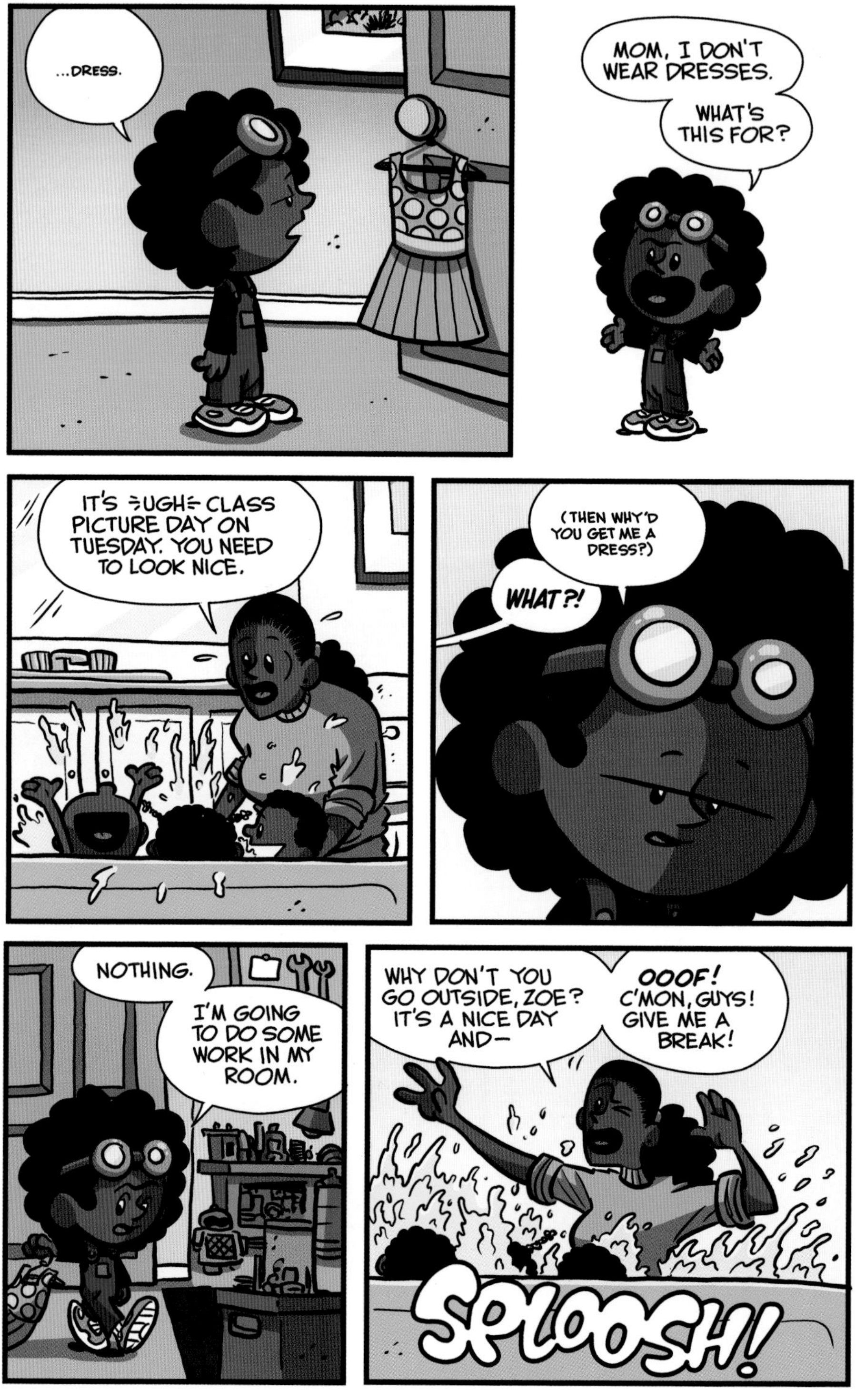
...DRESS.
MOM, I DON'T WEAR DRESSES.
WHAT'S THIS FOR?
IT'S =UGH= CLASS PICTURE DAY ON TUESDAY. YOU NEED TO LOOK NICE.
WHAT?!
(THEN WHY'D YOU GET ME A DRESS?)
NOTHING.
I'M GOING TO DO SOME WORK IN MY ROOM.
WHY DON'T YOU GO OUTSIDE, ZOE? IT'S A NICE DAY AND—
OOOF! C'MON, GUYS! GIVE ME A BREAK!
SPLOOSH!

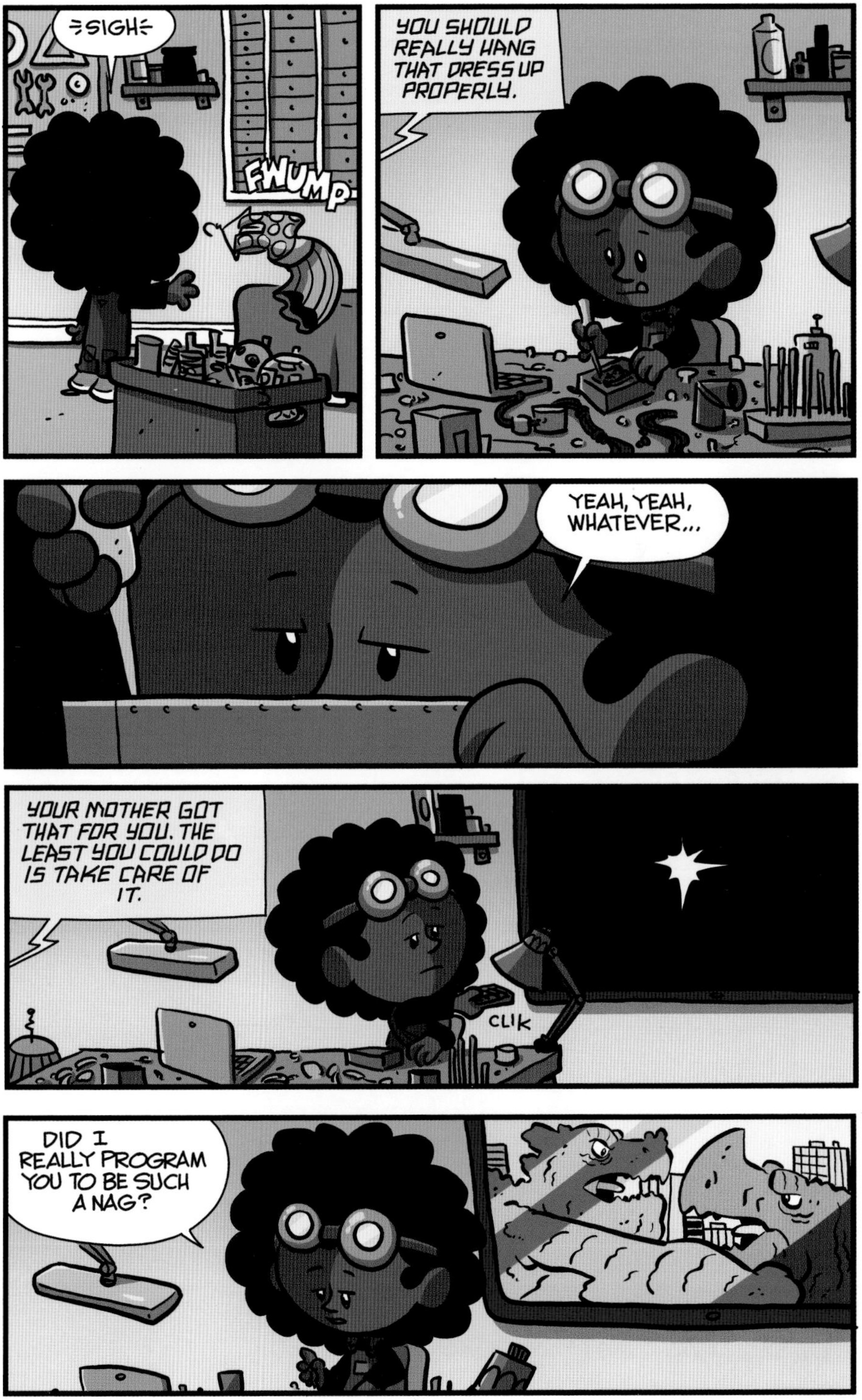

SIGH
FWUMP
YOU SHOULD REALLY HANG THAT DRESS UP PROPERLY.
YEAH, YEAH, WHATEVER...
YOUR MOTHER GOT THAT FOR YOU. THE LEAST YOU COULD DO IS TAKE CARE OF IT.
CLIK
DID I REALLY PROGRAM YOU TO BE SUCH A NAG?

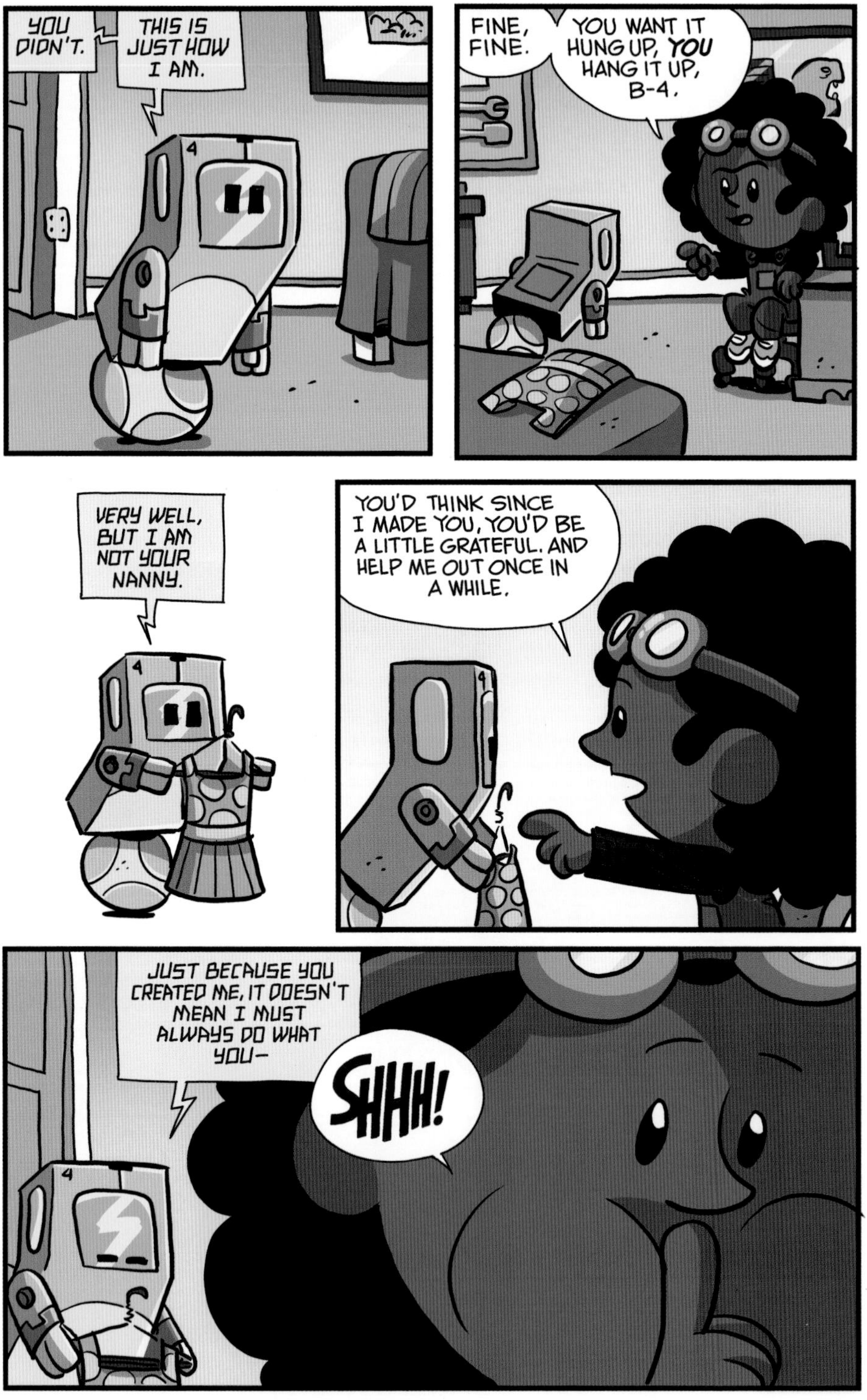
YOU DIDN'T.
THIS IS JUST HOW I AM.
FINE, FINE.
YOU WANT IT HUNG UP, **YOU** HANG IT UP, B-4.
VERY WELL, BUT I AM NOT YOUR NANNY.
YOU'D THINK SINCE I MADE YOU, YOU'D BE A LITTLE GRATEFUL. AND HELP ME OUT ONCE IN A WHILE.
JUST BECAUSE YOU CREATED ME, IT DOESN'T MEAN I MUST ALWAYS DO WHAT YOU—
SHHH!

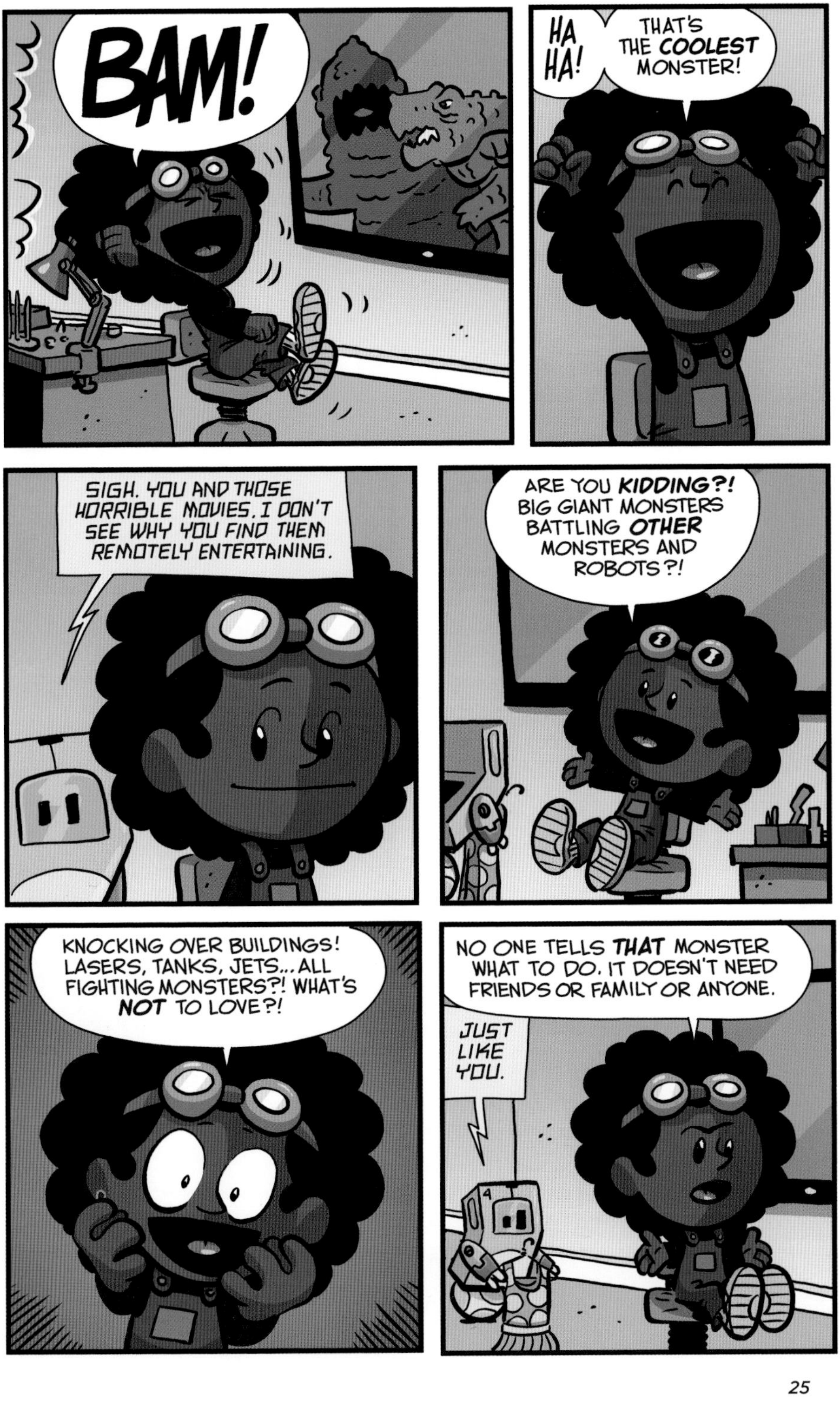

BAM!
HA HA!
THAT'S THE **COOLEST** MONSTER!
SIGH. YOU AND THOSE HORRIBLE MOVIES. I DON'T SEE WHY YOU FIND THEM REMOTELY ENTERTAINING.
ARE YOU **KIDDING?!** BIG GIANT MONSTERS BATTLING **OTHER** MONSTERS AND ROBOTS?!
KNOCKING OVER BUILDINGS! LASERS, TANKS, JETS... ALL FIGHTING MONSTERS?! WHAT'S **NOT** TO LOVE?!
NO ONE TELLS **THAT** MONSTER WHAT TO DO. IT DOESN'T NEED FRIENDS OR FAMILY OR ANYONE.
JUST LIKE YOU.

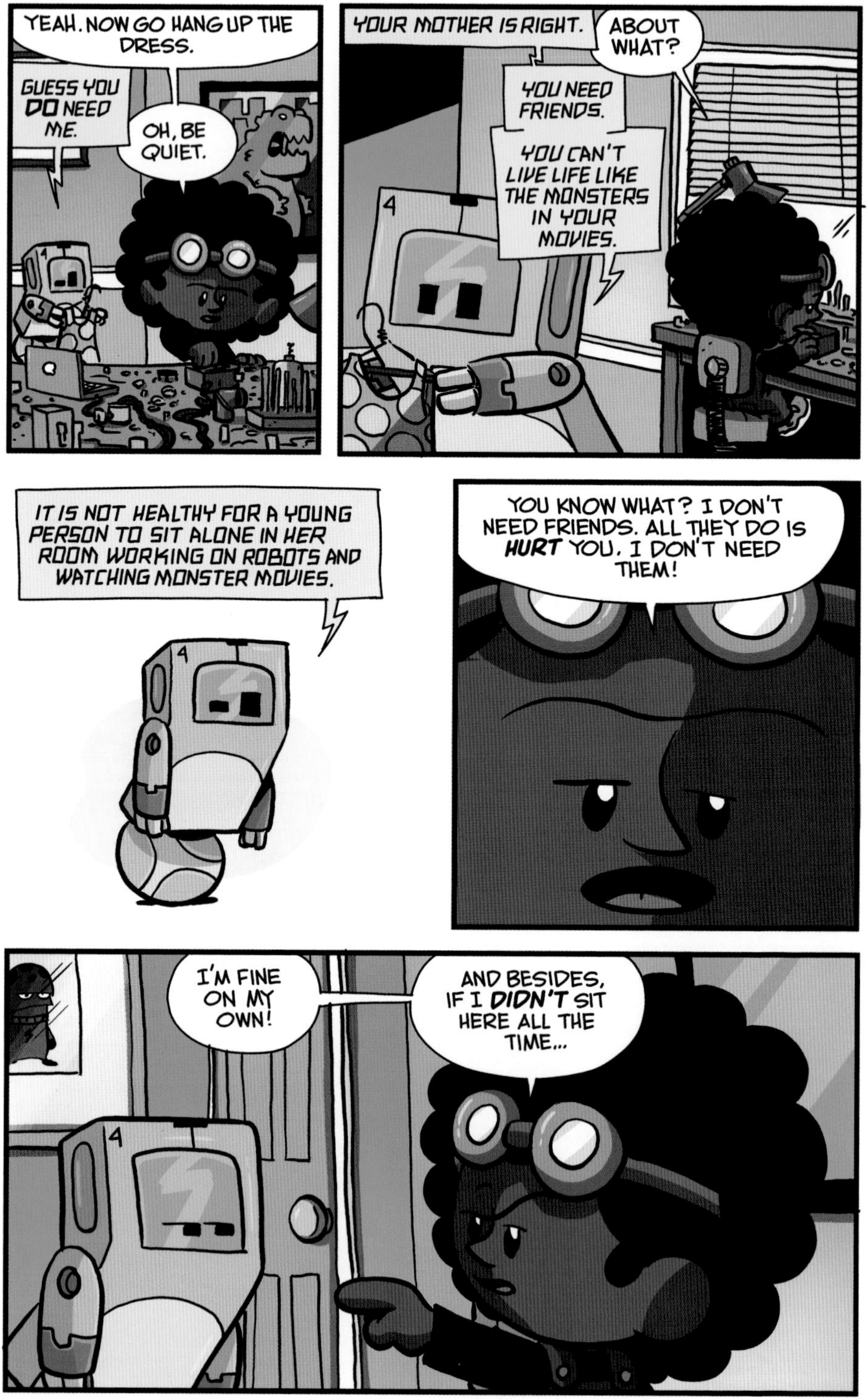
YEAH. NOW GO HANG UP THE DRESS.
GUESS YOU DO NEED ME.
OH, BE QUIET.
YOUR MOTHER IS RIGHT.
ABOUT WHAT?
YOU NEED FRIENDS.
YOU CAN'T LIVE LIFE LIKE THE MONSTERS IN YOUR MOVIES.
IT IS NOT HEALTHY FOR A YOUNG PERSON TO SIT ALONE IN HER ROOM WORKING ON ROBOTS AND WATCHING MONSTER MOVIES.
YOU KNOW WHAT? I DON'T NEED FRIENDS. ALL THEY DO IS HURT YOU. I DON'T NEED THEM!
I'M FINE ON MY OWN!
AND BESIDES, IF I DIDN'T SIT HERE ALL THE TIME...

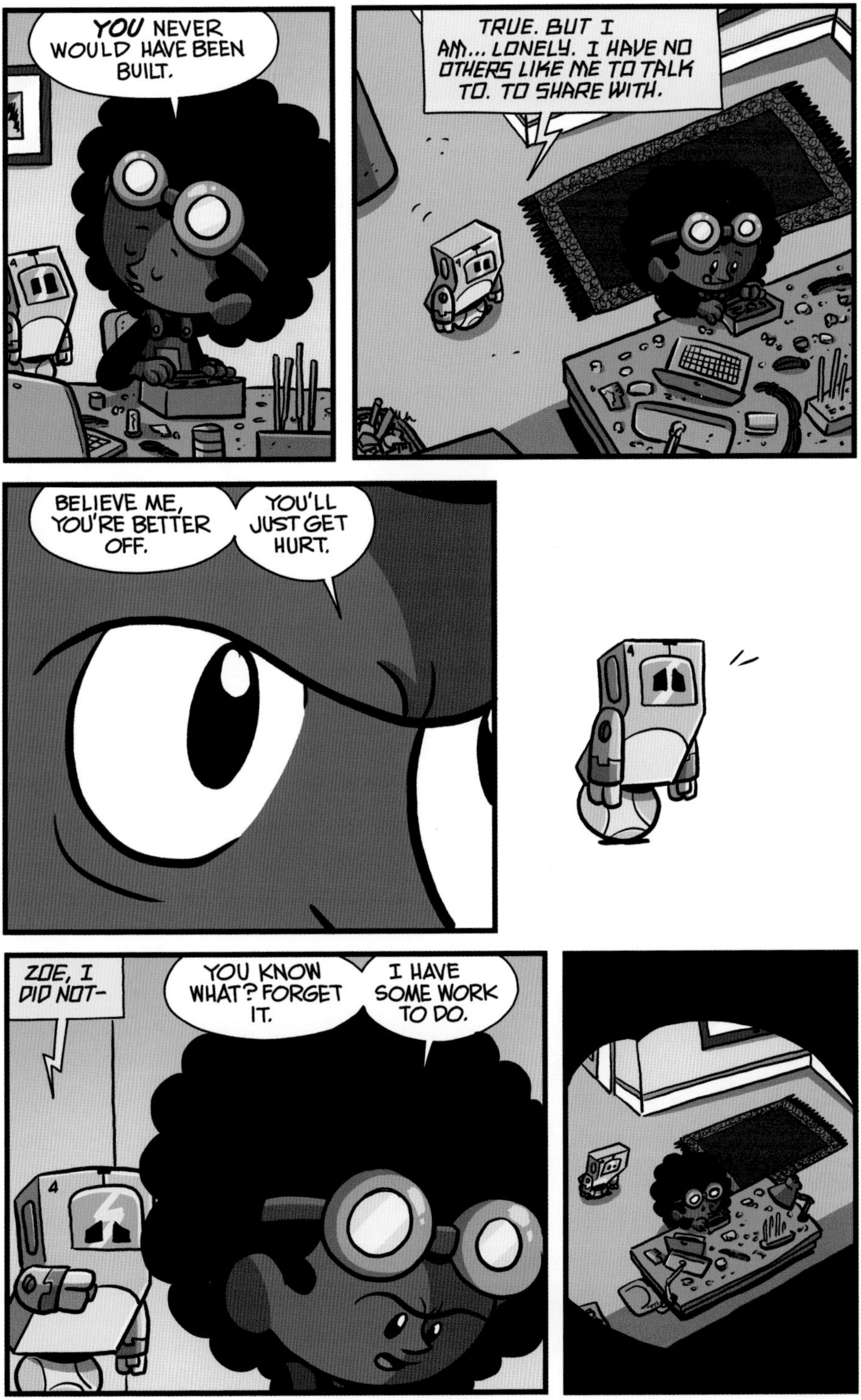
YOU NEVER WOULD HAVE BEEN BUILT.
TRUE. BUT I AM... LONELY. I HAVE NO OTHERS LIKE ME TO TALK TO. TO SHARE WITH.
BELIEVE ME, YOU'RE BETTER OFF.
YOU'LL JUST GET HURT.
ZOE, I DID NOT-
YOU KNOW WHAT? FORGET IT.
I HAVE SOME WORK TO DO.

CHAPTER 3 - GO BIG OR GO HOME

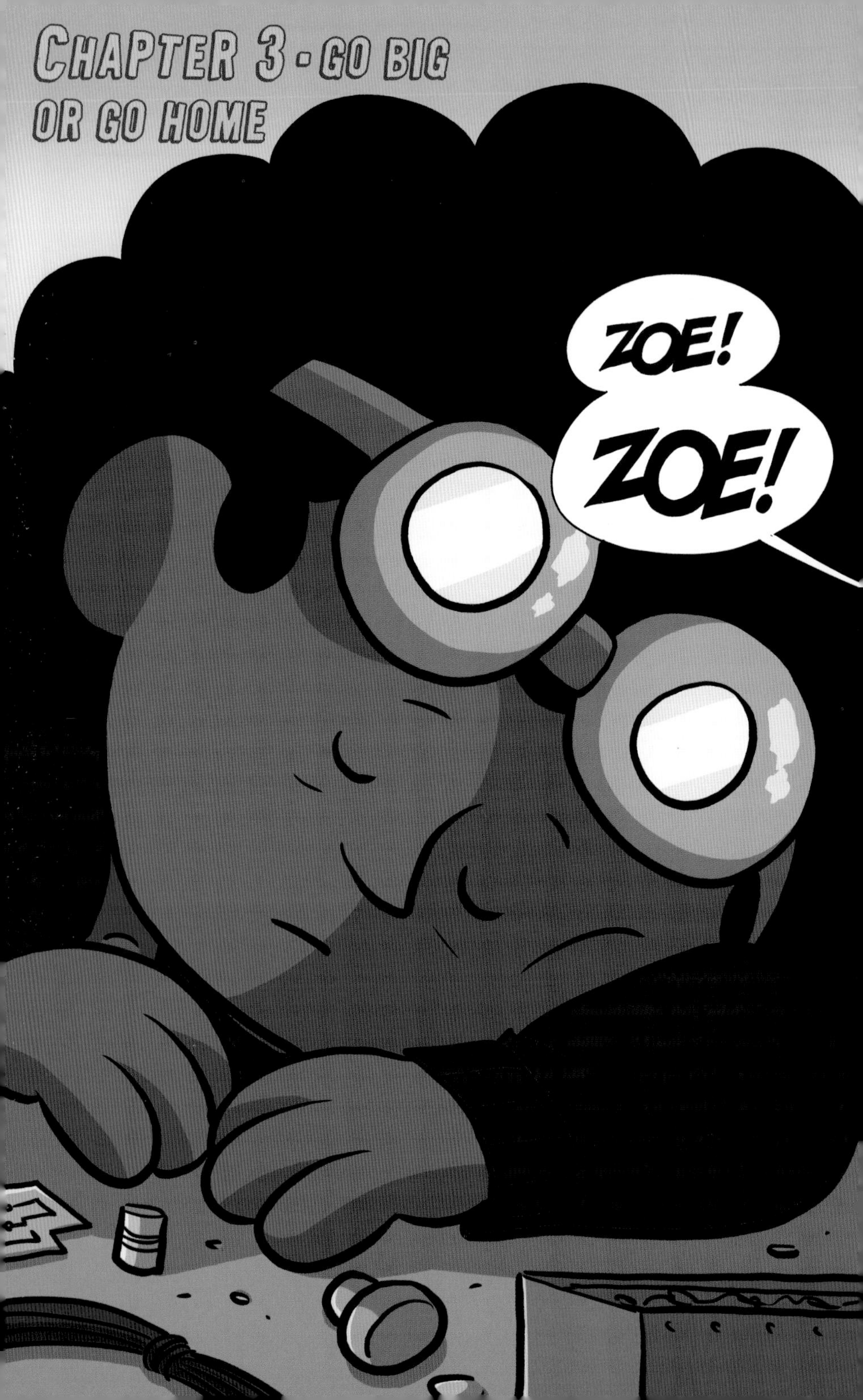

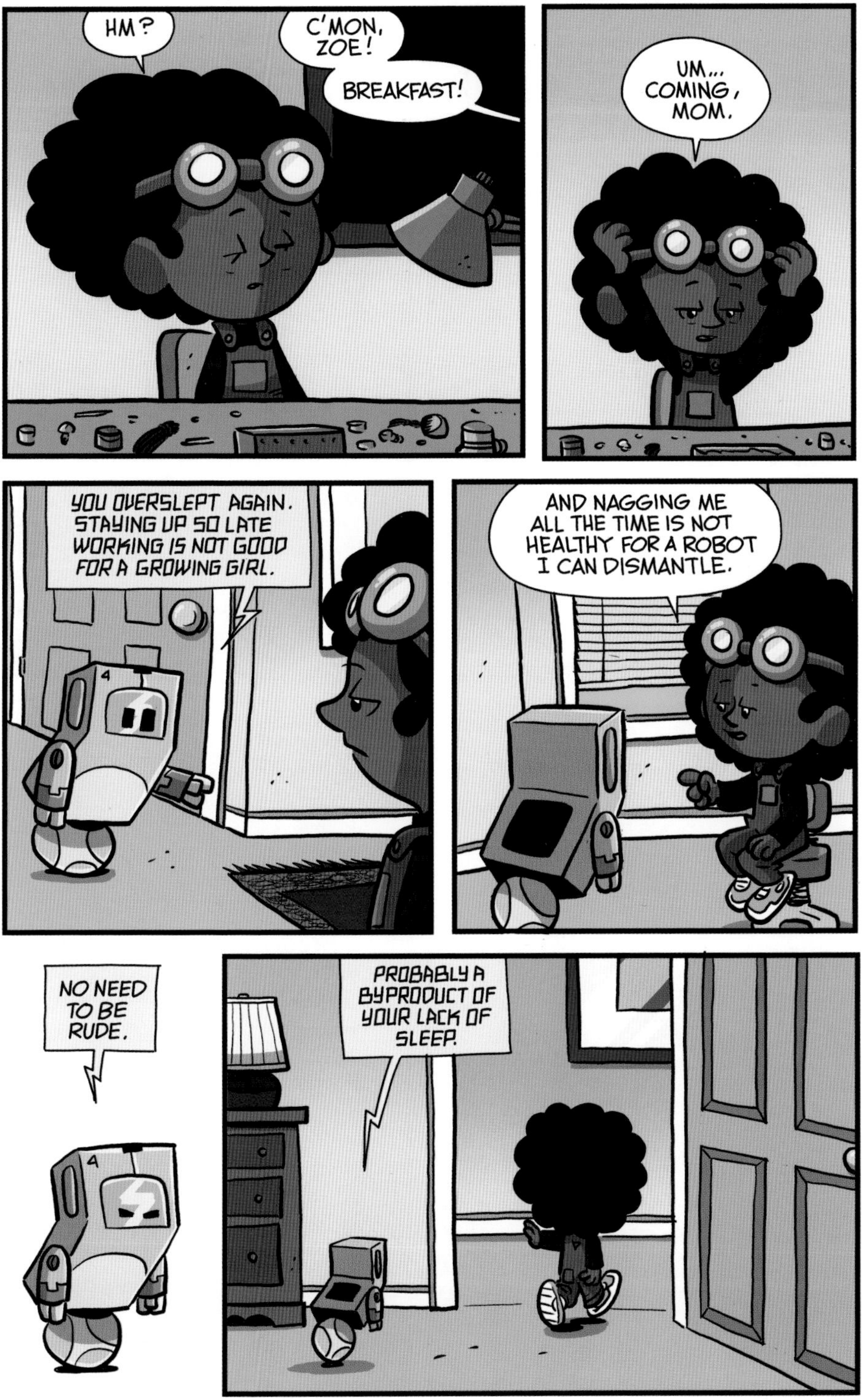
HM?
C'MON, ZOE!
BREAKFAST!
UM... COMING, MOM.
YOU OVERSLEPT AGAIN. STAYING UP SO LATE WORKING IS NOT GOOD FOR A GROWING GIRL.
AND NAGGING ME ALL THE TIME IS NOT HEALTHY FOR A ROBOT I CAN DISMANTLE.
NO NEED TO BE RUDE.
PROBABLY A BYPRODUCT OF YOUR LACK OF SLEEP.

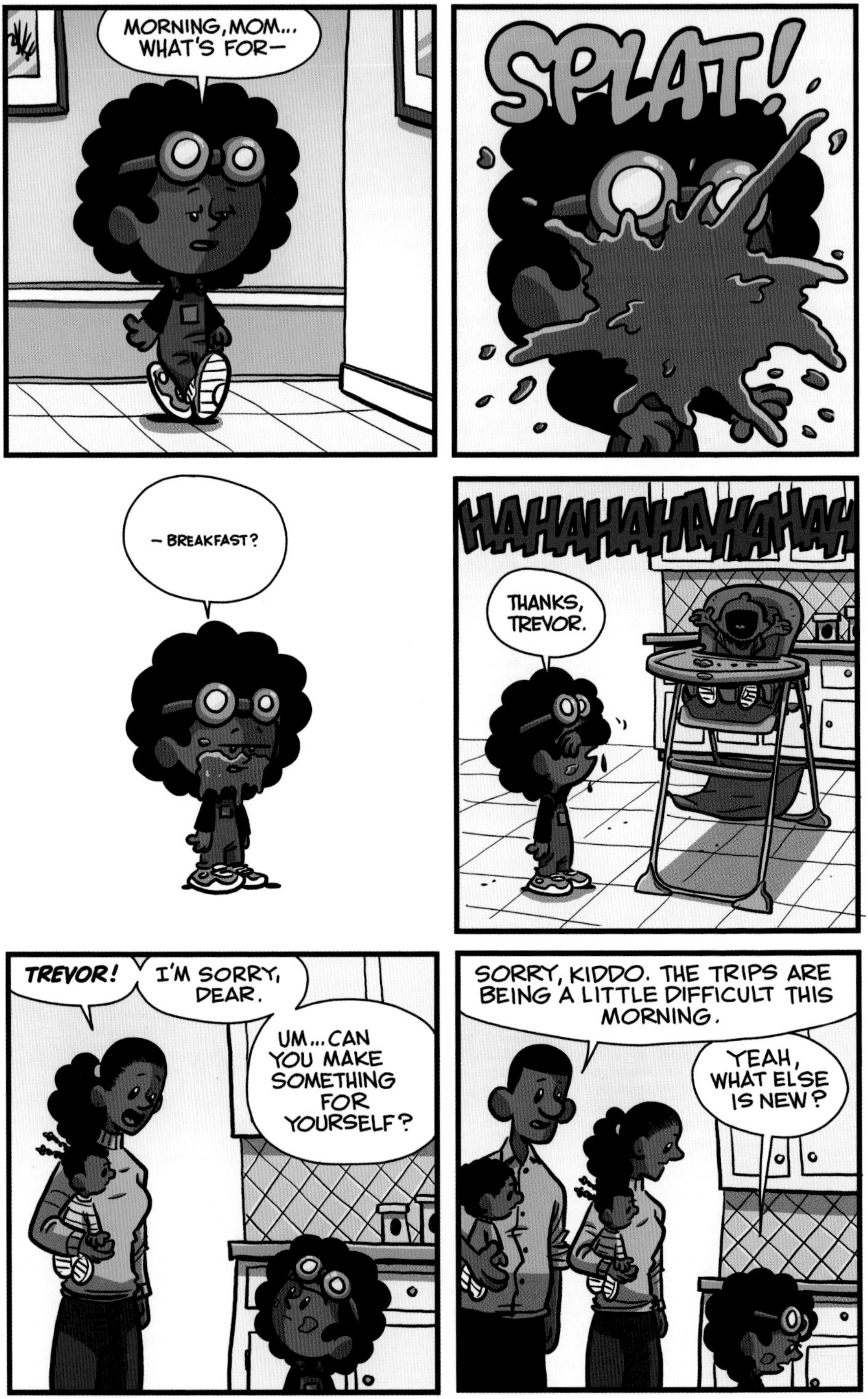
MORNING, MOM... WHAT'S FOR—
SPLAT!
—BREAKFAST?
HAHAHAHAHAHAHAH
THANKS, TREVOR.
TREVOR!
I'M SORRY, DEAR.
UM... CAN YOU MAKE SOMETHING FOR YOURSELF?
SORRY, KIDDO. THE TRIPS ARE BEING A LITTLE DIFFICULT THIS MORNING.
YEAH, WHAT ELSE IS NEW?

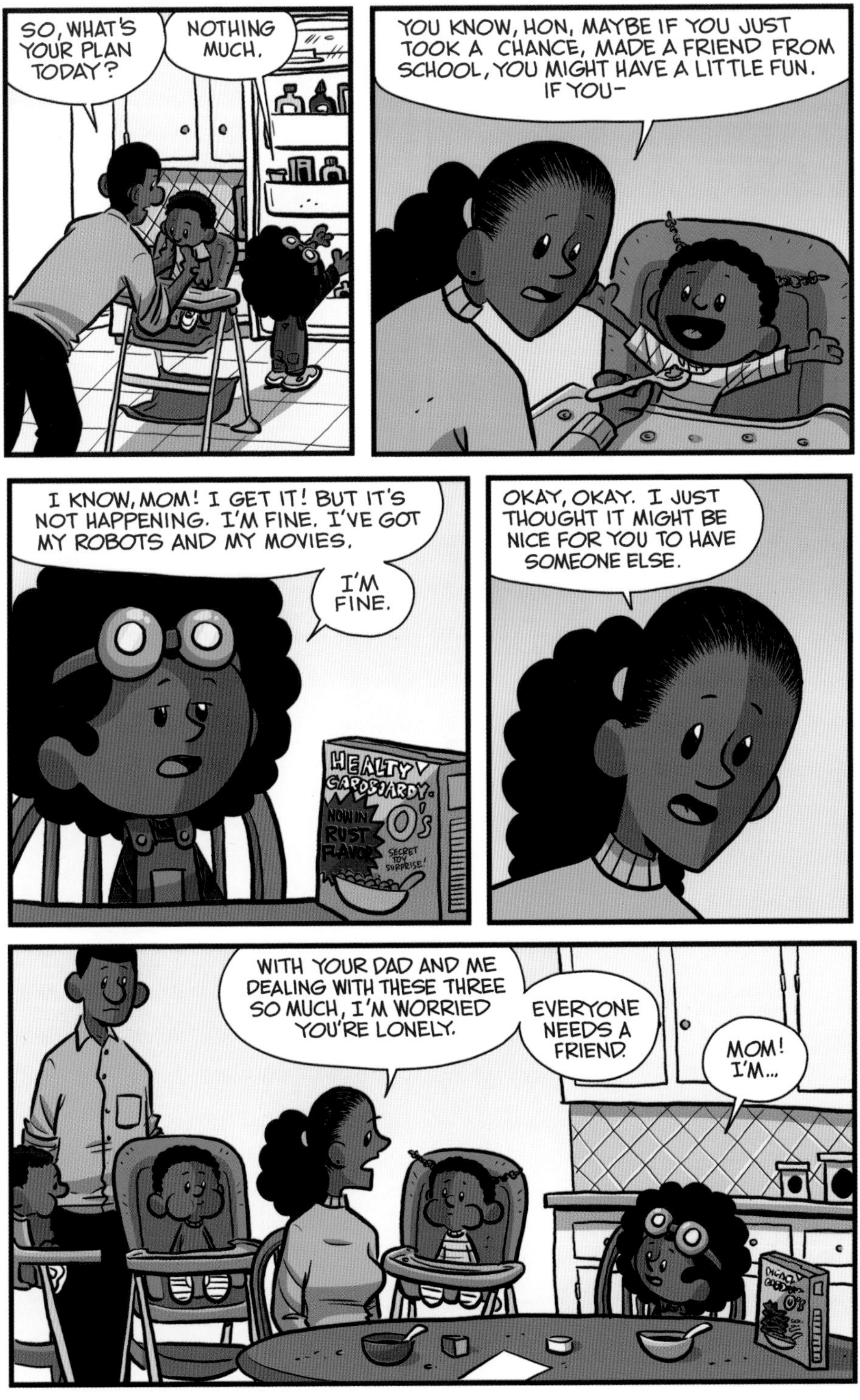
SO, WHAT'S YOUR PLAN TODAY?
NOTHING MUCH.
YOU KNOW, HON, MAYBE IF YOU JUST TOOK A CHANCE, MADE A FRIEND FROM SCHOOL, YOU MIGHT HAVE A LITTLE FUN. IF YOU–
I KNOW, MOM! I GET IT! BUT IT'S NOT HAPPENING. I'M FINE. I'VE GOT MY ROBOTS AND MY MOVIES.
I'M FINE.
HEALTY CARDBOARDY O's
NOW IN RUST FLAVOR
SECRET TOY SURPRISE!
OKAY, OKAY. I JUST THOUGHT IT MIGHT BE NICE FOR YOU TO HAVE SOMEONE ELSE.
WITH YOUR DAD AND ME DEALING WITH THESE THREE SO MUCH, I'M WORRIED YOU'RE LONELY.
EVERYONE NEEDS A FRIEND.
MOM! I'M...

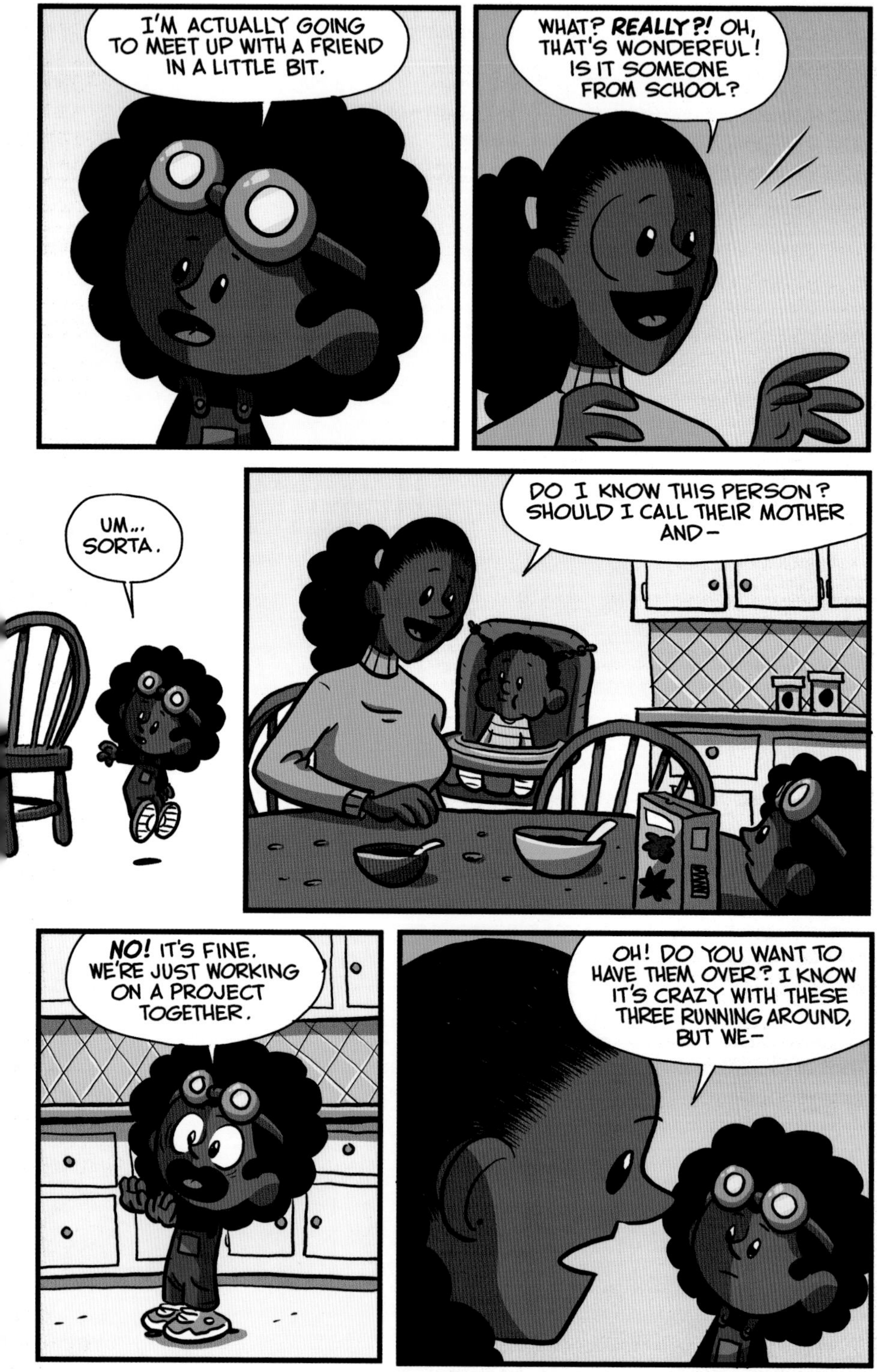
I'M ACTUALLY GOING TO MEET UP WITH A FRIEND IN A LITTLE BIT.
WHAT? **REALLY?!** OH, THAT'S WONDERFUL! IS IT SOMEONE FROM SCHOOL?
UM... SORTA.
DO I KNOW THIS PERSON? SHOULD I CALL THEIR MOTHER AND—
NO! IT'S FINE. WE'RE JUST WORKING ON A PROJECT TOGETHER.
OH! DO YOU WANT TO HAVE THEM OVER? I KNOW IT'S CRAZY WITH THESE THREE RUNNING AROUND, BUT WE—

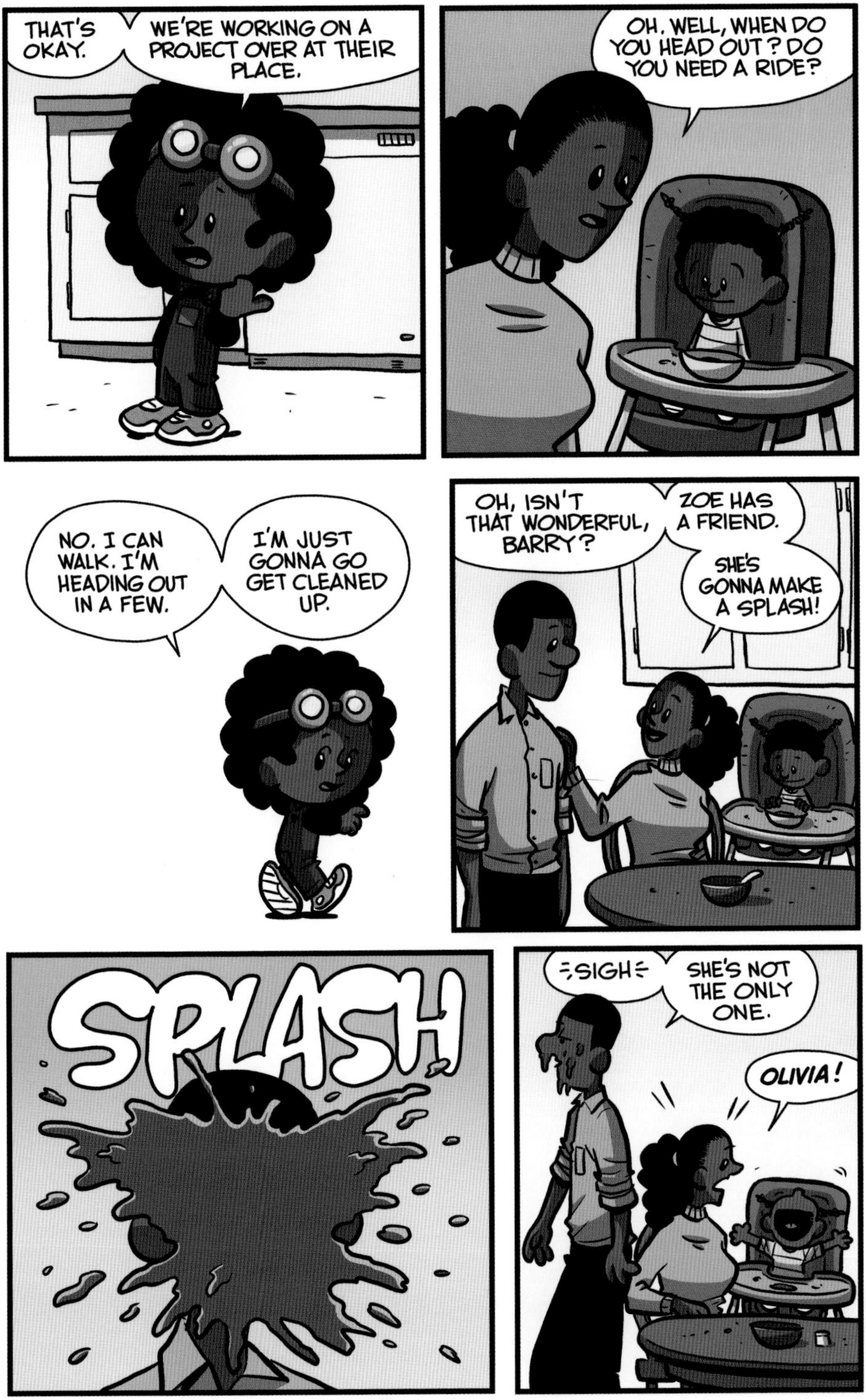
THAT'S OKAY.
WE'RE WORKING ON A PROJECT OVER AT THEIR PLACE.
OH. WELL, WHEN DO YOU HEAD OUT? DO YOU NEED A RIDE?
NO. I CAN WALK. I'M HEADING OUT IN A FEW.
I'M JUST GONNA GO GET CLEANED UP.
OH, ISN'T THAT WONDERFUL, BARRY?
ZOE HAS A FRIEND.
SHE'S GONNA MAKE A SPLASH!
SPLASH
=SIGH=
SHE'S NOT THE ONLY ONE.
OLIVIA!

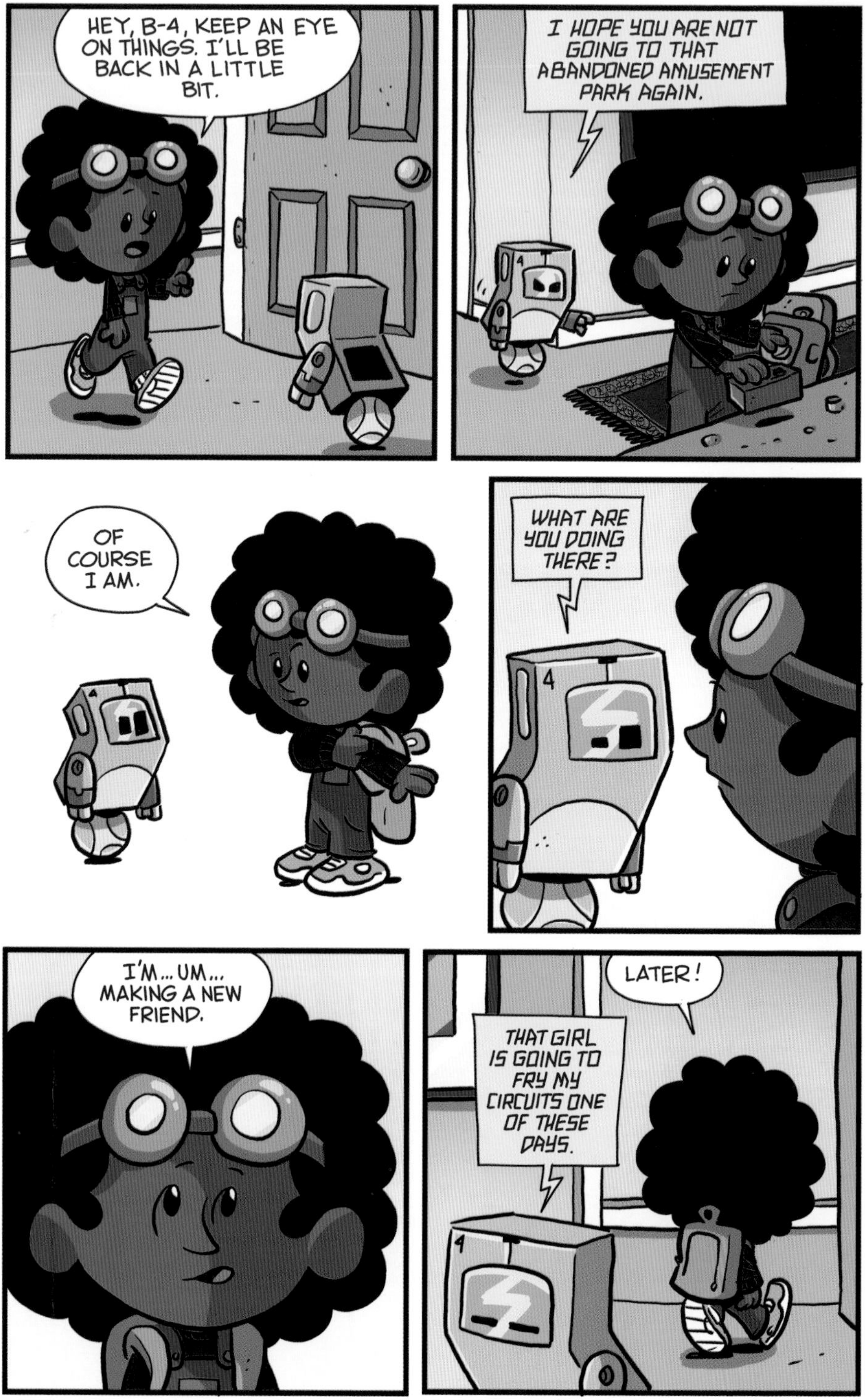
HEY, B-4, KEEP AN EYE ON THINGS. I'LL BE BACK IN A LITTLE BIT.
I HOPE YOU ARE NOT GOING TO THAT ABANDONED AMUSEMENT PARK AGAIN.
OF COURSE I AM.
WHAT ARE YOU DOING THERE?
I'M... UM... MAKING A NEW FRIEND.
LATER!
THAT GIRL IS GOING TO FRY MY CIRCUITS ONE OF THESE DAYS.

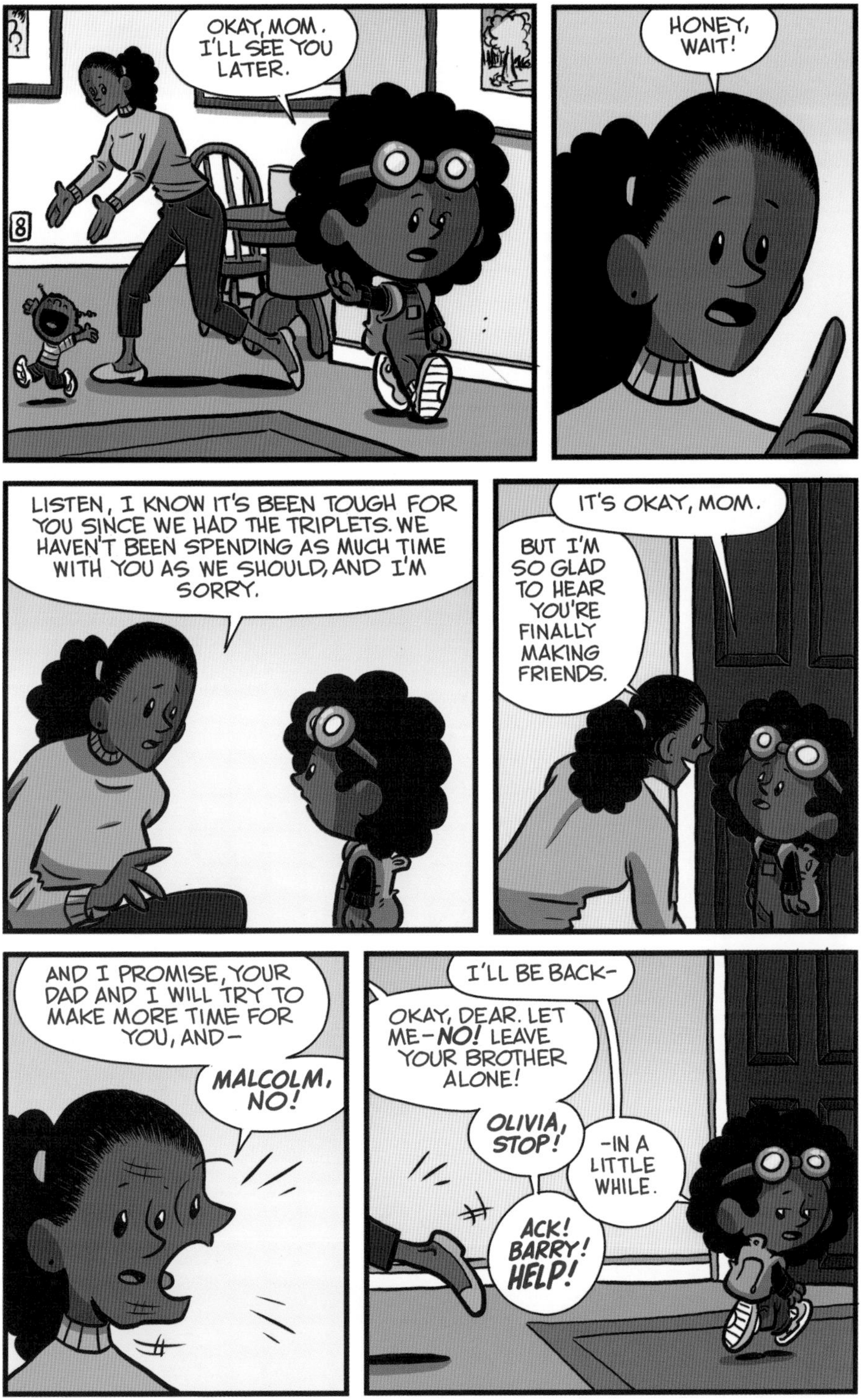
OKAY, MOM. I'LL SEE YOU LATER.
HONEY, WAIT!
LISTEN, I KNOW IT'S BEEN TOUGH FOR YOU SINCE WE HAD THE TRIPLETS. WE HAVEN'T BEEN SPENDING AS MUCH TIME WITH YOU AS WE SHOULD, AND I'M SORRY.
IT'S OKAY, MOM.
BUT I'M SO GLAD TO HEAR YOU'RE FINALLY MAKING FRIENDS.
AND I PROMISE, YOUR DAD AND I WILL TRY TO MAKE MORE TIME FOR YOU, AND—
MALCOLM, NO!
I'LL BE BACK—
OKAY, DEAR. LET ME—NO! LEAVE YOUR BROTHER ALONE!
OLIVIA, STOP!
—IN A LITTLE WHILE.
ACK! BARRY! HELP!

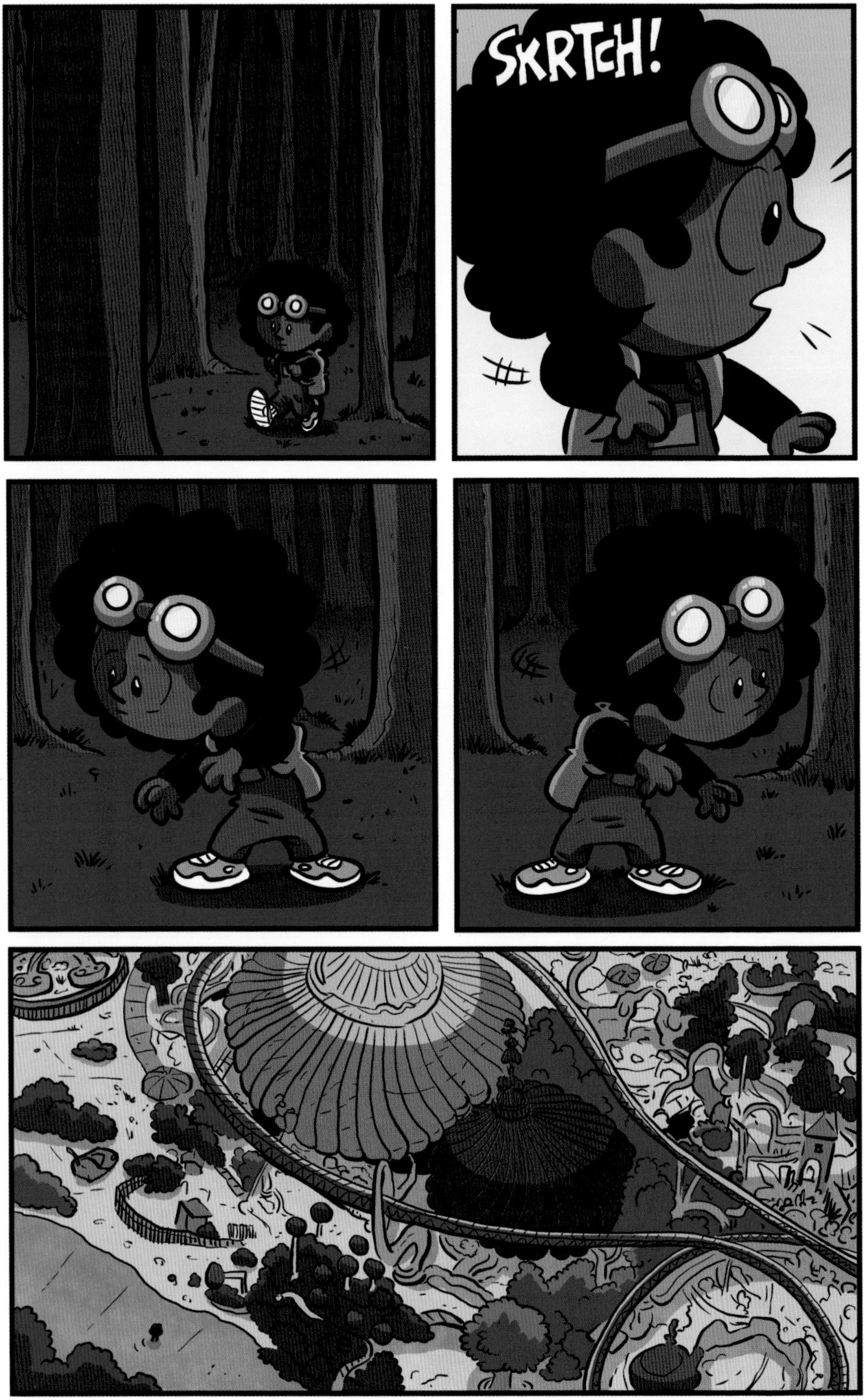
SKRTCH!

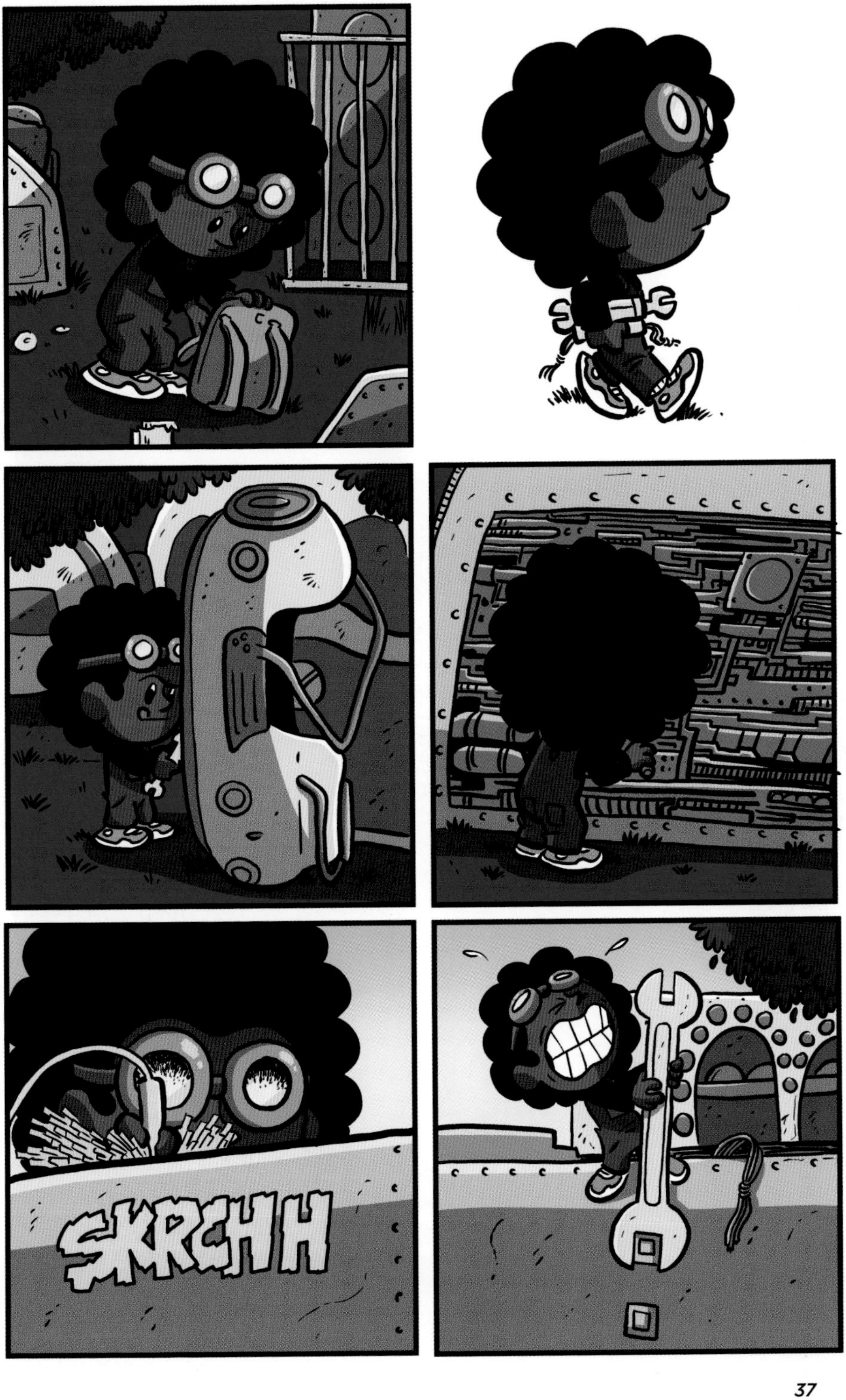
SKRCHH

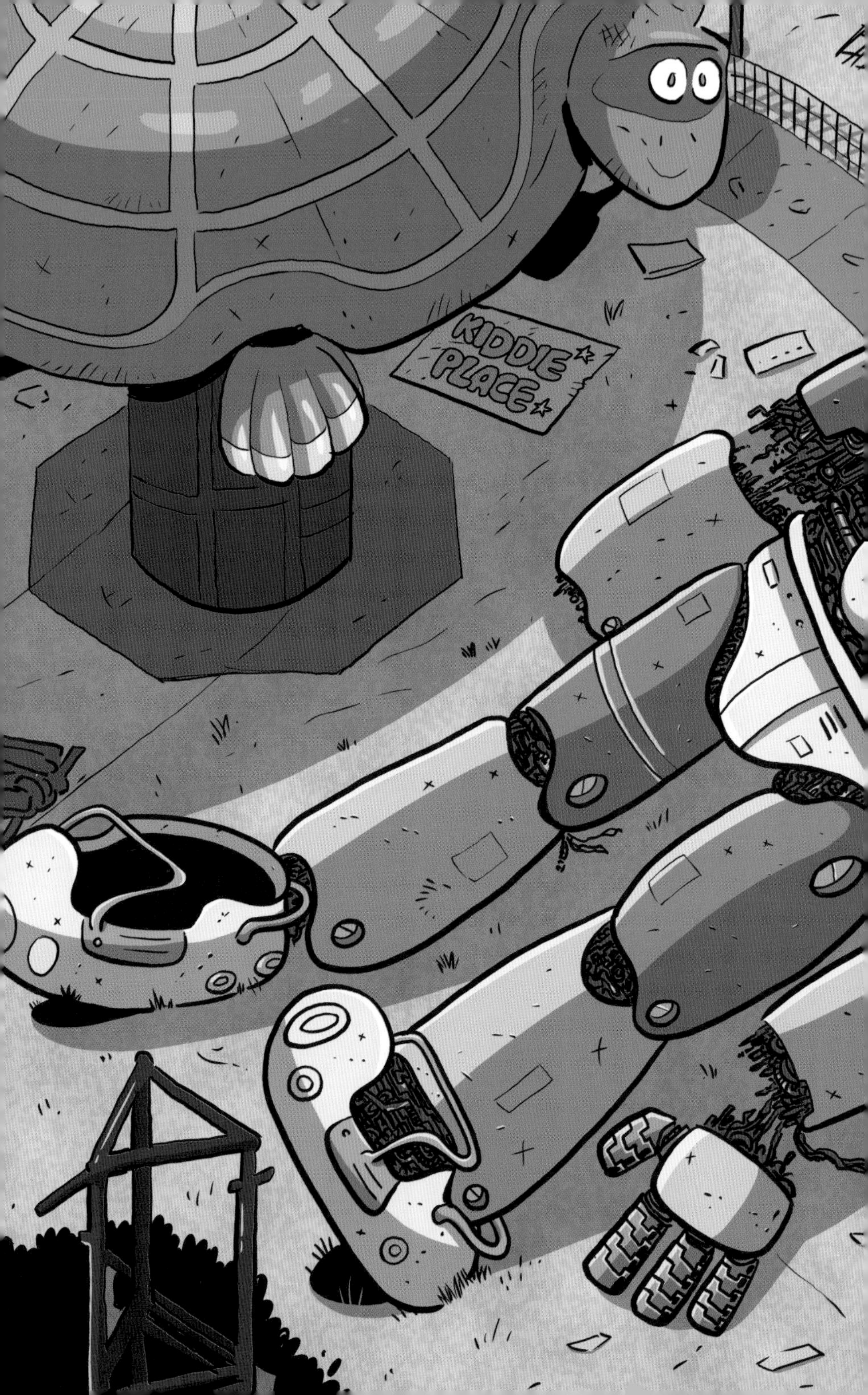
KIDDIE PLACE

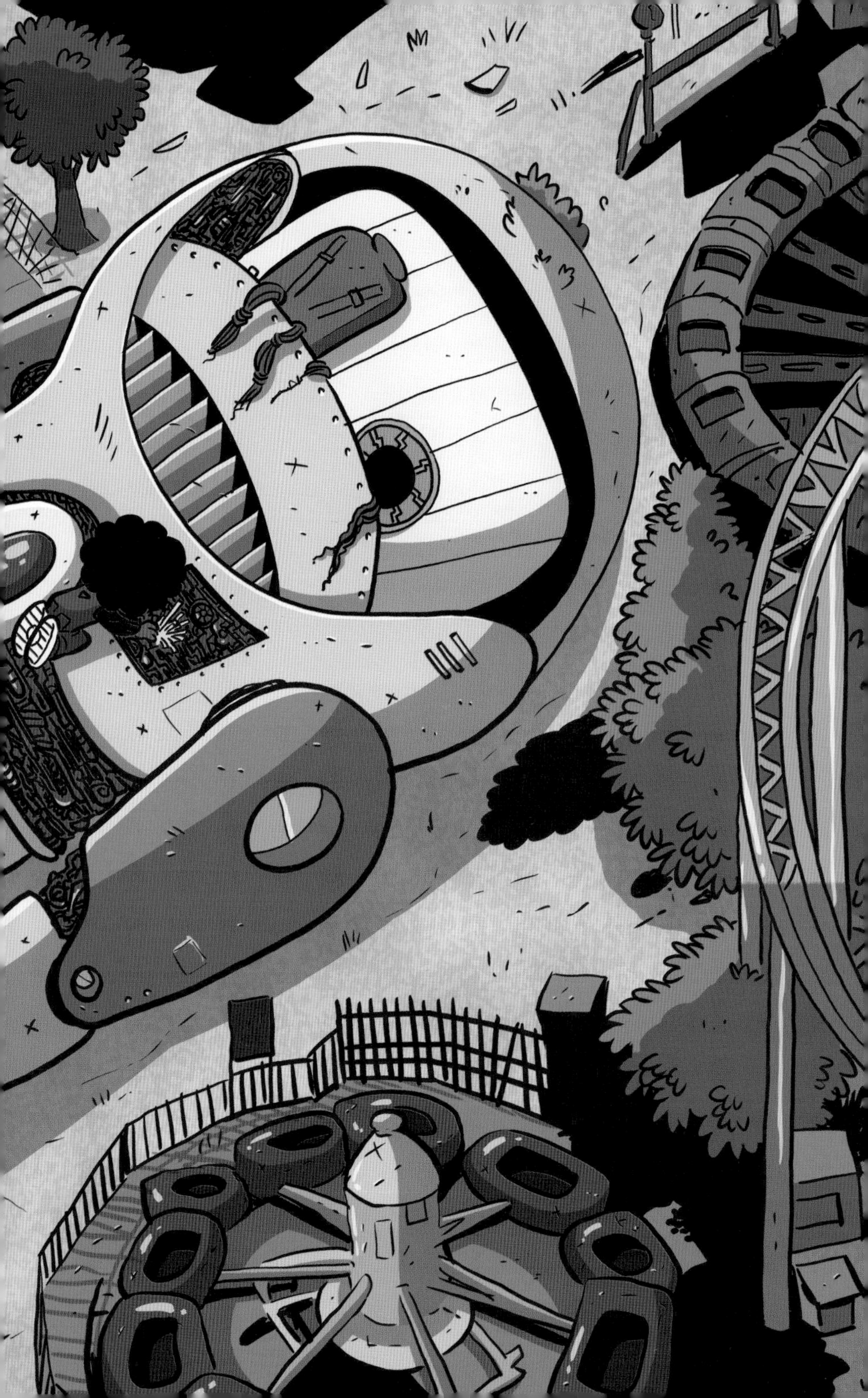

CHAPTER 4 - PICTURE DAY DISASTER

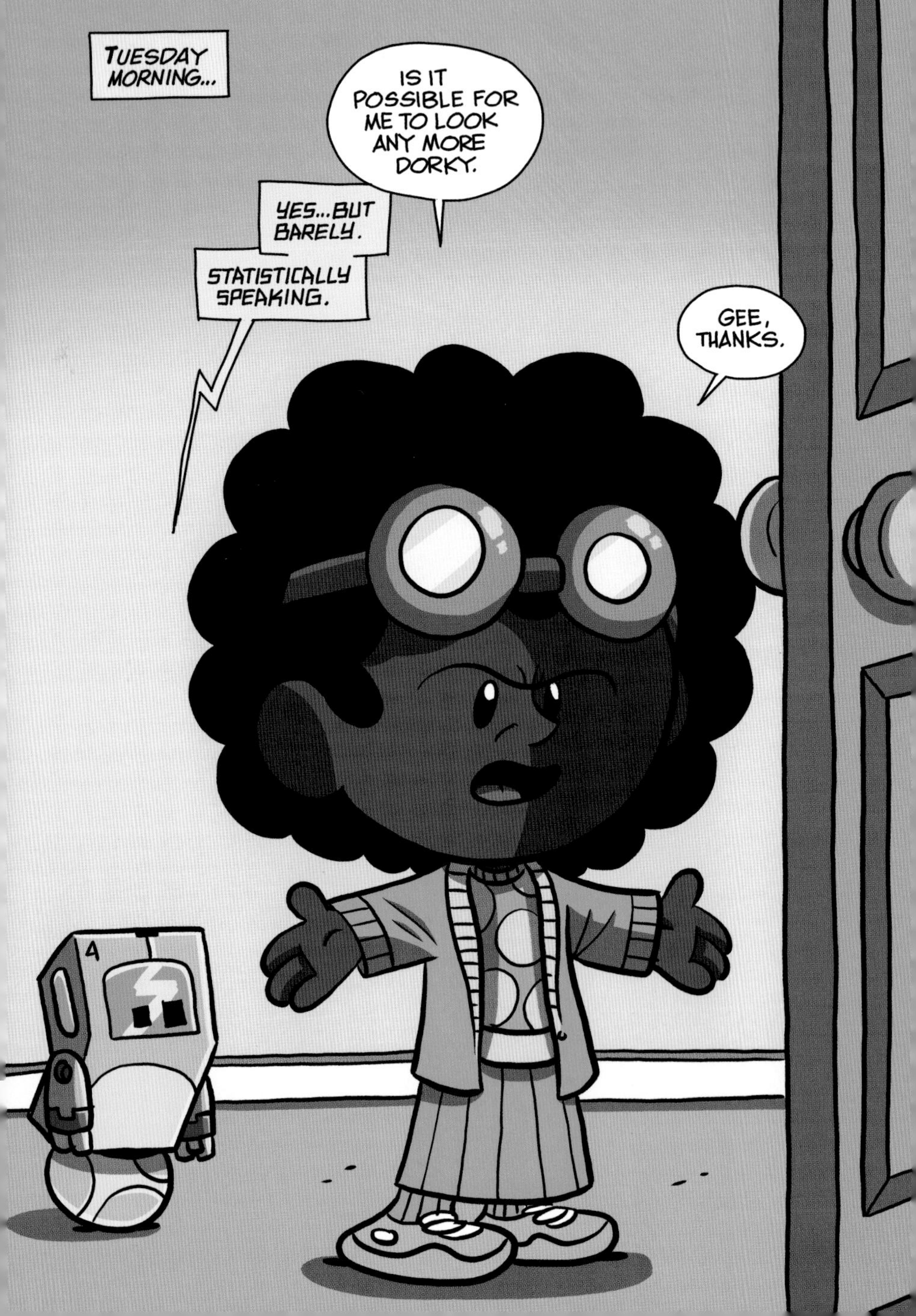
TUESDAY MORNING...
IS IT POSSIBLE FOR ME TO LOOK ANY MORE DORKY.
YES...BUT BARELY.
STATISTICALLY SPEAKING.
GEE, THANKS.
4

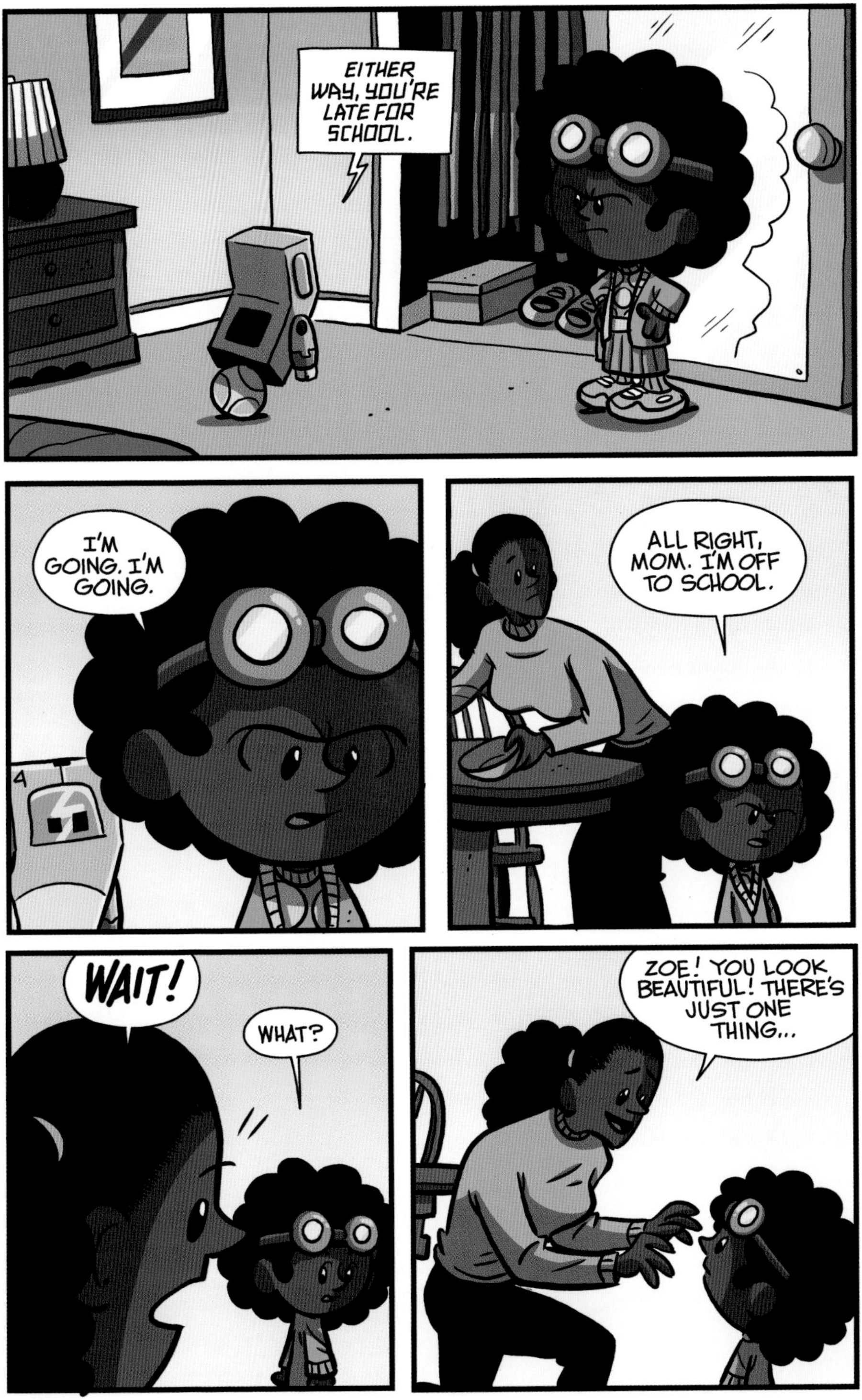
EITHER WAY, YOU'RE LATE FOR SCHOOL.
I'M GOING. I'M GOING.
ALL RIGHT, MOM. I'M OFF TO SCHOOL.
WAIT!
WHAT?
ZOE! YOU LOOK BEAUTIFUL! THERE'S JUST ONE THING...

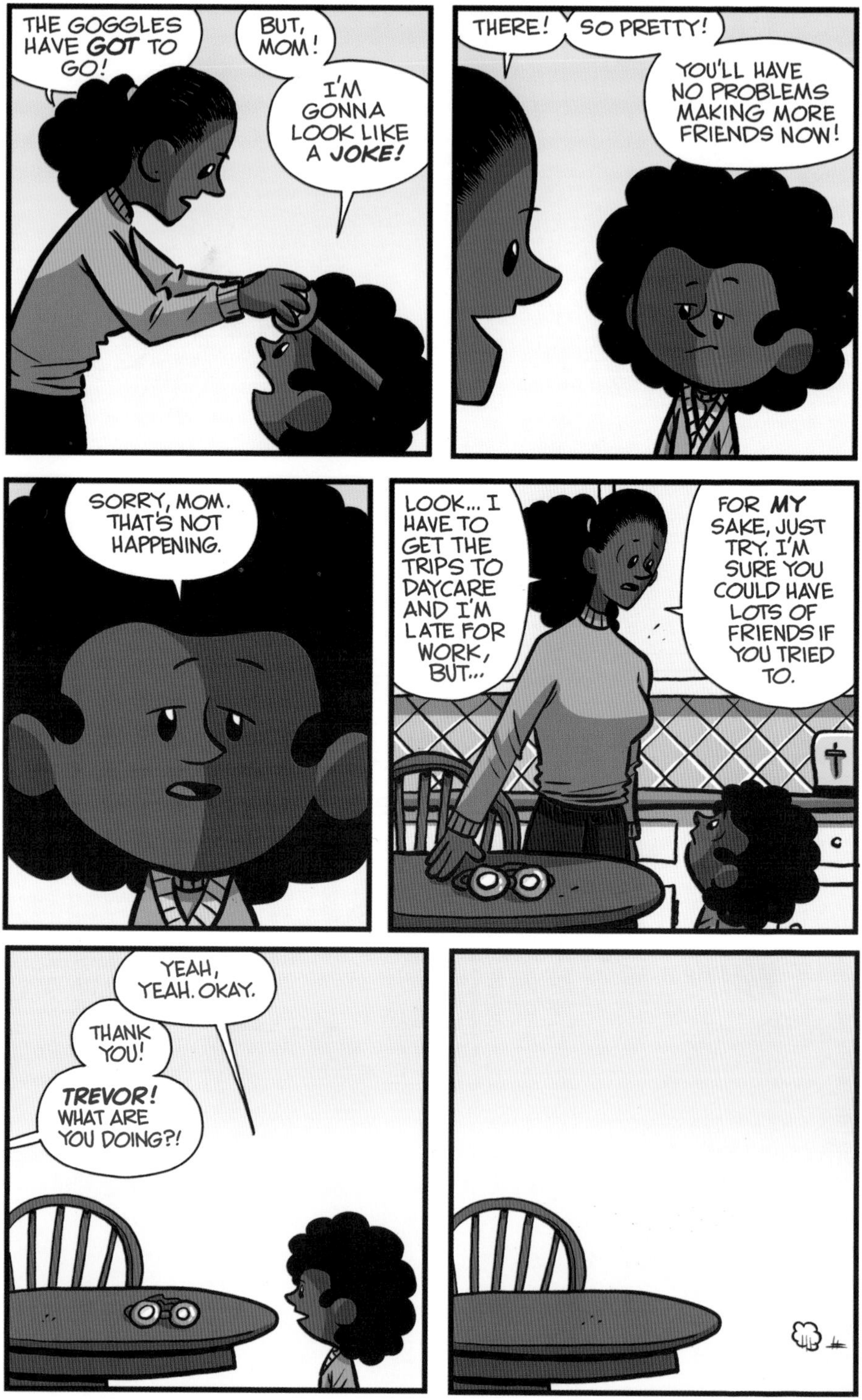
THE GOGGLES HAVE GOT TO GO!
BUT, MOM!
I'M GONNA LOOK LIKE A JOKE!
THERE!
SO PRETTY!
YOU'LL HAVE NO PROBLEMS MAKING MORE FRIENDS NOW!
SORRY, MOM. THAT'S NOT HAPPENING.
LOOK... I HAVE TO GET THE TRIPS TO DAYCARE AND I'M LATE FOR WORK, BUT...
FOR MY SAKE, JUST TRY. I'M SURE YOU COULD HAVE LOTS OF FRIENDS IF YOU TRIED TO.
YEAH, YEAH. OKAY.
THANK YOU!
TREVOR! WHAT ARE YOU DOING?!

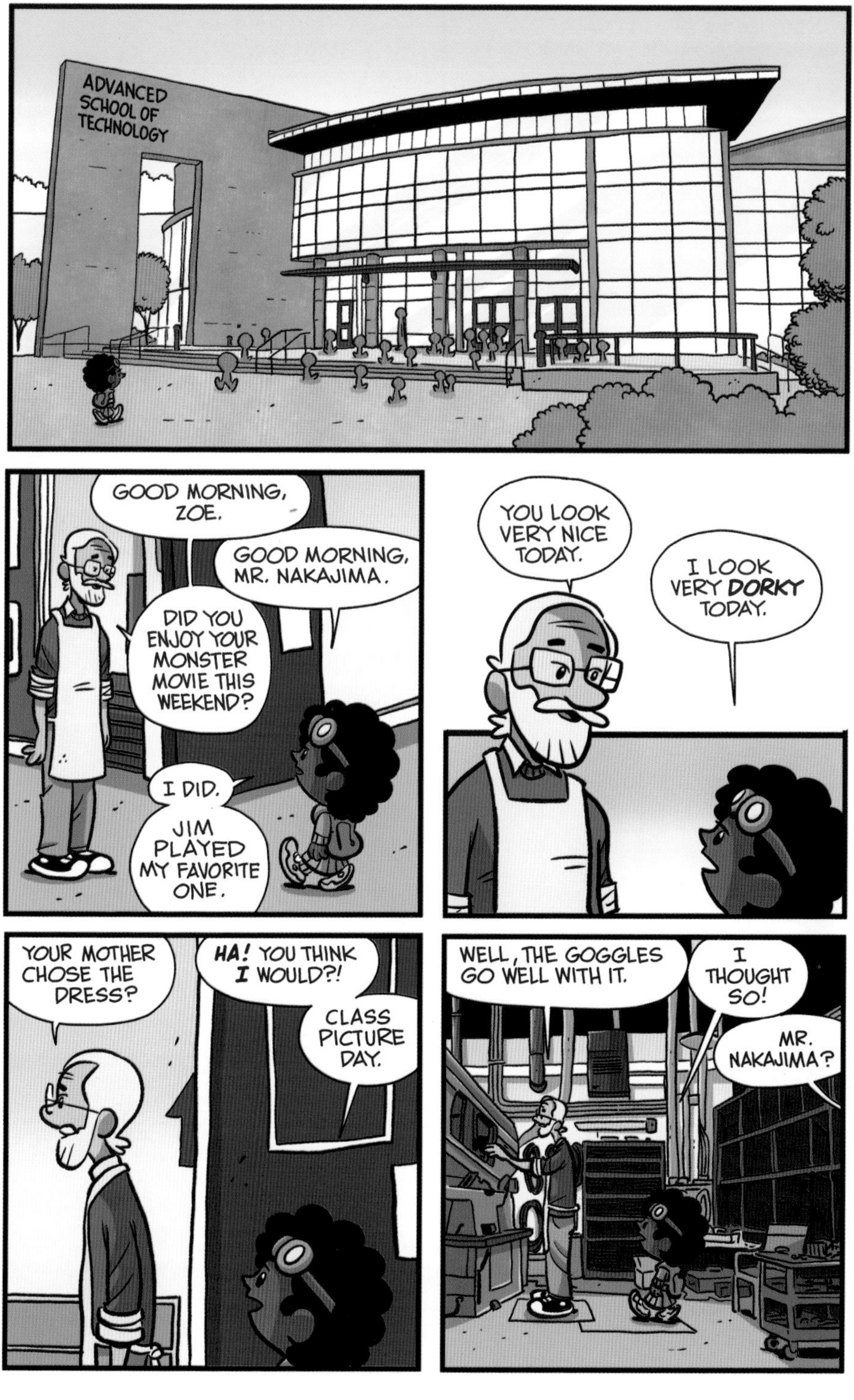
ADVANCED SCHOOL OF TECHNOLOGY
GOOD MORNING, ZOE.
GOOD MORNING, MR. NAKAJIMA.
DID YOU ENJOY YOUR MONSTER MOVIE THIS WEEKEND?
I DID.
JIM PLAYED MY FAVORITE ONE.
YOU LOOK VERY NICE TODAY.
I LOOK VERY **DORKY** TODAY.
YOUR MOTHER CHOSE THE DRESS?
HA! YOU THINK **I** WOULD?!
CLASS PICTURE DAY.
WELL, THE GOGGLES GO WELL WITH IT.
I THOUGHT SO!
MR. NAKAJIMA?

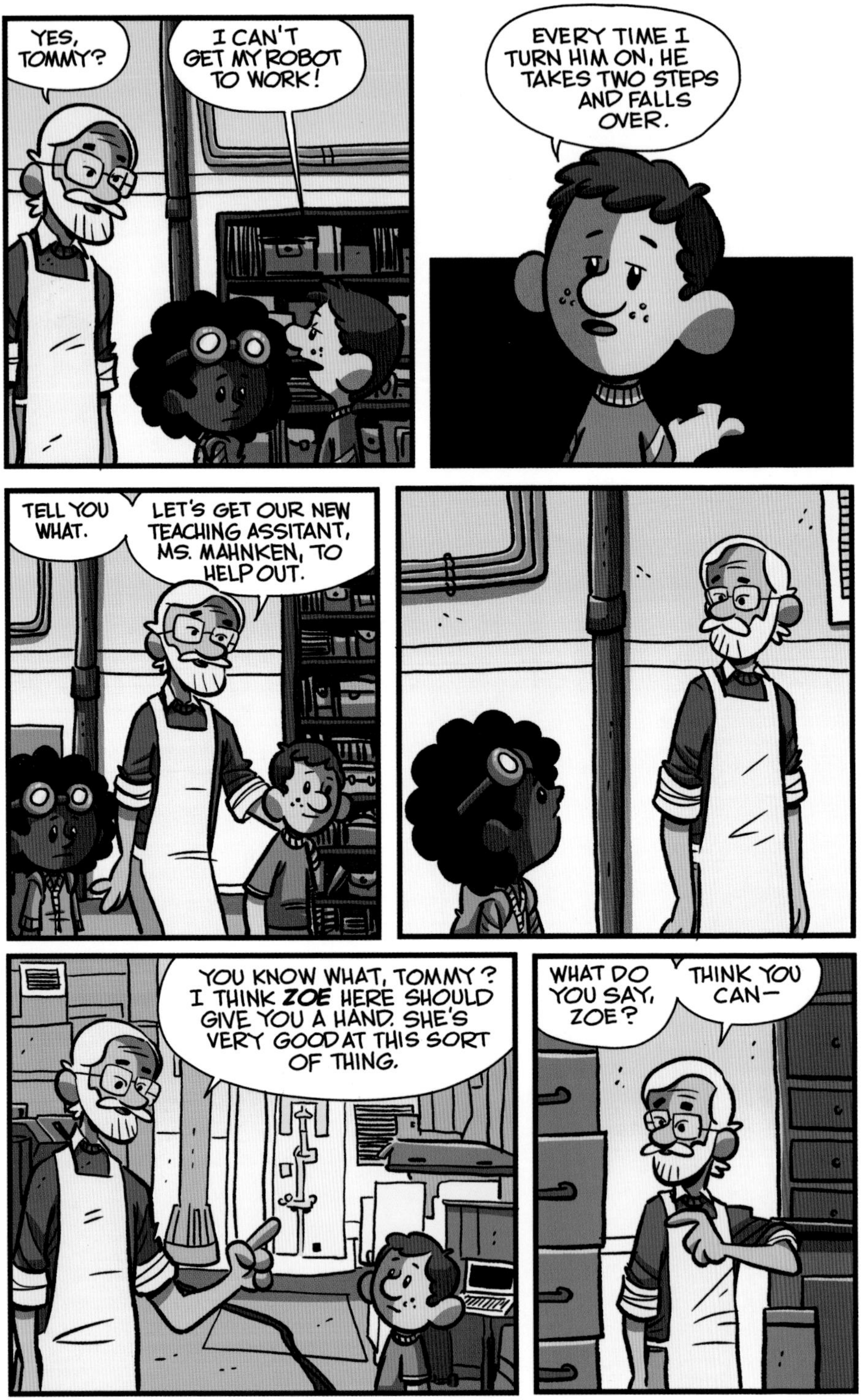
YES, TOMMY?
I CAN'T GET MY ROBOT TO WORK!
EVERY TIME I TURN HIM ON, HE TAKES TWO STEPS AND FALLS OVER.
TELL YOU WHAT.
LET'S GET OUR NEW TEACHING ASSITANT, MS. MAHNKEN, TO HELP OUT.
YOU KNOW WHAT, TOMMY? I THINK ZOE HERE SHOULD GIVE YOU A HAND. SHE'S VERY GOOD AT THIS SORT OF THING.
WHAT DO YOU SAY, ZOE?
THINK YOU CAN—

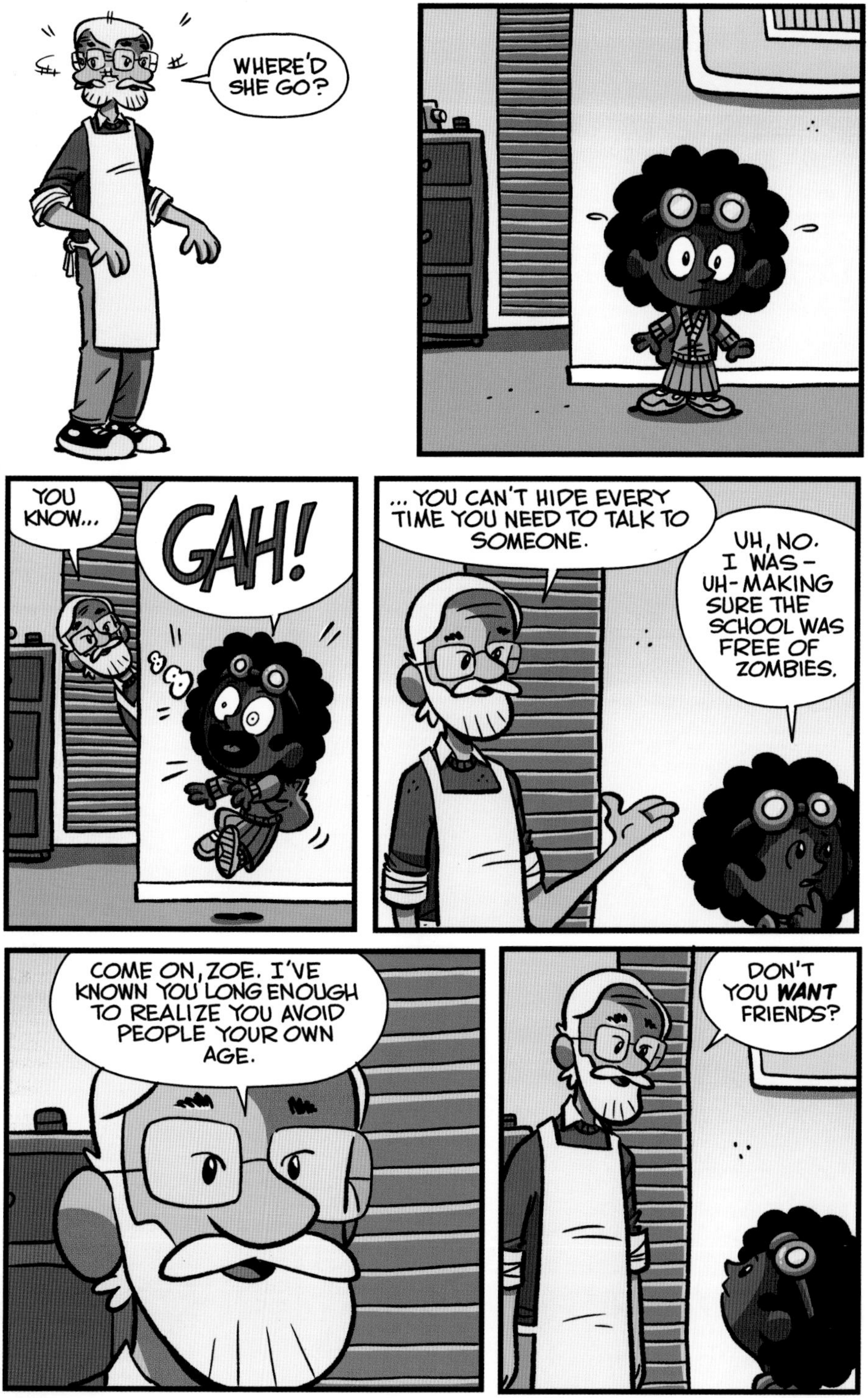
WHERE'D SHE GO?
YOU KNOW...
GAH!
...YOU CAN'T HIDE EVERY TIME YOU NEED TO TALK TO SOMEONE.
UH, NO. I WAS - UH - MAKING SURE THE SCHOOL WAS FREE OF ZOMBIES.
COME ON, ZOE. I'VE KNOWN YOU LONG ENOUGH TO REALIZE YOU AVOID PEOPLE YOUR OWN AGE.
DON'T YOU **WANT** FRIENDS?

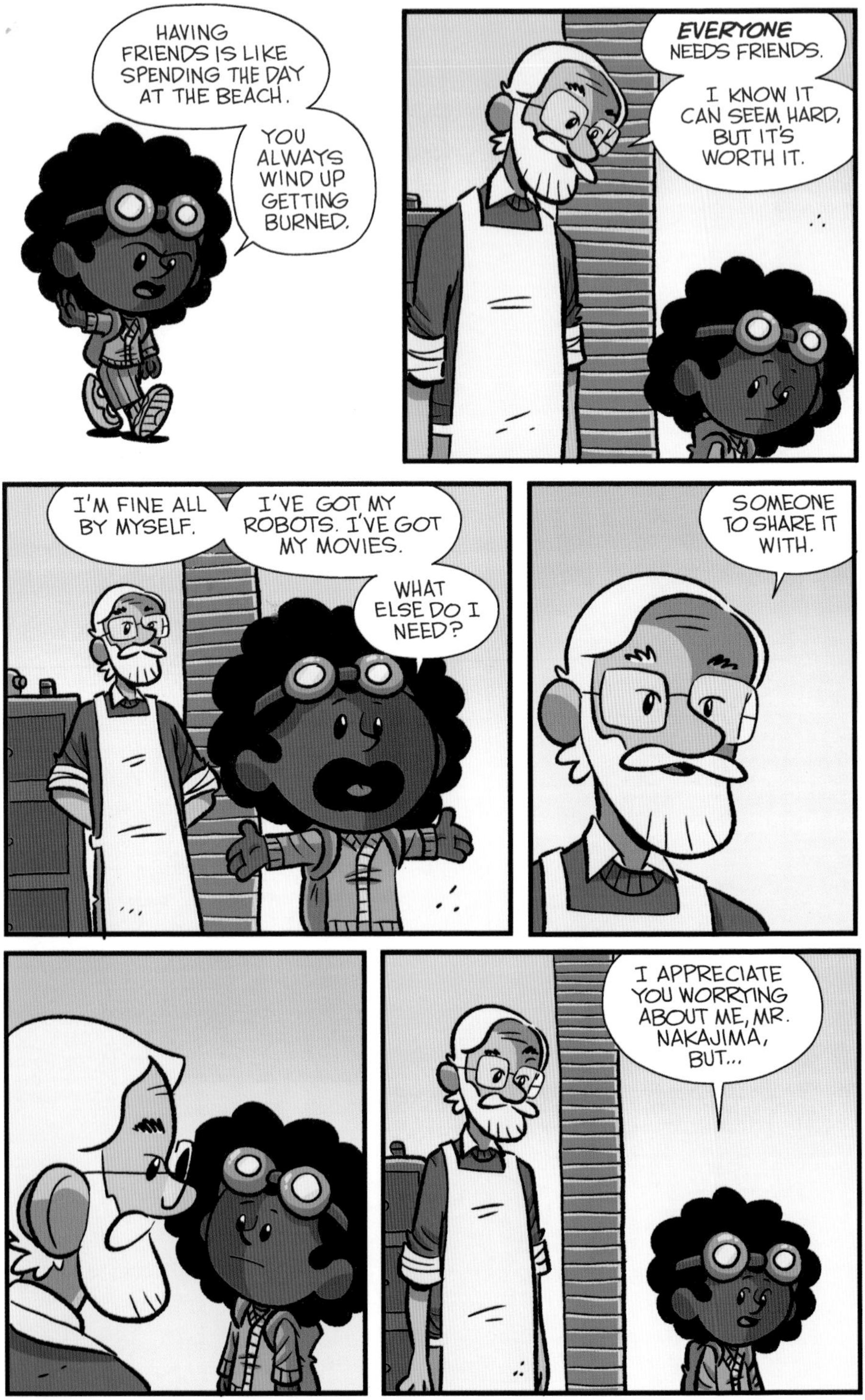
HAVING FRIENDS IS LIKE SPENDING THE DAY AT THE BEACH.
YOU ALWAYS WIND UP GETTING BURNED.
EVERYONE NEEDS FRIENDS.
I KNOW IT CAN SEEM HARD, BUT IT'S WORTH IT.
I'M FINE ALL BY MYSELF.
I'VE GOT MY ROBOTS. I'VE GOT MY MOVIES.
WHAT ELSE DO I NEED?
SOMEONE TO SHARE IT WITH.
I APPRECIATE YOU WORRYING ABOUT ME, MR. NAKAJIMA, BUT...

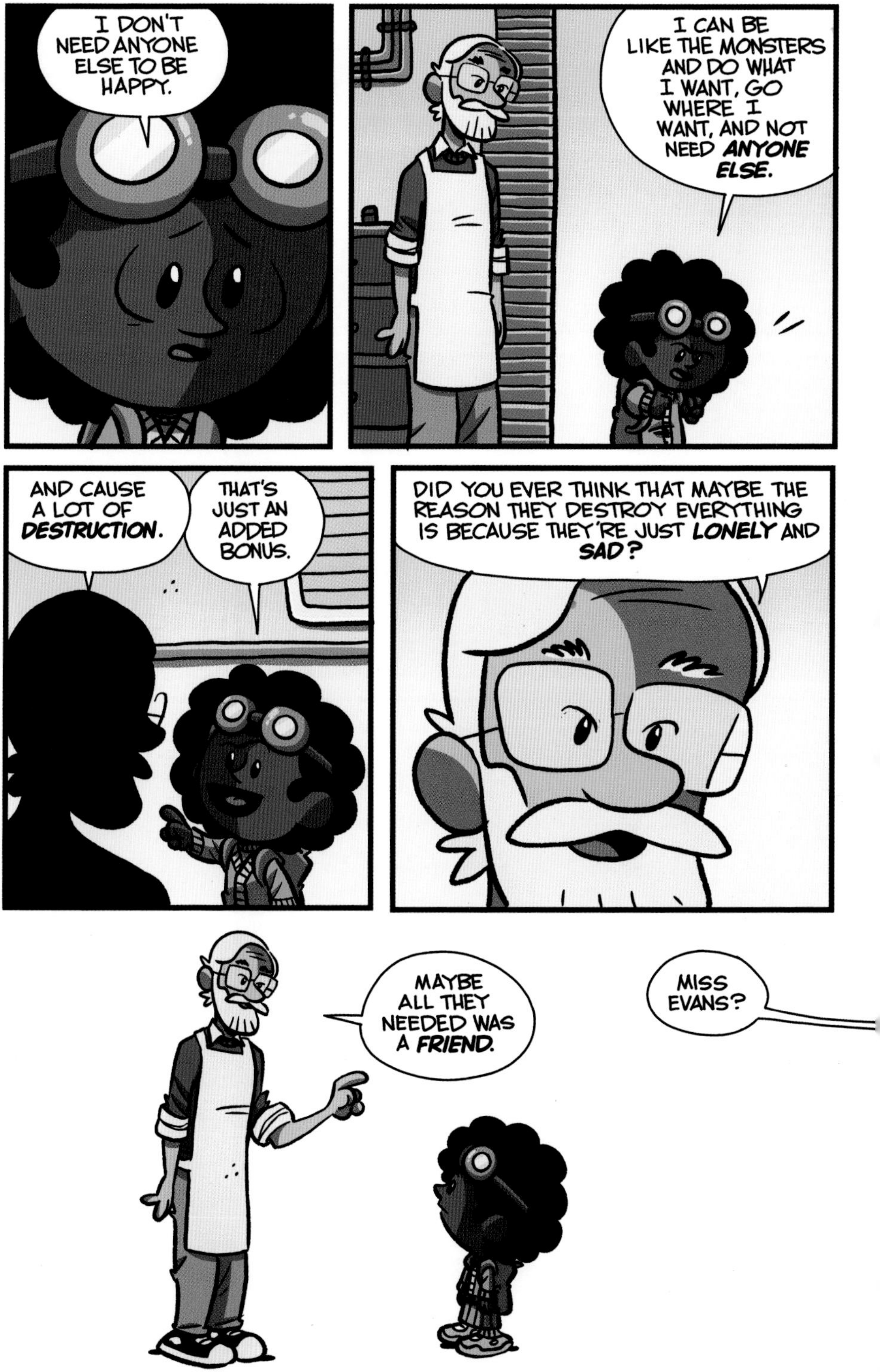
I DON'T NEED ANYONE ELSE TO BE HAPPY.
I CAN BE LIKE THE MONSTERS AND DO WHAT I WANT, GO WHERE I WANT, AND NOT NEED ANYONE ELSE.
AND CAUSE A LOT OF DESTRUCTION.
THAT'S JUST AN ADDED BONUS.
DID YOU EVER THINK THAT MAYBE THE REASON THEY DESTROY EVERYTHING IS BECAUSE THEY'RE JUST LONELY AND SAD?
MAYBE ALL THEY NEEDED WAS A FRIEND.
MISS EVANS?

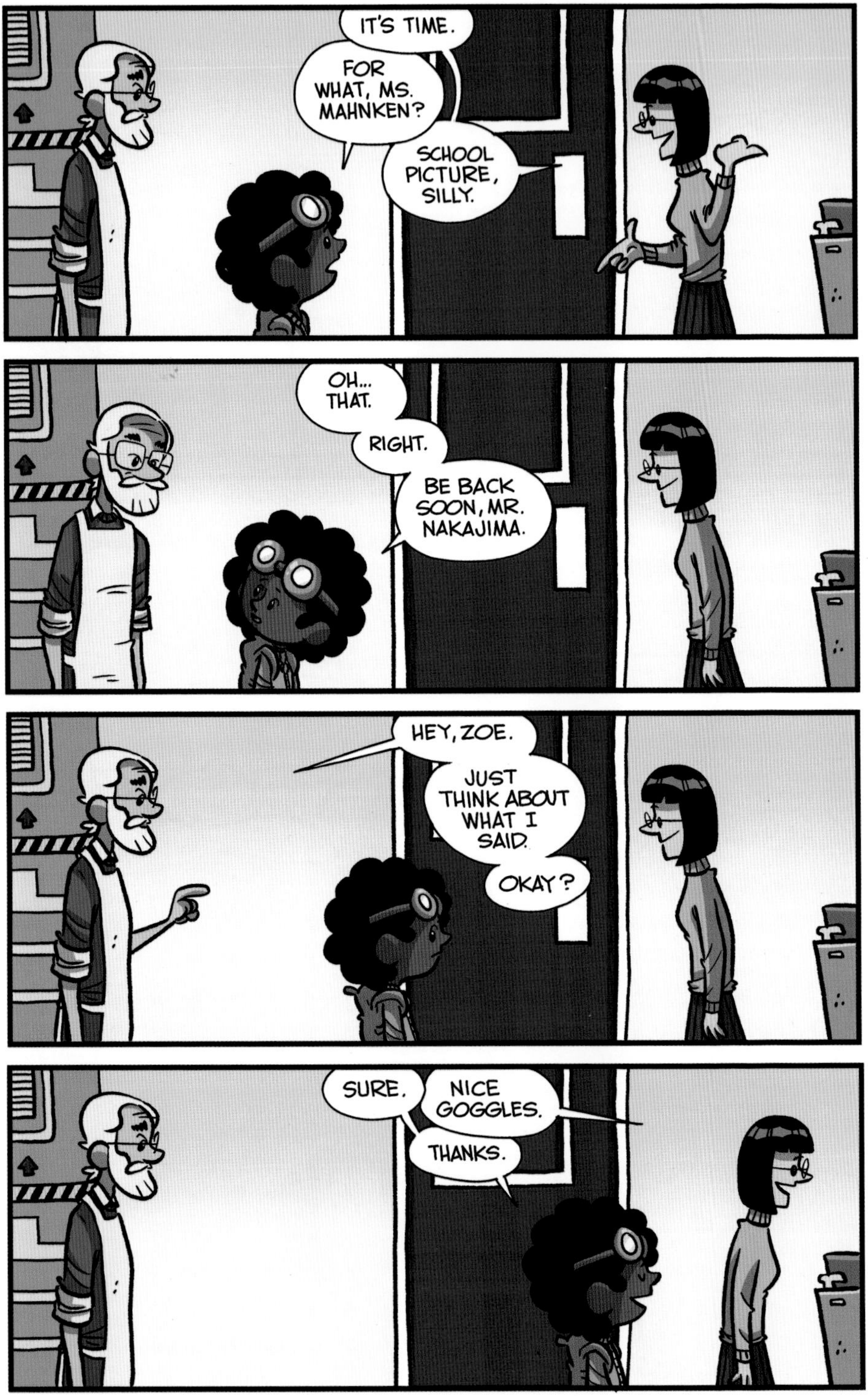
IT'S TIME.
FOR WHAT, MS. MAHNKEN?
SCHOOL PICTURE, SILLY.
OH... THAT.
RIGHT.
BE BACK SOON, MR. NAKAJIMA.
HEY, ZOE.
JUST THINK ABOUT WHAT I SAID.
OKAY?
SURE.
NICE GOGGLES.
THANKS.

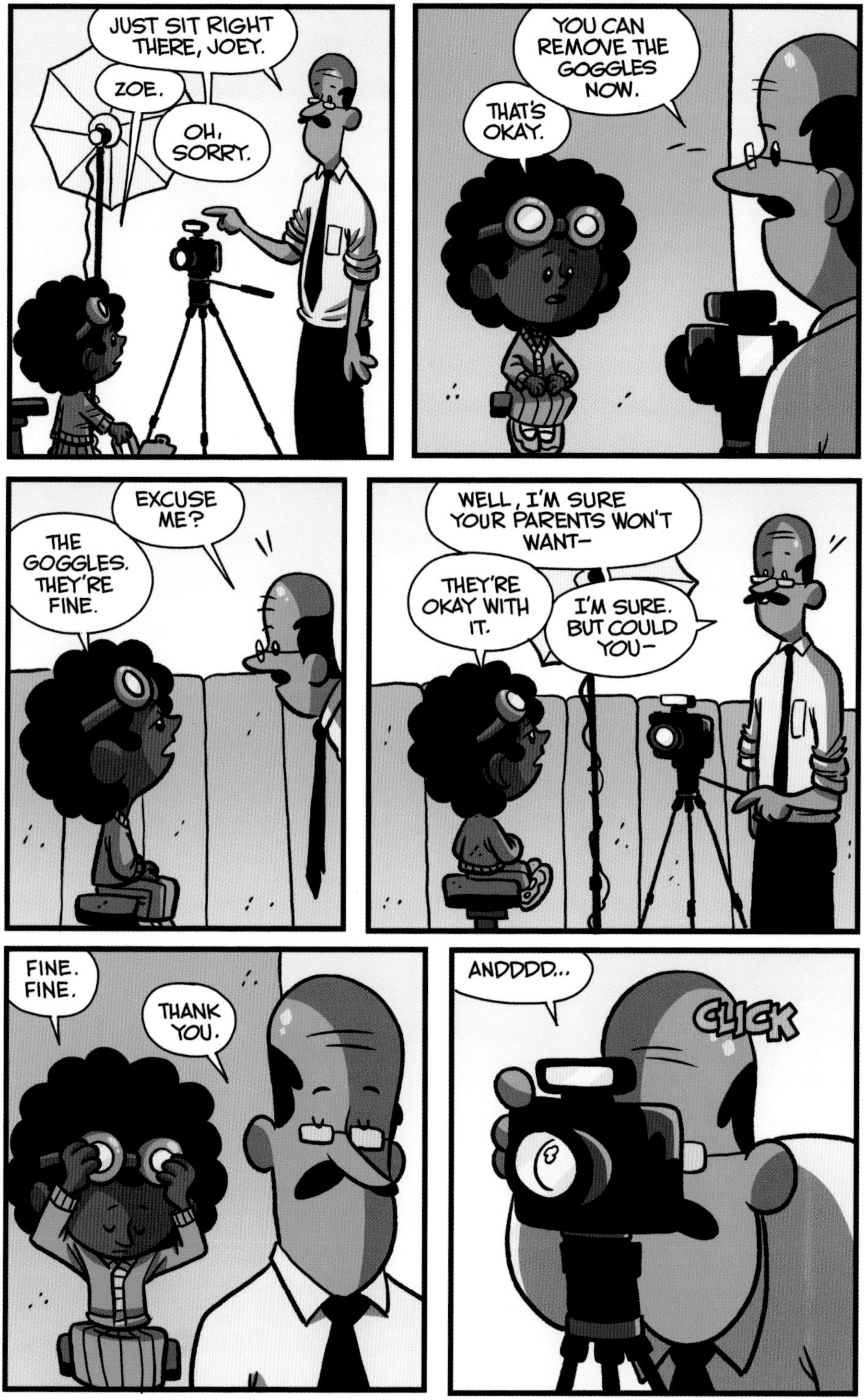
JUST SIT RIGHT THERE, JOEY.
ZOE.
OH, SORRY.
YOU CAN REMOVE THE GOGGLES NOW.
THAT'S OKAY.
EXCUSE ME?
THE GOGGLES. THEY'RE FINE.
WELL, I'M SURE YOUR PARENTS WON'T WANT–
THEY'RE OKAY WITH IT.
I'M SURE. BUT COULD YOU–
FINE. FINE.
THANK YOU.
ANDDDD...
CLICK

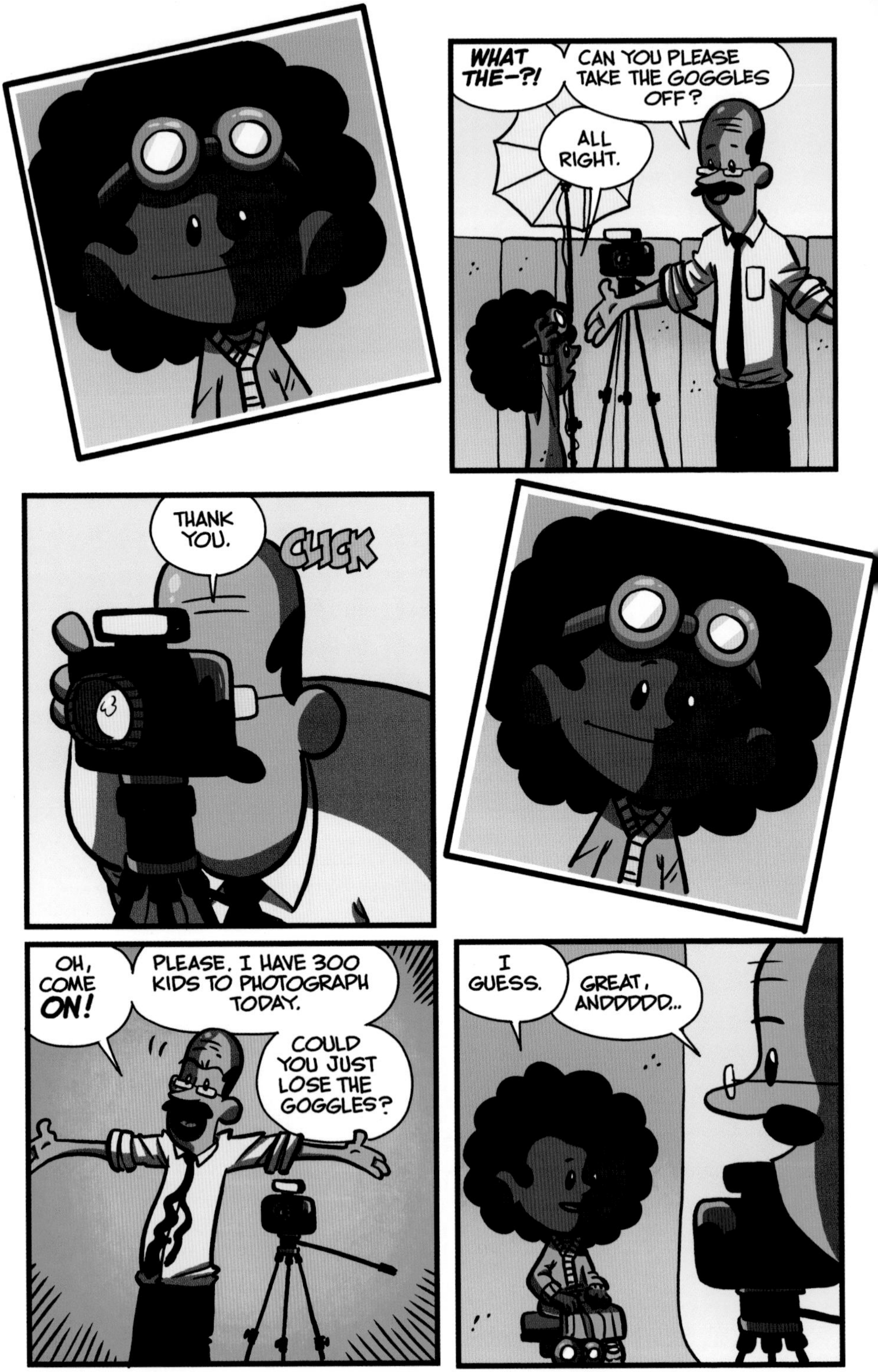
WHAT THE-?!
CAN YOU PLEASE TAKE THE GOGGLES OFF?
ALL RIGHT.
THANK YOU.
CLICK
OH, COME ON!
PLEASE. I HAVE 300 KIDS TO PHOTOGRAPH TODAY.
COULD YOU JUST LOSE THE GOGGLES?
I GUESS.
GREAT, ANDDDDD...

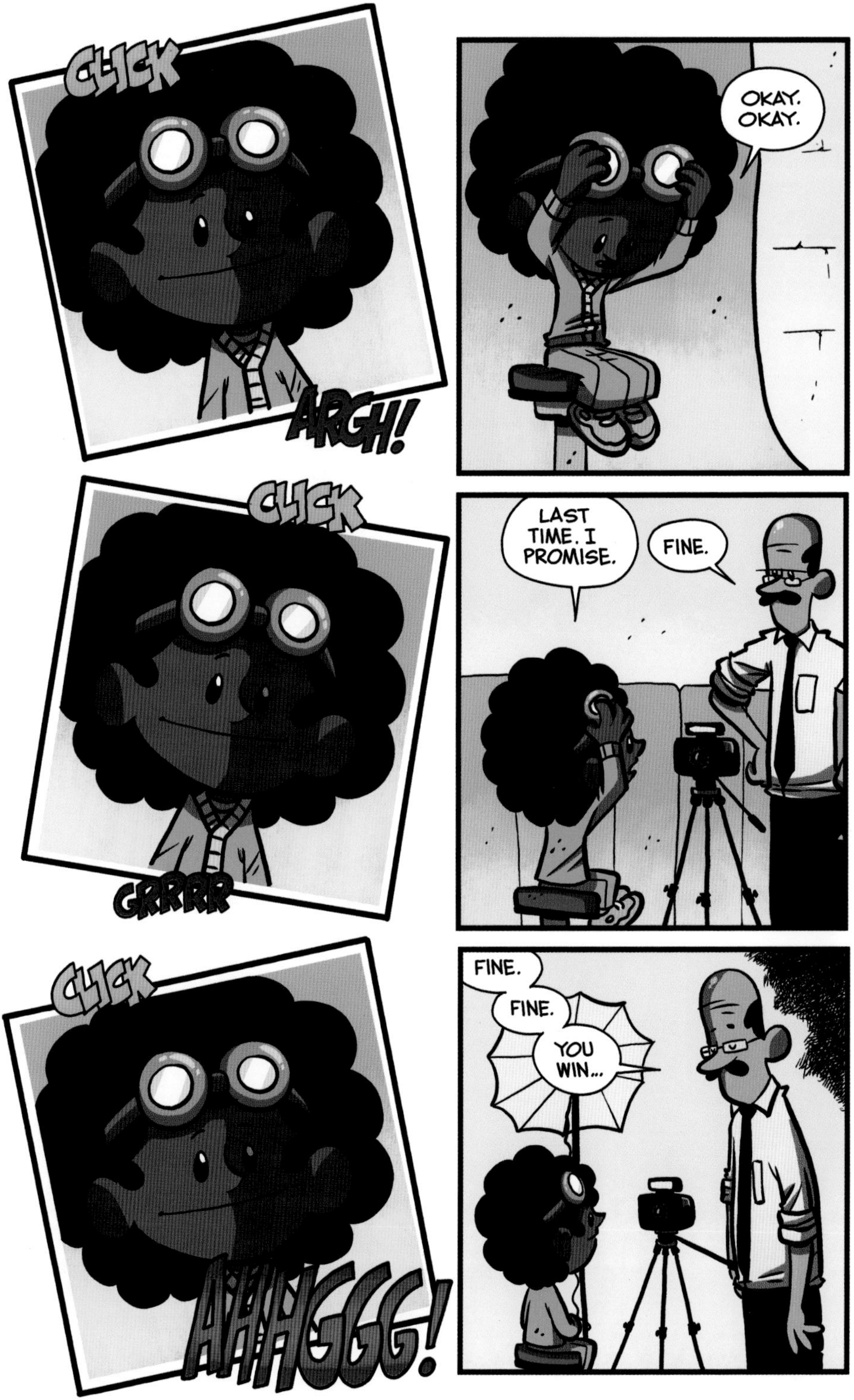
CLICK
ARGH!
OKAY. OKAY.
CLICK
GRRRR
LAST TIME. I PROMISE.
FINE.
CLICK
AHHGGG!
FINE.
FINE.
YOU WIN...

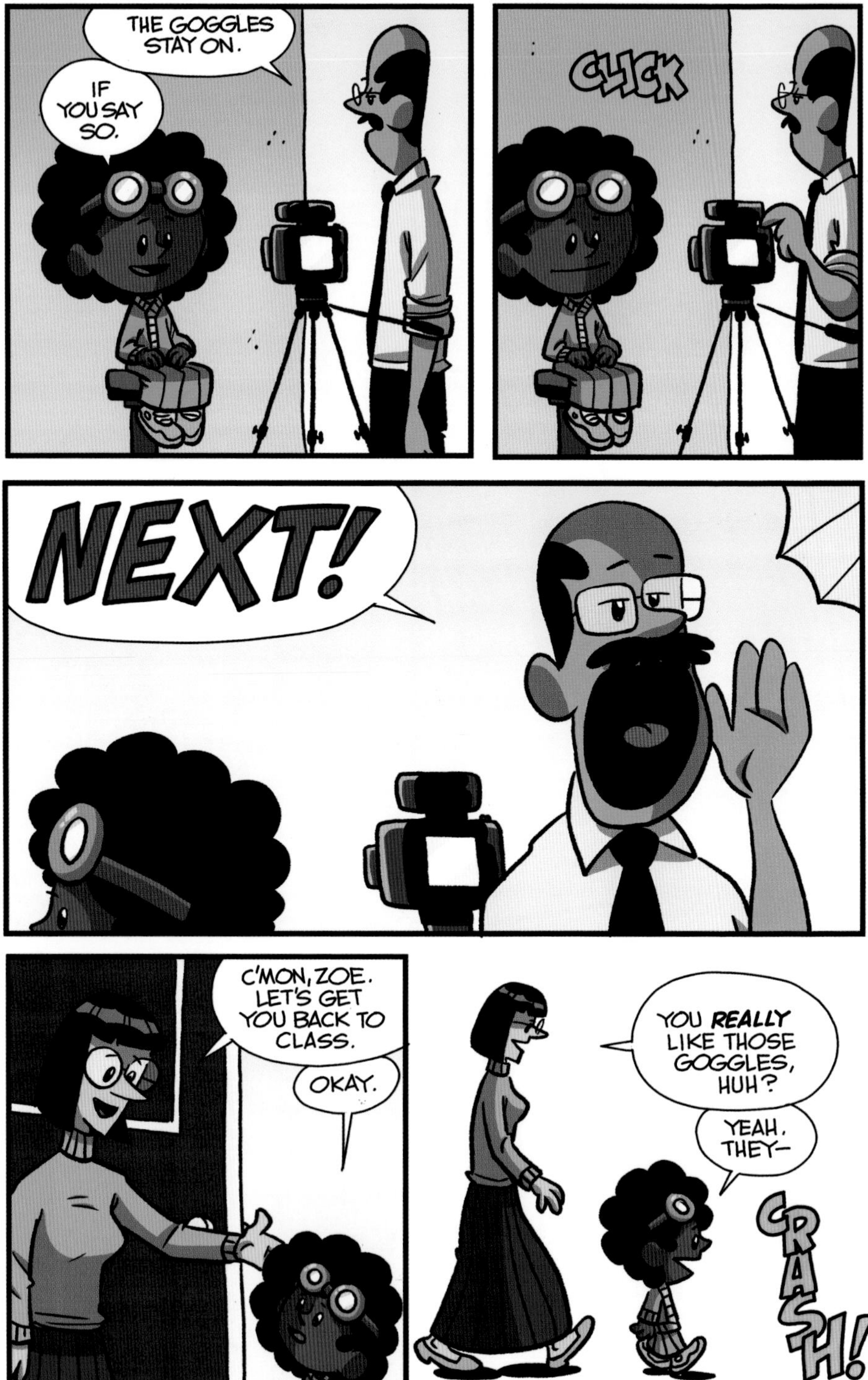
THE GOGGLES STAY ON.
IF YOU SAY SO.
CLICK
NEXT!
C'MON, ZOE. LET'S GET YOU BACK TO CLASS.
OKAY.
YOU **REALLY** LIKE THOSE GOGGLES, HUH?
YEAH. THEY—
CRASH!

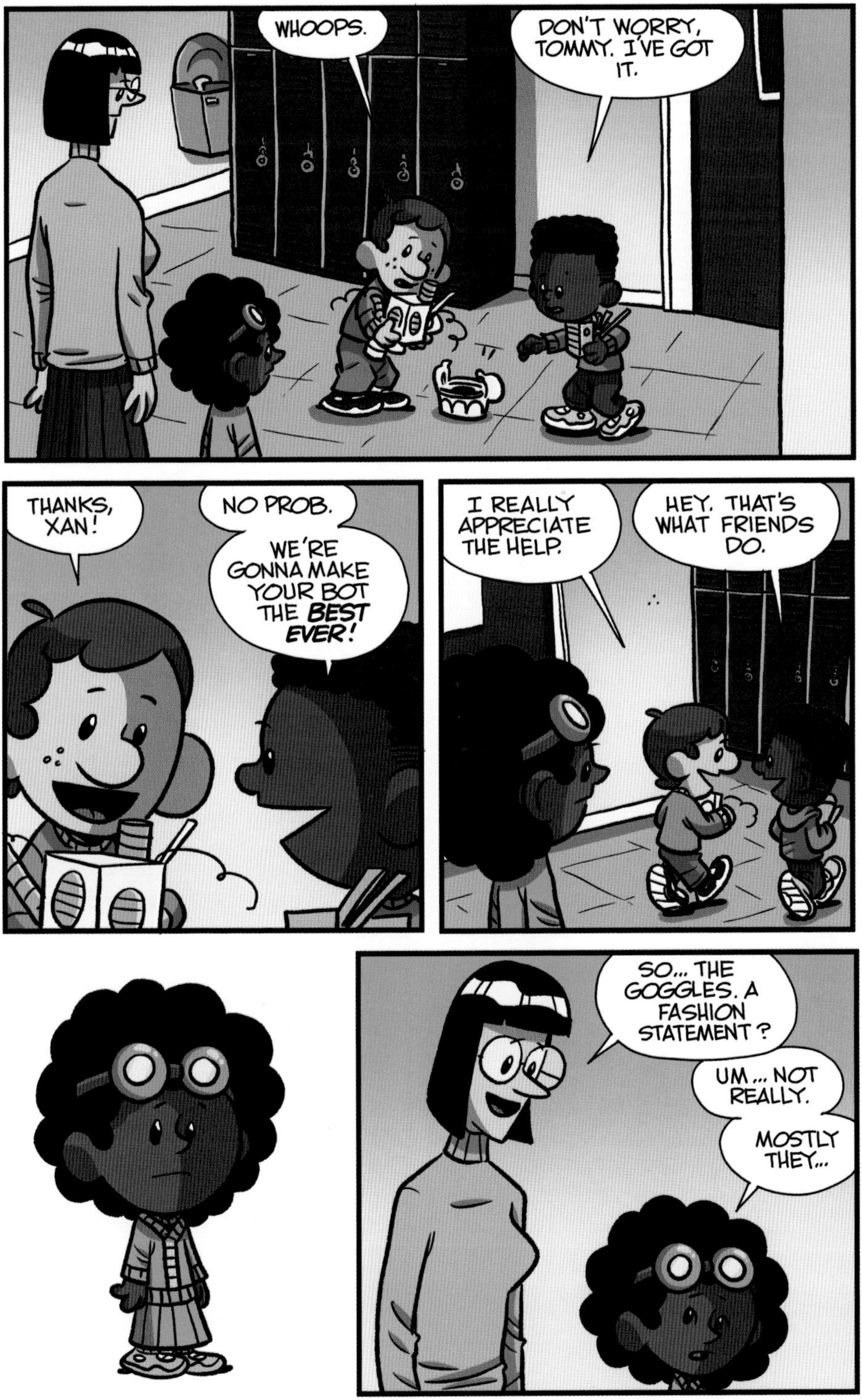
WHOOPS.
DON'T WORRY, TOMMY. I'VE GOT IT.
THANKS, XAN!
NO PROB.
WE'RE GONNA MAKE YOUR BOT THE **BEST EVER**!
I REALLY APPRECIATE THE HELP.
HEY. THAT'S WHAT FRIENDS DO.
SO... THE GOGGLES. A FASHION STATEMENT?
UM... NOT REALLY.
MOSTLY THEY...

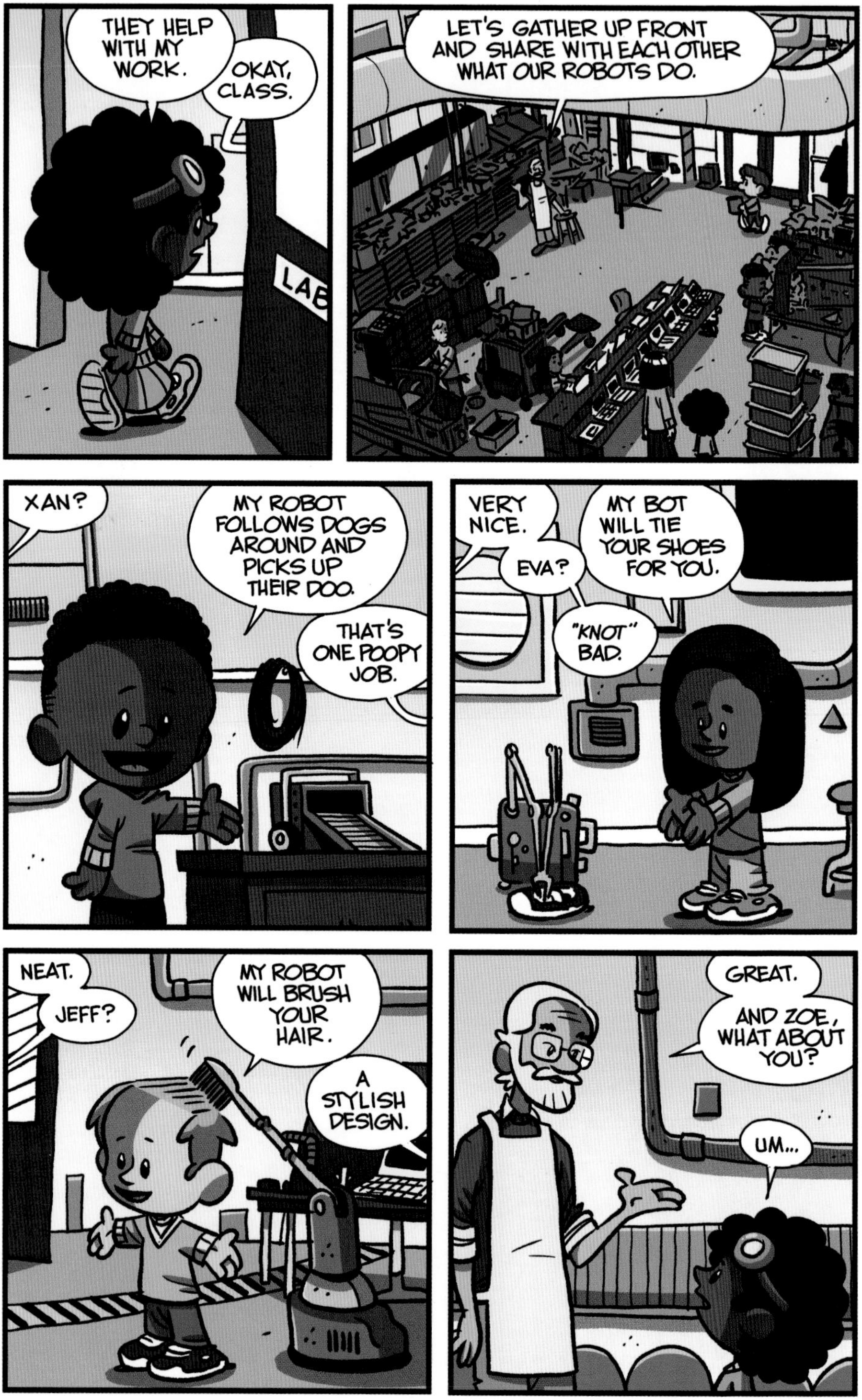
THEY HELP WITH MY WORK.
OKAY, CLASS.
LAB
LET'S GATHER UP FRONT AND SHARE WITH EACH OTHER WHAT OUR ROBOTS DO.
XAN?
MY ROBOT FOLLOWS DOGS AROUND AND PICKS UP THEIR DOO.
THAT'S ONE POOPY JOB.
VERY NICE.
EVA?
MY BOT WILL TIE YOUR SHOES FOR YOU.
"KNOT" BAD.
NEAT.
JEFF?
MY ROBOT WILL BRUSH YOUR HAIR.
A STYLISH DESIGN.
GREAT.
AND ZOE, WHAT ABOUT YOU?
UM...

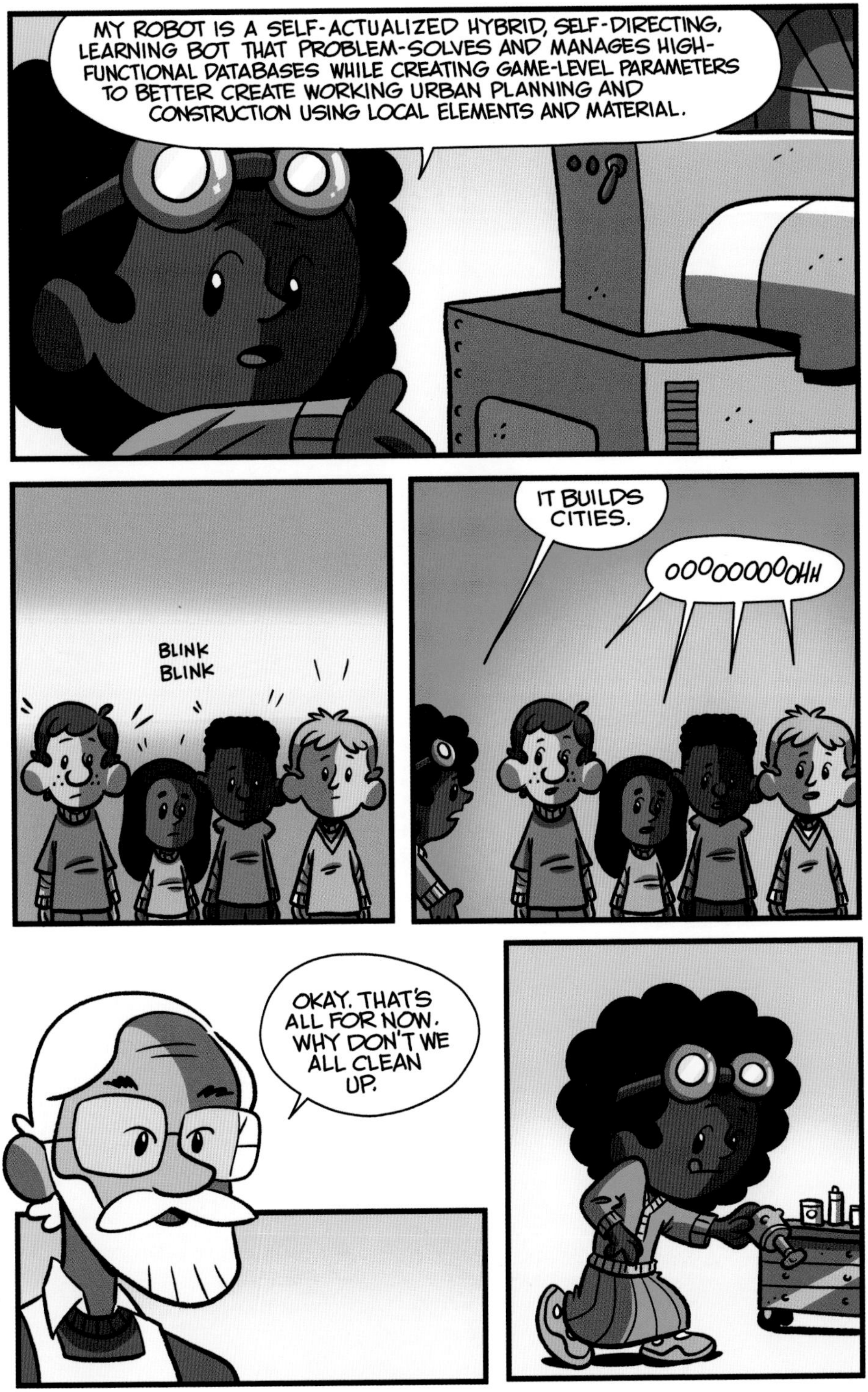
MY ROBOT IS A SELF-ACTUALIZED HYBRID, SELF-DIRECTING, LEARNING BOT THAT PROBLEM-SOLVES AND MANAGES HIGH-FUNCTIONAL DATABASES WHILE CREATING GAME-LEVEL PARAMETERS TO BETTER CREATE WORKING URBAN PLANNING AND CONSTRUCTION USING LOCAL ELEMENTS AND MATERIAL.
BLINK BLINK
IT BUILDS CITIES.
OOOOOOOOOHH
OKAY. THAT'S ALL FOR NOW. WHY DON'T WE ALL CLEAN UP.

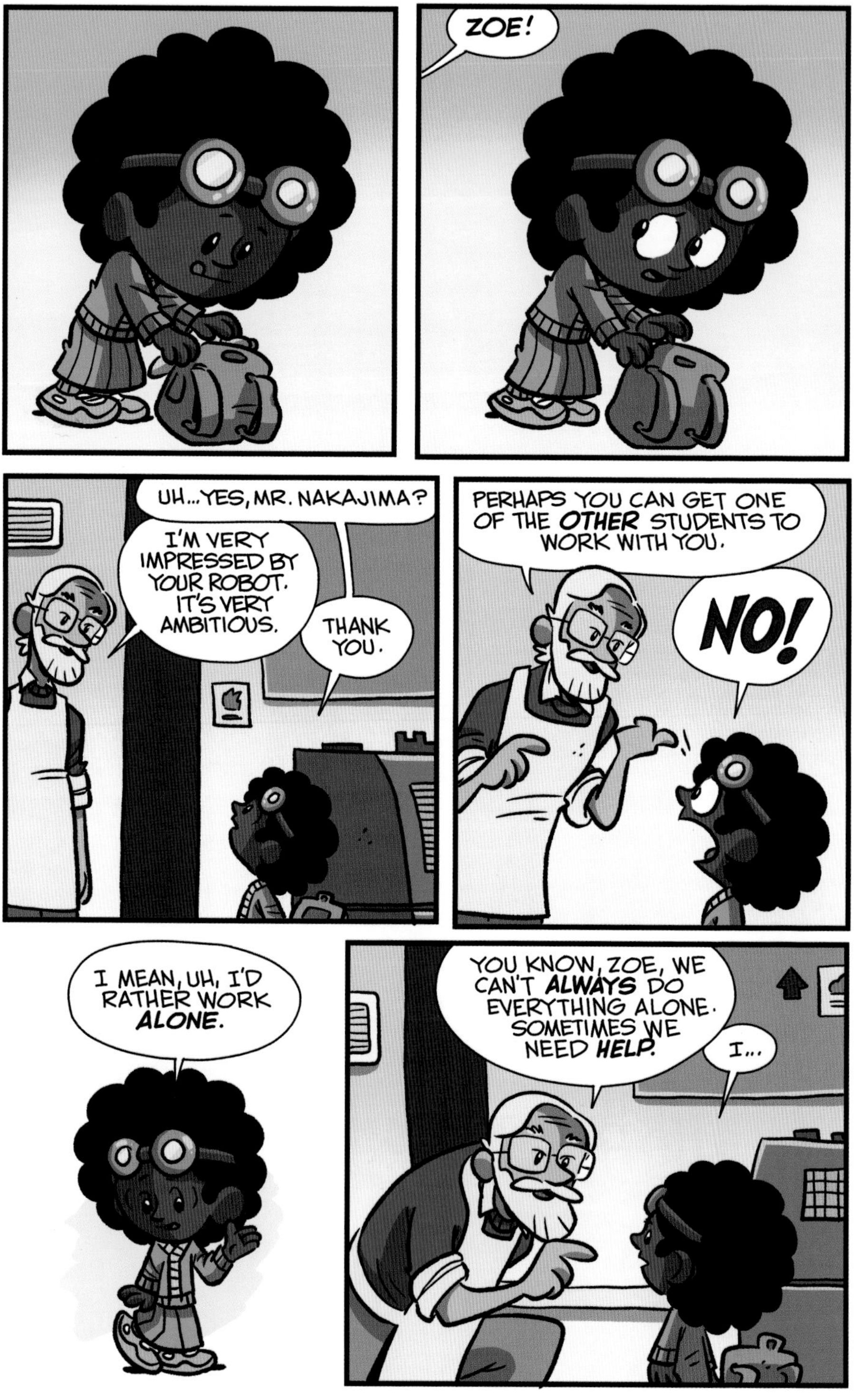

ZOE!
UH... YES, MR. NAKAJIMA?
I'M VERY IMPRESSED BY YOUR ROBOT. IT'S VERY AMBITIOUS.
THANK YOU.
PERHAPS YOU CAN GET ONE OF THE OTHER STUDENTS TO WORK WITH YOU.
NO!
I MEAN, UH, I'D RATHER WORK ALONE.
YOU KNOW, ZOE, WE CAN'T ALWAYS DO EVERYTHING ALONE. SOMETIMES WE NEED HELP.
I...

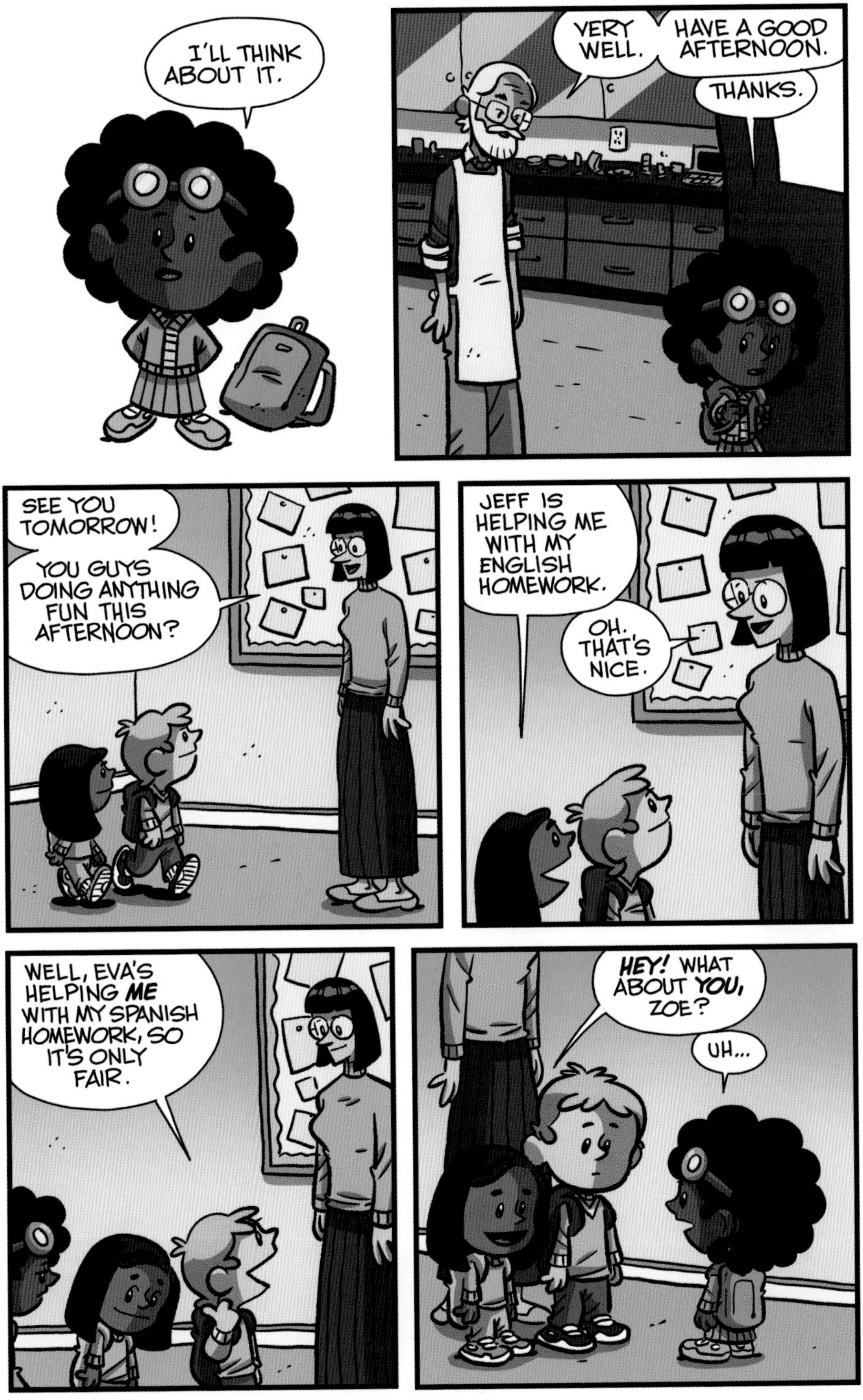
I'LL THINK ABOUT IT.
VERY WELL.
HAVE A GOOD AFTERNOON.
THANKS.
SEE YOU TOMORROW!
YOU GUYS DOING ANYTHING FUN THIS AFTERNOON?
JEFF IS HELPING ME WITH MY ENGLISH HOMEWORK.
OH. THAT'S NICE.
WELL, EVA'S HELPING **ME** WITH MY SPANISH HOMEWORK, SO IT'S ONLY FAIR.
HEY! WHAT ABOUT **YOU,** ZOE?
UH...

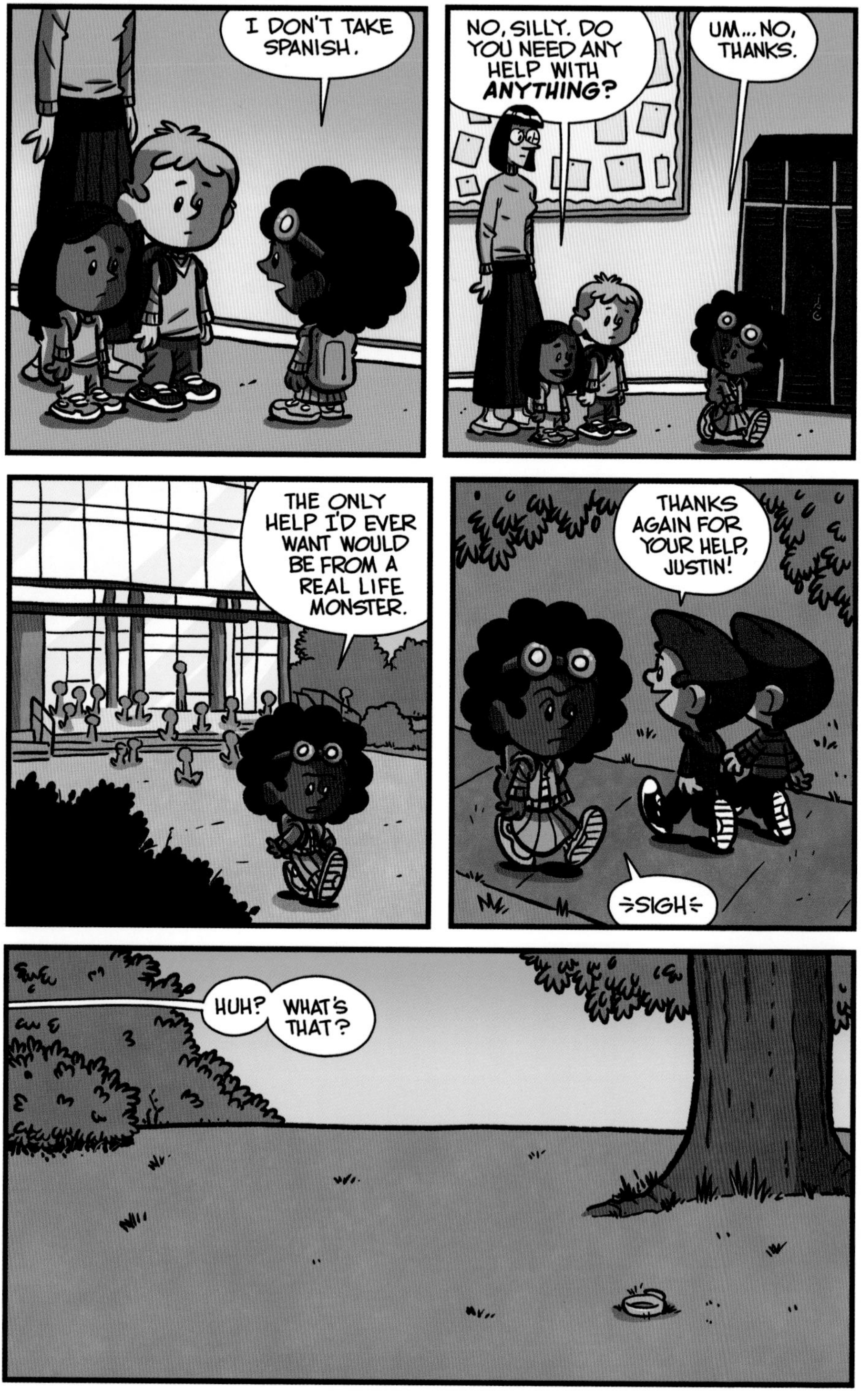
I DON'T TAKE SPANISH.
NO, SILLY. DO YOU NEED ANY HELP WITH **ANYTHING?**
UM... NO, THANKS.
THE ONLY HELP I'D EVER WANT WOULD BE FROM A REAL LIFE MONSTER.
THANKS AGAIN FOR YOUR HELP, JUSTIN!
SIGH
HUH?
WHAT'S THAT?

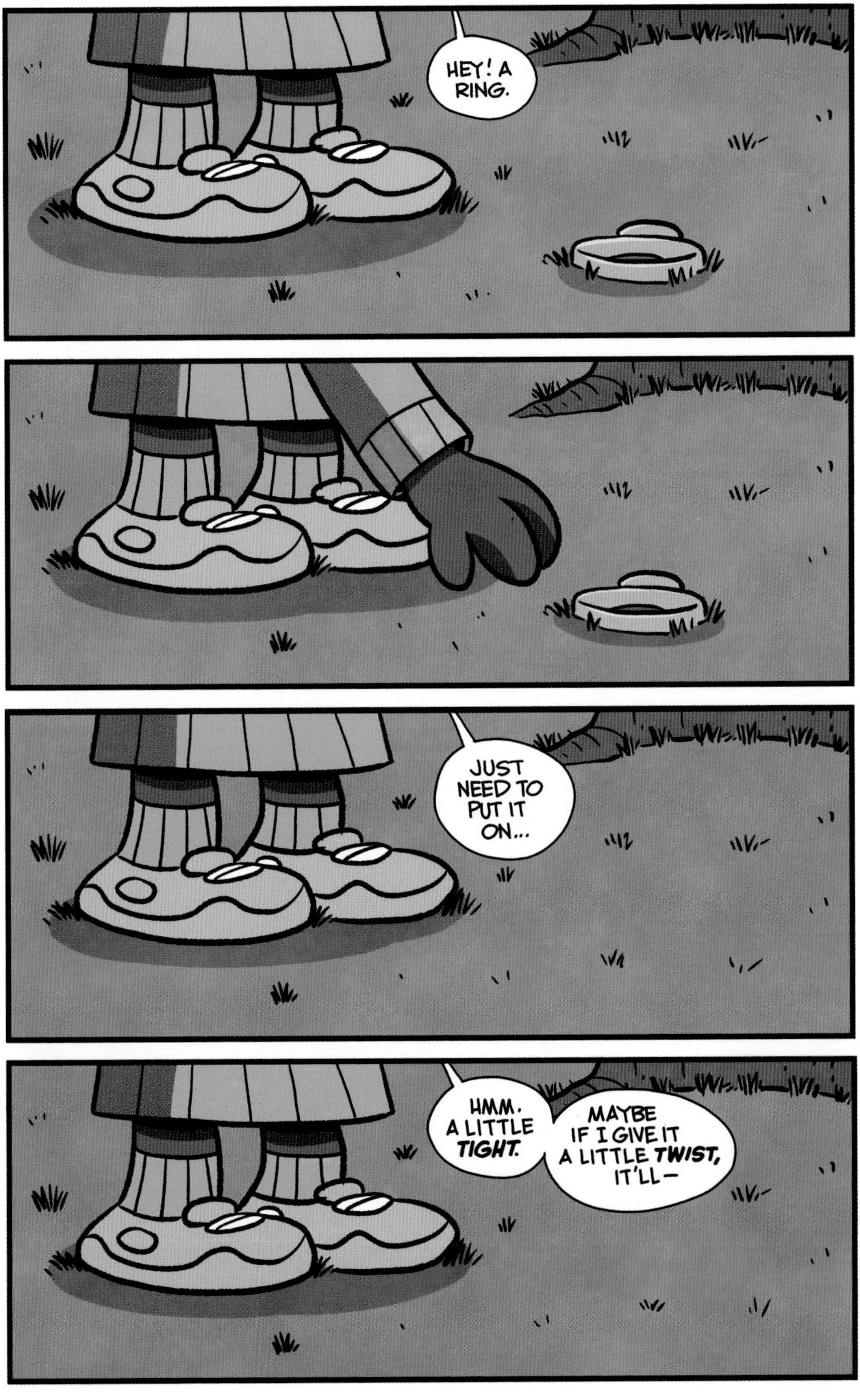
HEY! A RING.
JUST NEED TO PUT IT ON...
HMM. A LITTLE *TIGHT*.
MAYBE IF I GIVE IT A LITTLE *TWIST*, IT'LL—

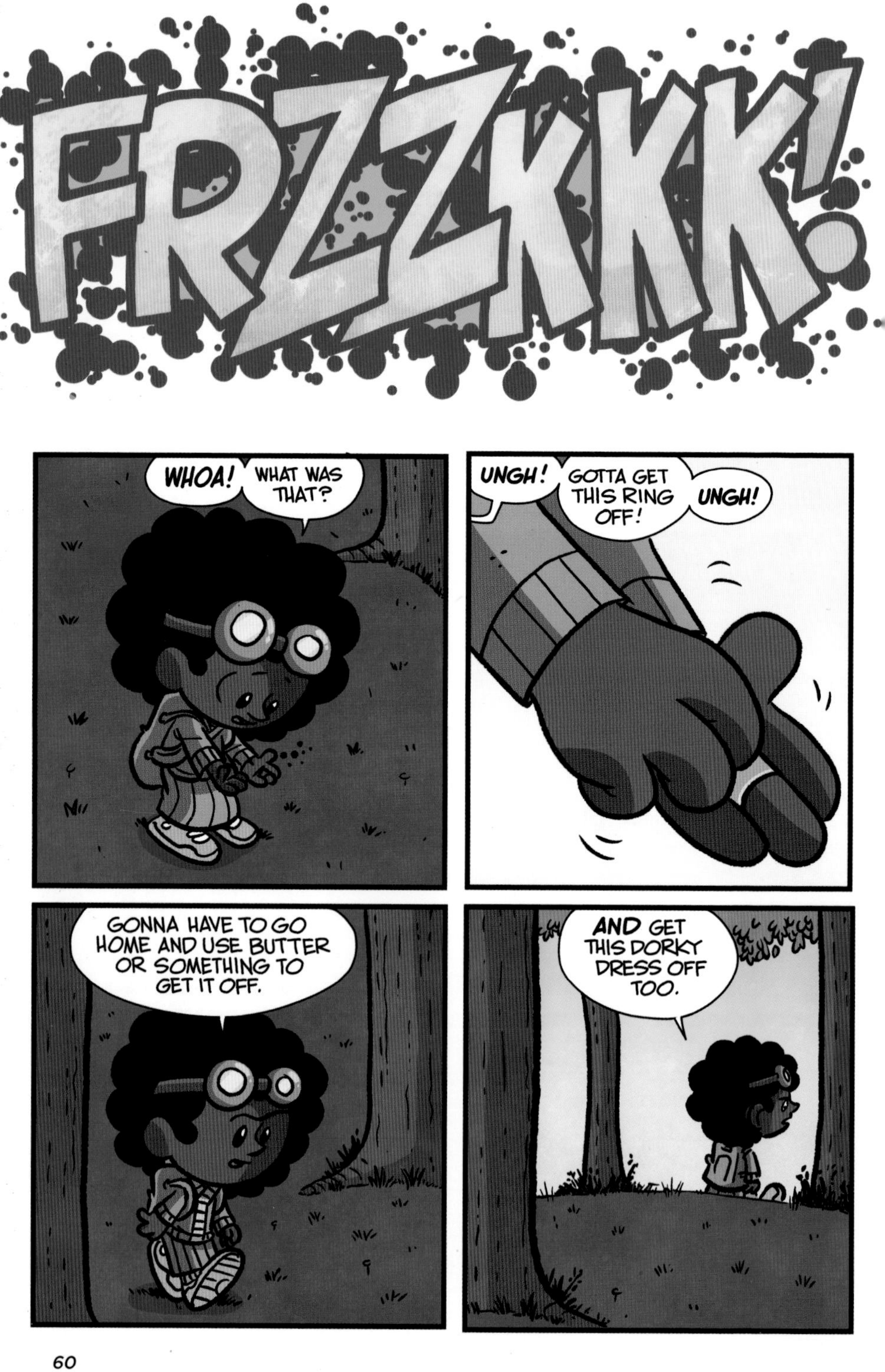
FRZKKK!
WHOA!
WHAT WAS THAT?
UNGH!
GOTTA GET THIS RING OFF!
UNGH!
GONNA HAVE TO GO HOME AND USE BUTTER OR SOMETHING TO GET IT OFF.
AND GET THIS DORKY DRESS OFF TOO.

CHAPTER 5 - A MONSTROUS DAY

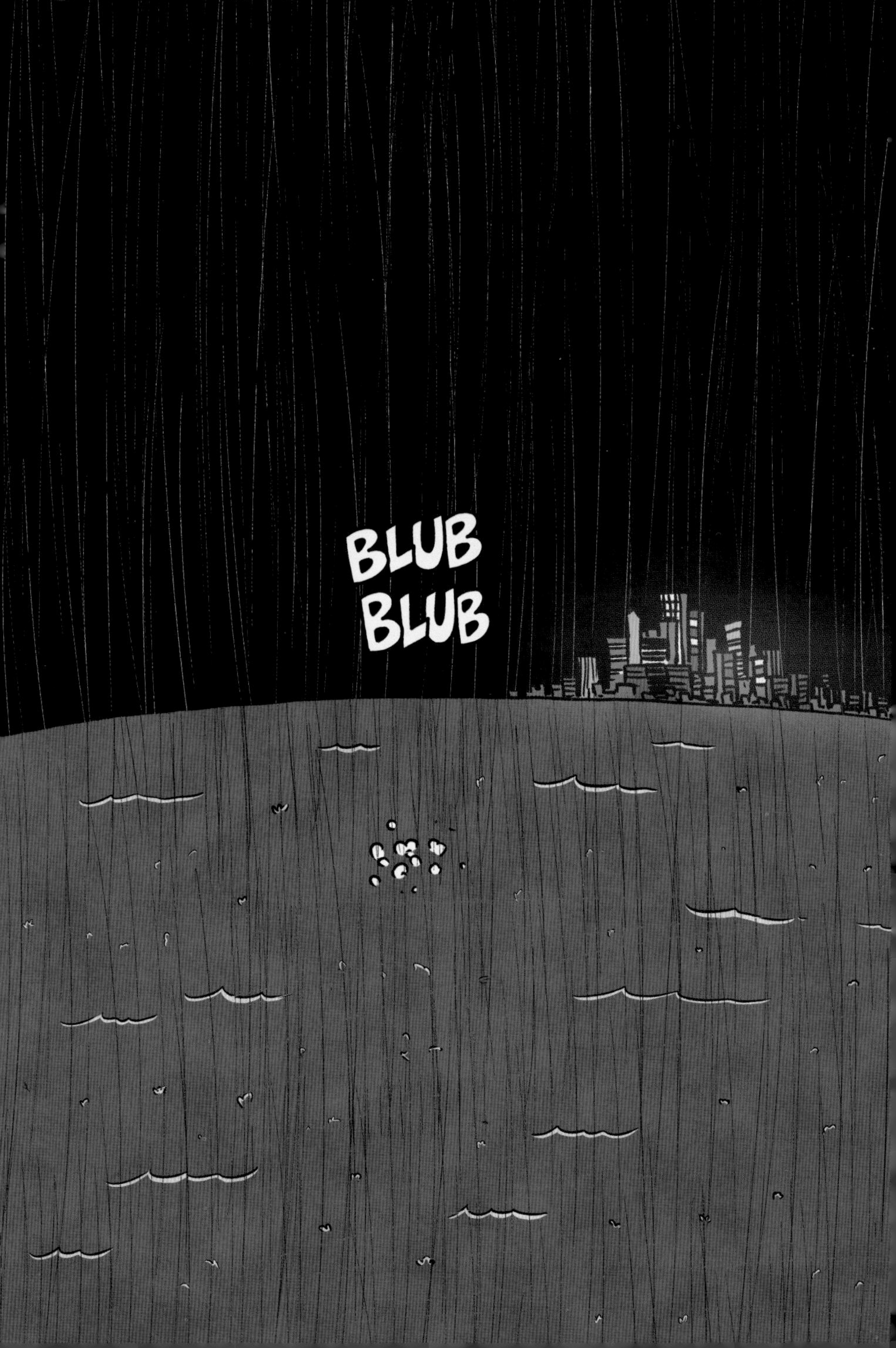
BLUB
BLUB

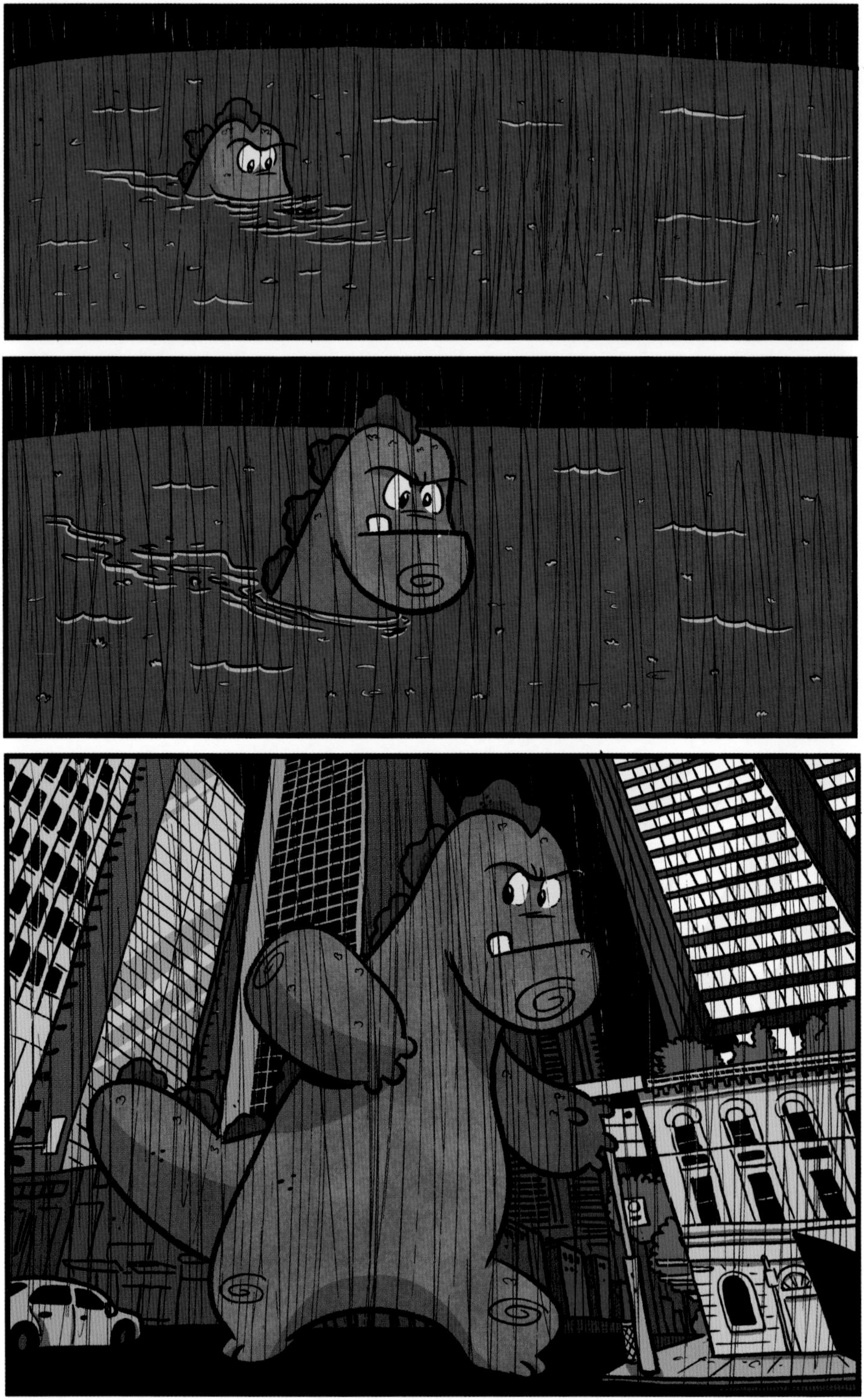

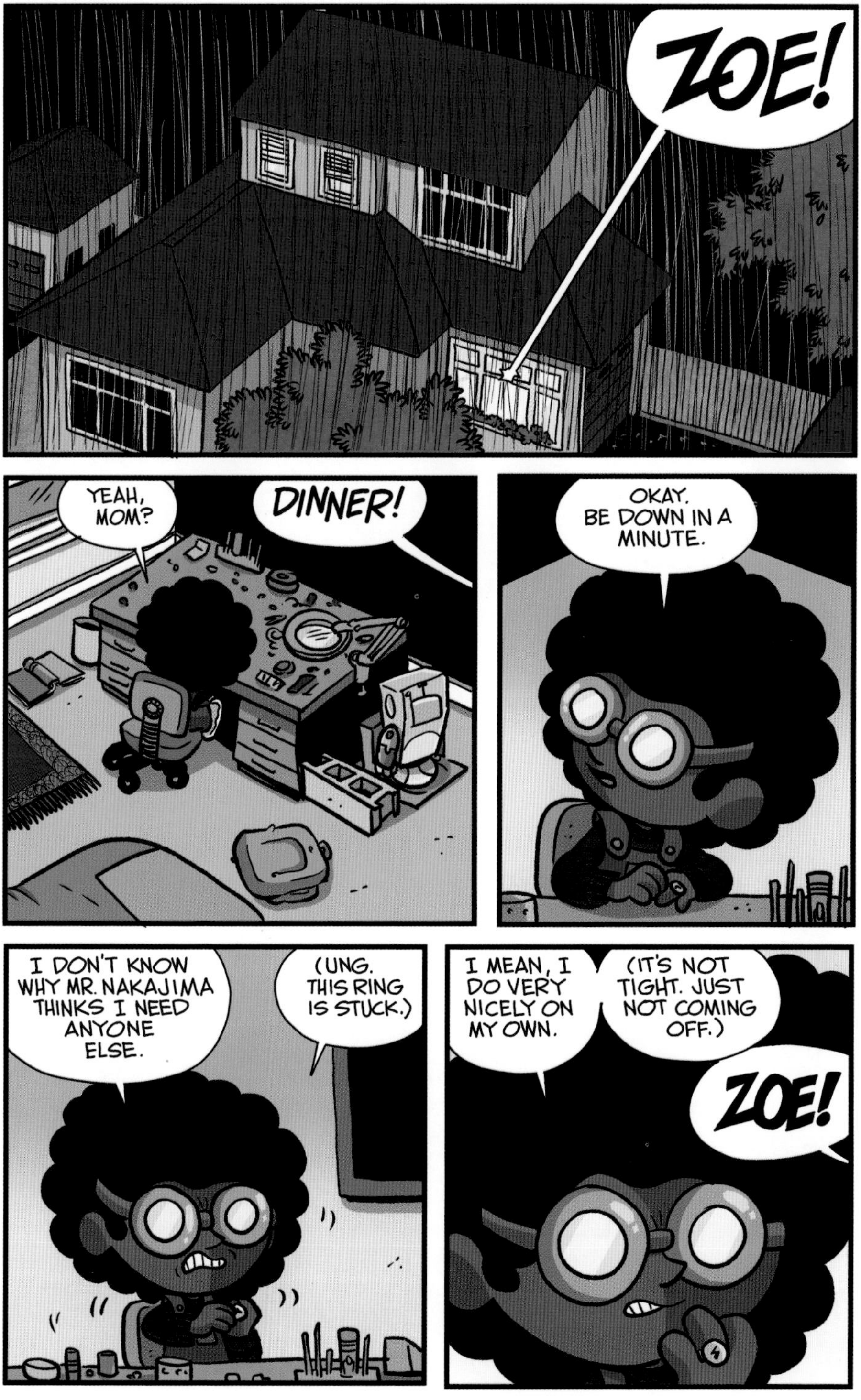
ZOE!
YEAH, MOM?
DINNER!
OKAY. BE DOWN IN A MINUTE.
I DON'T KNOW WHY MR. NAKAJIMA THINKS I NEED ANYONE ELSE.
(UNG. THIS RING IS STUCK.)
I MEAN, I DO VERY NICELY ON MY OWN.
(IT'S NOT TIGHT. JUST NOT COMING OFF.)
ZOE!

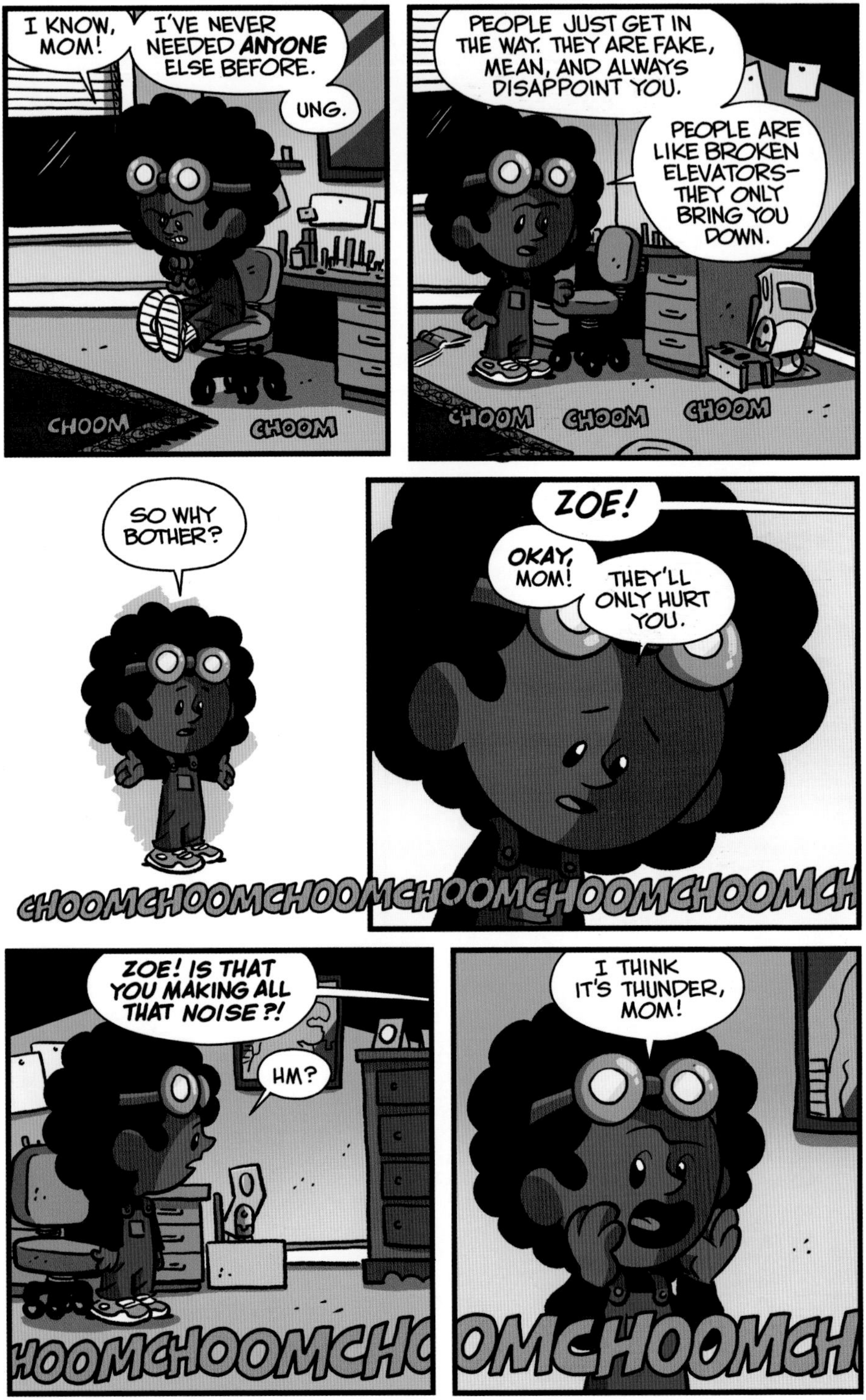

I KNOW, MOM!
I'VE NEVER NEEDED ANYONE ELSE BEFORE.
UNG.
CHOOM
CHOOM
PEOPLE JUST GET IN THE WAY. THEY ARE FAKE, MEAN, AND ALWAYS DISAPPOINT YOU.
PEOPLE ARE LIKE BROKEN ELEVATORS— THEY ONLY BRING YOU DOWN.
CHOOM
CHOOM
CHOOM
SO WHY BOTHER?
ZOE!
OKAY, MOM!
THEY'LL ONLY HURT YOU.
CHOOMCHOOMCHOOMCHOOMCHOOMCHOOMCH
ZOE! IS THAT YOU MAKING ALL THAT NOISE?!
HM?
I THINK IT'S THUNDER, MOM!
HOOMCHOOMCHC
OMCHOOMCH

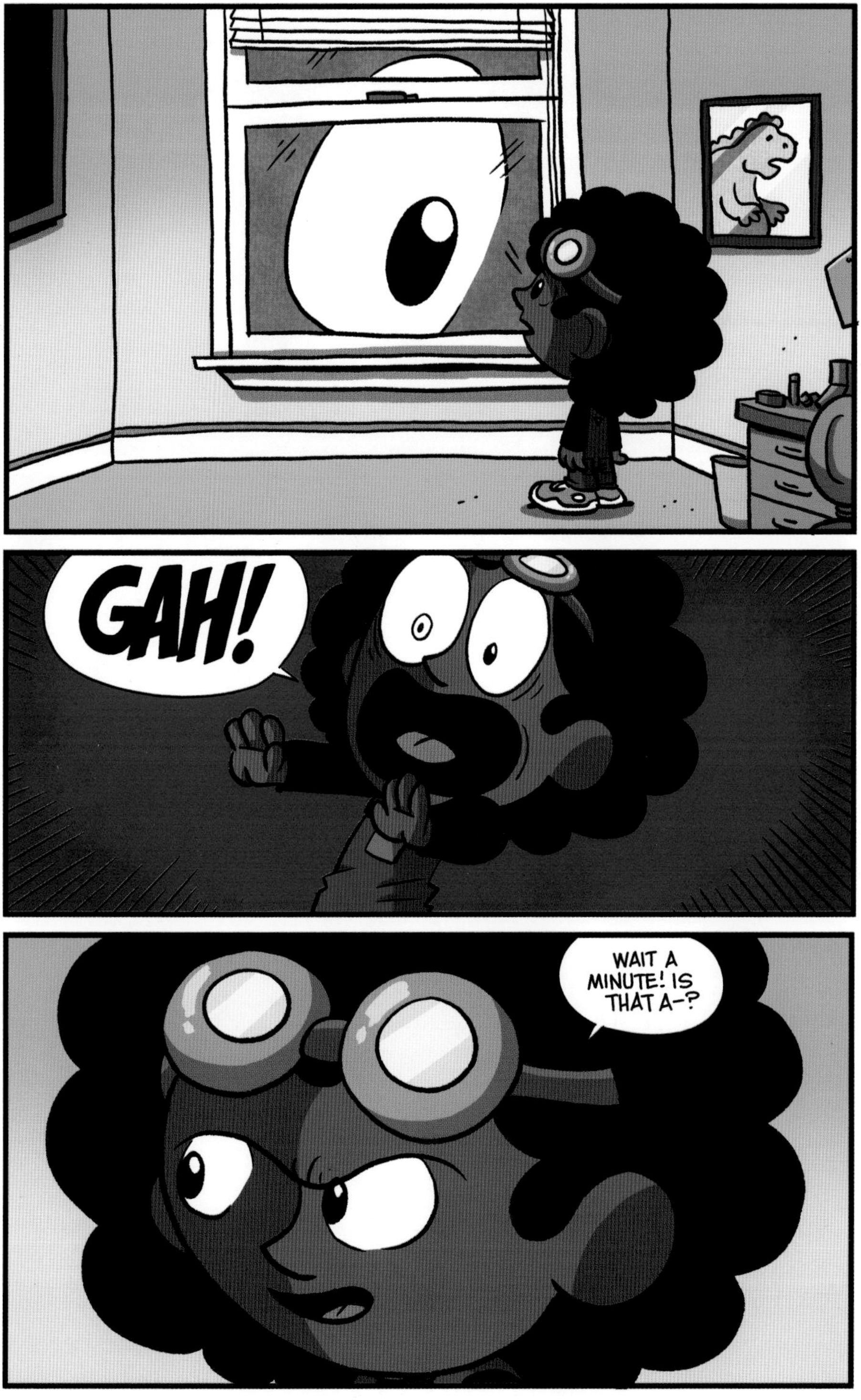
GAH!
WAIT A MINUTE! IS THAT A-?

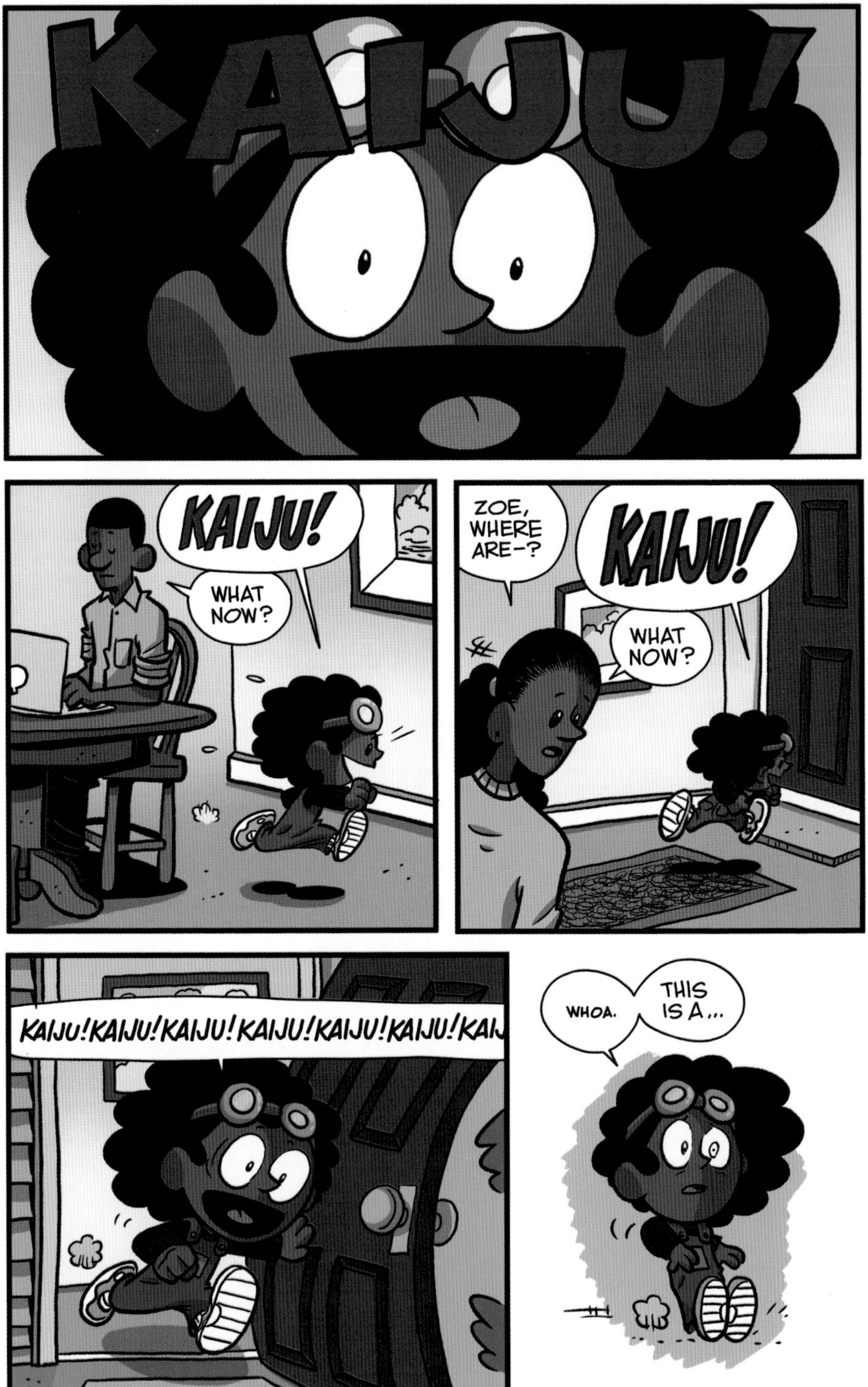
KAIJU!
KAIJU!
WHAT NOW?
ZOE, WHERE ARE-?
KAIJU!
WHAT NOW?
KAIJU!KAIJU!KAIJU!KAIJU!KAIJU!KAIJU!KAI
WHOA.
THIS IS A...

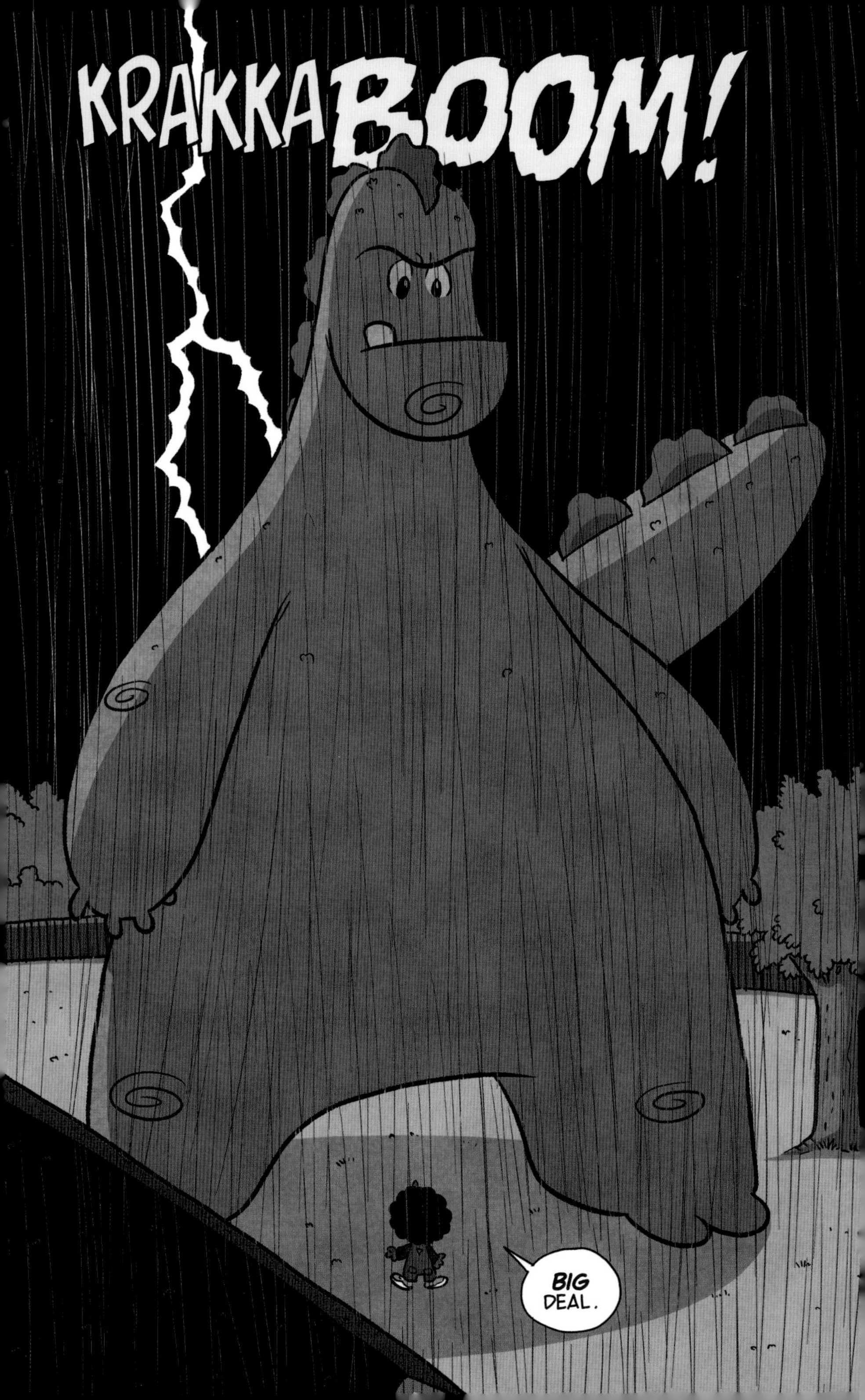
KRAKKA BOOM!
BIG DEAL.

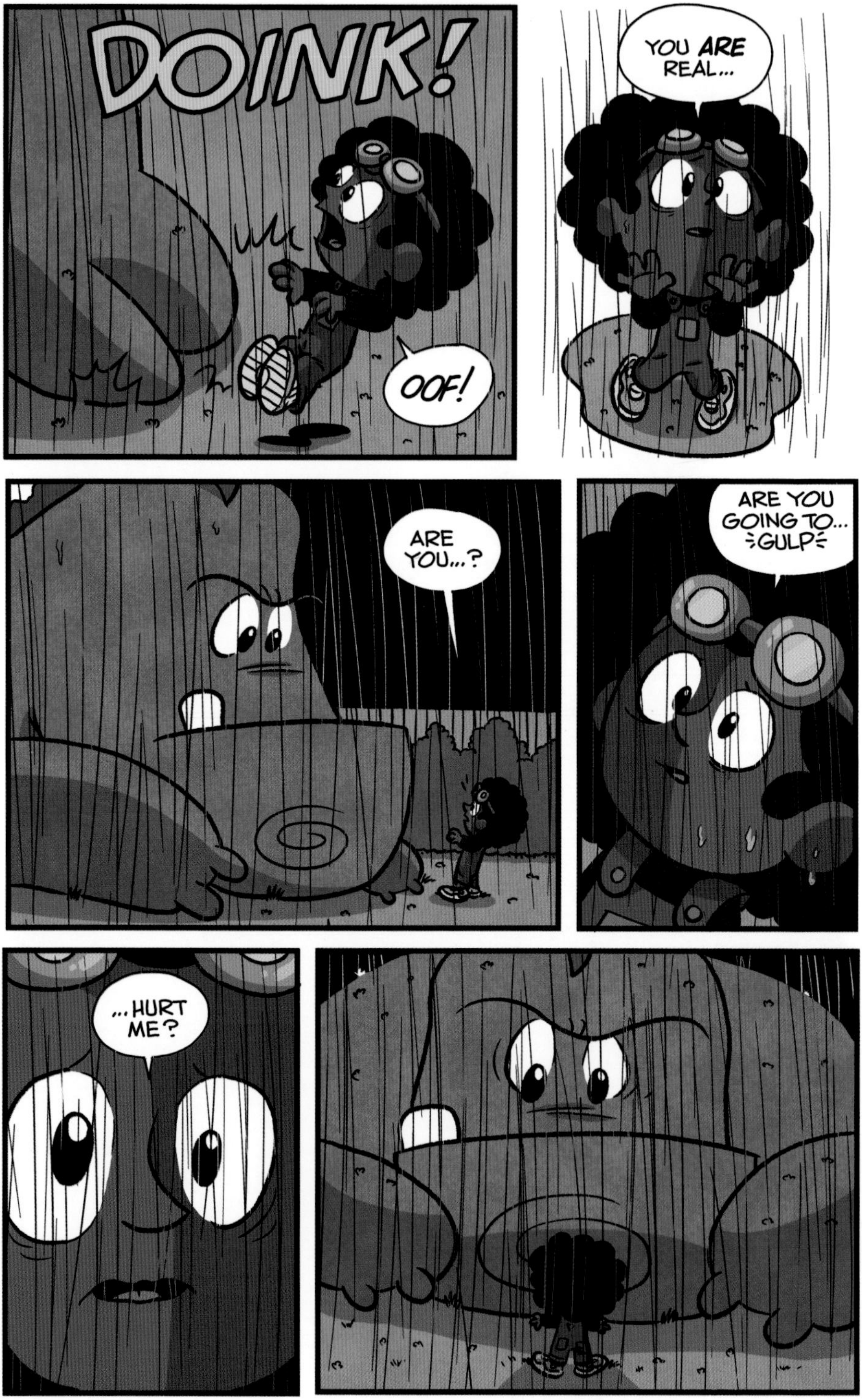
DOINK!
ULK
OOF!
YOU ARE REAL...
ARE YOU...?
ARE YOU GOING TO... GULP
...HURT ME?

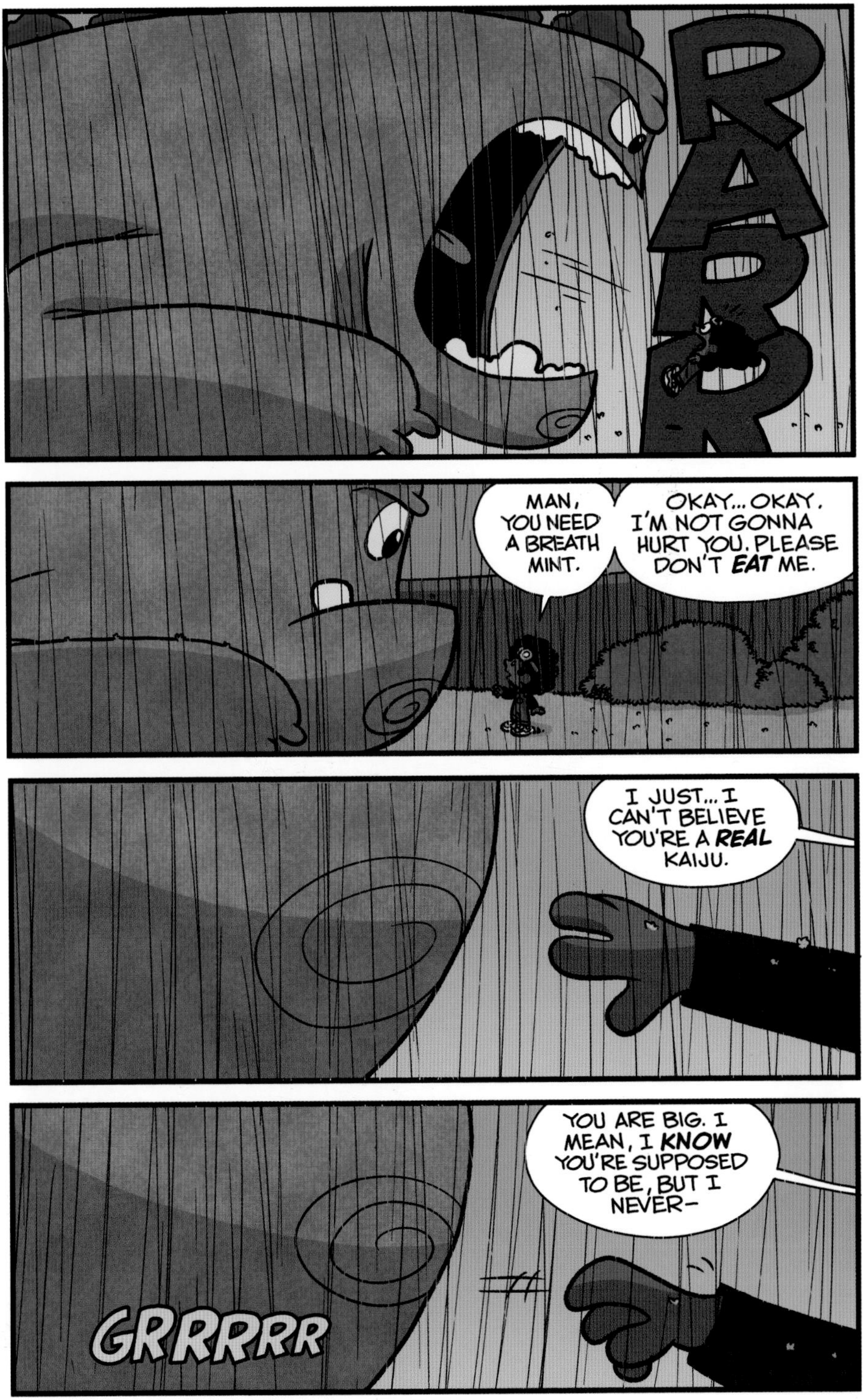
RARRR
MAN, YOU NEED A BREATH MINT.
OKAY... OKAY. I'M NOT GONNA HURT YOU. PLEASE DON'T **EAT** ME.
I JUST... I CAN'T BELIEVE YOU'RE A **REAL** KAIJU.
YOU ARE BIG. I MEAN, I **KNOW** YOU'RE SUPPOSED TO BE, BUT I NEVER–
GRRRRR

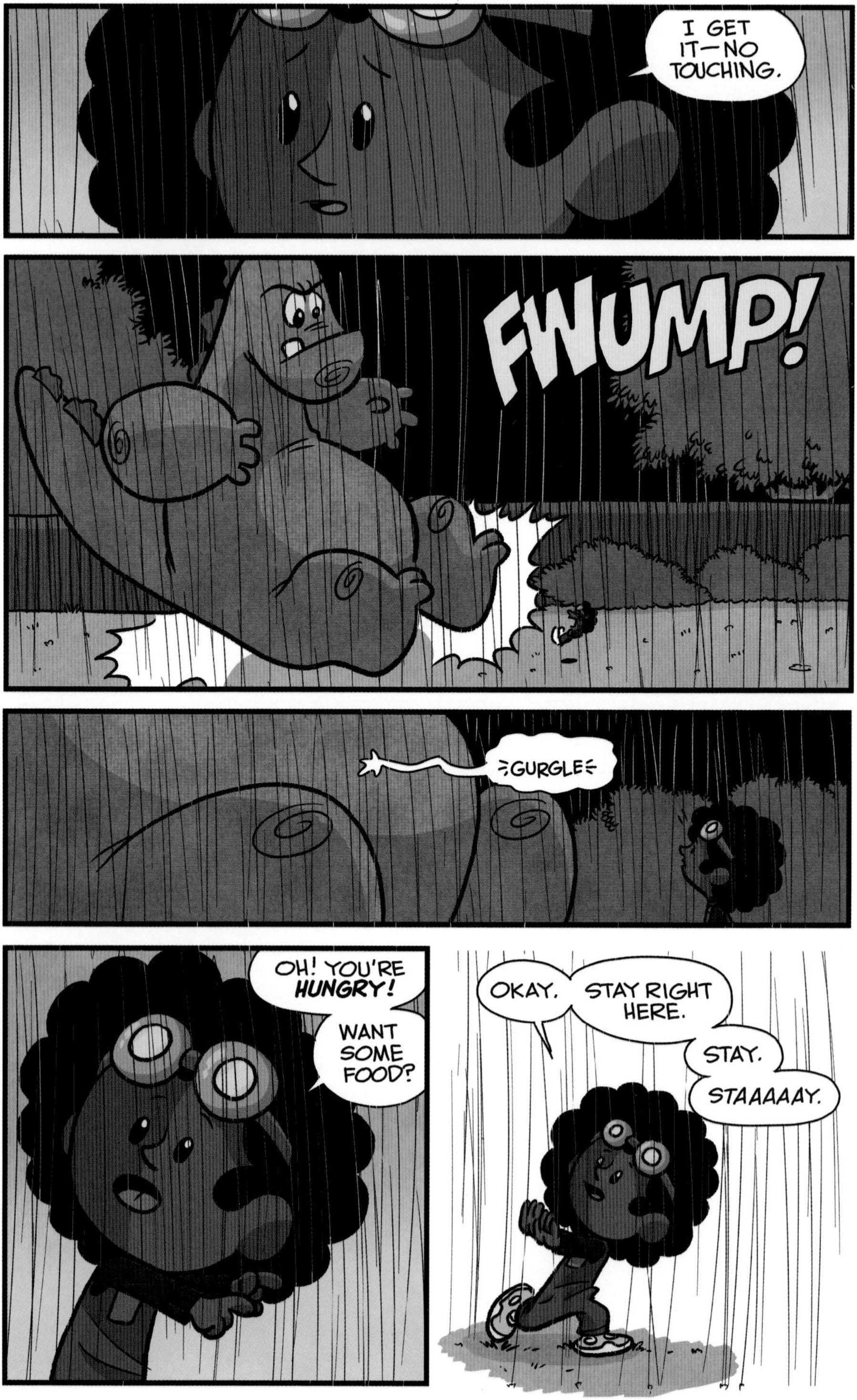
I GET IT—NO TOUCHING.
FWUMP!
GURGLE
OH! YOU'RE HUNGRY!
WANT SOME FOOD?
OKAY.
STAY RIGHT HERE.
STAY.
STAAAAAY.

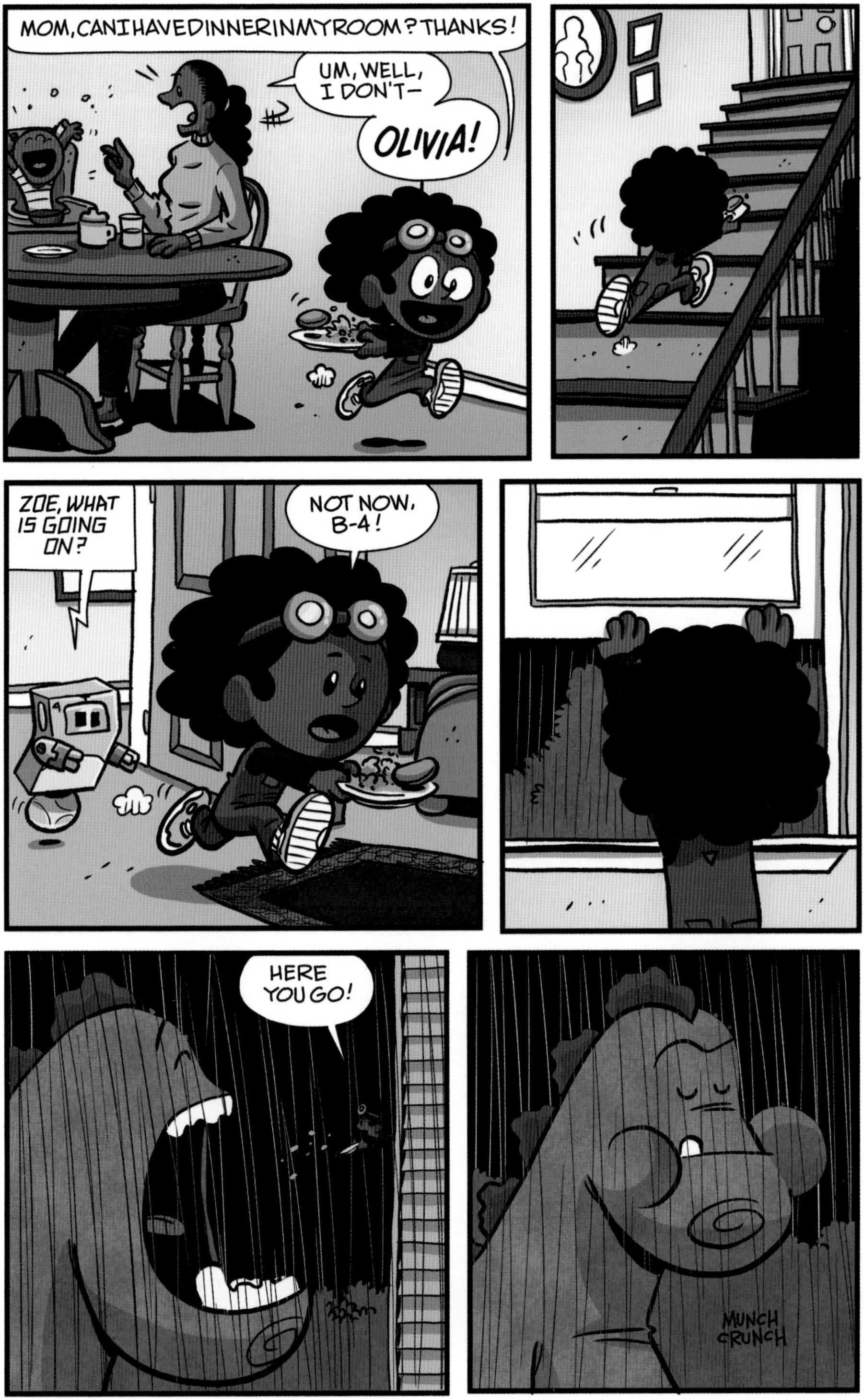
MOM, CANIHAVEDINNERINMYROOM? THANKS!
UM, WELL, I DON'T—
OLIVIA!
ZOE, WHAT IS GOING ON?
NOT NOW, B-4!
HERE YOU GO!
MUNCH CRUNCH

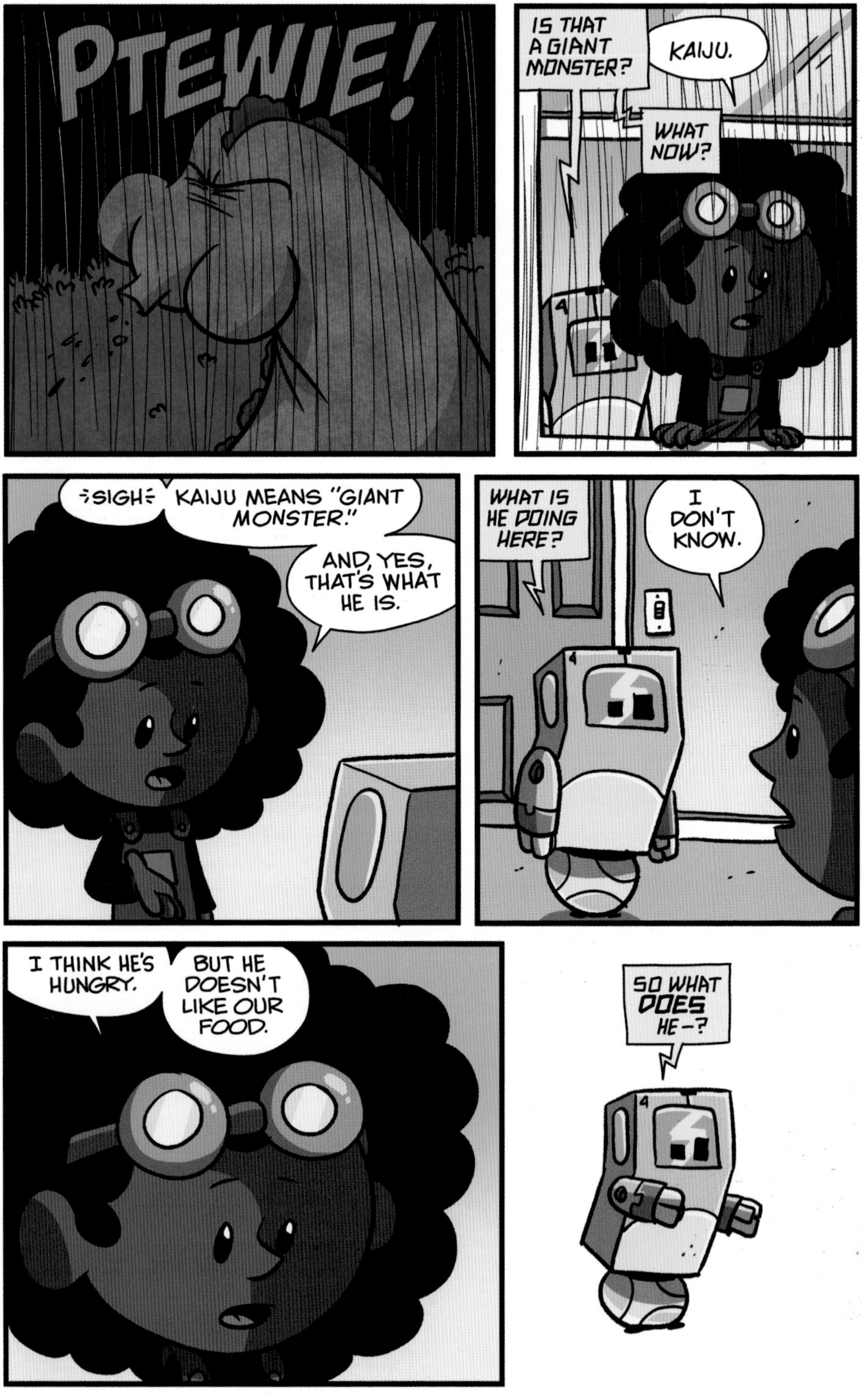
PTEWIE!
IS THAT A GIANT MONSTER?
KAIJU.
WHAT NOW?
-SIGH-
KAIJU MEANS "GIANT MONSTER."
AND, YES, THAT'S WHAT HE IS.
WHAT IS HE DOING HERE?
I DON'T KNOW.
I THINK HE'S HUNGRY.
BUT HE DOESN'T LIKE OUR FOOD.
SO WHAT DOES HE—?

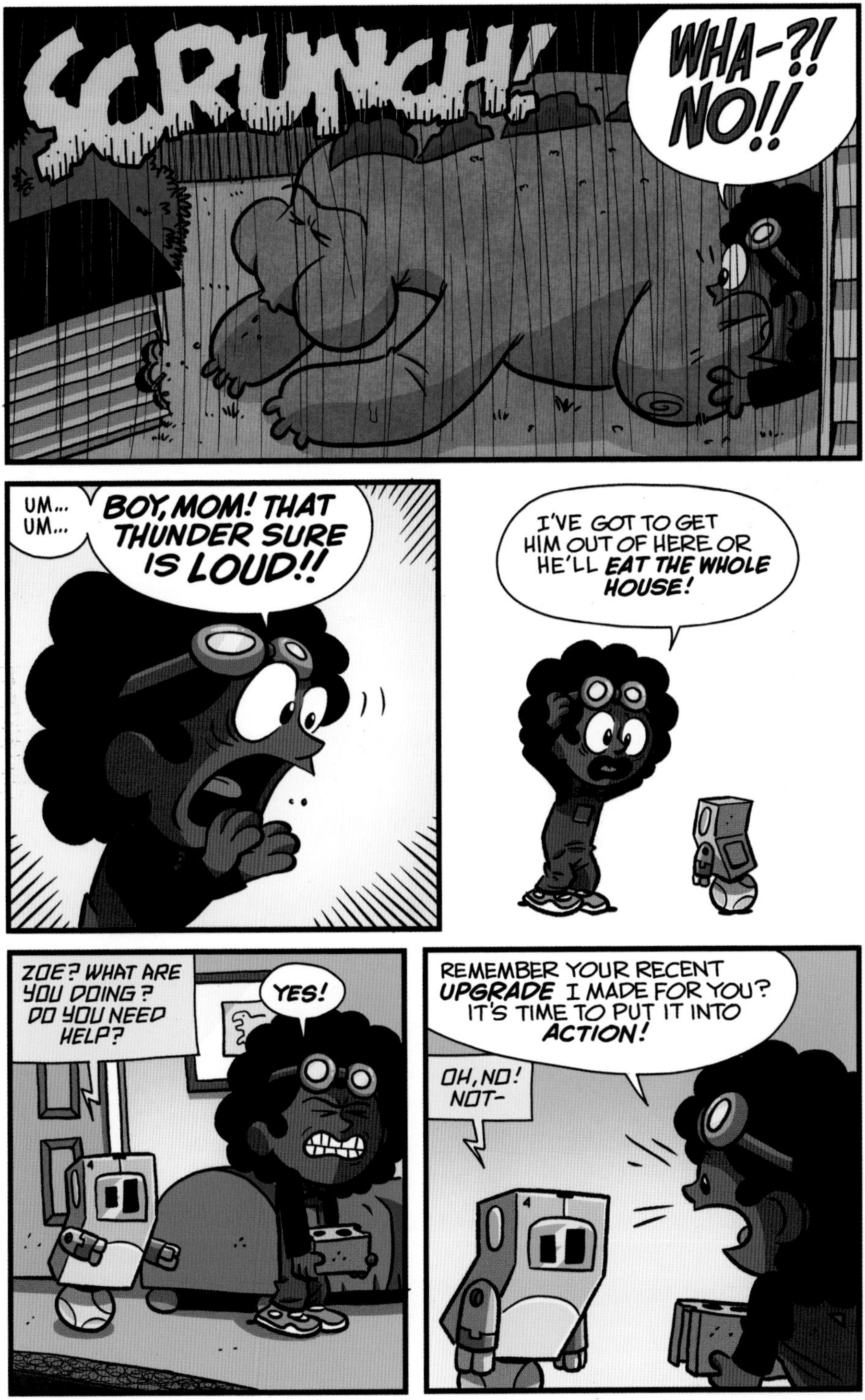
SCRUNCH!
WHA-?! NO!!
UM... UM...
BOY, MOM! THAT THUNDER SURE IS LOUD!!
I'VE GOT TO GET HIM OUT OF HERE OR HE'LL EAT THE WHOLE HOUSE!
ZOE? WHAT ARE YOU DOING? DO YOU NEED HELP?
YES!
REMEMBER YOUR RECENT UPGRADE I MADE FOR YOU? IT'S TIME TO PUT IT INTO ACTION!
OH, NO! NOT-

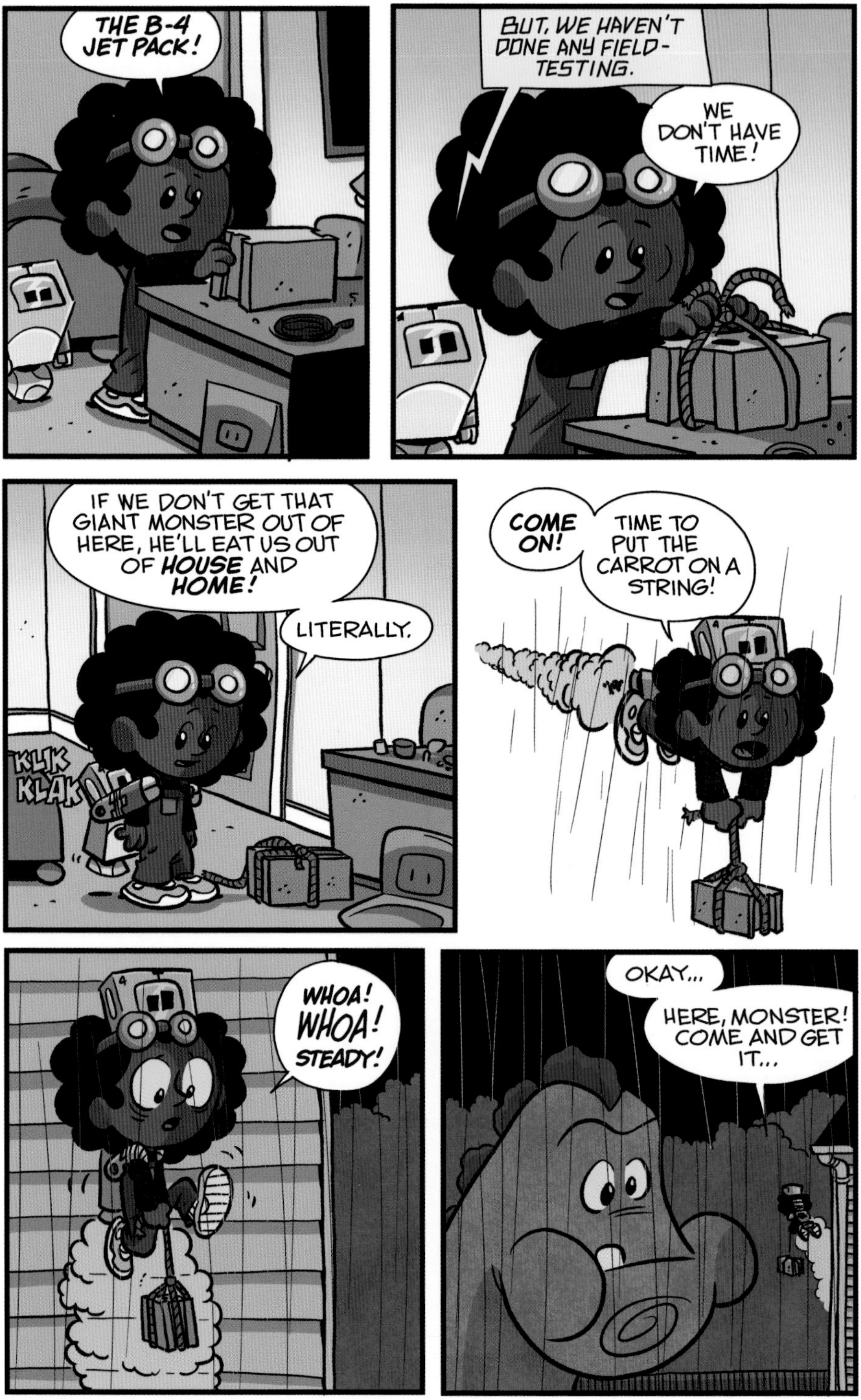
THE B-4 JET PACK!
BUT, WE HAVEN'T DONE ANY FIELD-TESTING.
WE DON'T HAVE TIME!
IF WE DON'T GET THAT GIANT MONSTER OUT OF HERE, HE'LL EAT US OUT OF HOUSE AND HOME!
LITERALLY.
KLIK KLAK
COME ON!
TIME TO PUT THE CARROT ON A STRING!
WHOA! WHOA! STEADY!
OKAY...
HERE, MONSTER! COME AND GET IT...

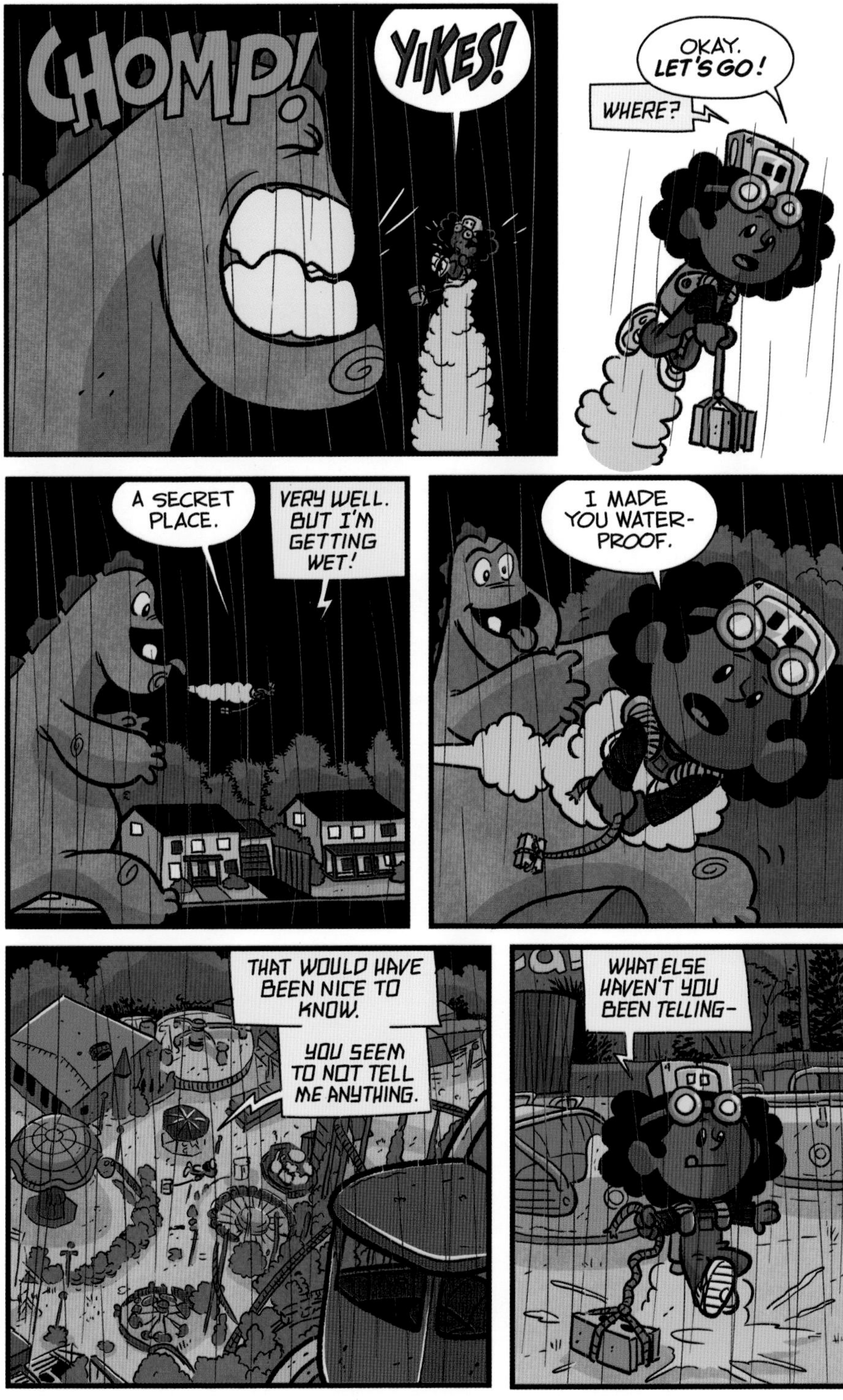
CHOMP!
YIKES!
OKAY. LET'S GO!
WHERE?
A SECRET PLACE.
VERY WELL. BUT I'M GETTING WET!
I MADE YOU WATER-PROOF.
THAT WOULD HAVE BEEN NICE TO KNOW.
YOU SEEM TO NOT TELL ME ANYTHING.
WHAT ELSE HAVEN'T YOU BEEN TELLING-

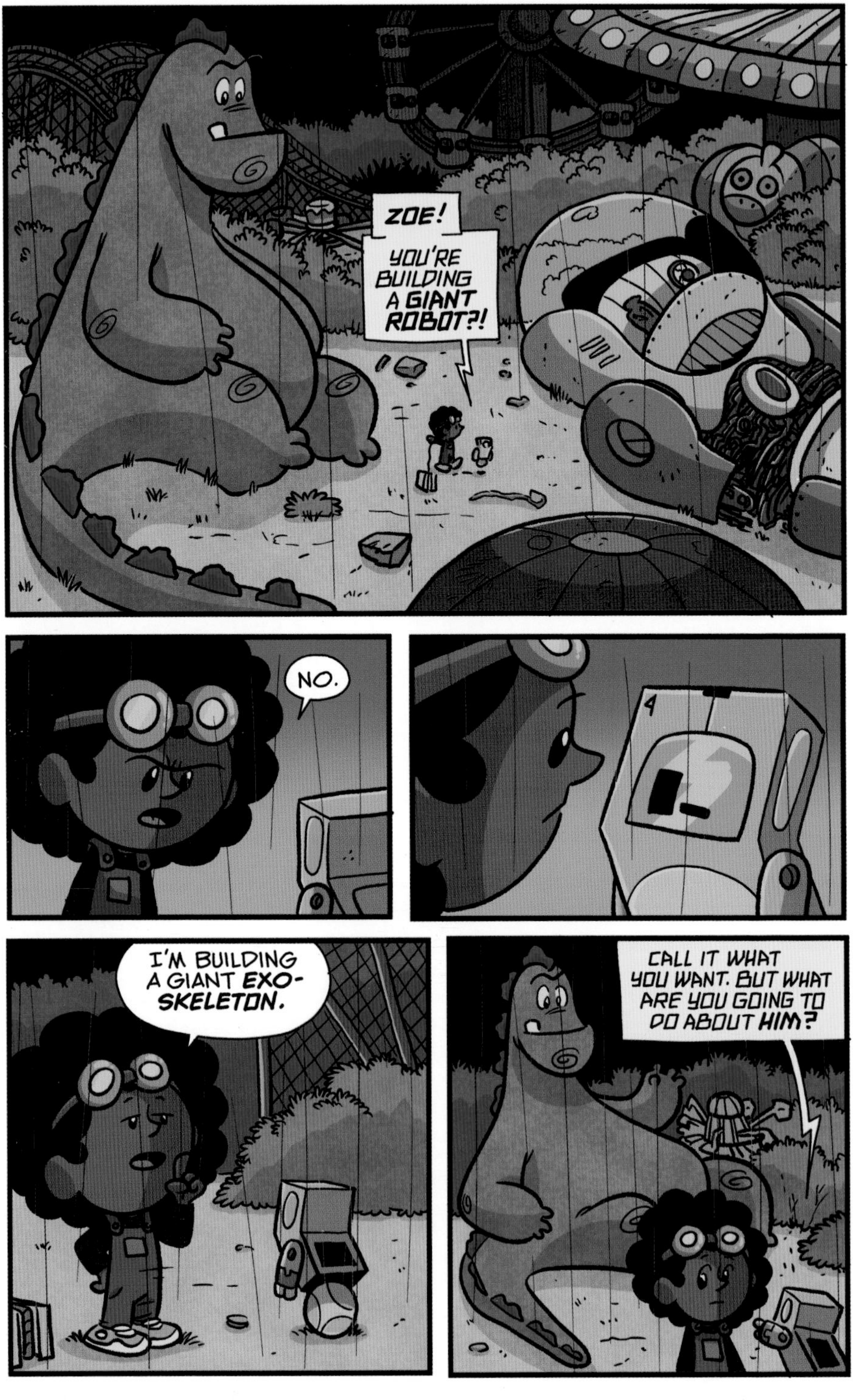
ZOE!
YOU'RE BUILDING A GIANT ROBOT?!
NO.
4
I'M BUILDING A GIANT EXO-SKELETON.
CALL IT WHAT YOU WANT. BUT WHAT ARE YOU GOING TO DO ABOUT HIM?

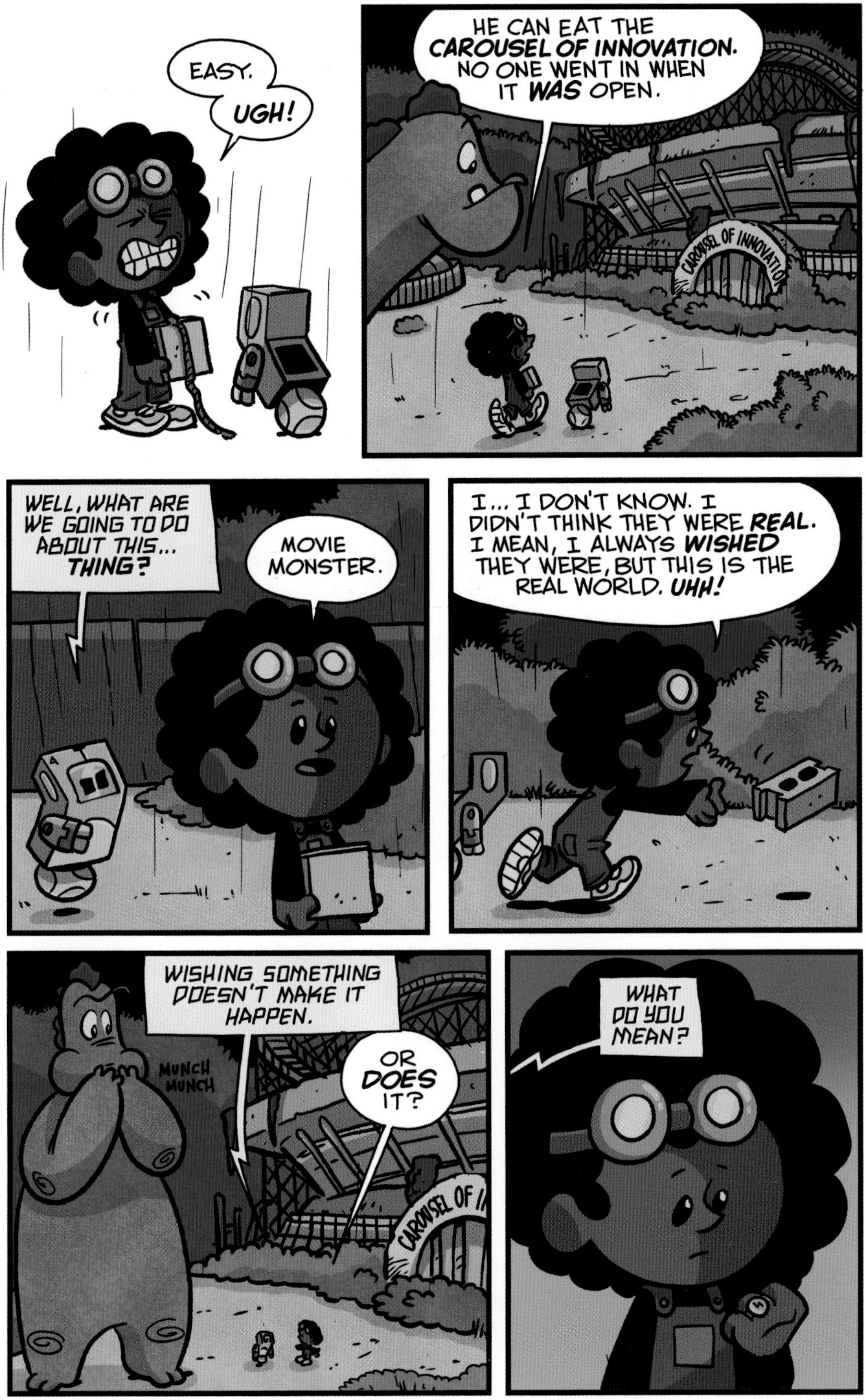
EASY.
UGH!
HE CAN EAT THE CAROUSEL OF INNOVATION. NO ONE WENT IN WHEN IT WAS OPEN.
CAROUSEL OF INNOVATION
WELL, WHAT ARE WE GOING TO DO ABOUT THIS... THING?
MOVIE MONSTER.
I... I DON'T KNOW. I DIDN'T THINK THEY WERE REAL. I MEAN, I ALWAYS WISHED THEY WERE, BUT THIS IS THE REAL WORLD. UHH!
WISHING SOMETHING DOESN'T MAKE IT HAPPEN.
MUNCH MUNCH
OR DOES IT?
WHAT DO YOU MEAN?

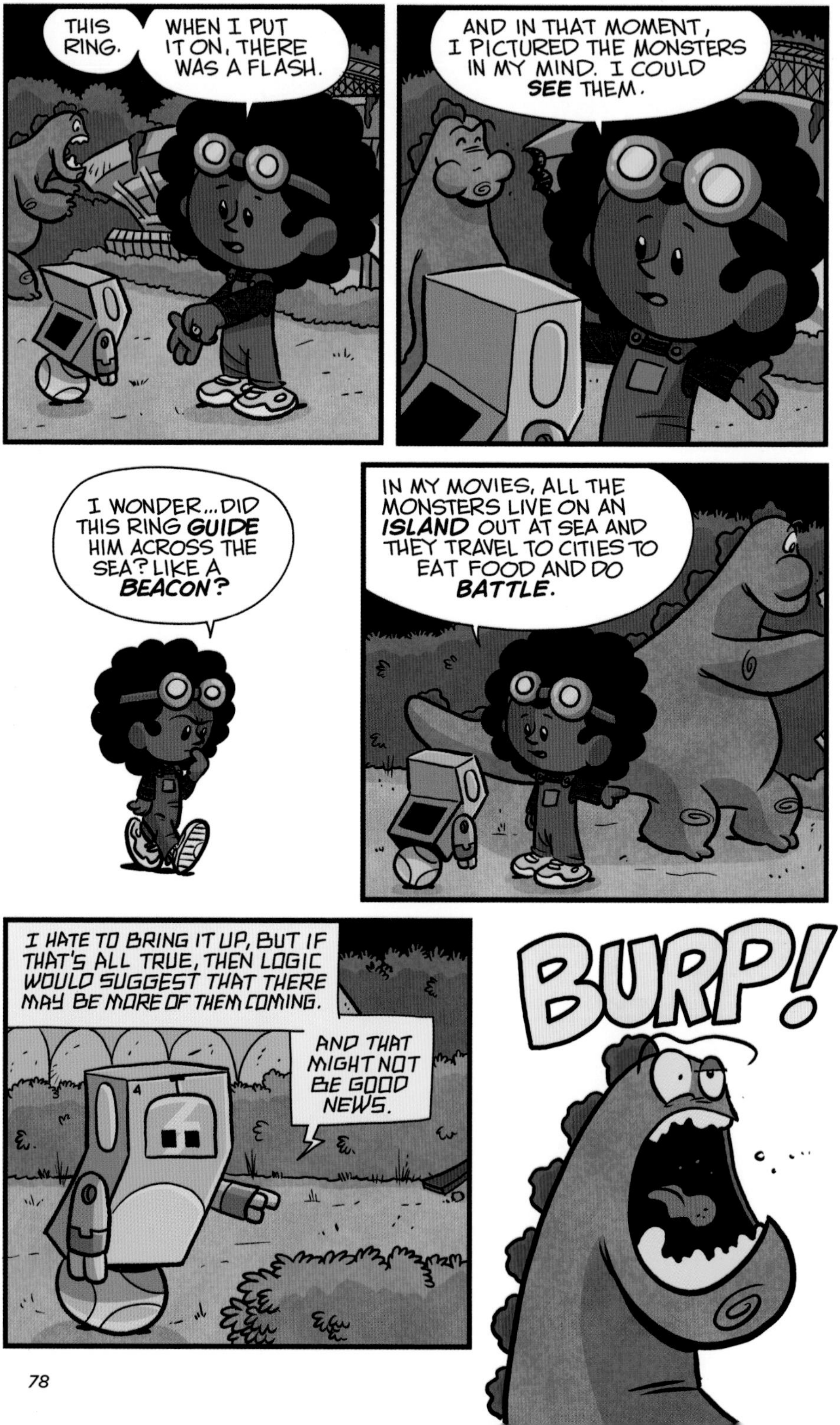
THIS RING.
WHEN I PUT IT ON, THERE WAS A FLASH.
AND IN THAT MOMENT, I PICTURED THE MONSTERS IN MY MIND. I COULD **SEE** THEM.
I WONDER...DID THIS RING **GUIDE** HIM ACROSS THE SEA? LIKE A **BEACON**?
IN MY MOVIES, ALL THE MONSTERS LIVE ON AN **ISLAND** OUT AT SEA AND THEY TRAVEL TO CITIES TO EAT FOOD AND DO **BATTLE**.
I HATE TO BRING IT UP, BUT IF THAT'S ALL TRUE, THEN LOGIC WOULD SUGGEST THAT THERE MAY BE MORE OF THEM COMING.
AND THAT MIGHT NOT BE GOOD NEWS.
BURP!

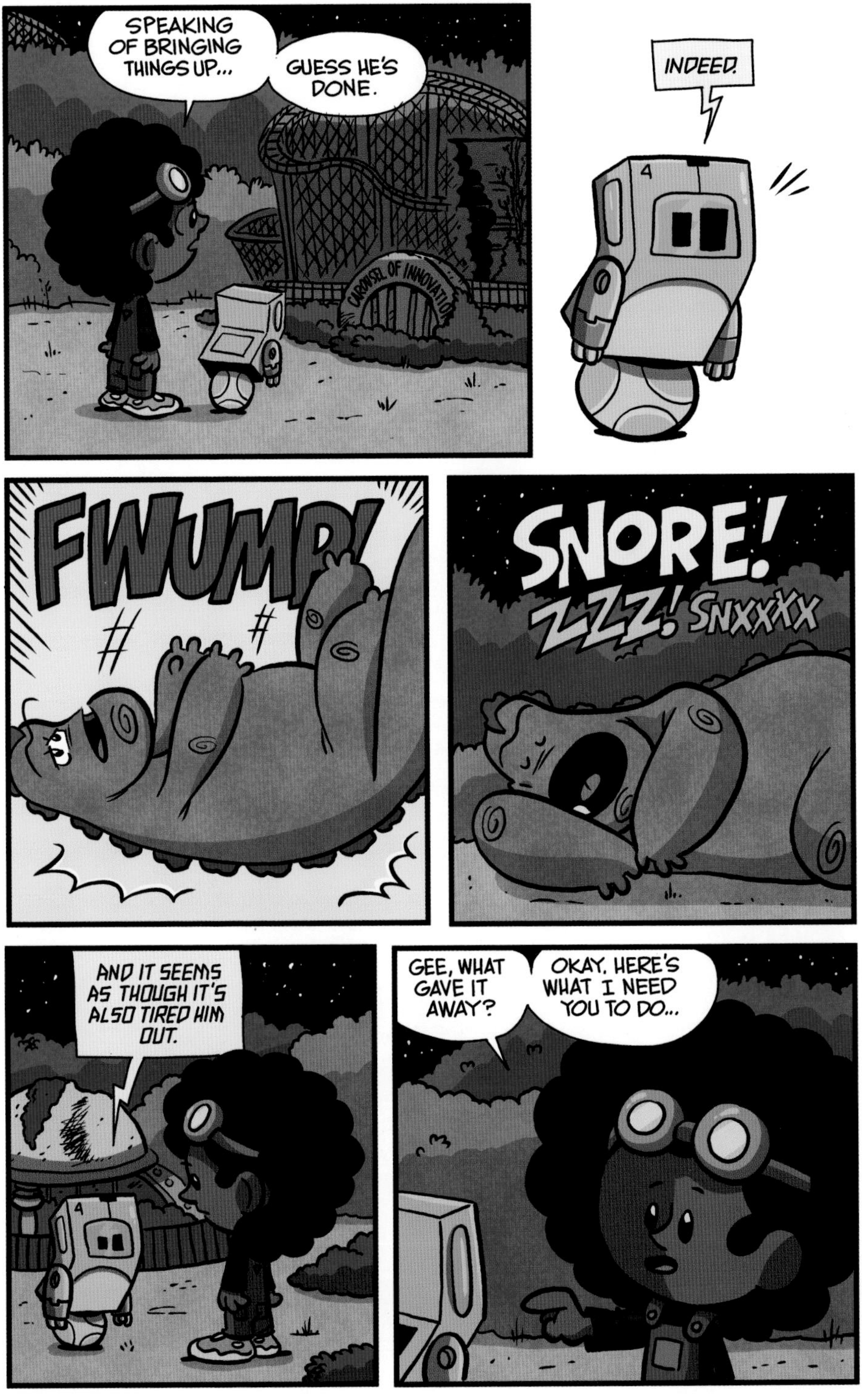
SPEAKING OF BRINGING THINGS UP...
GUESS HE'S DONE.
INDEED.
FWUMP!
SNORE!
ZZZ!
SNXXXX
AND IT SEEMS AS THOUGH IT'S ALSO TIRED HIM OUT.
GEE, WHAT GAVE IT AWAY?
OKAY. HERE'S WHAT I NEED YOU TO DO...

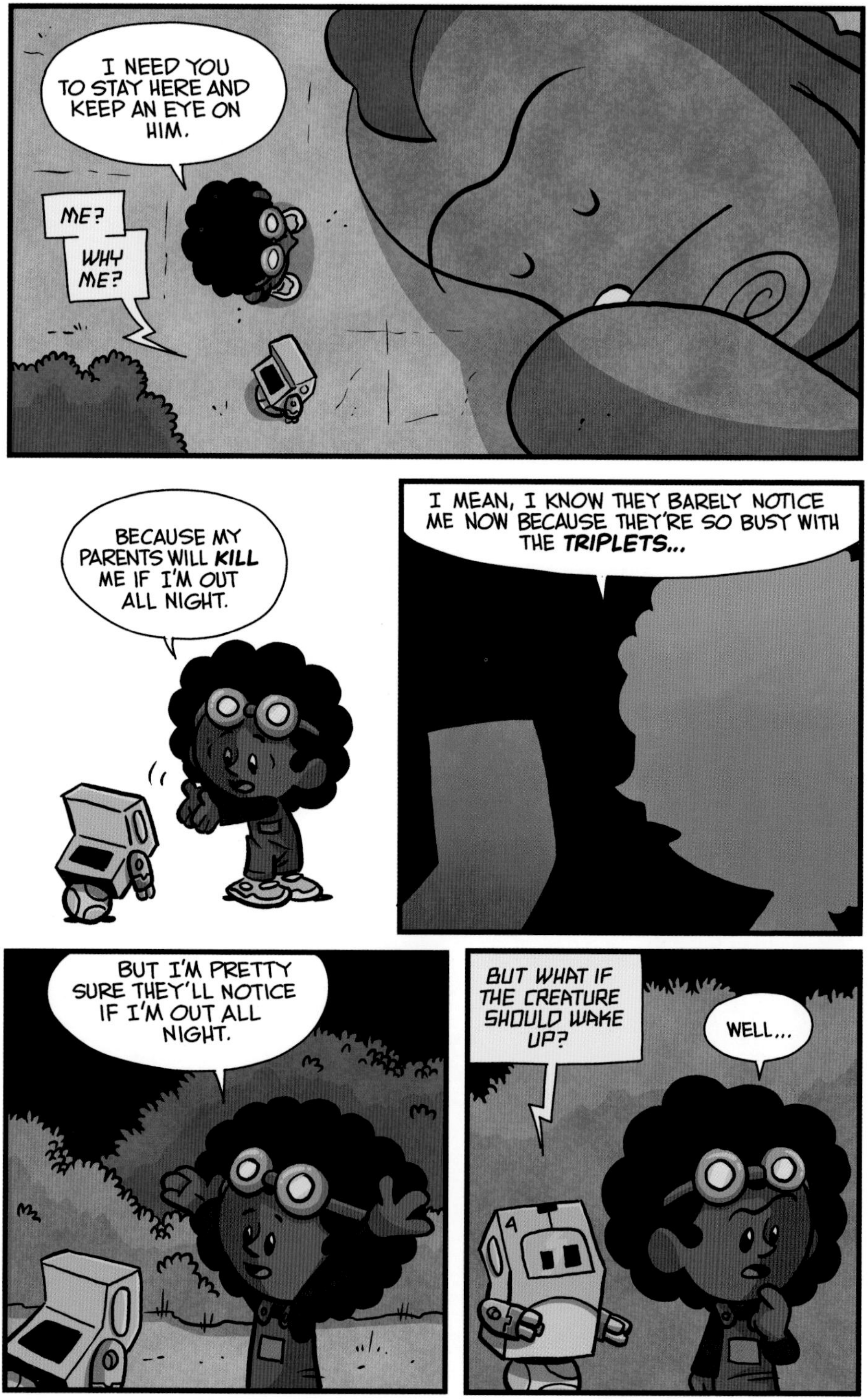
I NEED YOU TO STAY HERE AND KEEP AN EYE ON HIM.
ME?
WHY ME?
BECAUSE MY PARENTS WILL **KILL** ME IF I'M OUT ALL NIGHT.
I MEAN, I KNOW THEY BARELY NOTICE ME NOW BECAUSE THEY'RE SO BUSY WITH THE ***TRIPLETS...***
BUT I'M PRETTY SURE THEY'LL NOTICE IF I'M OUT ALL NIGHT.
BUT WHAT IF THE CREATURE SHOULD WAKE UP?
WELL...

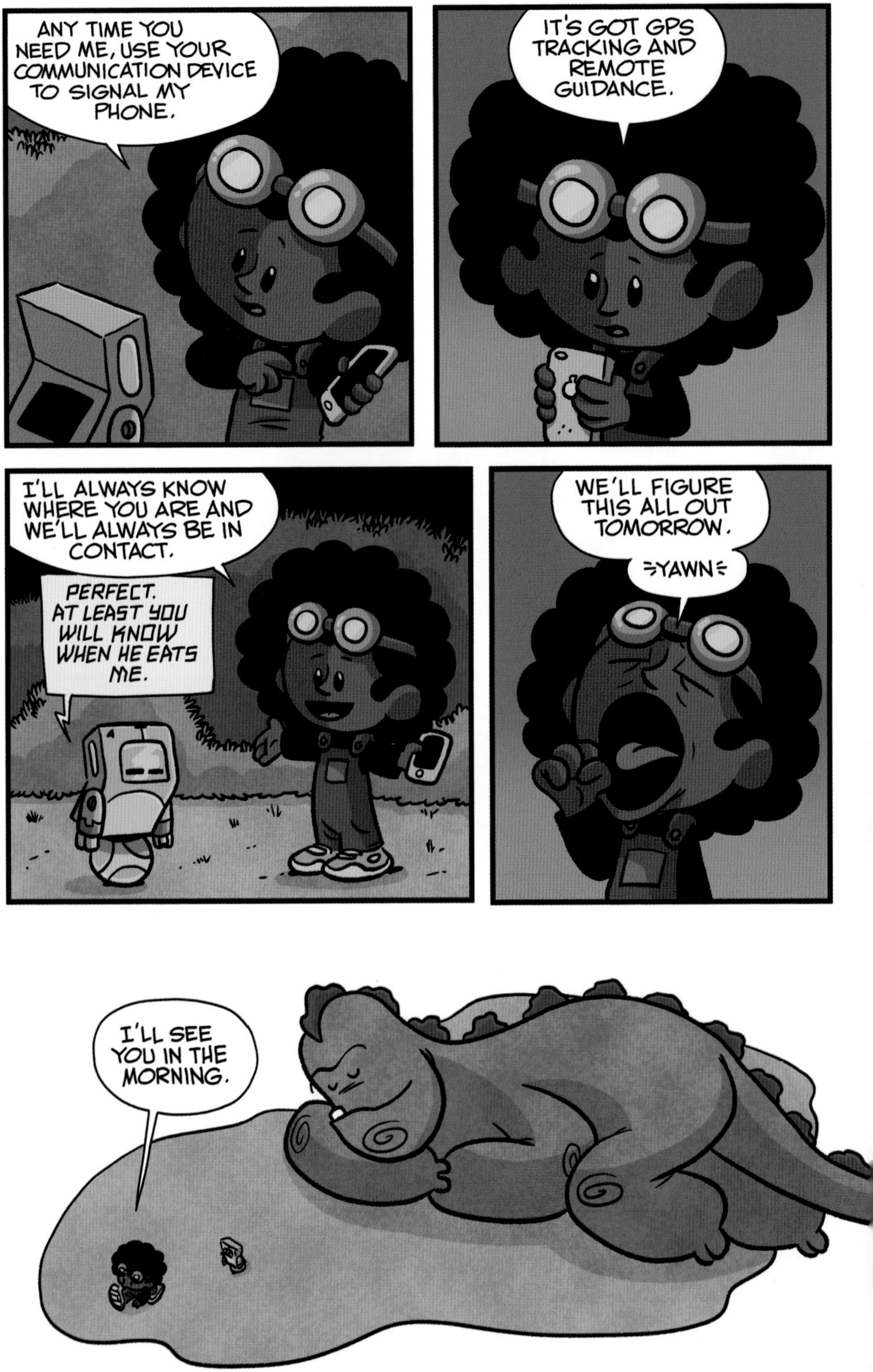
ANY TIME YOU NEED ME, USE YOUR COMMUNICATION DEVICE TO SIGNAL MY PHONE.
IT'S GOT GPS TRACKING AND REMOTE GUIDANCE.
I'LL ALWAYS KNOW WHERE YOU ARE AND WE'LL ALWAYS BE IN CONTACT.
PERFECT. AT LEAST YOU WILL KNOW WHEN HE EATS ME.
WE'LL FIGURE THIS ALL OUT TOMORROW.
YAWN
I'LL SEE YOU IN THE MORNING.

CHAPTER 6 - CHOMP

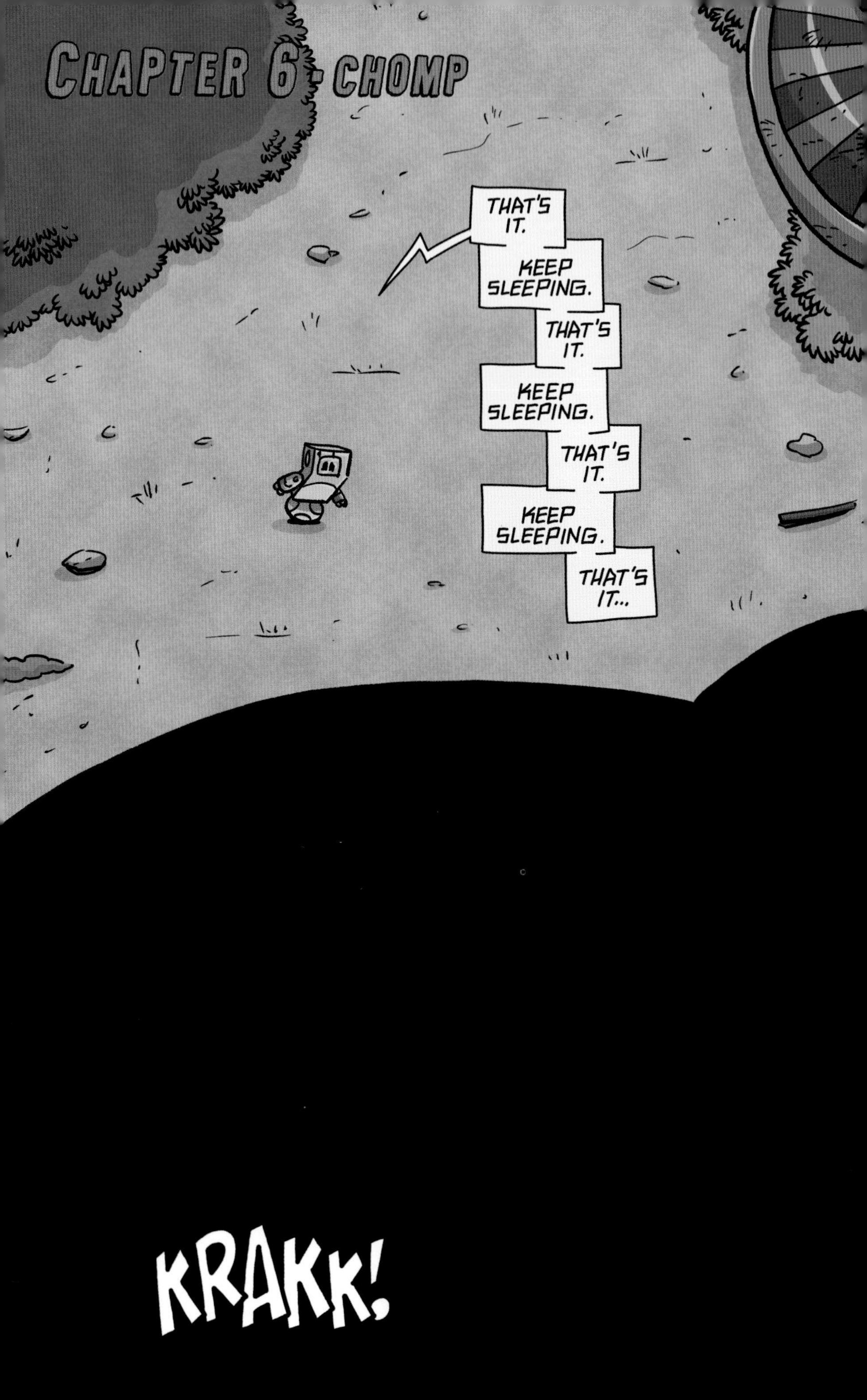
THAT'S IT.
KEEP SLEEPING.
THAT'S IT.
KEEP SLEEPING.
THAT'S IT.
KEEP SLEEPING.
THAT'S IT...
KRAKK!

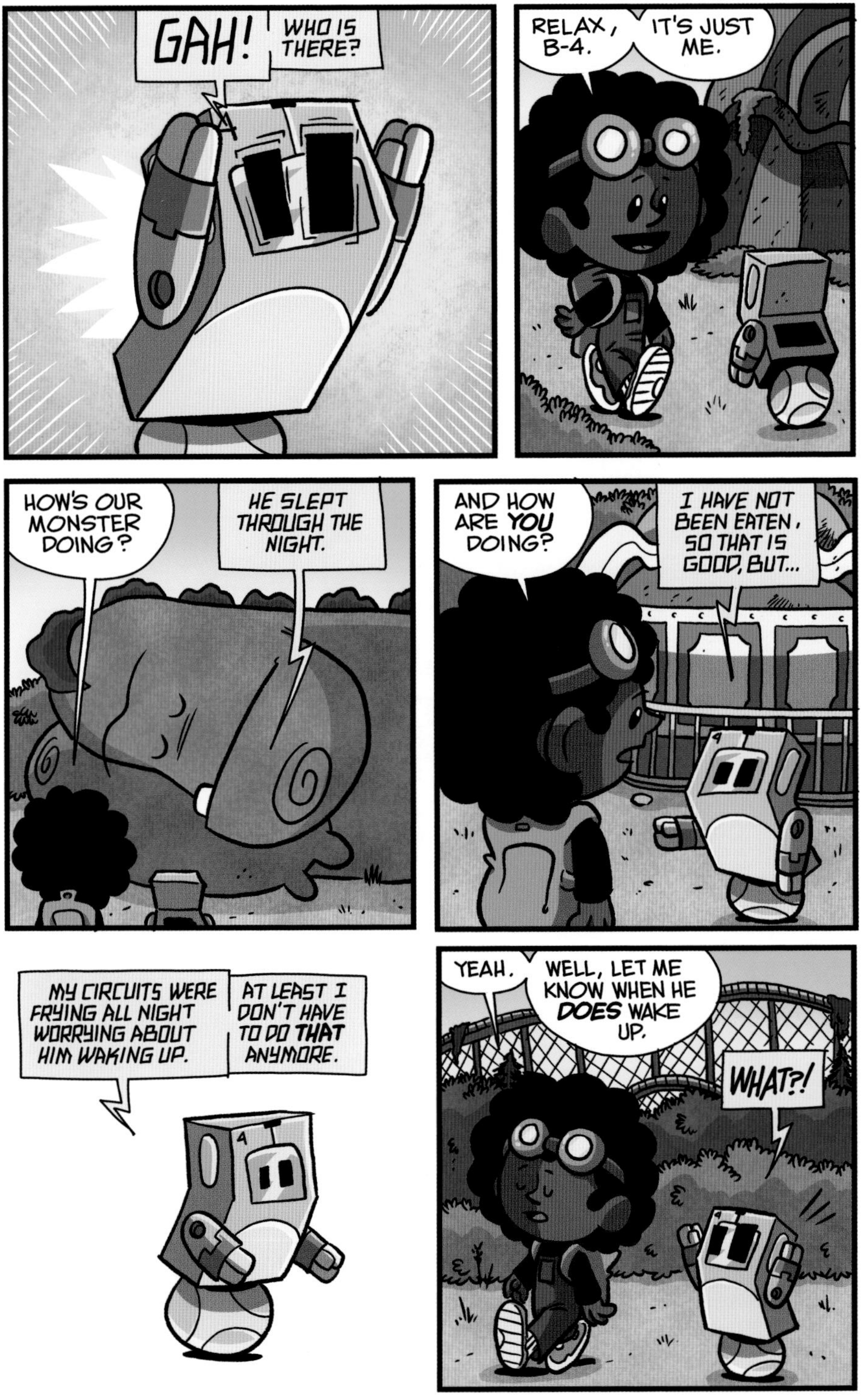
GAH!
WHO IS THERE?
RELAX, B-4.
IT'S JUST ME.
HOW'S OUR MONSTER DOING?
HE SLEPT THROUGH THE NIGHT.
AND HOW ARE **YOU** DOING?
I HAVE NOT BEEN EATEN, SO THAT IS GOOD, BUT...
MY CIRCUITS WERE FRYING ALL NIGHT WORRYING ABOUT HIM WAKING UP.
AT LEAST I DON'T HAVE TO DO **THAT** ANYMORE.
YEAH.
WELL, LET ME KNOW WHEN HE **DOES** WAKE UP.
WHAT?!

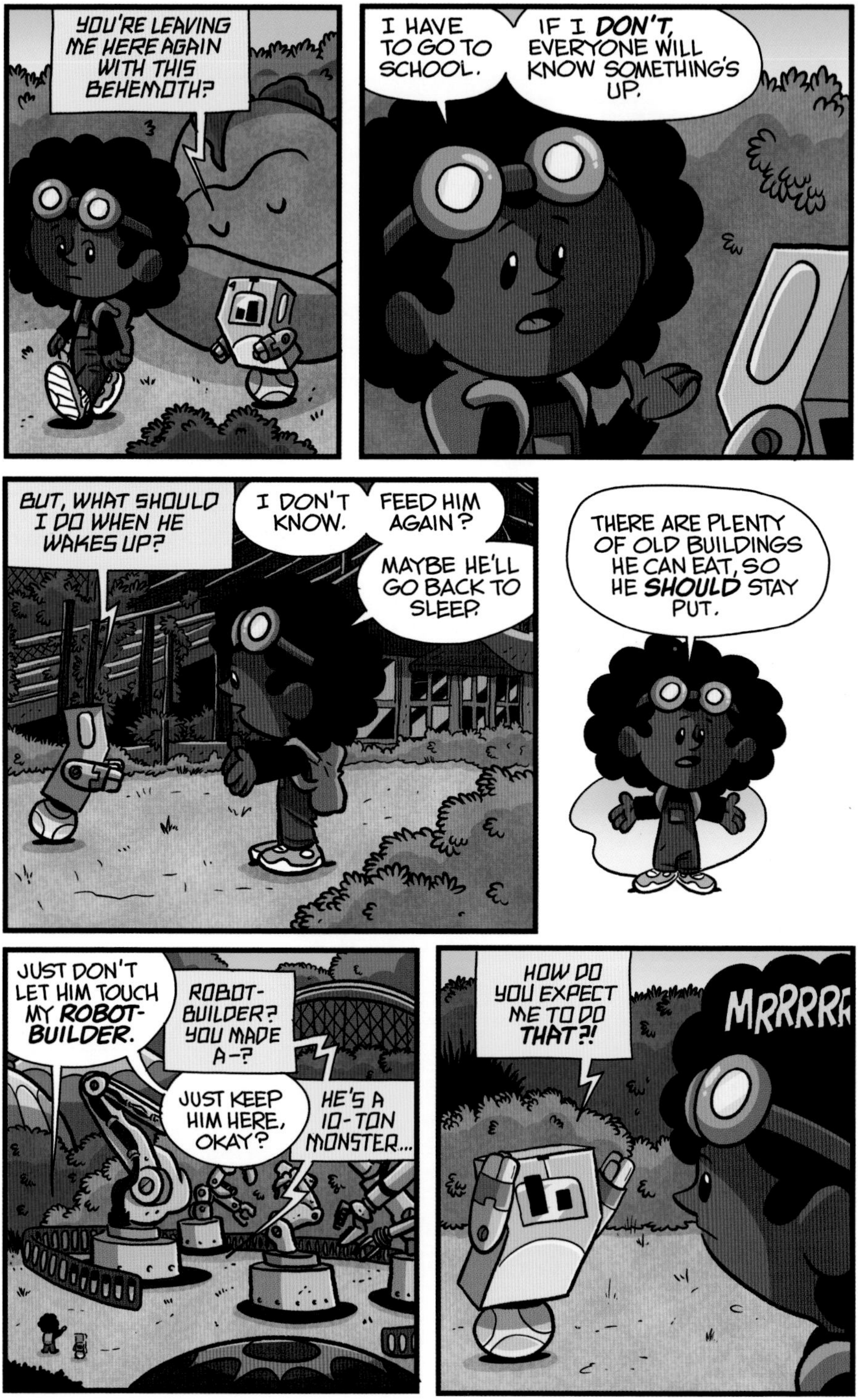
YOU'RE LEAVING ME HERE AGAIN WITH THIS BEHEMOTH?
I HAVE TO GO TO SCHOOL.
IF I DON'T, EVERYONE WILL KNOW SOMETHING'S UP.
BUT, WHAT SHOULD I DO WHEN HE WAKES UP?
I DON'T KNOW.
FEED HIM AGAIN?
MAYBE HE'LL GO BACK TO SLEEP.
THERE ARE PLENTY OF OLD BUILDINGS HE CAN EAT, SO HE SHOULD STAY PUT.
JUST DON'T LET HIM TOUCH MY ROBOT-BUILDER.
ROBOT-BUILDER? YOU MADE A–?
JUST KEEP HIM HERE, OKAY?
HE'S A 10-TON MONSTER...
HOW DO YOU EXPECT ME TO DO THAT?!
MRRRRR

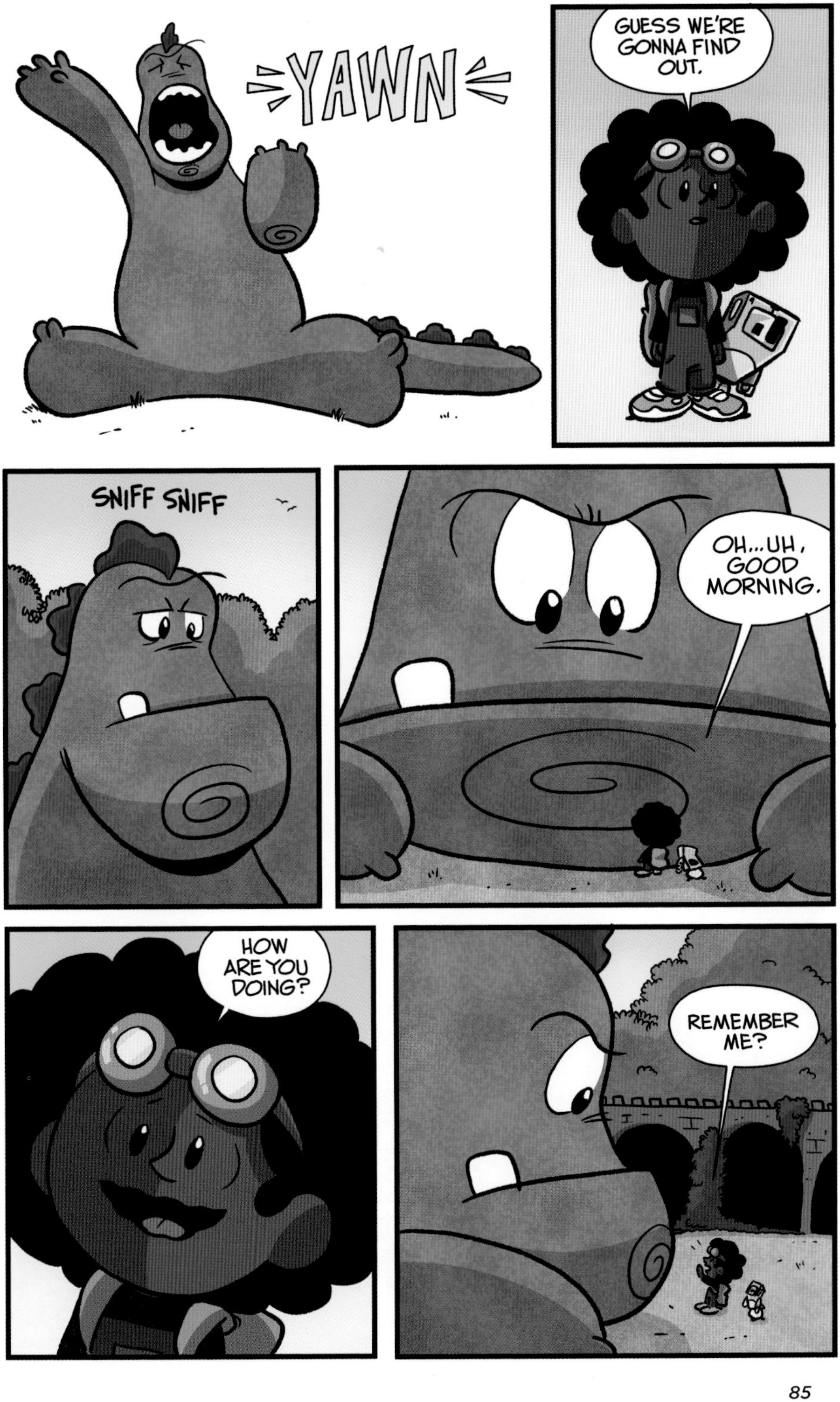
YAWN
GUESS WE'RE GONNA FIND OUT.
SNIFF SNIFF
OH...UH, GOOD MORNING.
HOW ARE YOU DOING?
REMEMBER ME?

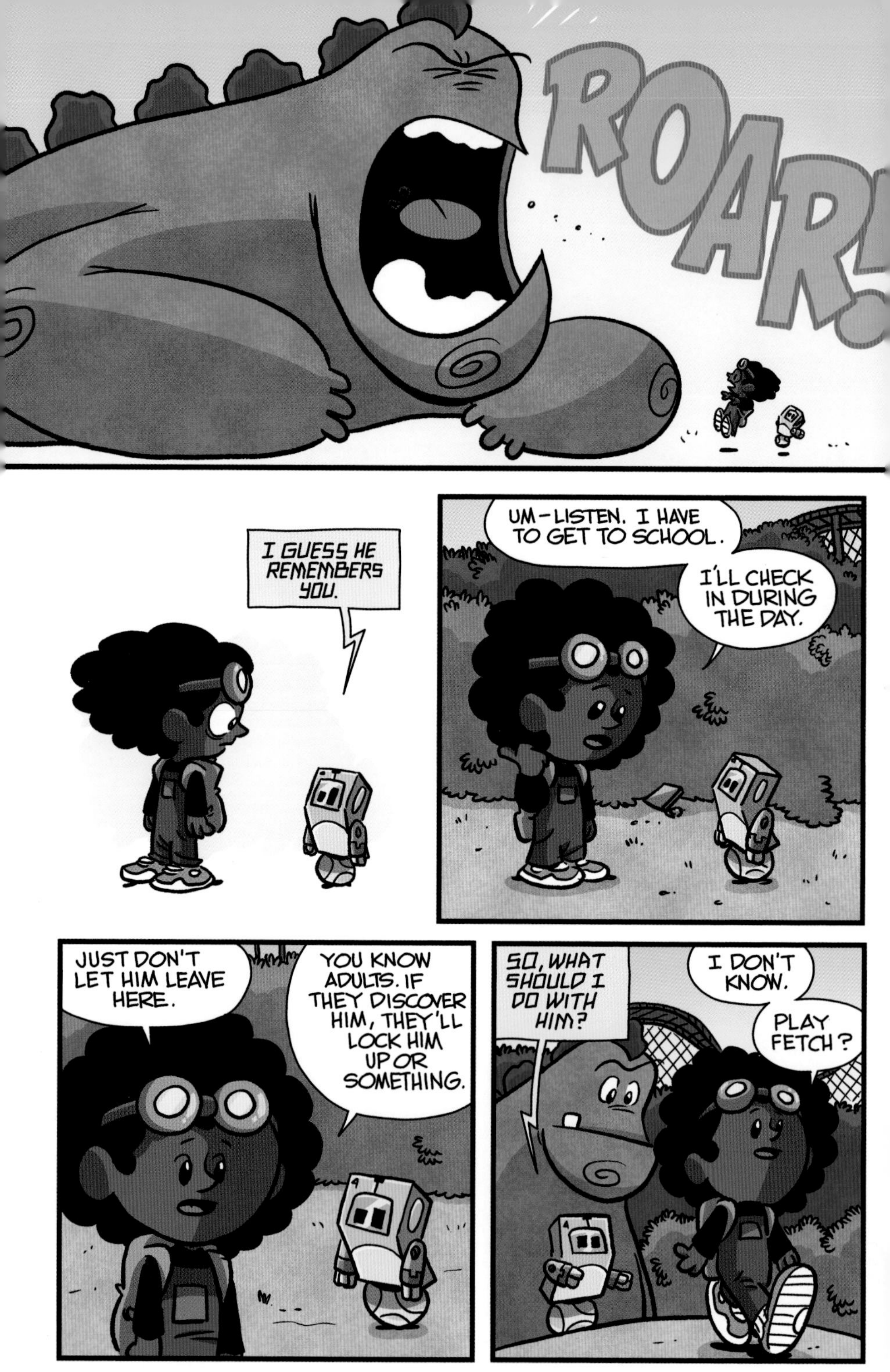
ROAR!
I GUESS HE REMEMBERS YOU.
UM–LISTEN. I HAVE TO GET TO SCHOOL.
I'LL CHECK IN DURING THE DAY.
JUST DON'T LET HIM LEAVE HERE.
YOU KNOW ADULTS. IF THEY DISCOVER HIM, THEY'LL LOCK HIM UP OR SOMETHING.
SO, WHAT SHOULD I DO WITH HIM?
I DON'T KNOW.
PLAY FETCH?

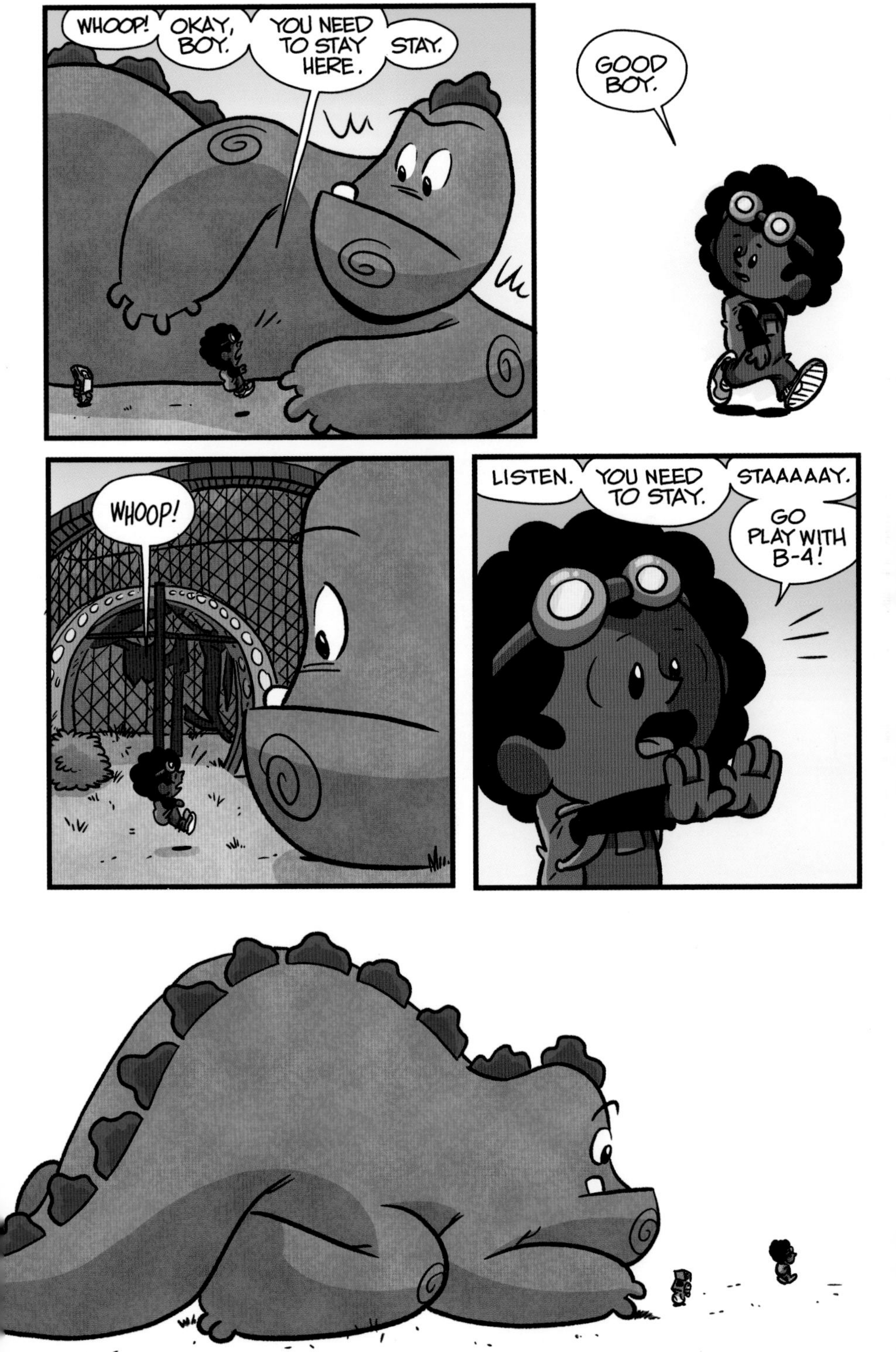
WHOOP!
OKAY, BOY.
YOU NEED TO STAY HERE.
STAY.
GOOD BOY.
WHOOP!
LISTEN.
YOU NEED TO STAY.
STAAAAAY.
GO PLAY WITH B-4!

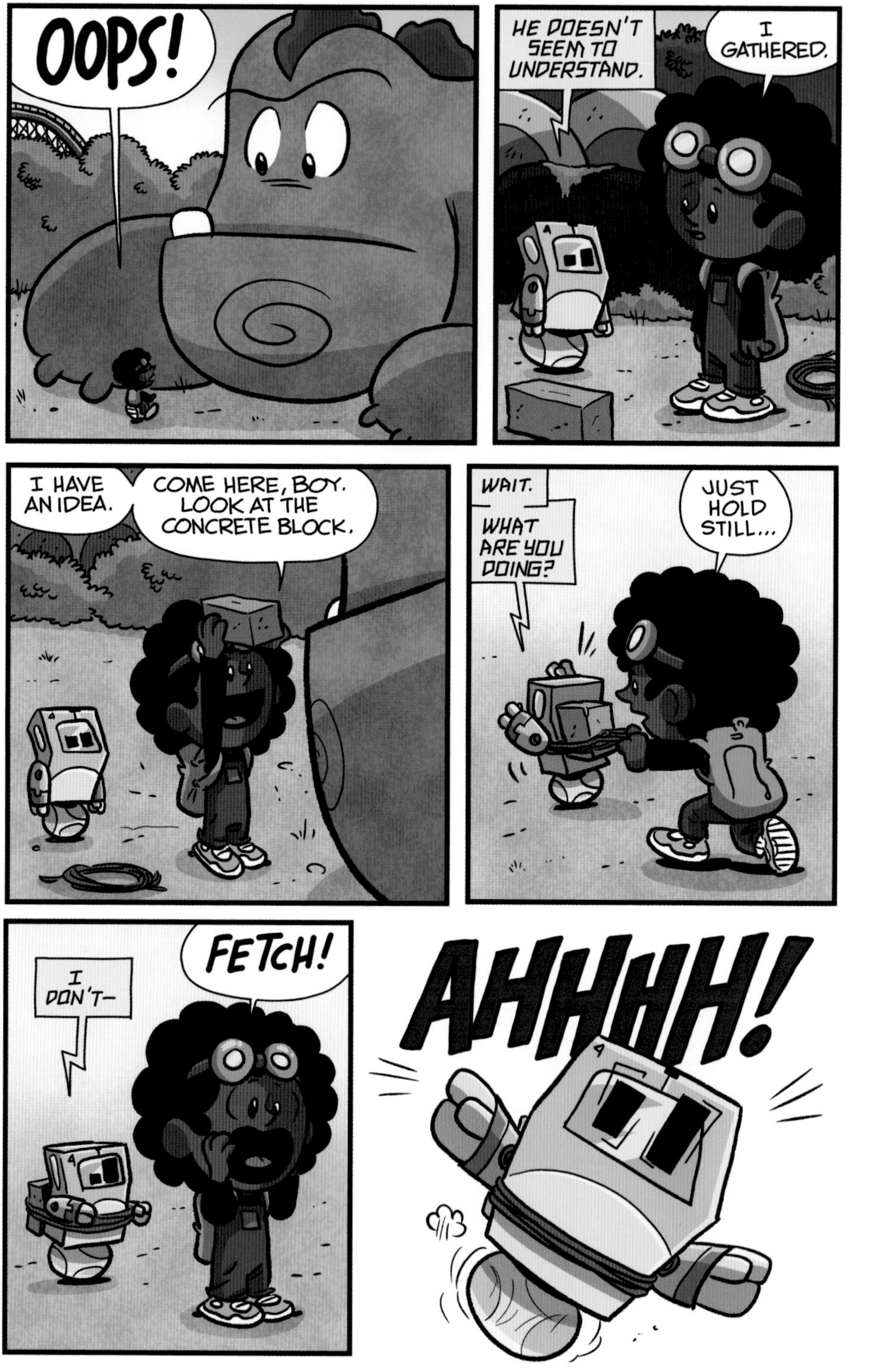
OOPS!
HE DOESN'T SEEM TO UNDERSTAND.
I GATHERED.
I HAVE AN IDEA.
COME HERE, BOY. LOOK AT THE CONCRETE BLOCK.
WAIT.
WHAT ARE YOU DOING?
JUST HOLD STILL...
I DON'T—
FETCH!
AHHHH!

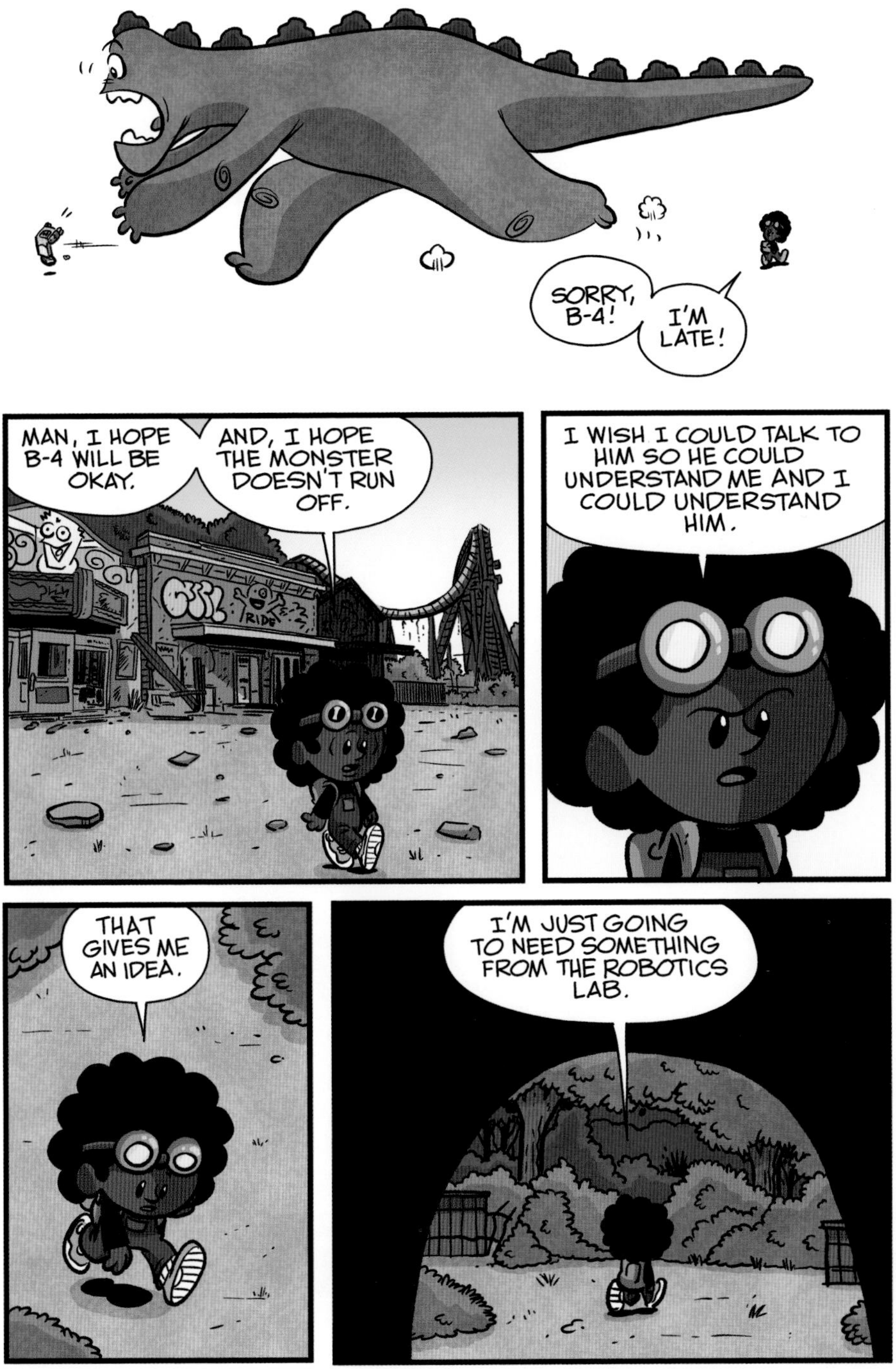
SORRY, B-4!
I'M LATE!
MAN, I HOPE B-4 WILL BE OKAY.
AND, I HOPE THE MONSTER DOESN'T RUN OFF.
RIDE
I WISH I COULD TALK TO HIM SO HE COULD UNDERSTAND ME AND I COULD UNDERSTAND HIM.
THAT GIVES ME AN IDEA.
I'M JUST GOING TO NEED SOMETHING FROM THE ROBOTICS LAB.

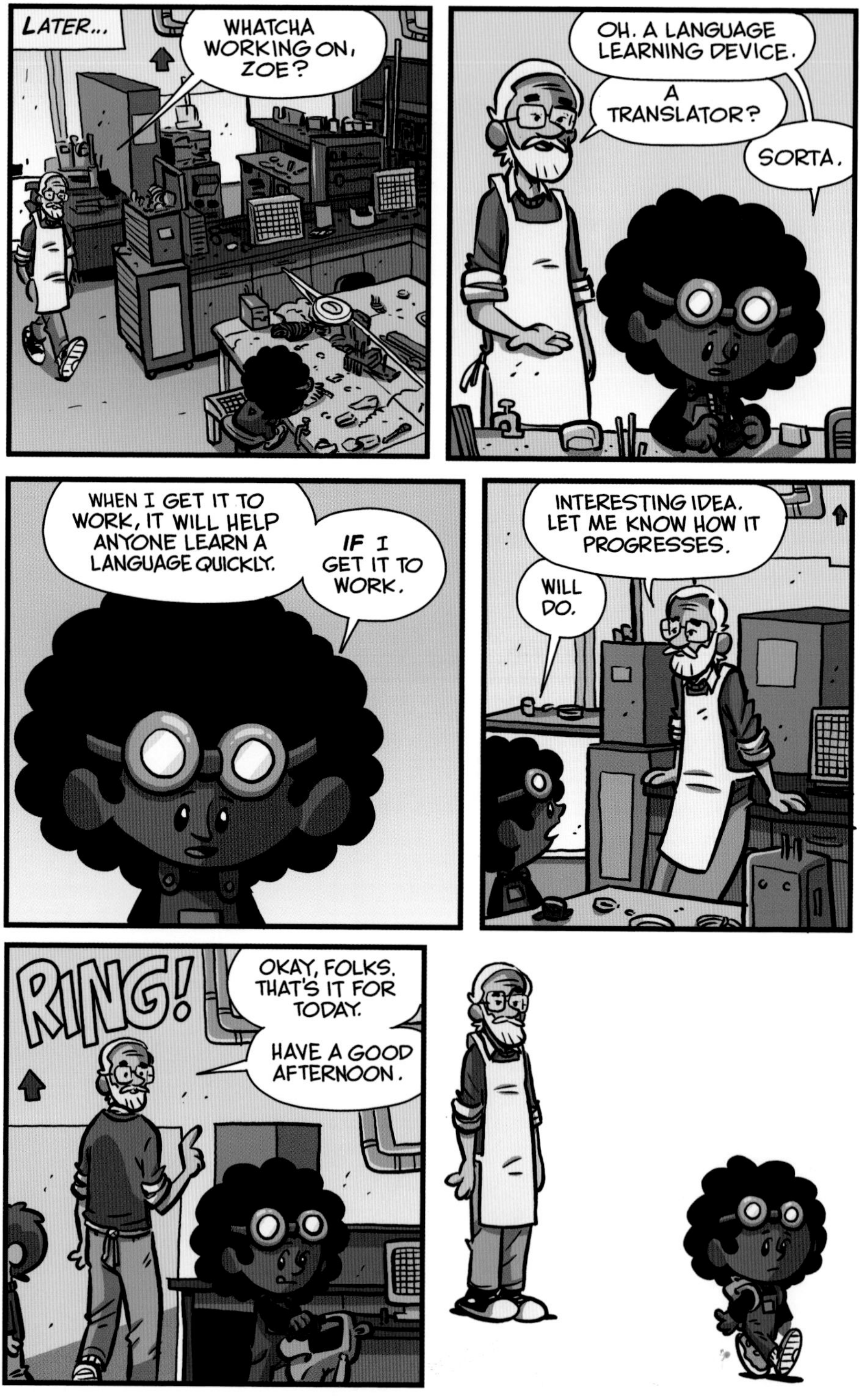
LATER...
WHATCHA WORKING ON, ZOE?
OH. A LANGUAGE LEARNING DEVICE.
A TRANSLATOR?
SORTA.
WHEN I GET IT TO WORK, IT WILL HELP ANYONE LEARN A LANGUAGE QUICKLY.
IF I GET IT TO WORK.
INTERESTING IDEA. LET ME KNOW HOW IT PROGRESSES.
WILL DO.
RING!
OKAY, FOLKS. THAT'S IT FOR TODAY.
HAVE A GOOD AFTERNOON.

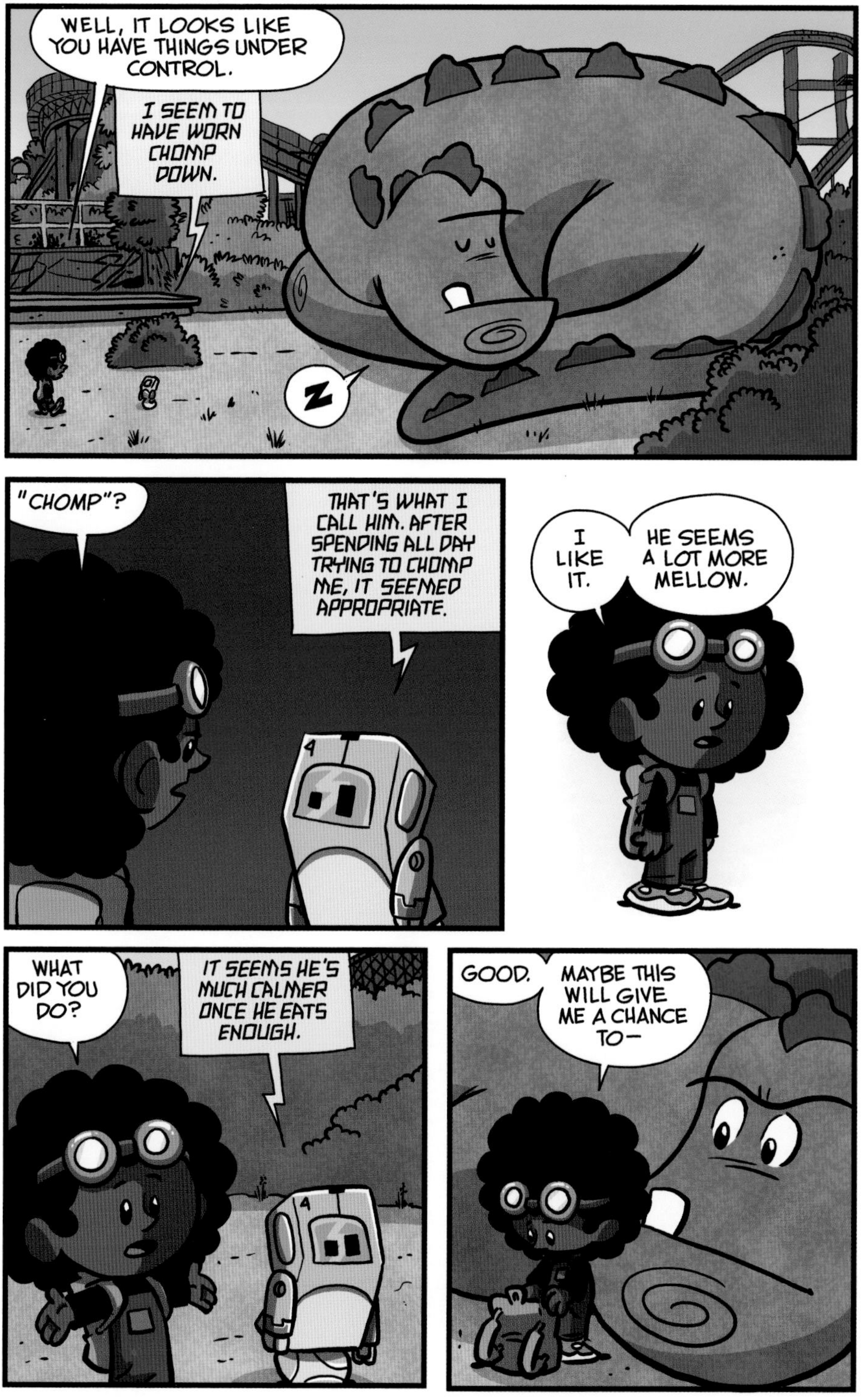
WELL, IT LOOKS LIKE YOU HAVE THINGS UNDER CONTROL.
I SEEM TO HAVE WORN CHOMP DOWN.
Z
"CHOMP"?
THAT'S WHAT I CALL HIM. AFTER SPENDING ALL DAY TRYING TO CHOMP ME, IT SEEMED APPROPRIATE.
I LIKE IT.
HE SEEMS A LOT MORE MELLOW.
WHAT DID YOU DO?
IT SEEMS HE'S MUCH CALMER ONCE HE EATS ENOUGH.
GOOD.
MAYBE THIS WILL GIVE ME A CHANCE TO—

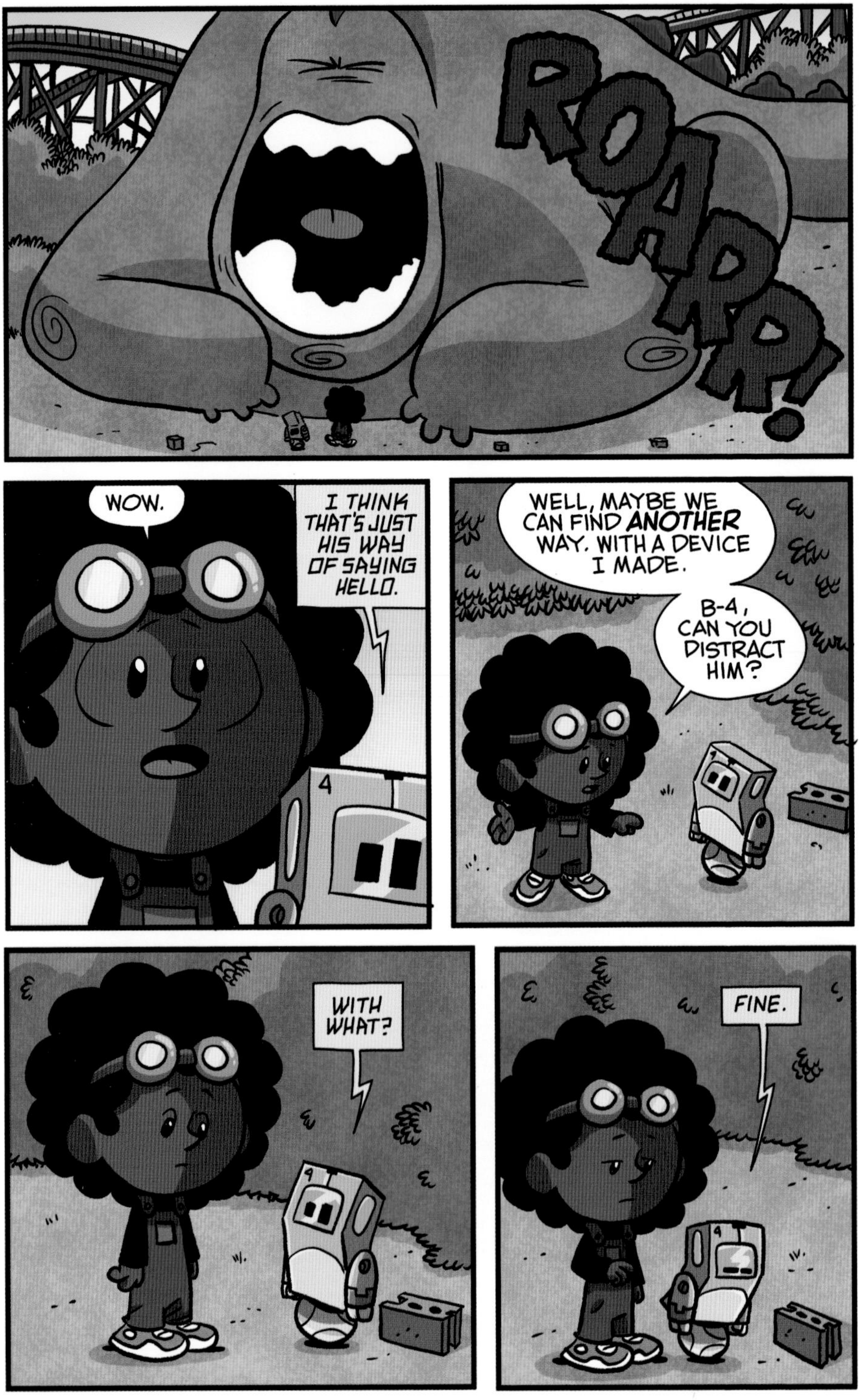
ROARR!
WOW.
I THINK THAT'S JUST HIS WAY OF SAYING HELLO.
WELL, MAYBE WE CAN FIND **ANOTHER** WAY. WITH A DEVICE I MADE.
B-4, CAN YOU DISTRACT HIM?
WITH WHAT?
FINE.

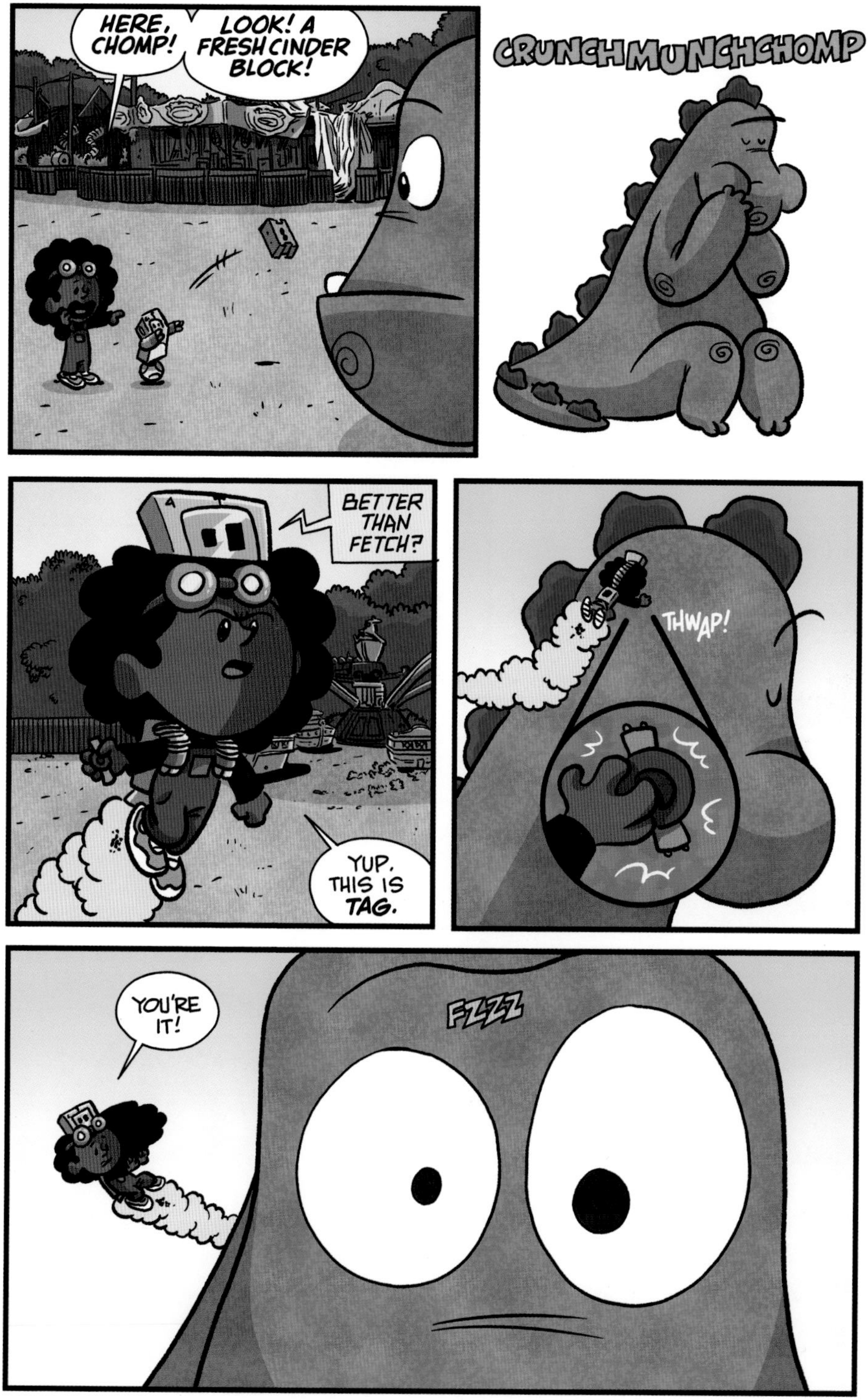
HERE, CHOMP!
LOOK! A FRESH CINDER BLOCK!
CRUNCHMUNCHCHOMP
BETTER THAN FETCH?
YUP. THIS IS TAG.
THWAP!
YOU'RE IT!
FZZZ

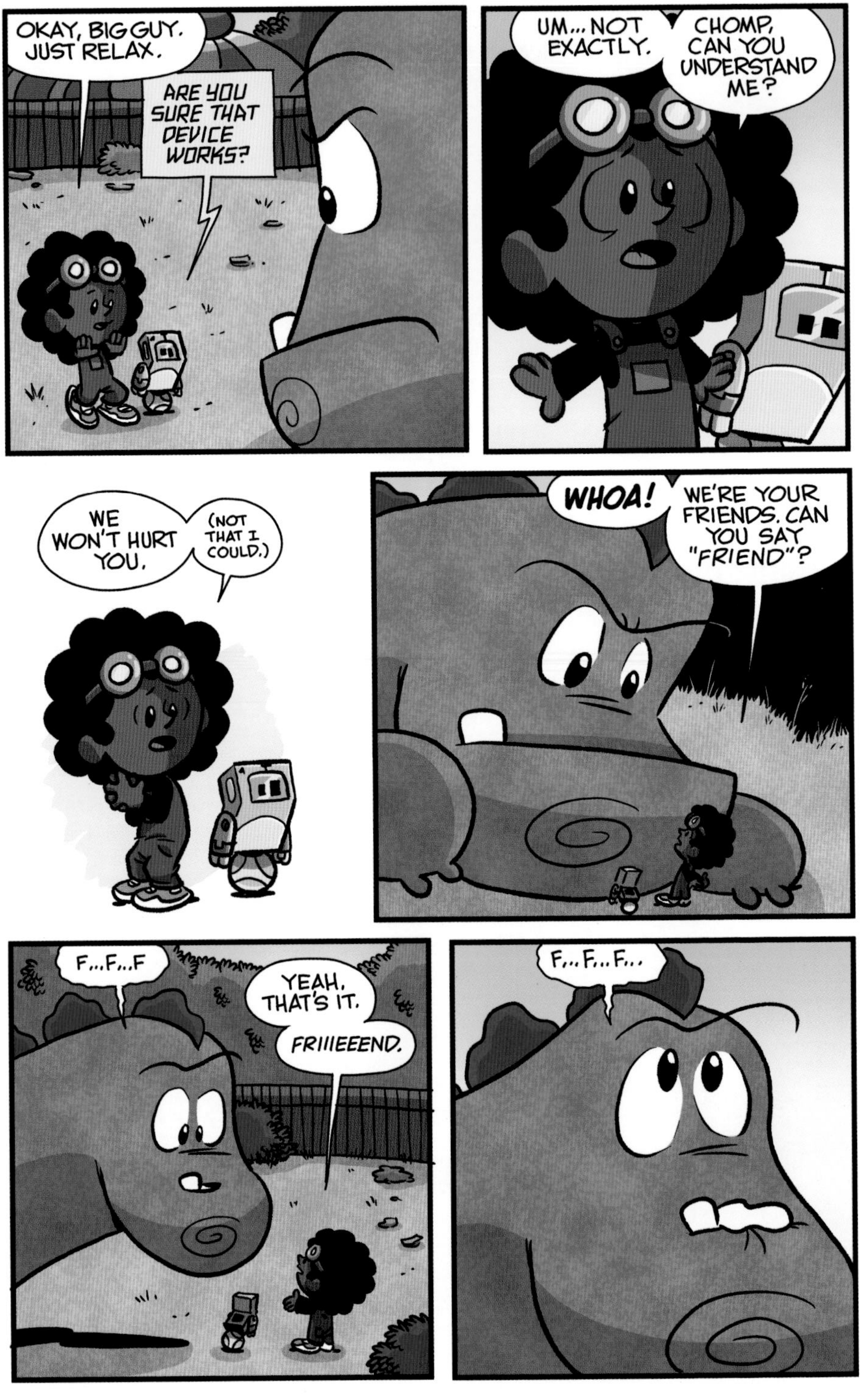
OKAY, BIG GUY. JUST RELAX.
ARE YOU SURE THAT DEVICE WORKS?
UM... NOT EXACTLY.
CHOMP, CAN YOU UNDERSTAND ME?
WE WON'T HURT YOU.
(NOT THAT I COULD.)
WHOA!
WE'RE YOUR FRIENDS. CAN YOU SAY "FRIEND"?
F...F...F
YEAH, THAT'S IT.
FRIIIEEEND.
F... F... F...

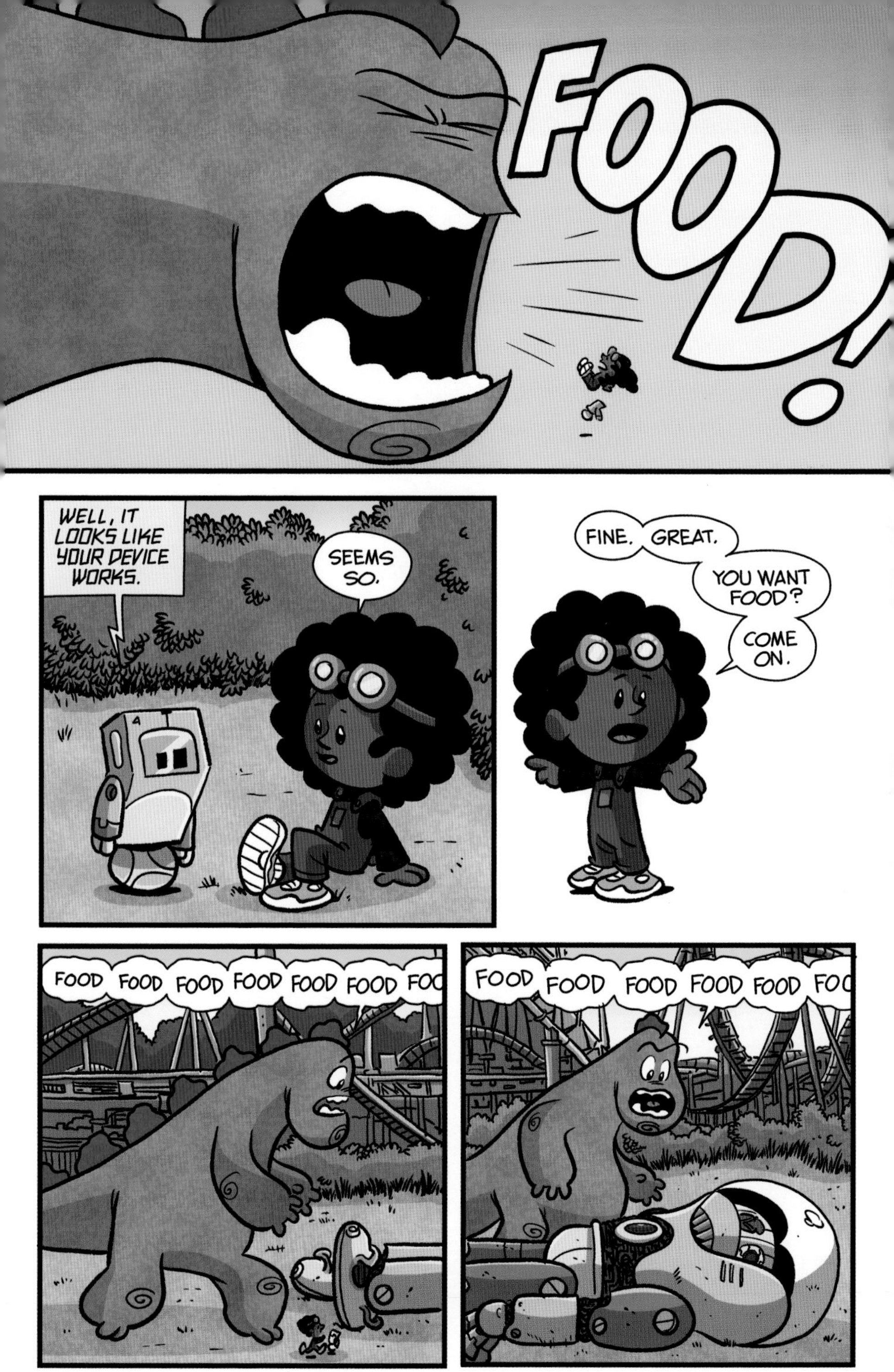
FOOD!
WELL, IT LOOKS LIKE YOUR DEVICE WORKS.
SEEMS SO.
FINE. GREAT.
YOU WANT FOOD?
COME ON.
FOOD FOOD FOOD FOOD FOOD FOOD
FOOD FOOD FOOD FOOD FOOD

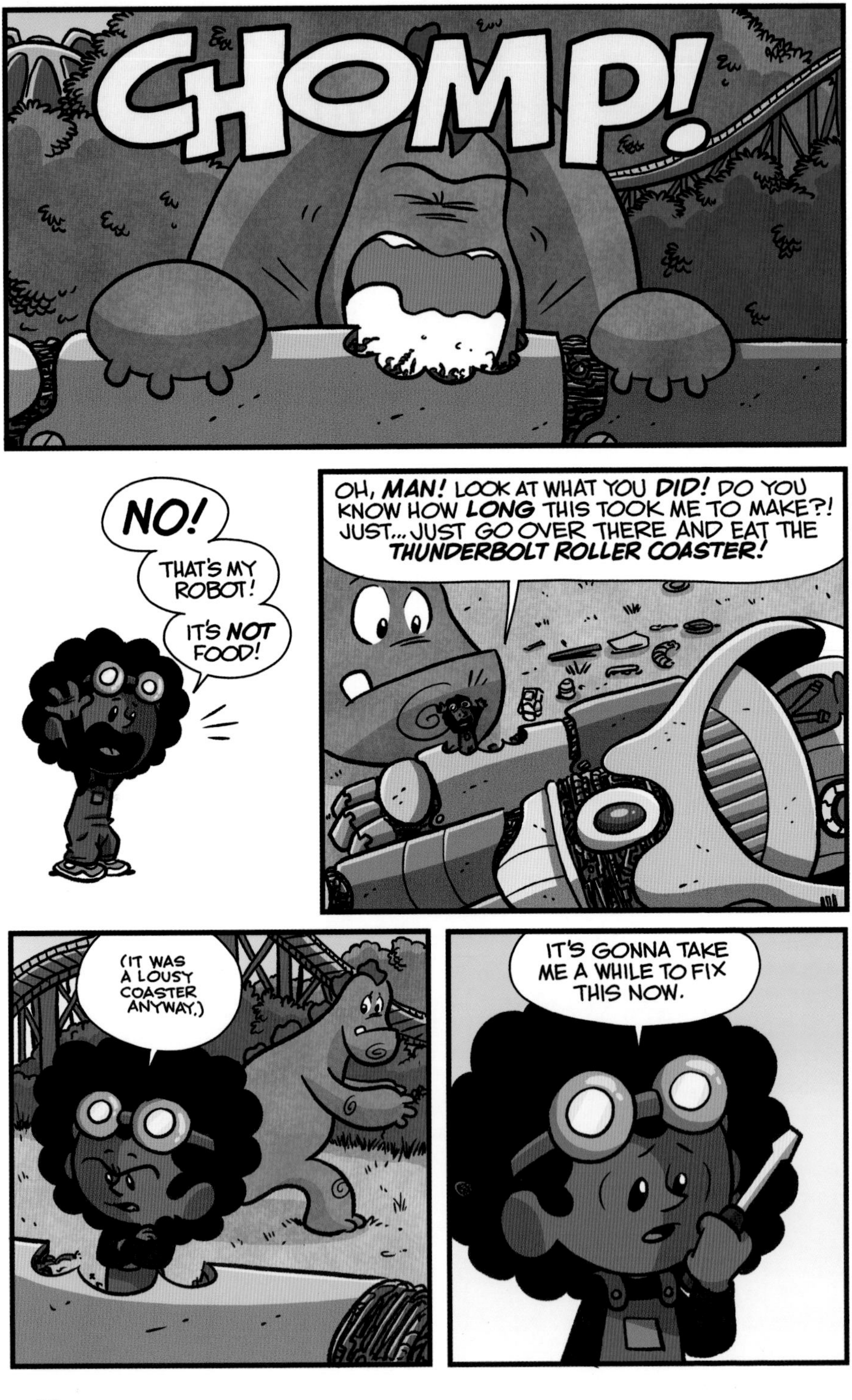
CHOMP!
NO!
THAT'S MY ROBOT!
IT'S NOT FOOD!
OH, MAN! LOOK AT WHAT YOU DID! DO YOU KNOW HOW LONG THIS TOOK ME TO MAKE?! JUST... JUST GO OVER THERE AND EAT THE THUNDERBOLT ROLLER COASTER!
(IT WAS A LOUSY COASTER ANYWAY.)
IT'S GONNA TAKE ME A WHILE TO FIX THIS NOW.

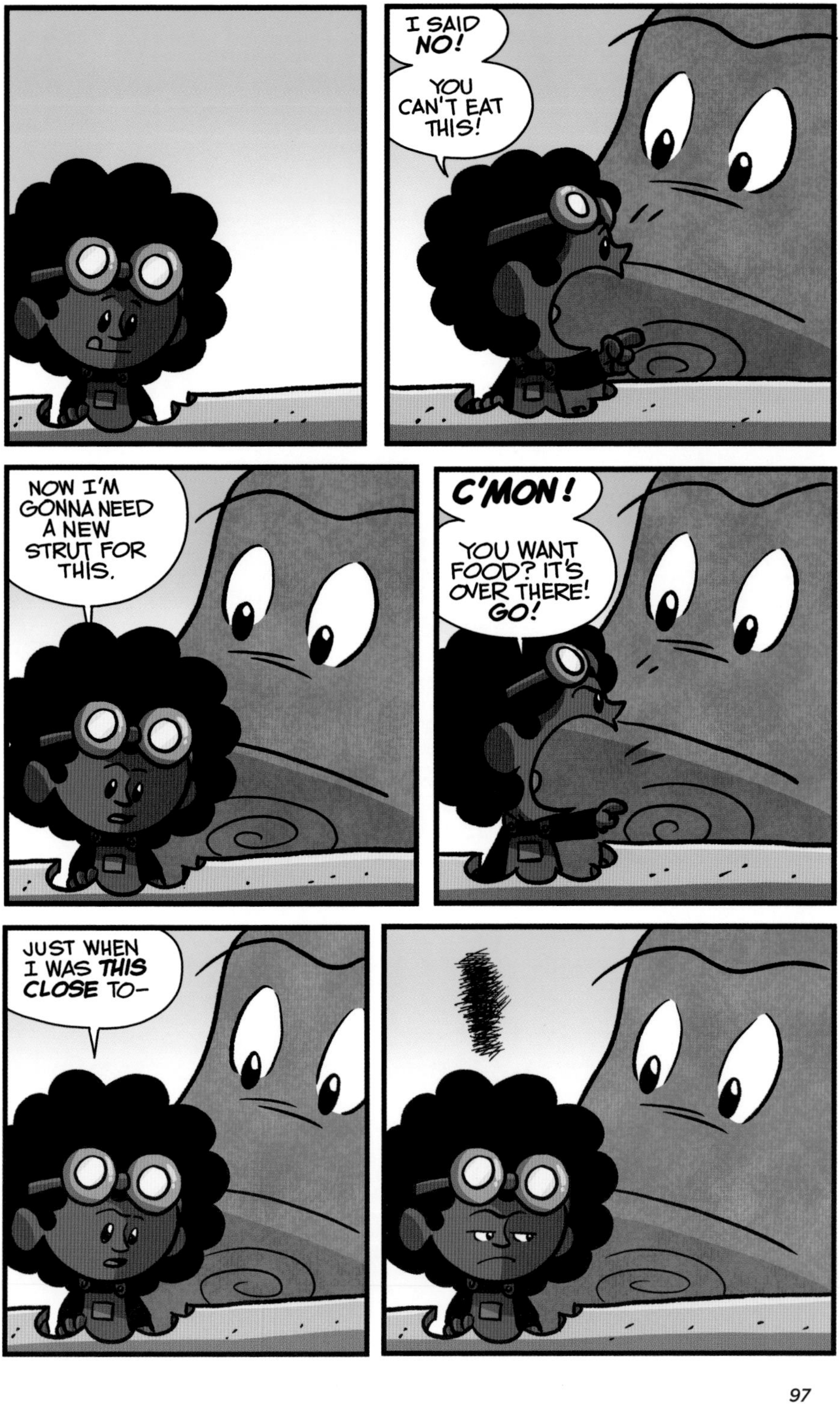
I SAID **NO!**
YOU CAN'T EAT THIS!
NOW I'M GONNA NEED A NEW STRUT FOR THIS.
C'MON!
YOU WANT FOOD? IT'S OVER THERE! **GO!**
JUST WHEN I WAS **THIS CLOSE** TO-

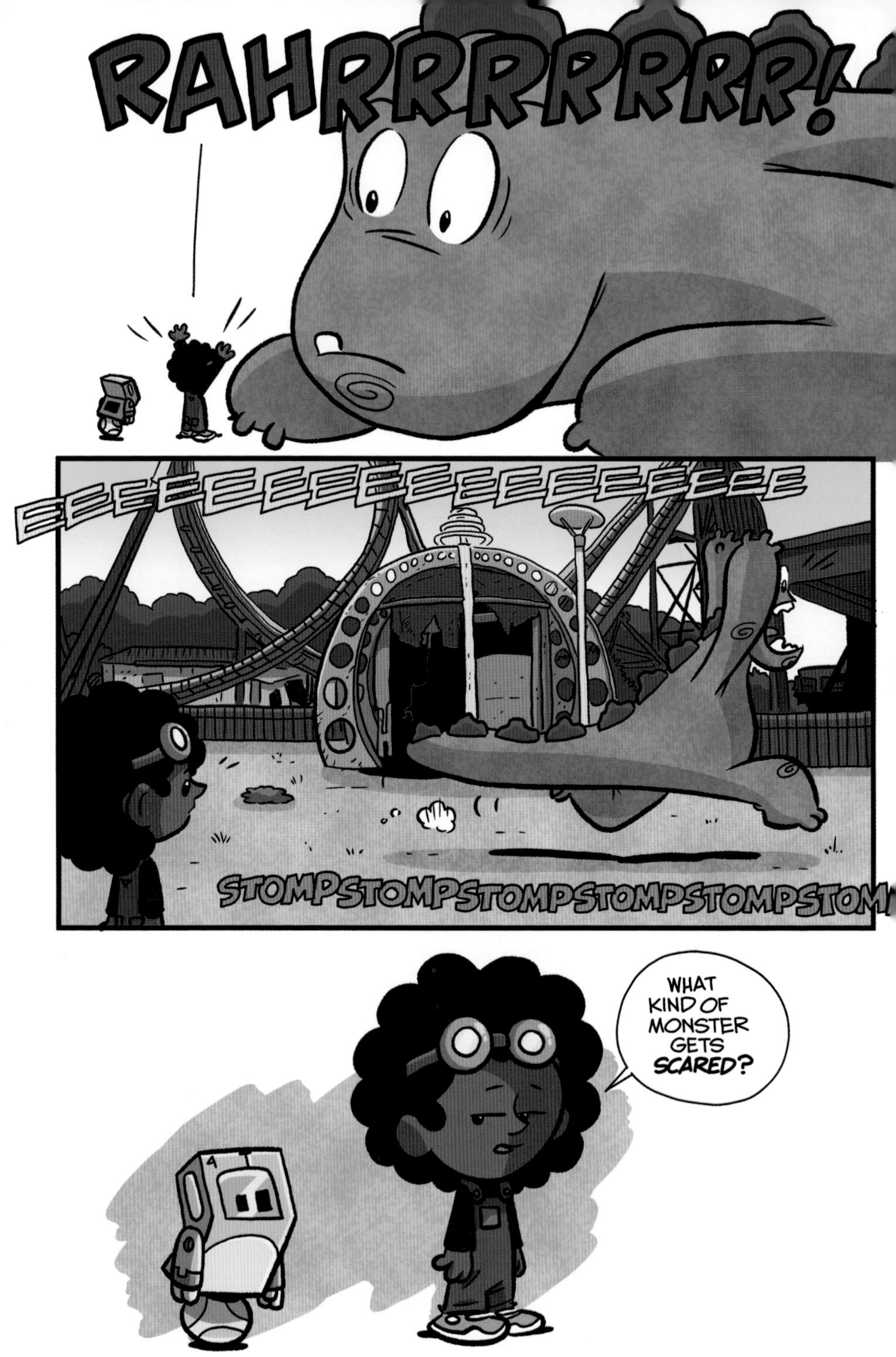
RAHRRRRRRRR!
EEEEEEEEEEEEEEEEEEEE
STOMPSTOMPSTOMPSTOMPSTOMPSTOM
WHAT KIND OF MONSTER GETS SCARED?

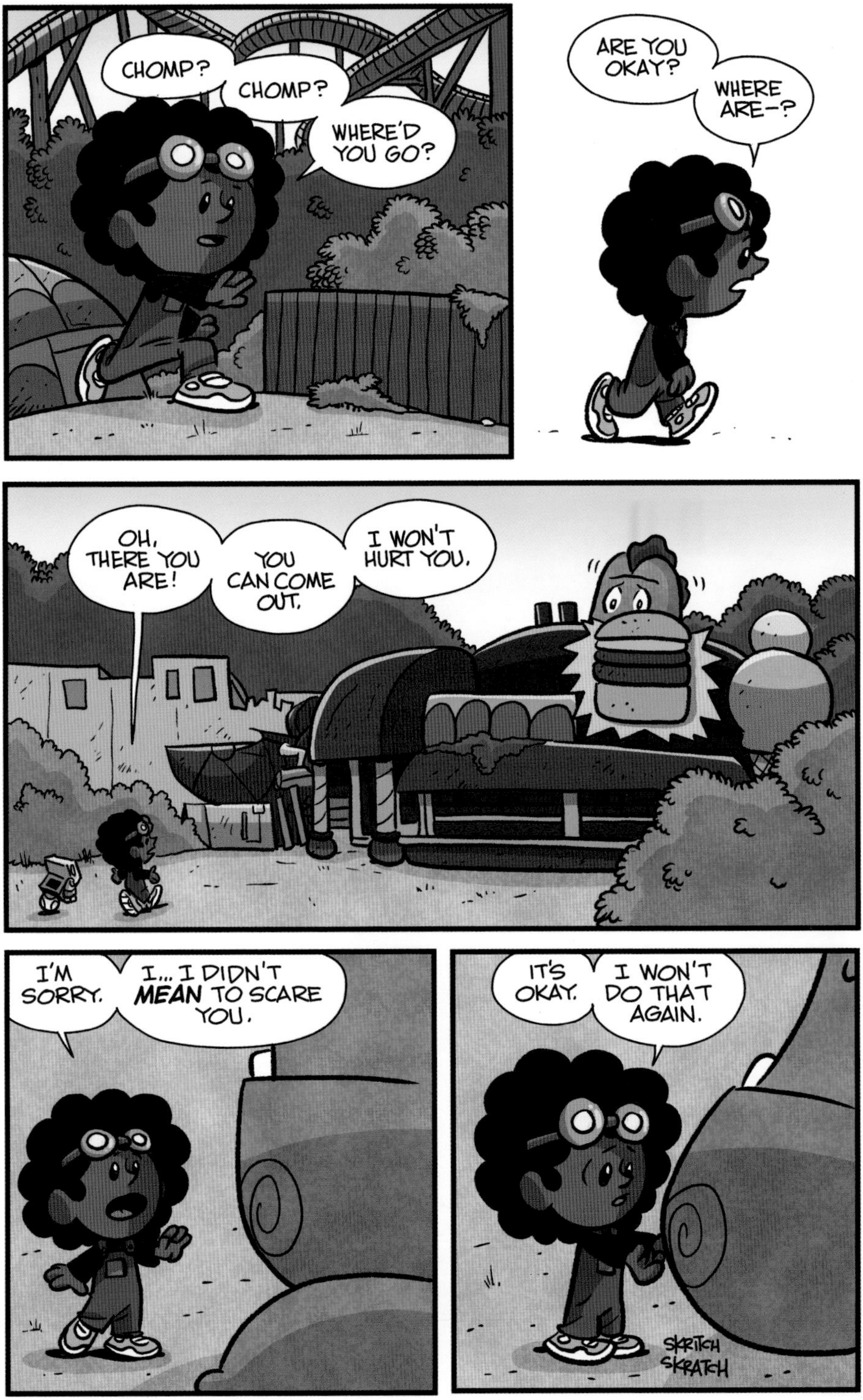
CHOMP?
CHOMP?
WHERE'D YOU GO?
ARE YOU OKAY?
WHERE ARE–?
OH, THERE YOU ARE!
YOU CAN COME OUT.
I WON'T HURT YOU.
I'M SORRY.
I... I DIDN'T **MEAN** TO SCARE YOU.
IT'S OKAY.
I WON'T DO THAT AGAIN.
SKRITCH SKRATCH

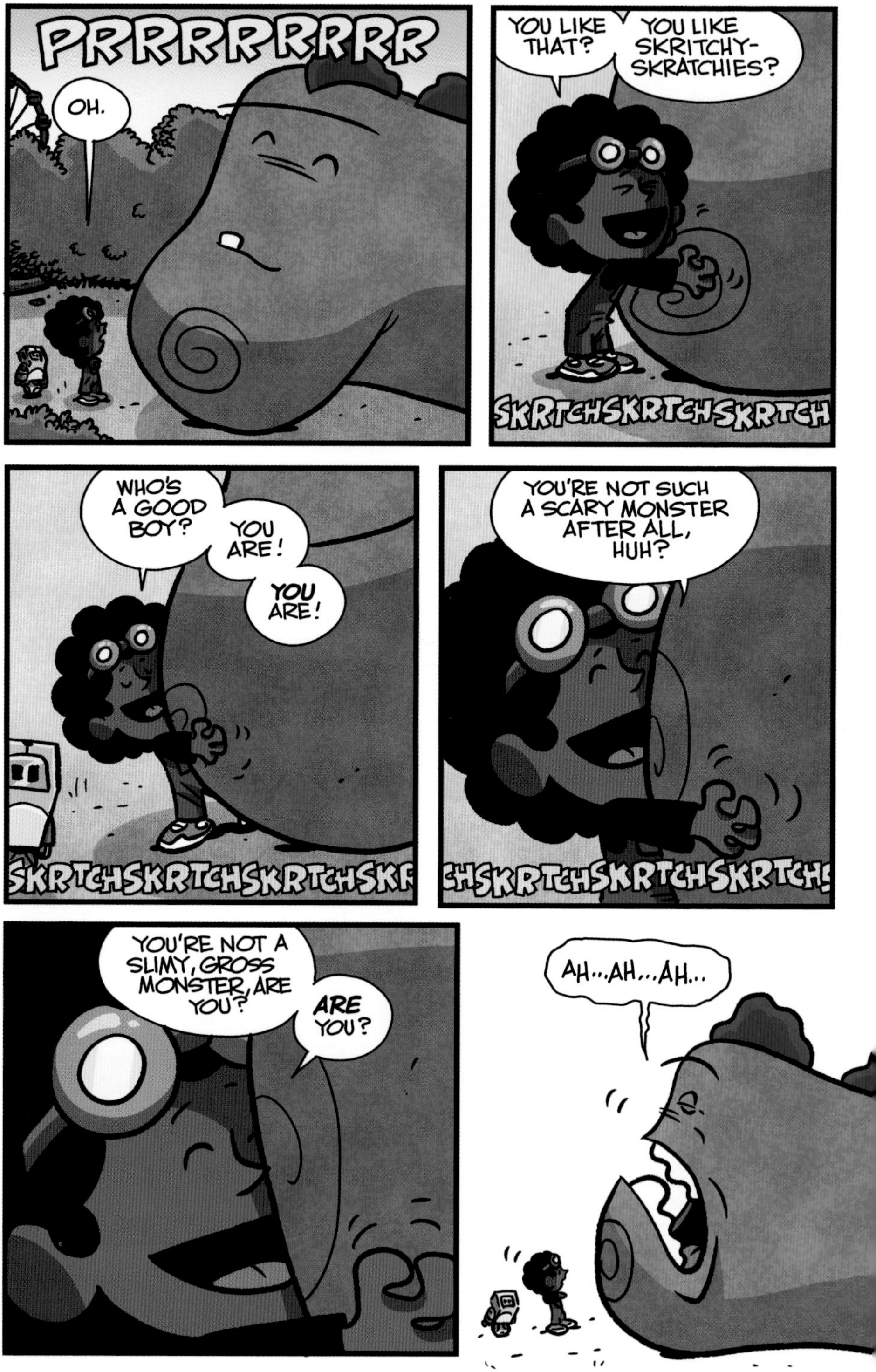
PRRRRRRRRR
OH.
YOU LIKE THAT?
YOU LIKE SKRITCHY-SKRATCHIES?
SKRTCHSKRTCHSKRTCH
WHO'S A GOOD BOY?
YOU ARE!
YOU ARE!
SKRTCHSKRTCHSKRTCHSKR
YOU'RE NOT SUCH A SCARY MONSTER AFTER ALL, HUH?
CHSKRTCHSKRTCHSKRTCH
YOU'RE NOT A SLIMY, GROSS MONSTER, ARE YOU?
ARE YOU?
AH...AH...AH...

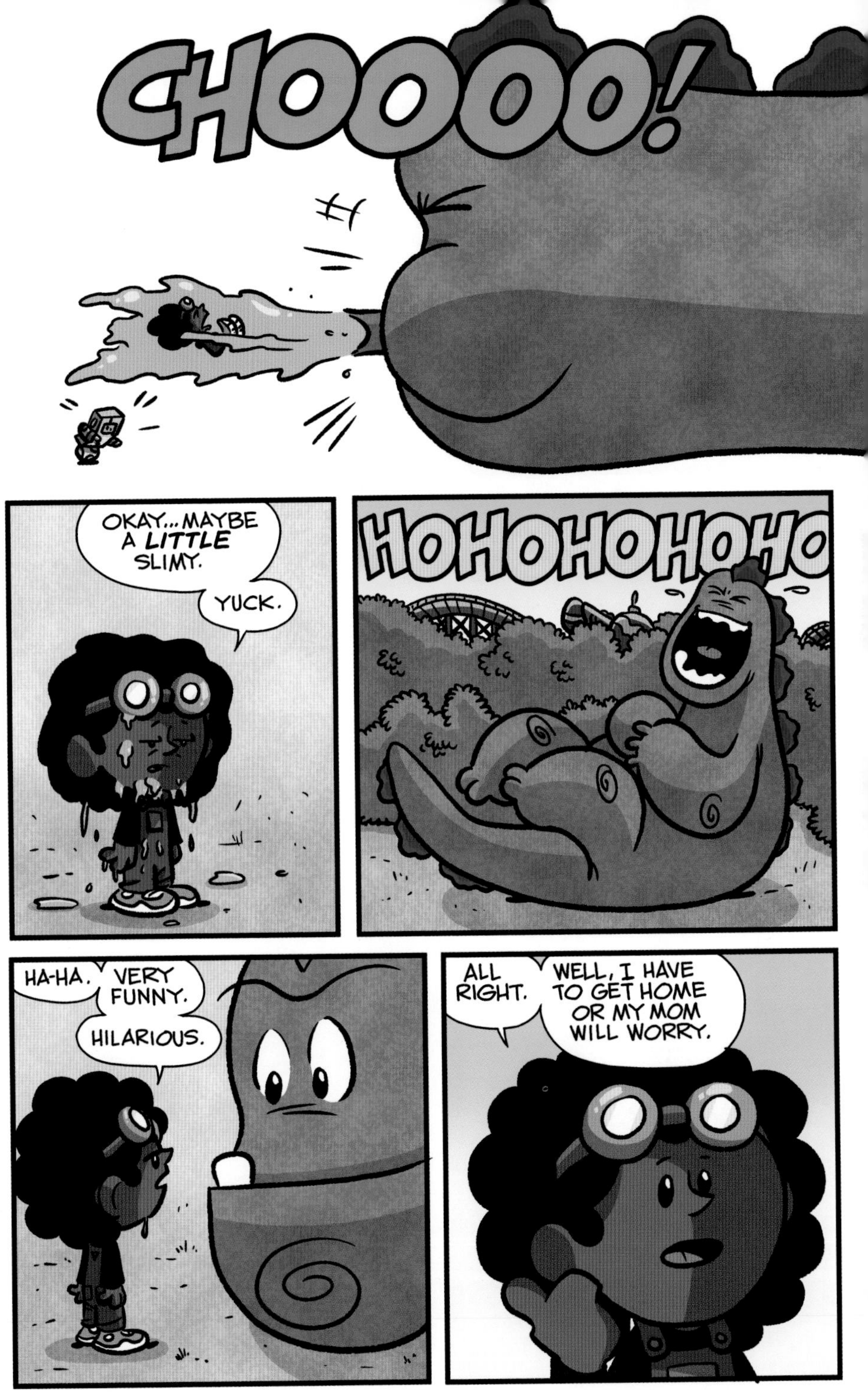
CHOOOO!
OKAY... MAYBE A *LITTLE* SLIMY.
YUCK.
HOHOHOHOHOHO
HA-HA.
VERY FUNNY.
HILARIOUS.
ALL RIGHT.
WELL, I HAVE TO GET HOME OR MY MOM WILL WORRY.

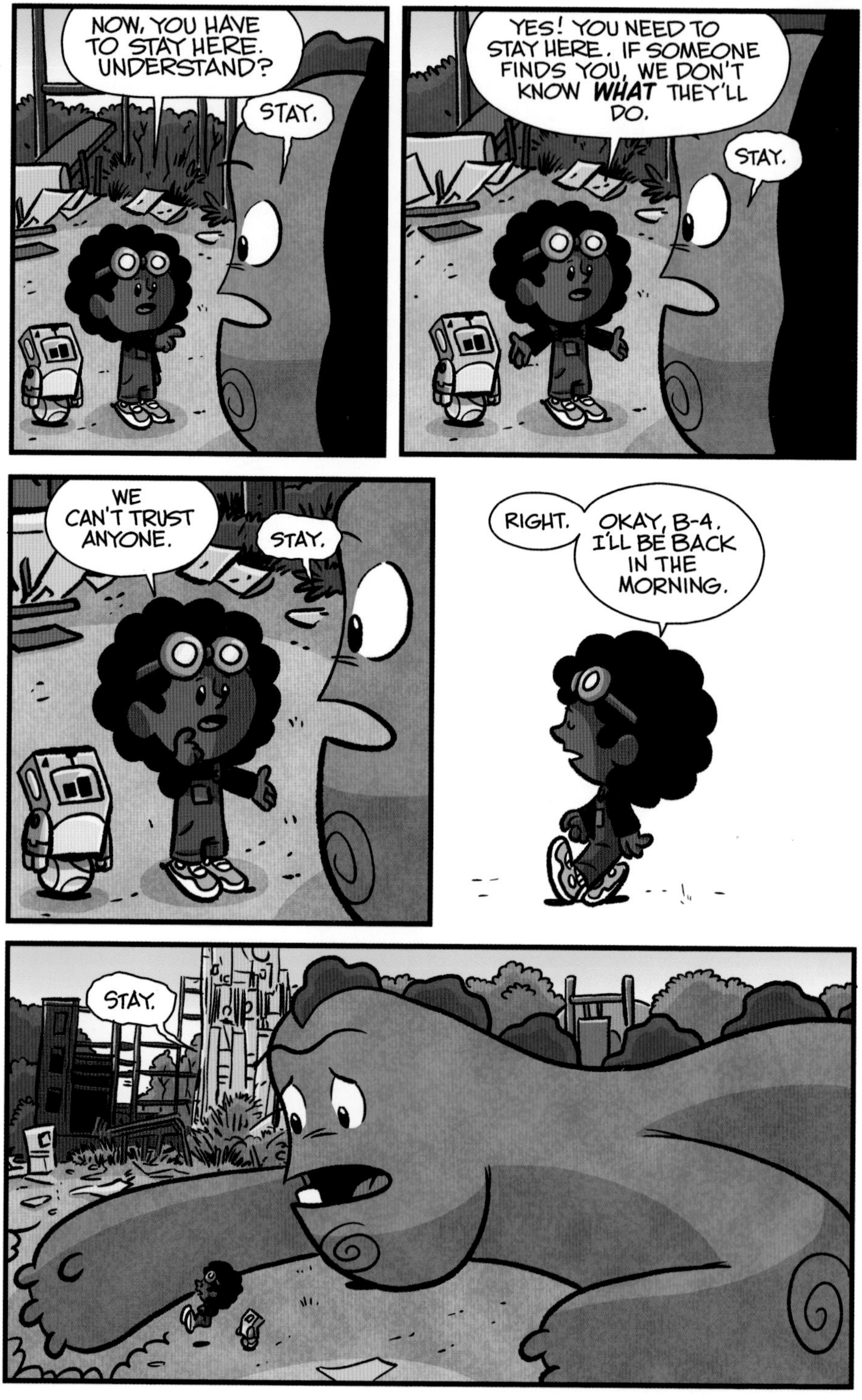
NOW, YOU HAVE TO STAY HERE. UNDERSTAND?
STAY.
YES! YOU NEED TO STAY HERE. IF SOMEONE FINDS YOU, WE DON'T KNOW **WHAT** THEY'LL DO.
STAY.
WE CAN'T TRUST ANYONE.
STAY.
RIGHT.
OKAY, B-4. I'LL BE BACK IN THE MORNING.
STAY.

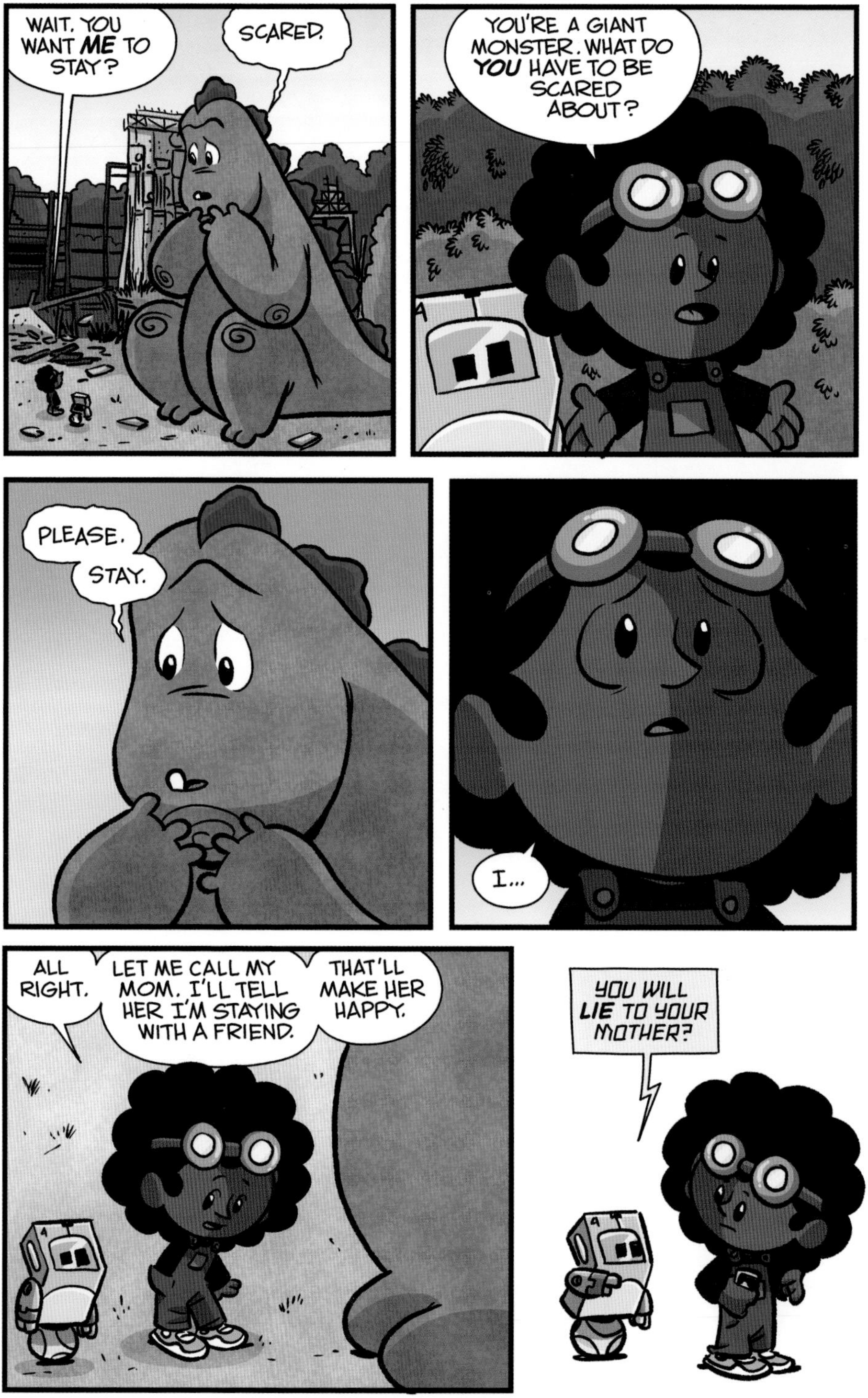
WAIT. YOU WANT ME TO STAY?
SCARED.
YOU'RE A GIANT MONSTER. WHAT DO YOU HAVE TO BE SCARED ABOUT?
PLEASE.
STAY.
I...
ALL RIGHT.
LET ME CALL MY MOM. I'LL TELL HER I'M STAYING WITH A FRIEND.
THAT'LL MAKE HER HAPPY.
YOU WILL LIE TO YOUR MOTHER?

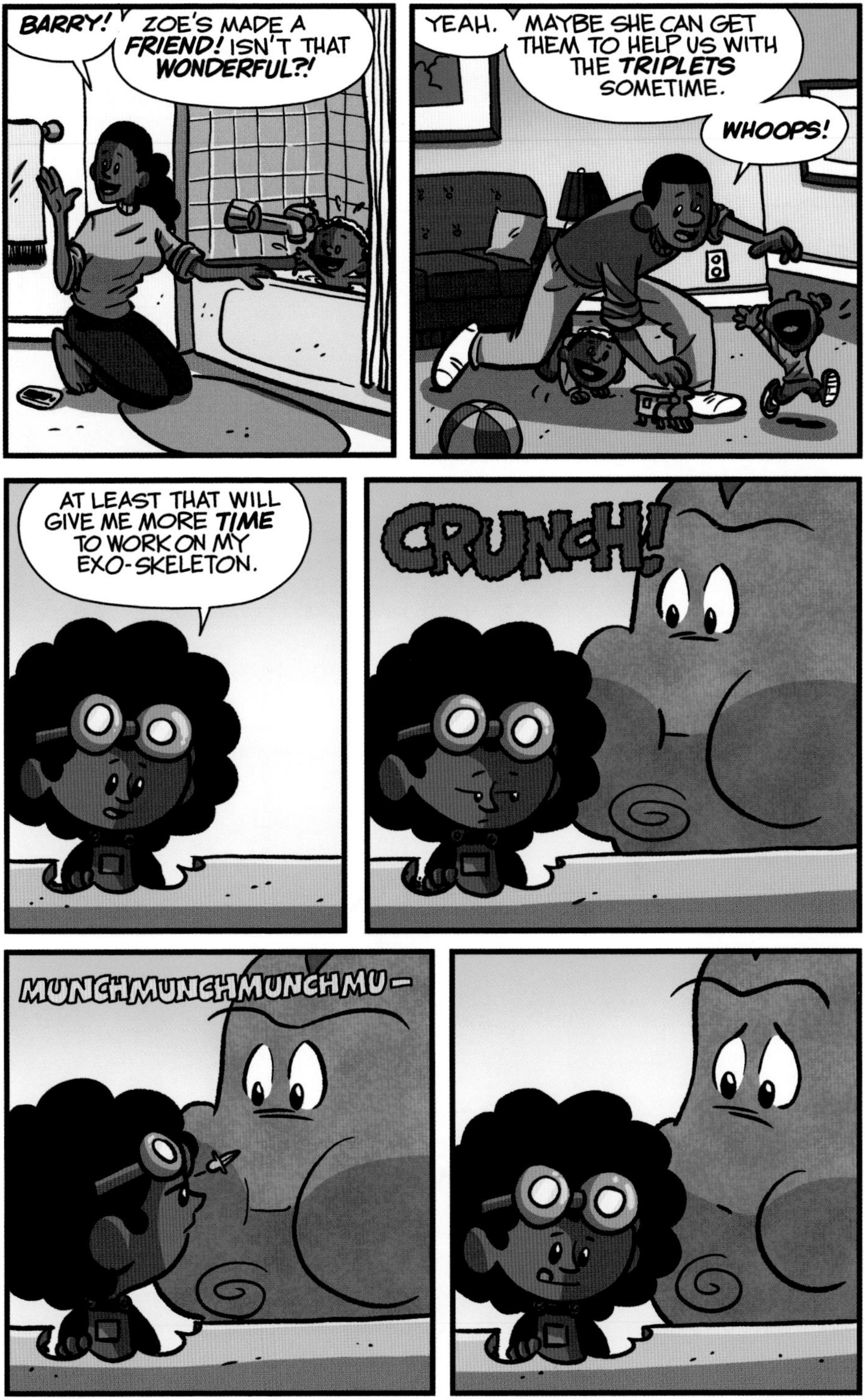
BARRY!
ZOE'S MADE A FRIEND! ISN'T THAT WONDERFUL?!
YEAH.
MAYBE SHE CAN GET THEM TO HELP US WITH THE TRIPLETS SOMETIME.
WHOOPS!
AT LEAST THAT WILL GIVE ME MORE TIME TO WORK ON MY EXO-SKELETON.
CRUNCH!
MUNCHMUNCHMUNCHMU-

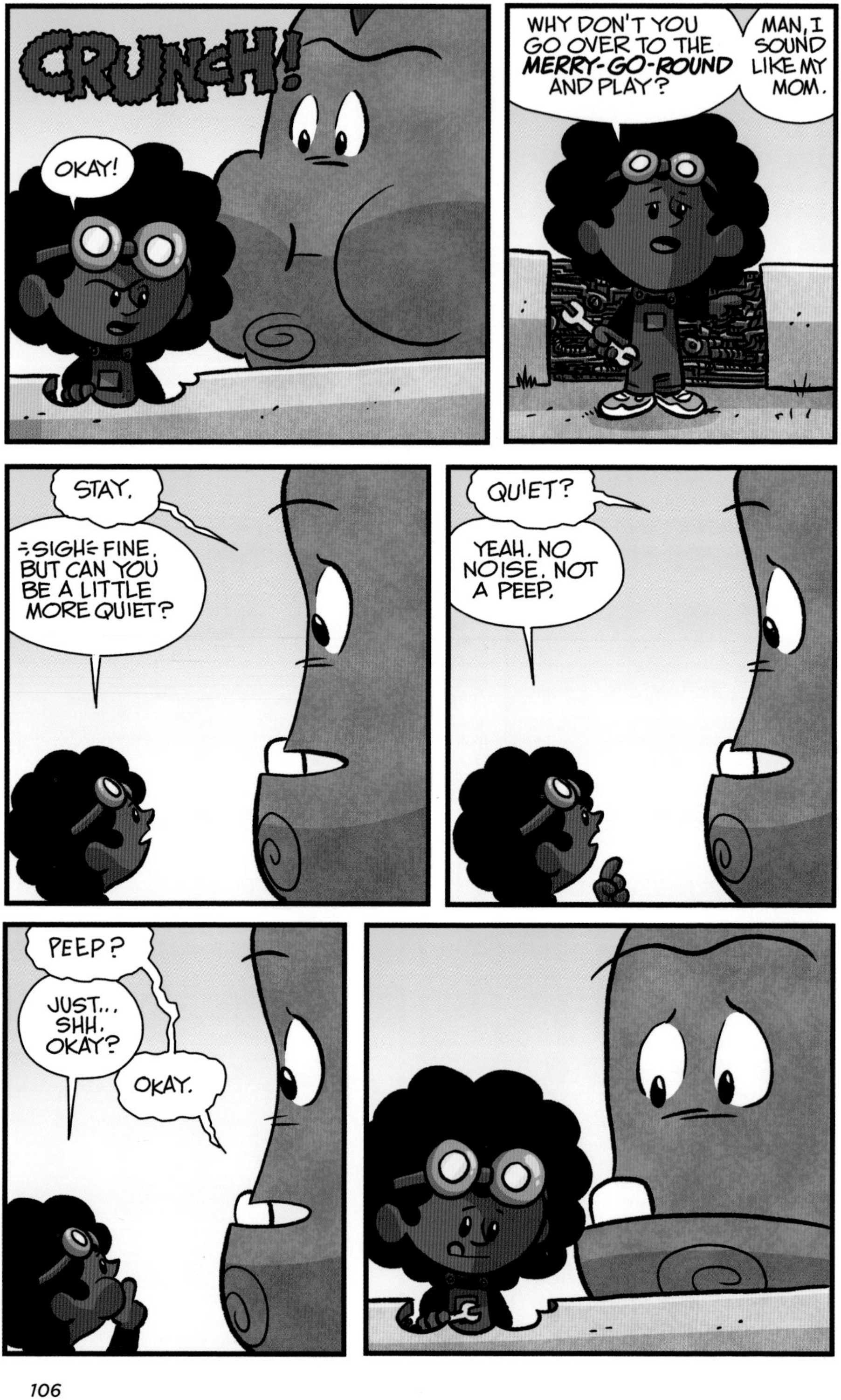

CRUNCH!
OKAY!
WHY DON'T YOU GO OVER TO THE MERRY-GO-ROUND AND PLAY?
MAN, I SOUND LIKE MY MOM.
STAY.
=SIGH= FINE. BUT CAN YOU BE A LITTLE MORE QUIET?
QUIET?
YEAH. NO NOISE. NOT A PEEP.
PEEP?
JUST... SHH. OKAY?
OKAY.

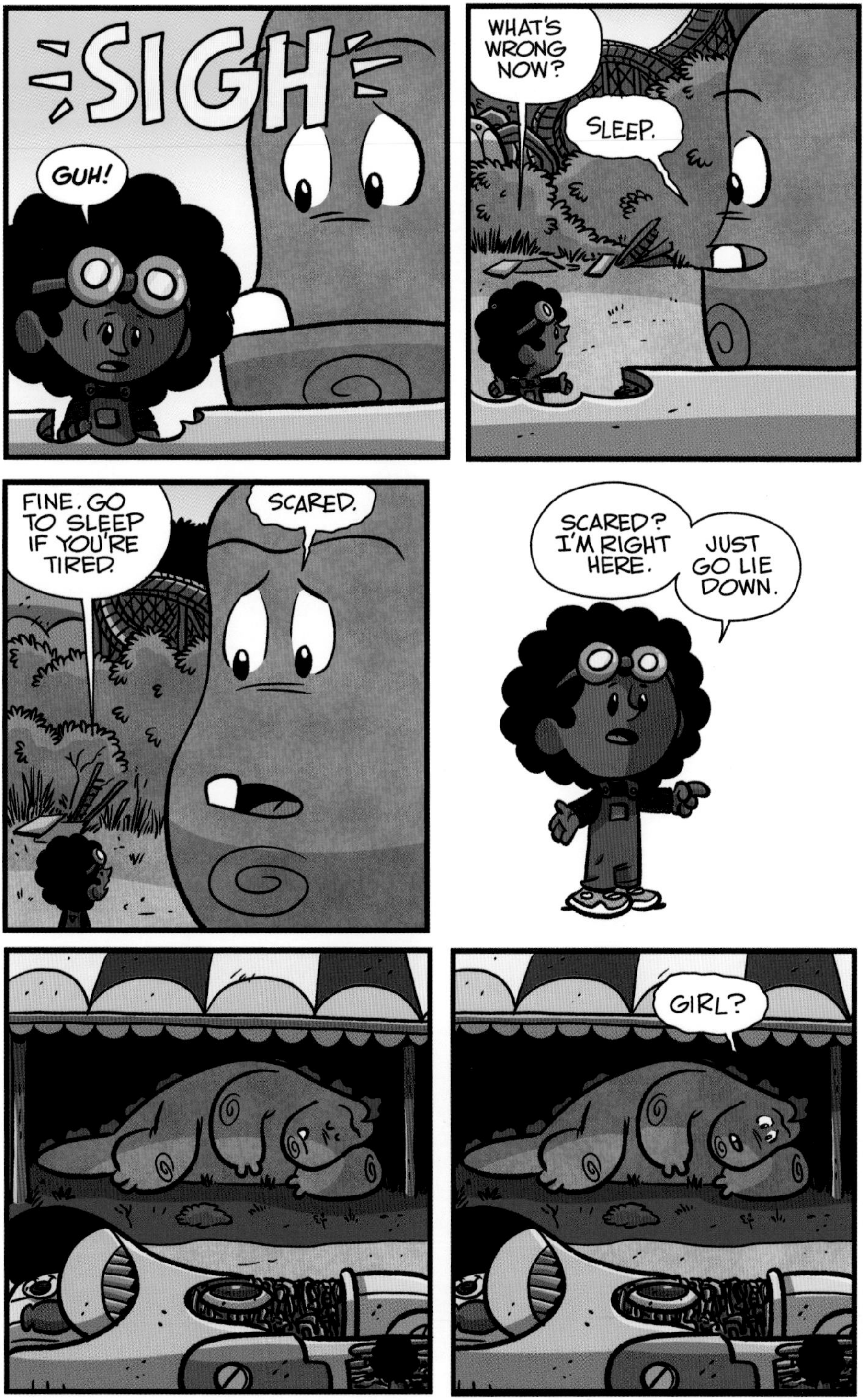
SIGH
GUH!
WHAT'S WRONG NOW?
SLEEP.
FINE. GO TO SLEEP IF YOU'RE TIRED.
SCARED.
SCARED? I'M RIGHT HERE.
JUST GO LIE DOWN.
GIRL?

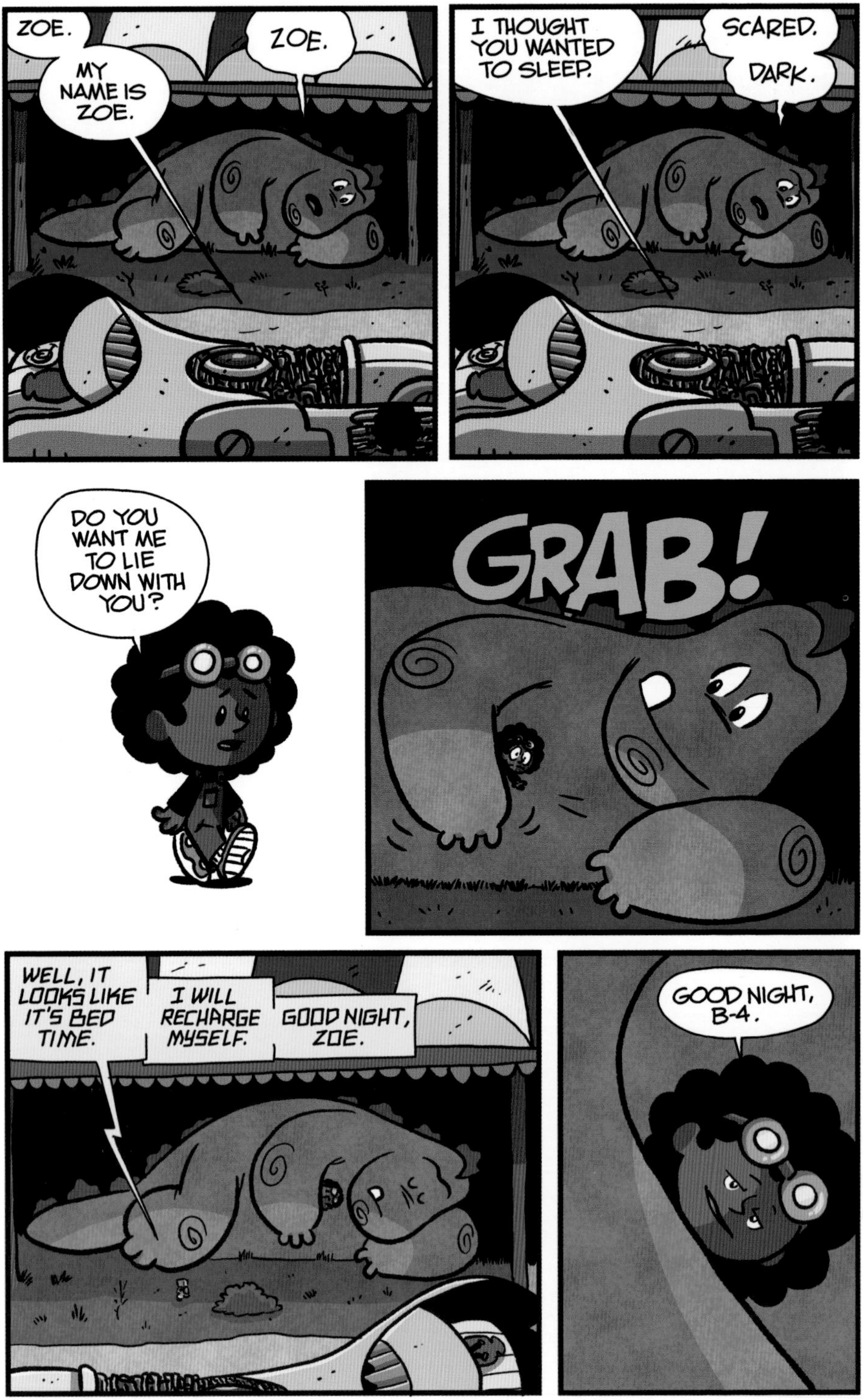
ZOE.
MY NAME IS ZOE.
ZOE.
I THOUGHT YOU WANTED TO SLEEP.
SCARED.
DARK.
DO YOU WANT ME TO LIE DOWN WITH YOU?
GRAB!
WELL, IT LOOKS LIKE IT'S BED TIME.
I WILL RECHARGE MYSELF.
GOOD NIGHT, ZOE.
GOOD NIGHT, B-4.

CHAPTER 7 - MORE MONSTERS

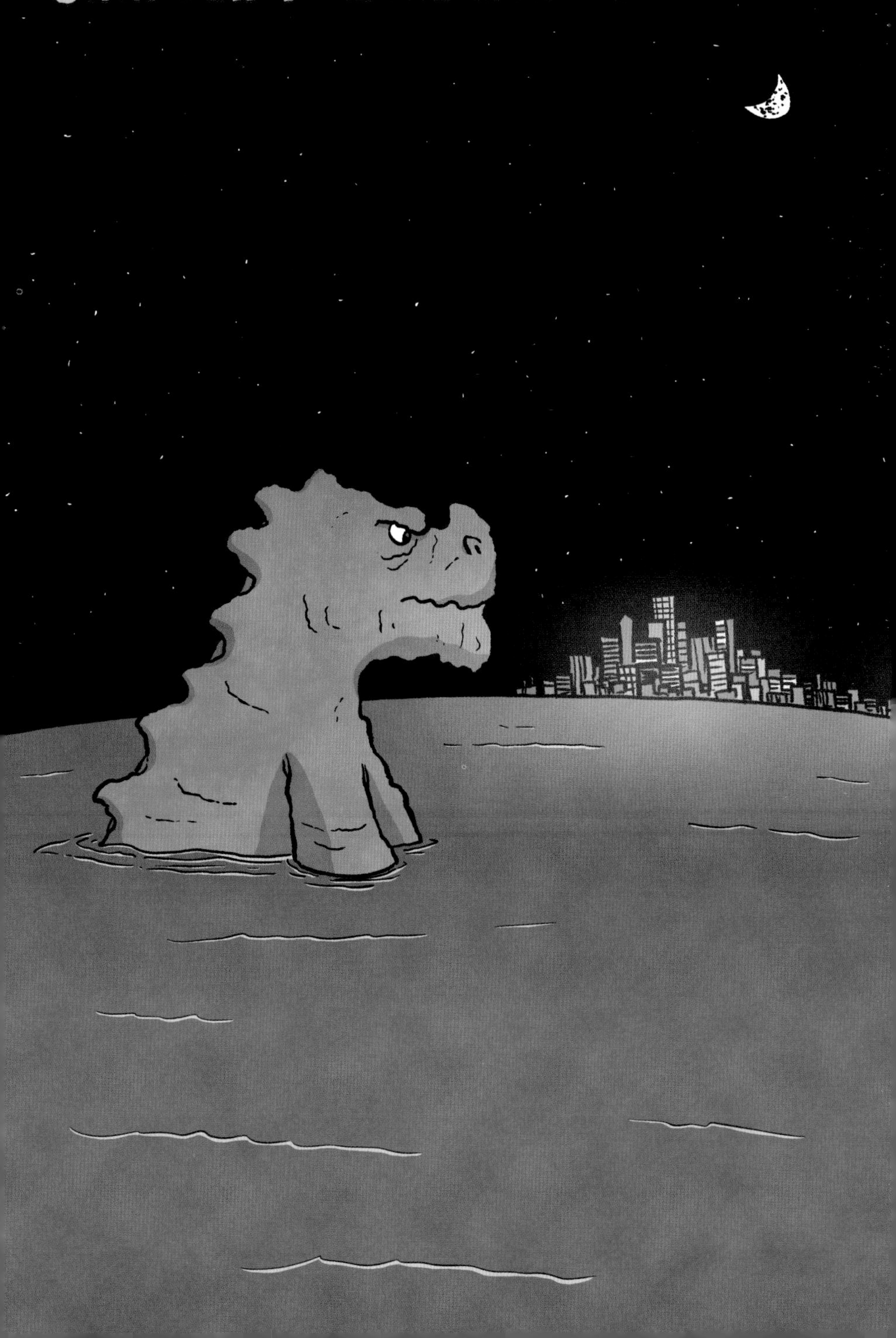

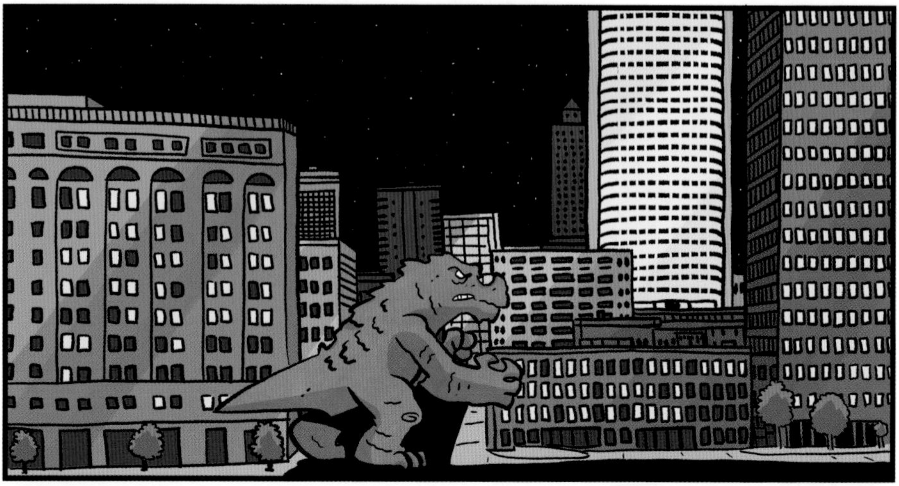

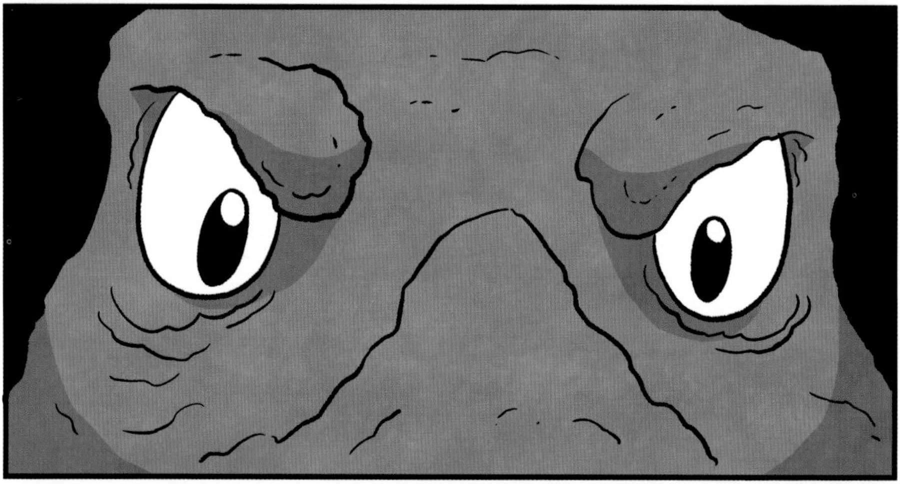

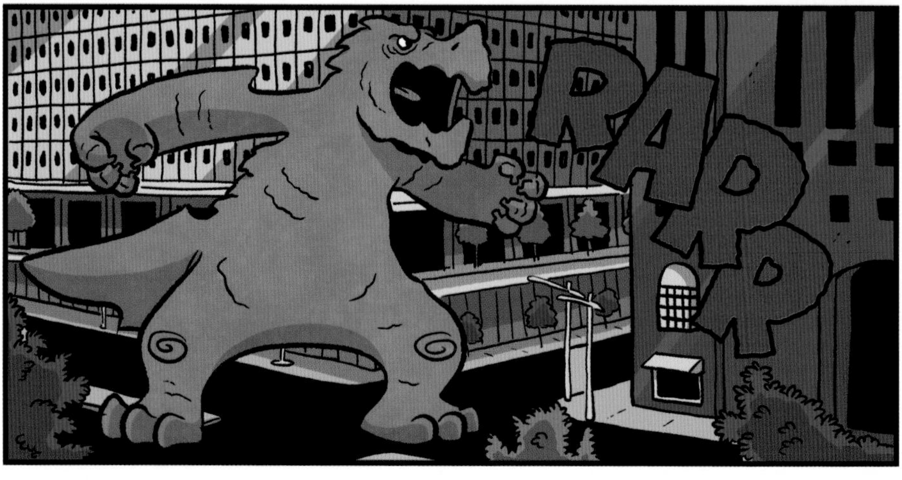
RAAP

CHAPTER 8 - ONCE BITTEN

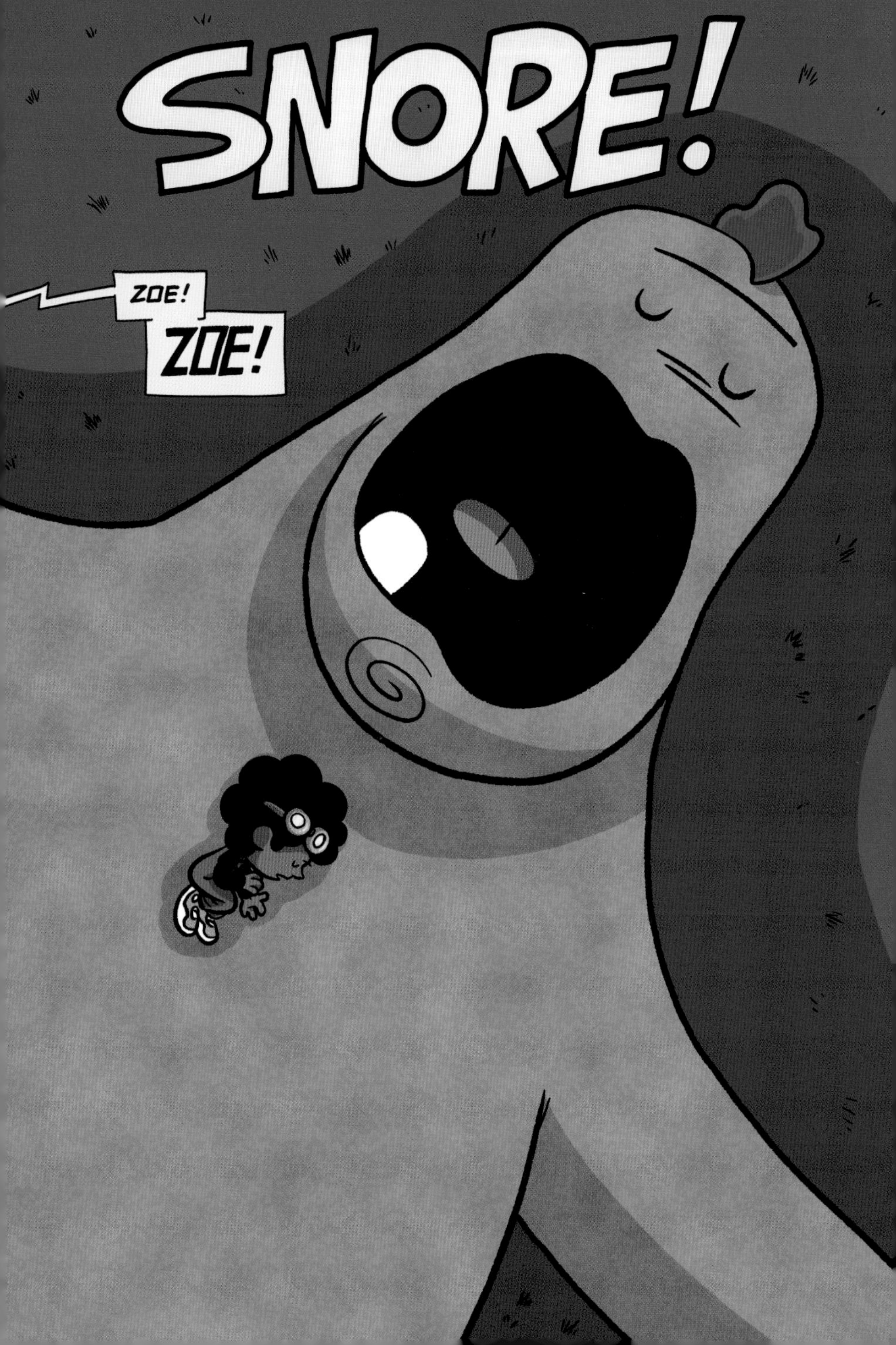
SNORE!
ZOE!
ZOE!

113

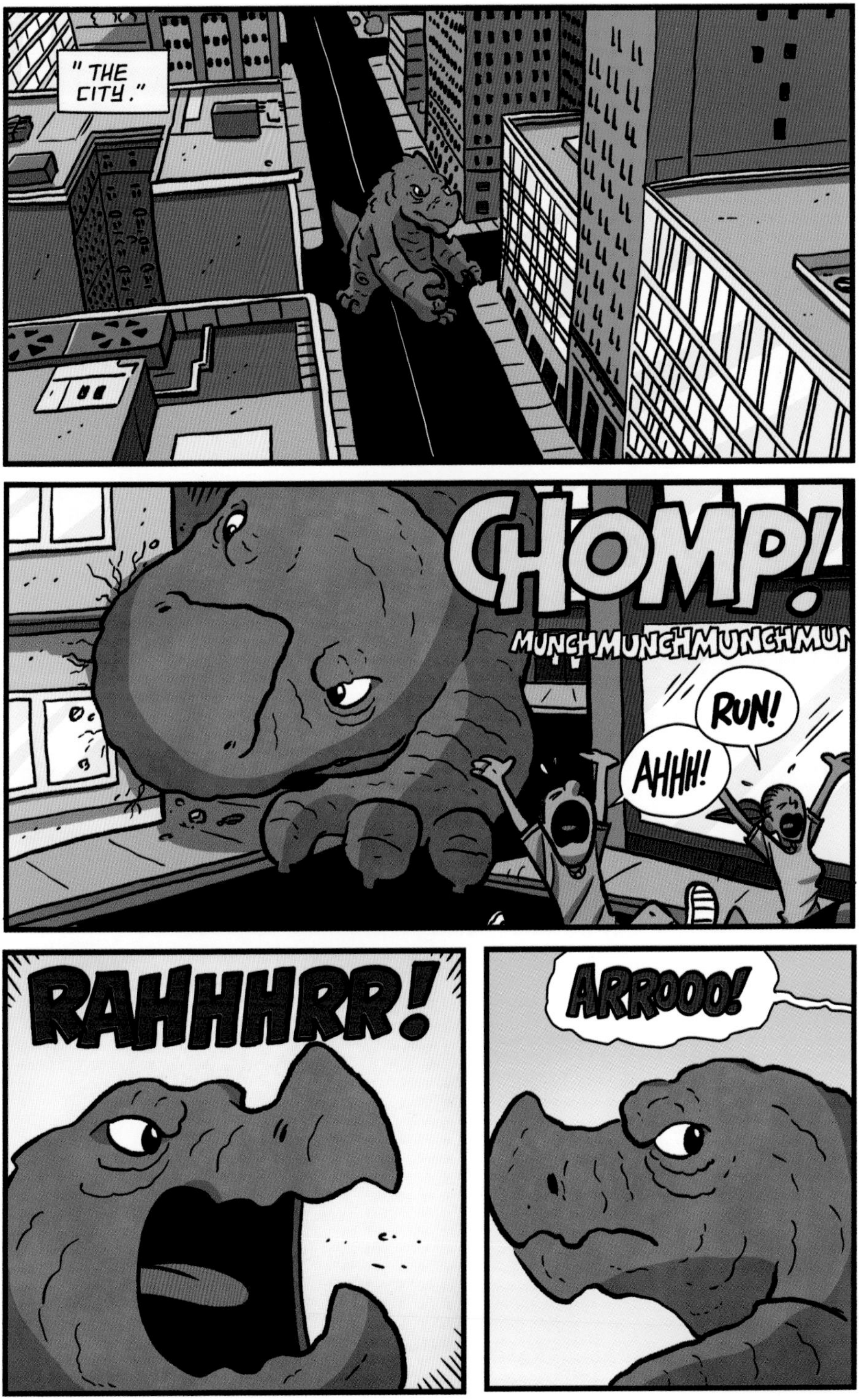
"THE CITY."
CHOMP!
MUNCHMUNCHMUNCHMUN
RUN!
AHHH!
RAHHHRR!
ARROOO!

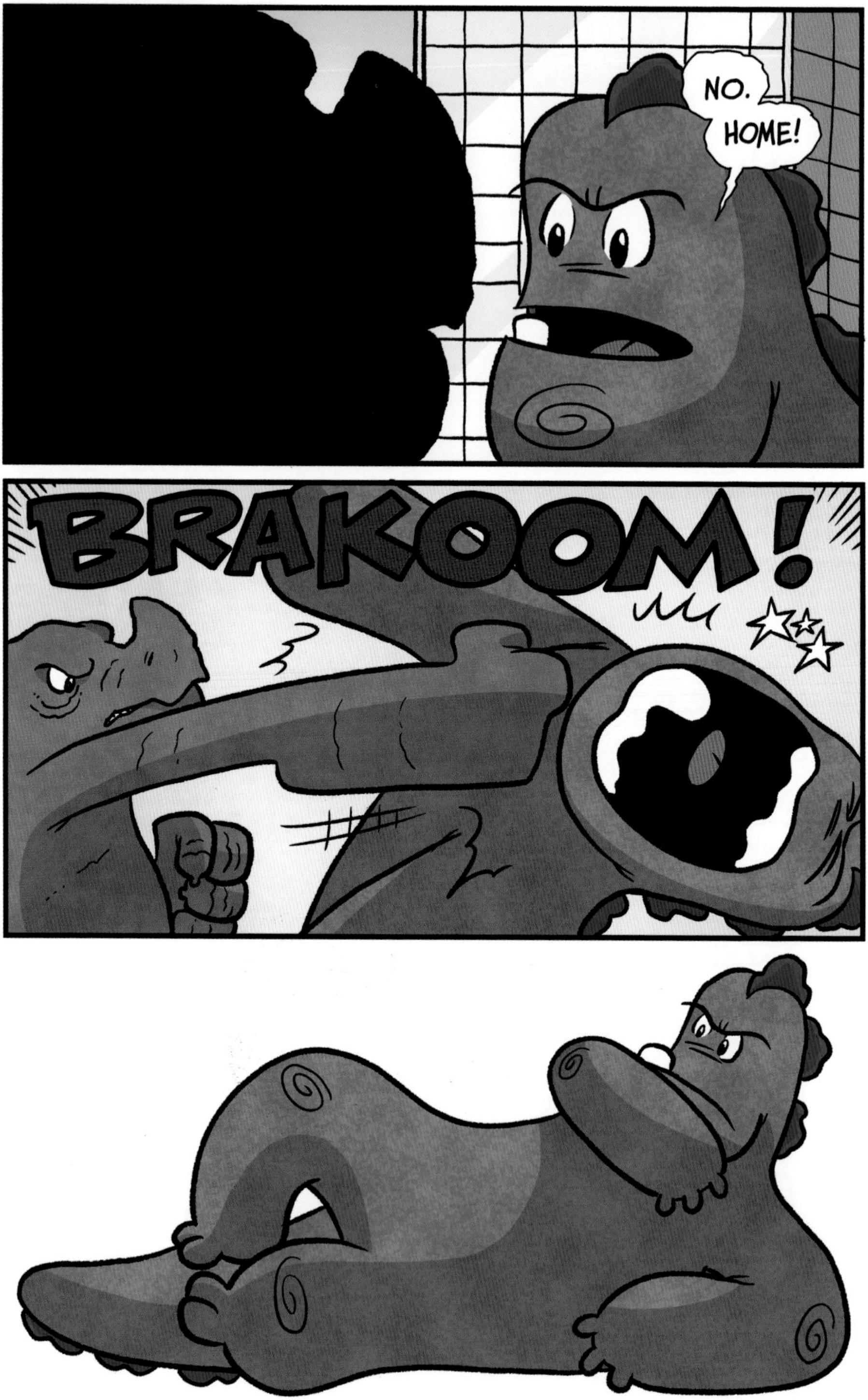
NO. HOME!
BRAKOOM!

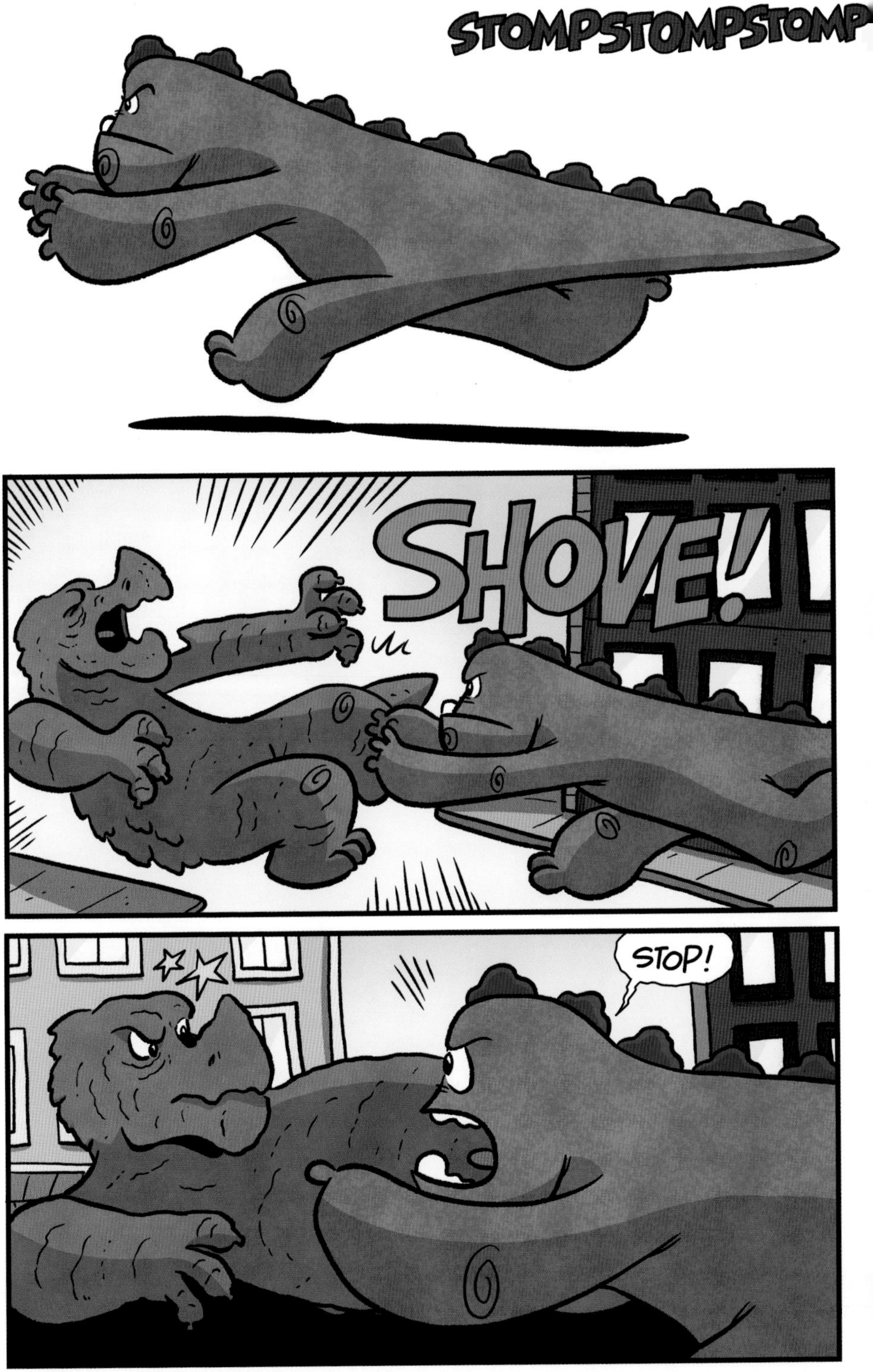
STOMPSTOMPSTOMP
SHOVE!!
STOP!

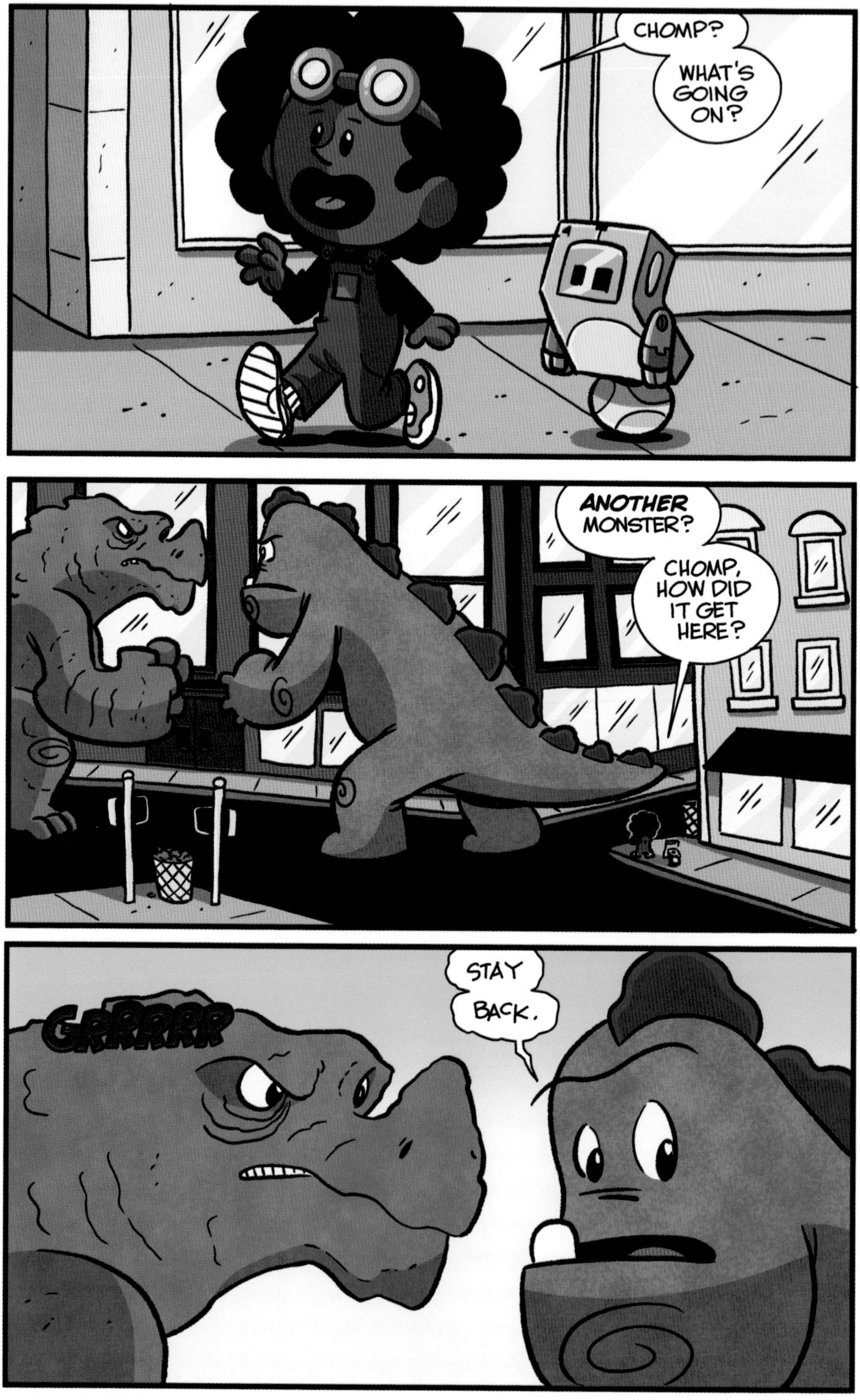
CHOMP?
WHAT'S GOING ON?
ANOTHER MONSTER?
CHOMP, HOW DID IT GET HERE?
GRRRRR
STAY BACK.

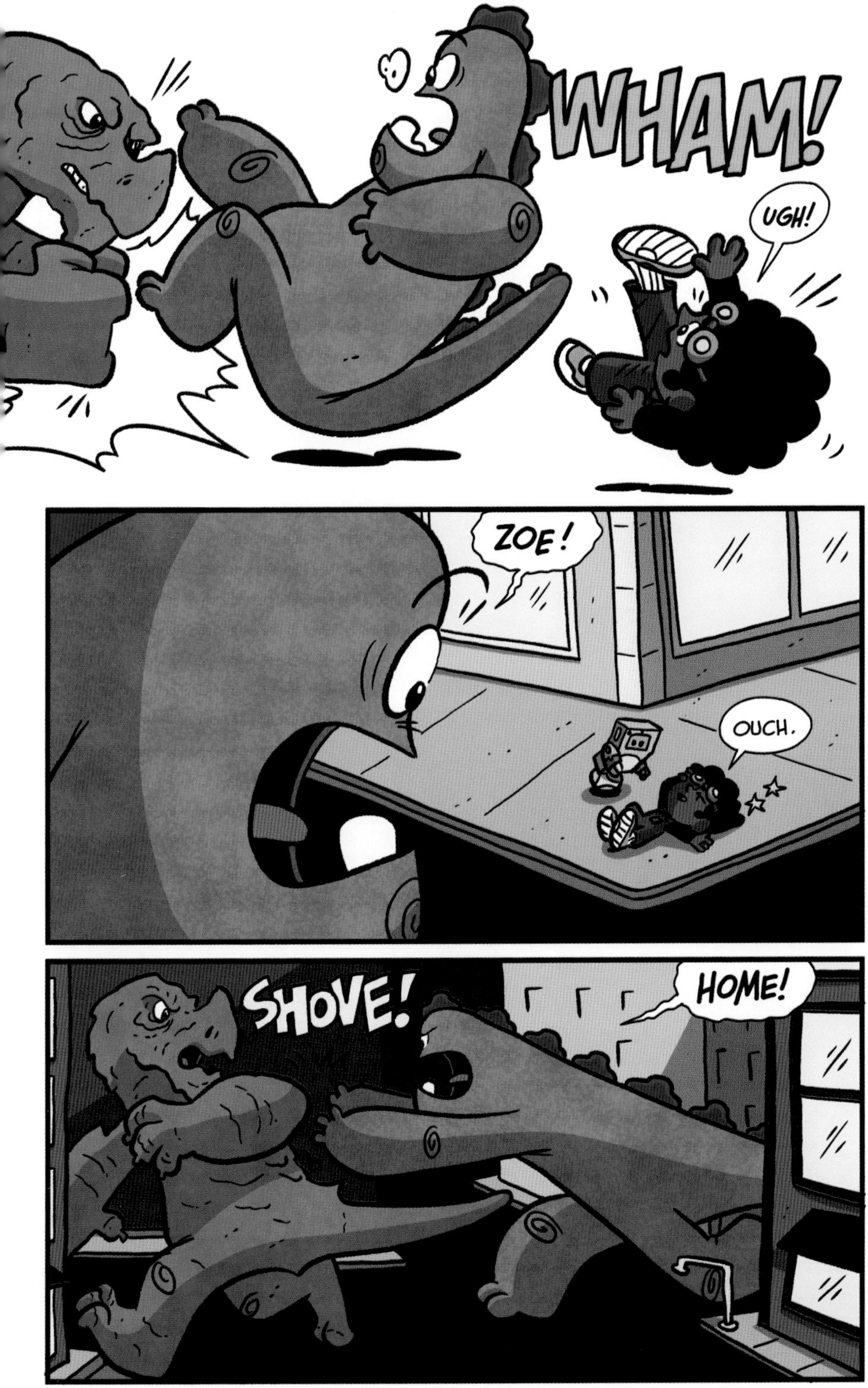

WHAM!
UGH!
ZOE!
OUCH.
SHOVE!
HOME!

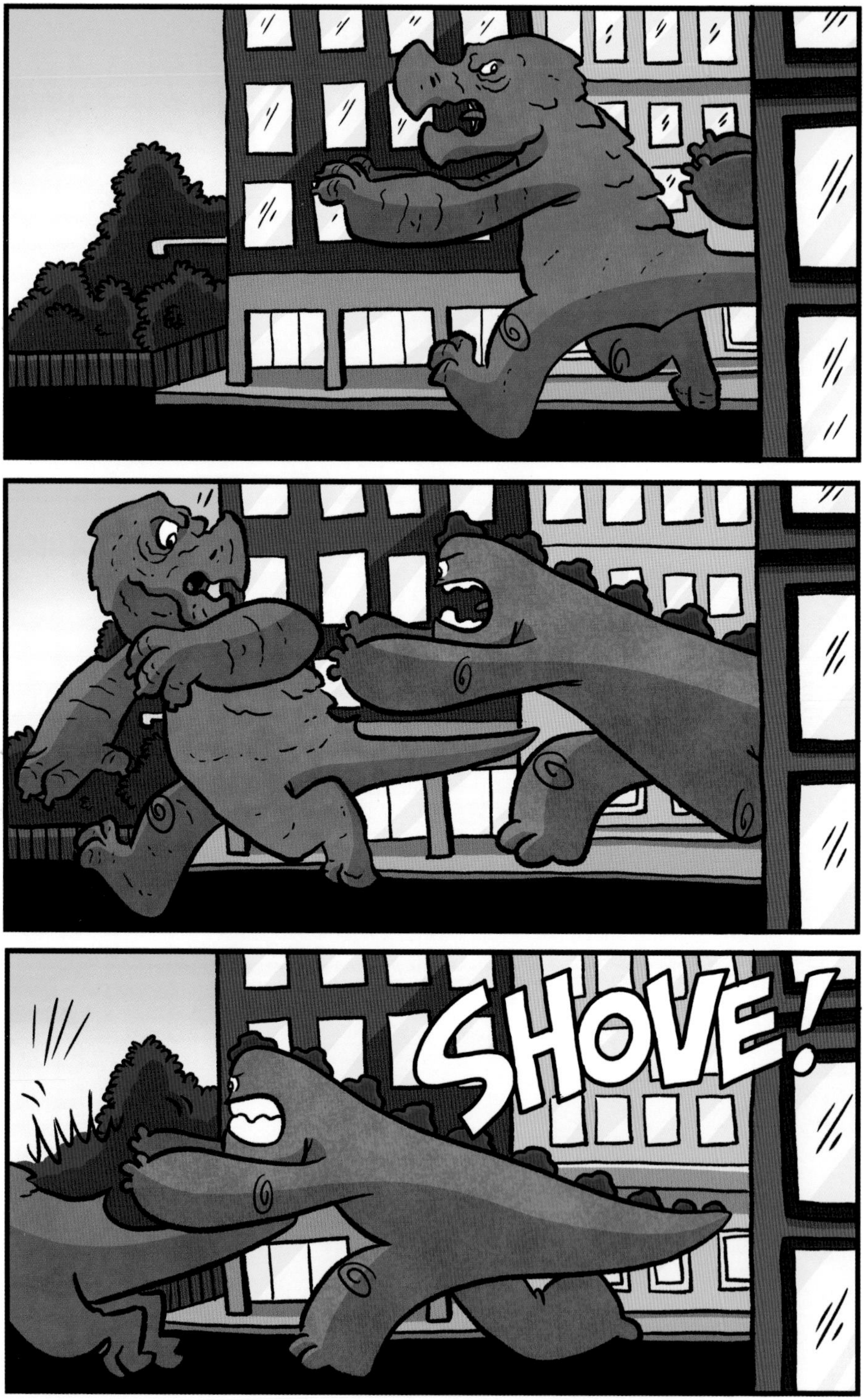
SHOVE!

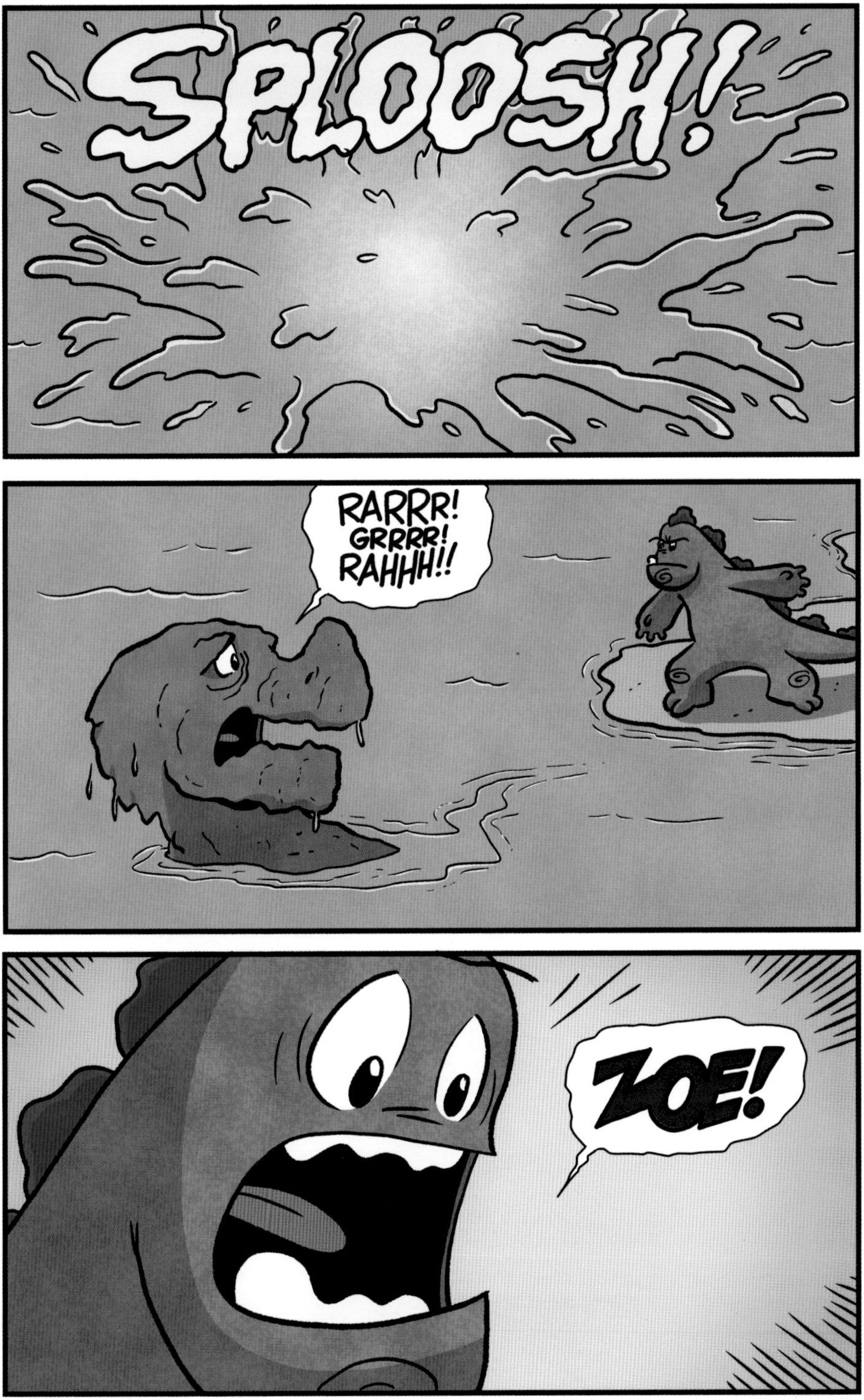
SPLOOSH!
RARRR! GRRRR! RAHHH!!
ZOE!

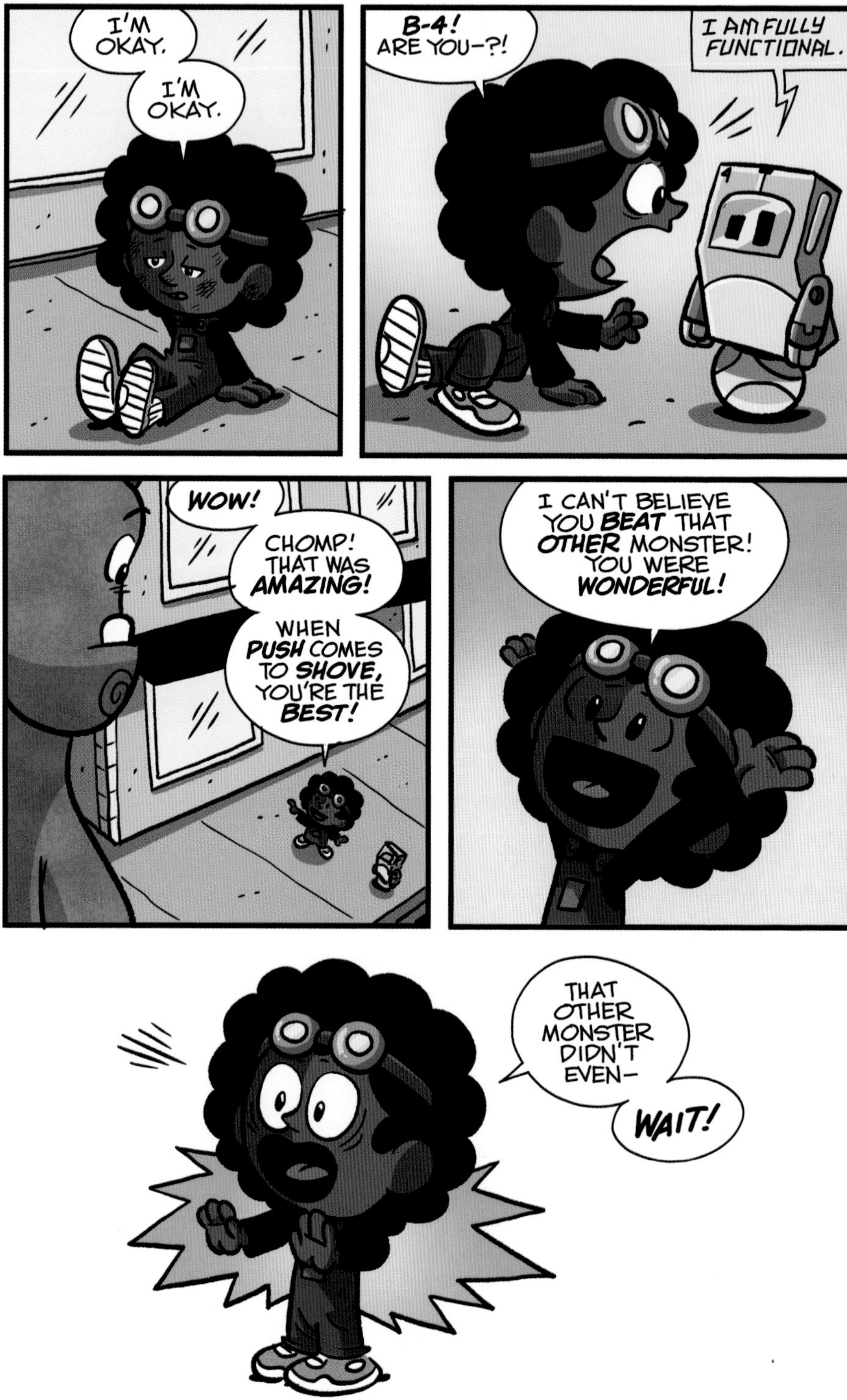
I'M OKAY.
I'M OKAY.
B-4! ARE YOU-?!
I AM FULLY FUNCTIONAL.
WOW!
CHOMP! THAT WAS **AMAZING!**
WHEN **PUSH** COMES TO **SHOVE,** YOU'RE THE **BEST!**
I CAN'T BELIEVE YOU **BEAT** THAT **OTHER** MONSTER! YOU WERE **WONDERFUL!**
THAT OTHER MONSTER DIDN'T EVEN-
WAIT!

124

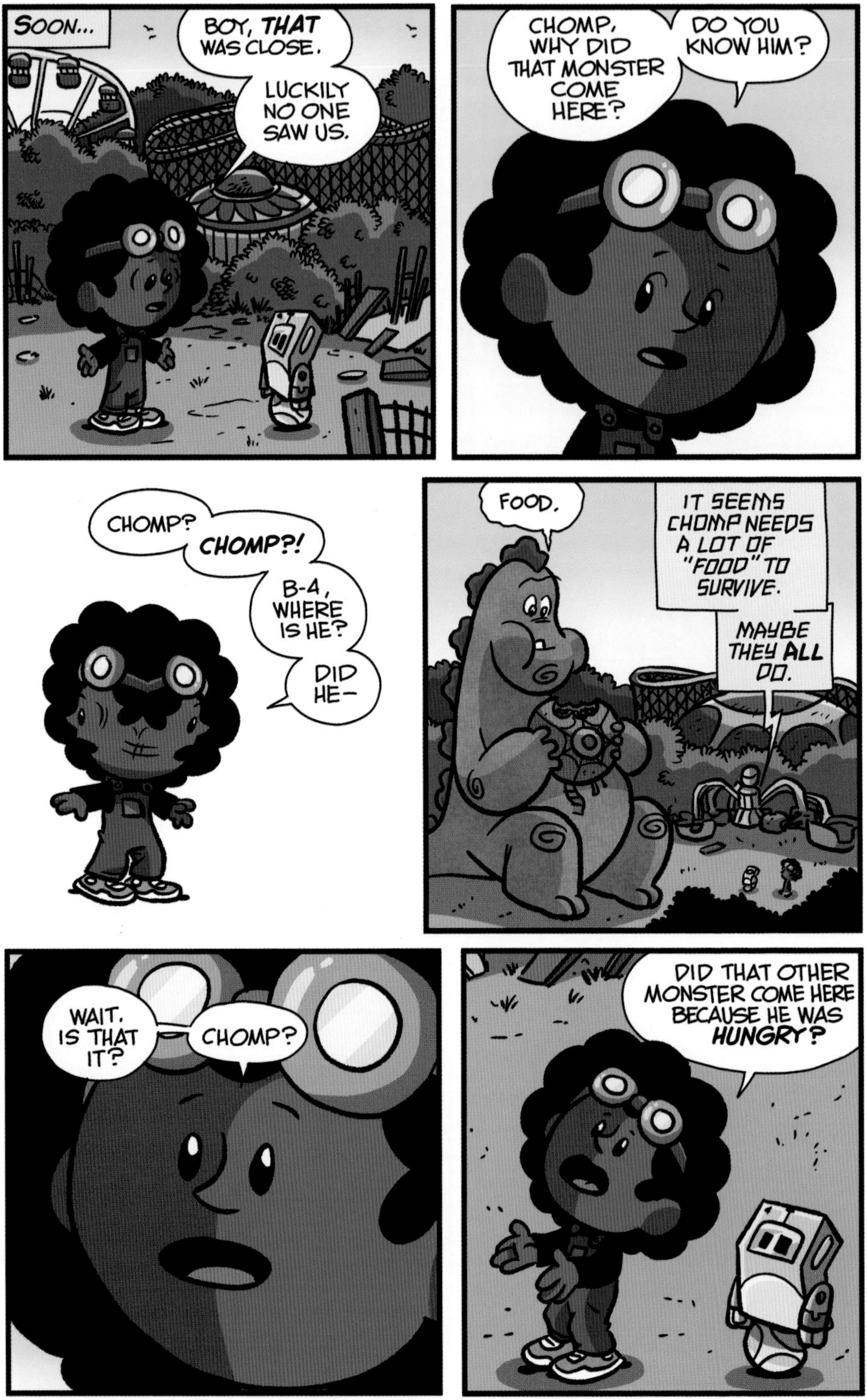
SOON...
BOY, THAT WAS CLOSE.
LUCKILY NO ONE SAW US.
CHOMP, WHY DID THAT MONSTER COME HERE?
DO YOU KNOW HIM?
CHOMP?
CHOMP?!
B-4, WHERE IS HE?
DID HE–
FOOD.
IT SEEMS CHOMP NEEDS A LOT OF "FOOD" TO SURVIVE.
MAYBE THEY ALL DO.
WAIT. IS THAT IT?
CHOMP?
DID THAT OTHER MONSTER COME HERE BECAUSE HE WAS HUNGRY?

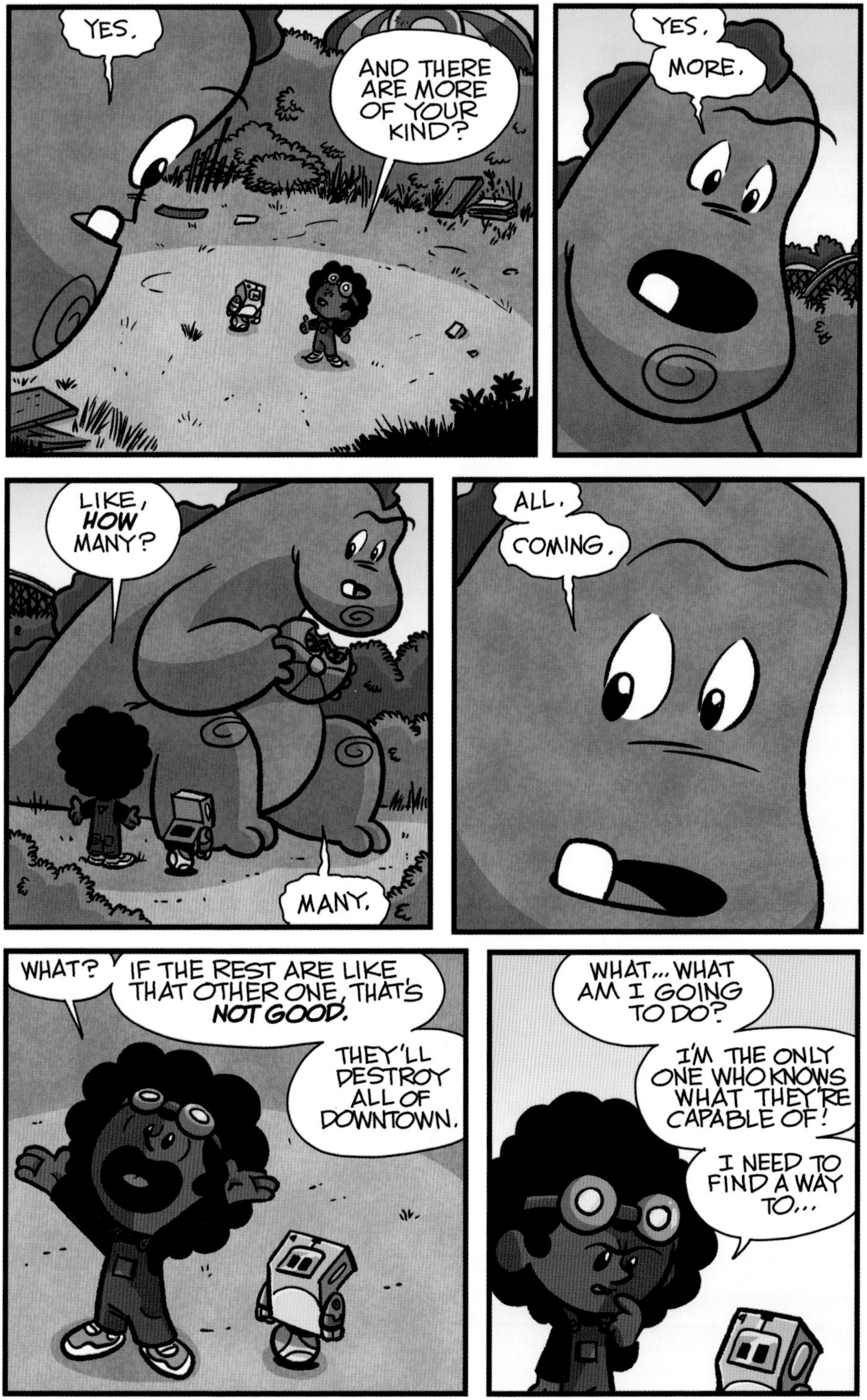
YES.
AND THERE ARE MORE OF YOUR KIND?
YES.
MORE.
LIKE, **HOW** MANY?
MANY.
ALL.
COMING.
WHAT?
IF THE REST ARE LIKE THAT OTHER ONE, THAT'S **NOT GOOD.**
THEY'LL DESTROY ALL OF DOWNTOWN.
WHAT... WHAT AM I GOING TO DO?
I'M THE ONLY ONE WHO KNOWS WHAT THEY'RE CAPABLE OF!
I NEED TO FIND A WAY TO...

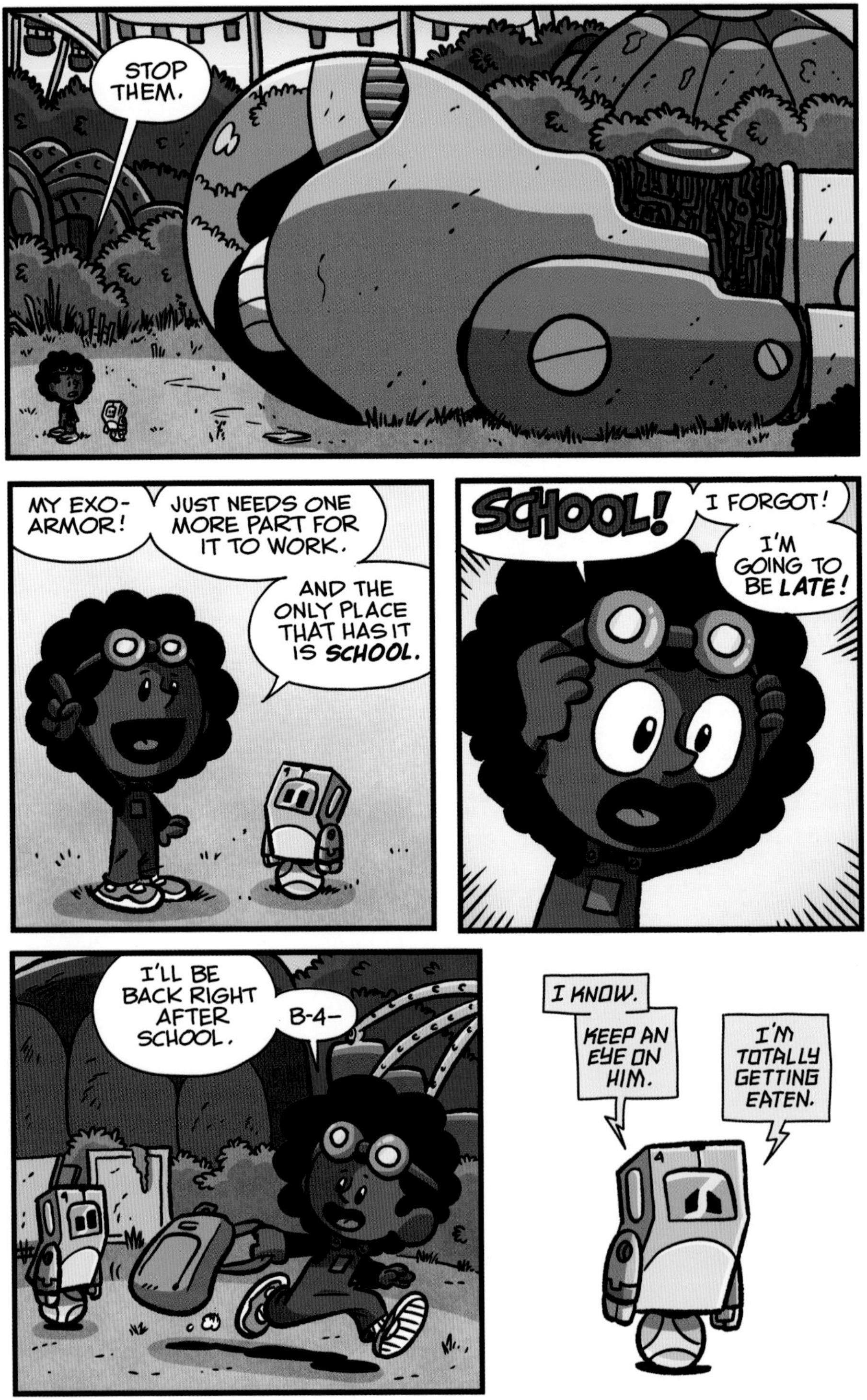
STOP THEM.
MY EXO-ARMOR!
JUST NEEDS ONE MORE PART FOR IT TO WORK.
AND THE ONLY PLACE THAT HAS IT IS **SCHOOL**.
SCHOOL!
I FORGOT!
I'M GOING TO BE **LATE**!
I'LL BE BACK RIGHT AFTER SCHOOL.
B-4-
I KNOW.
KEEP AN EYE ON HIM.
I'M TOTALLY GETTING EATEN.

CHAPTER 9 - GATHERING STORM

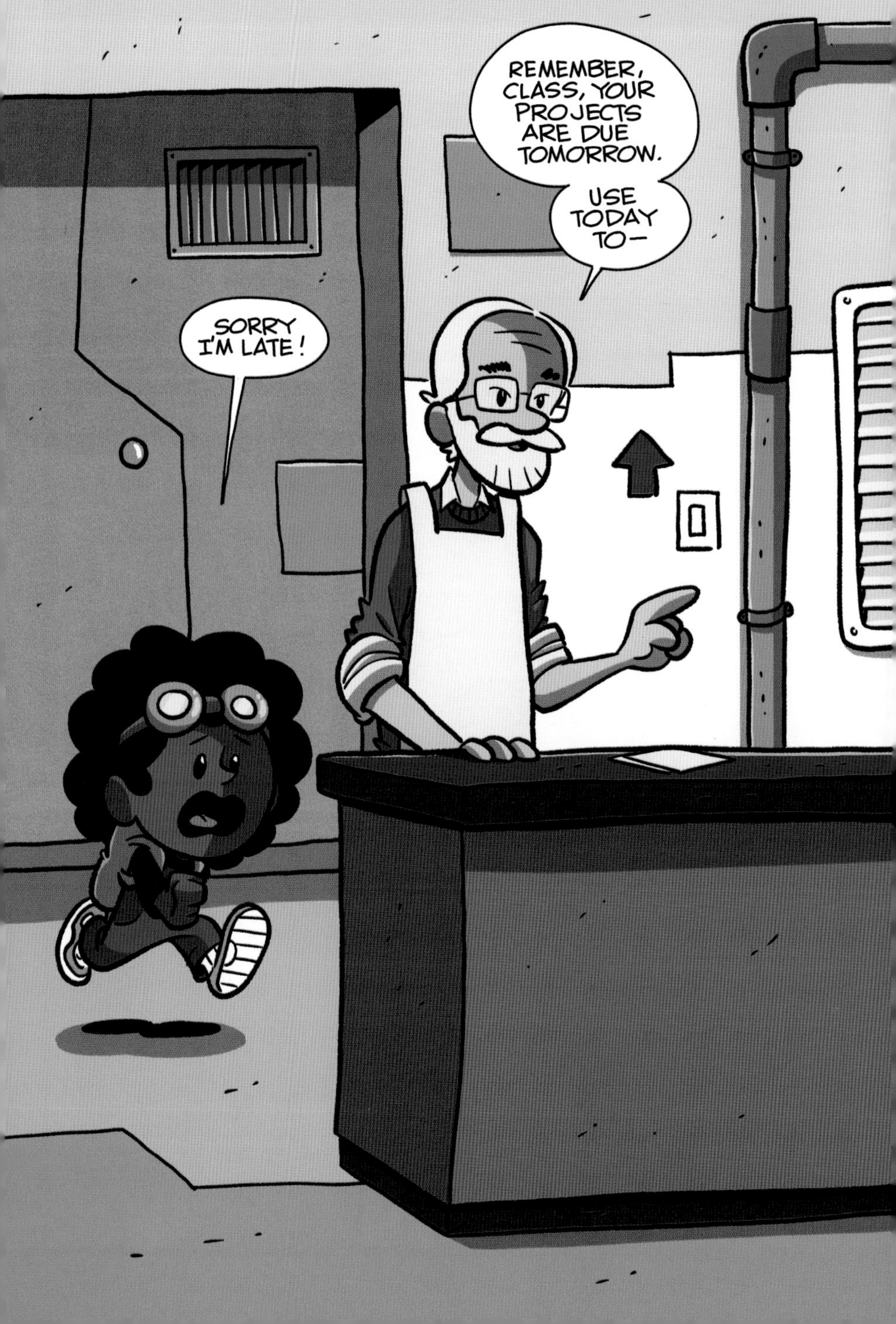
REMEMBER, CLASS, YOUR PROJECTS ARE DUE TOMORROW.
USE TODAY TO—
SORRY I'M LATE!

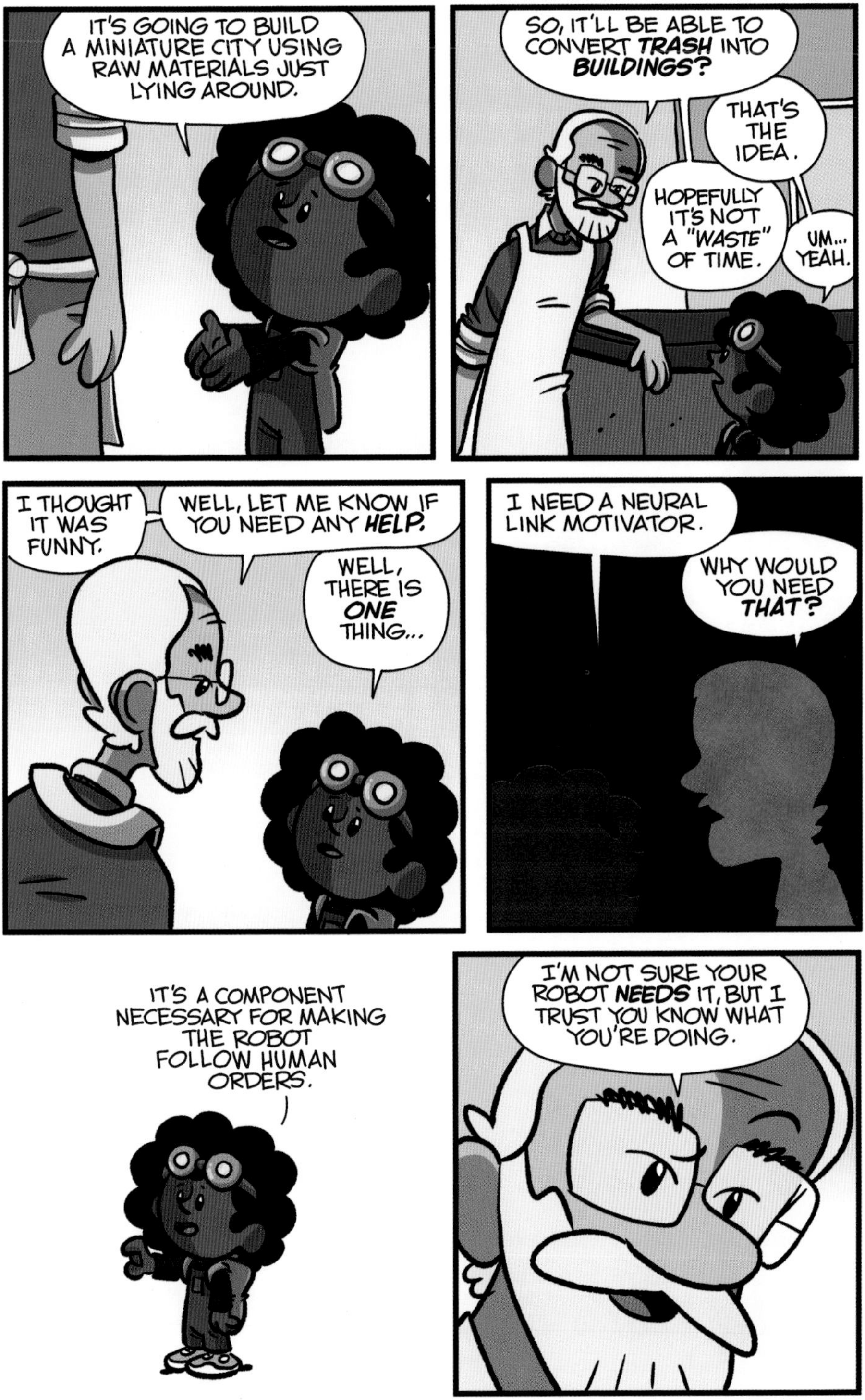
IT'S GOING TO BUILD A MINIATURE CITY USING RAW MATERIALS JUST LYING AROUND.
SO, IT'LL BE ABLE TO CONVERT TRASH INTO BUILDINGS?
THAT'S THE IDEA.
HOPEFULLY IT'S NOT A "WASTE" OF TIME.
UM... YEAH.
I THOUGHT IT WAS FUNNY.
WELL, LET ME KNOW IF YOU NEED ANY HELP.
WELL, THERE IS ONE THING...
I NEED A NEURAL LINK MOTIVATOR.
WHY WOULD YOU NEED THAT?
IT'S A COMPONENT NECESSARY FOR MAKING THE ROBOT FOLLOW HUMAN ORDERS.
I'M NOT SURE YOUR ROBOT NEEDS IT, BUT I TRUST YOU KNOW WHAT YOU'RE DOING.

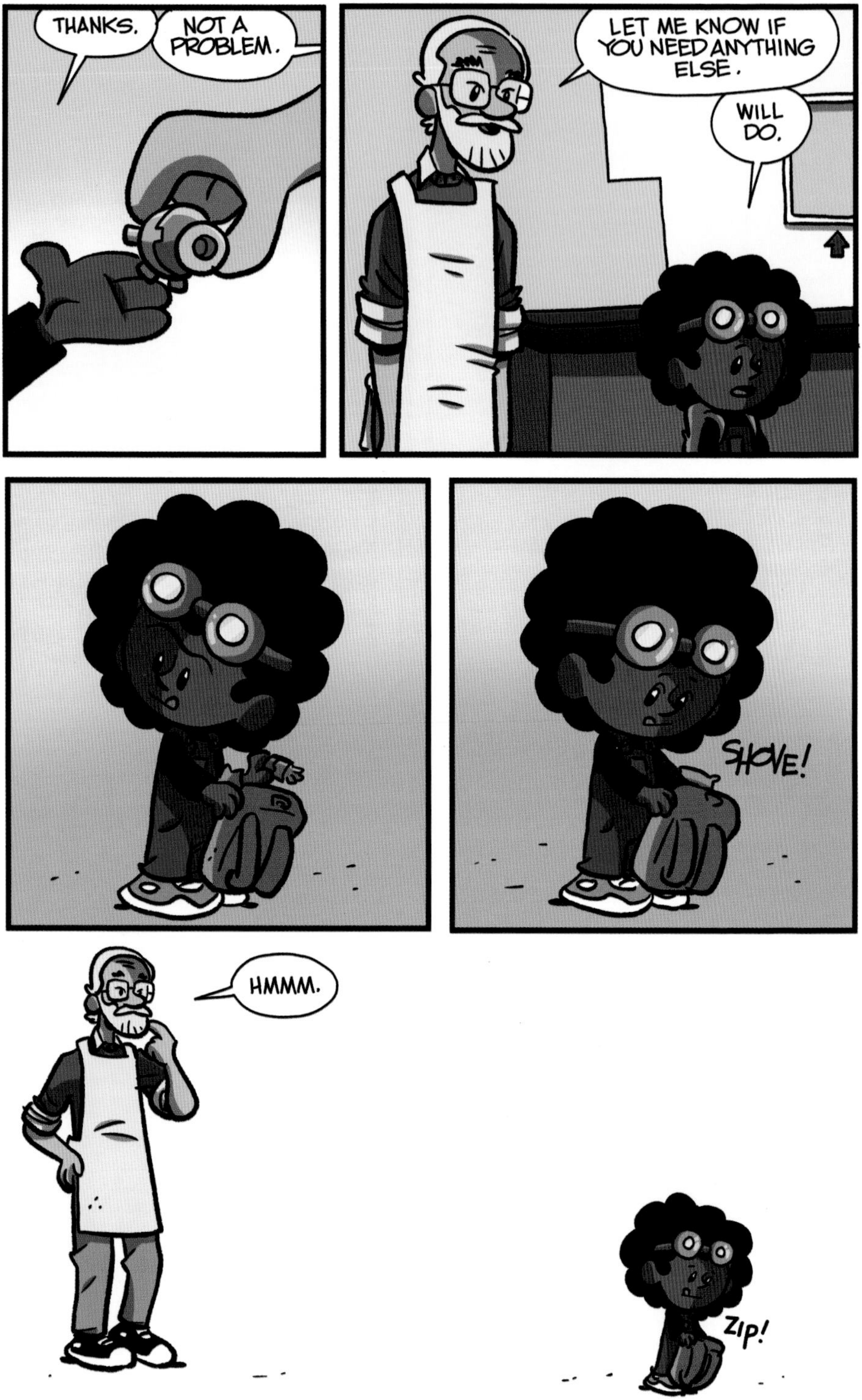
THANKS.
NOT A PROBLEM.
LET ME KNOW IF YOU NEED ANYTHING ELSE.
WILL DO.
SHOVE!
HMMM.
ZIP!

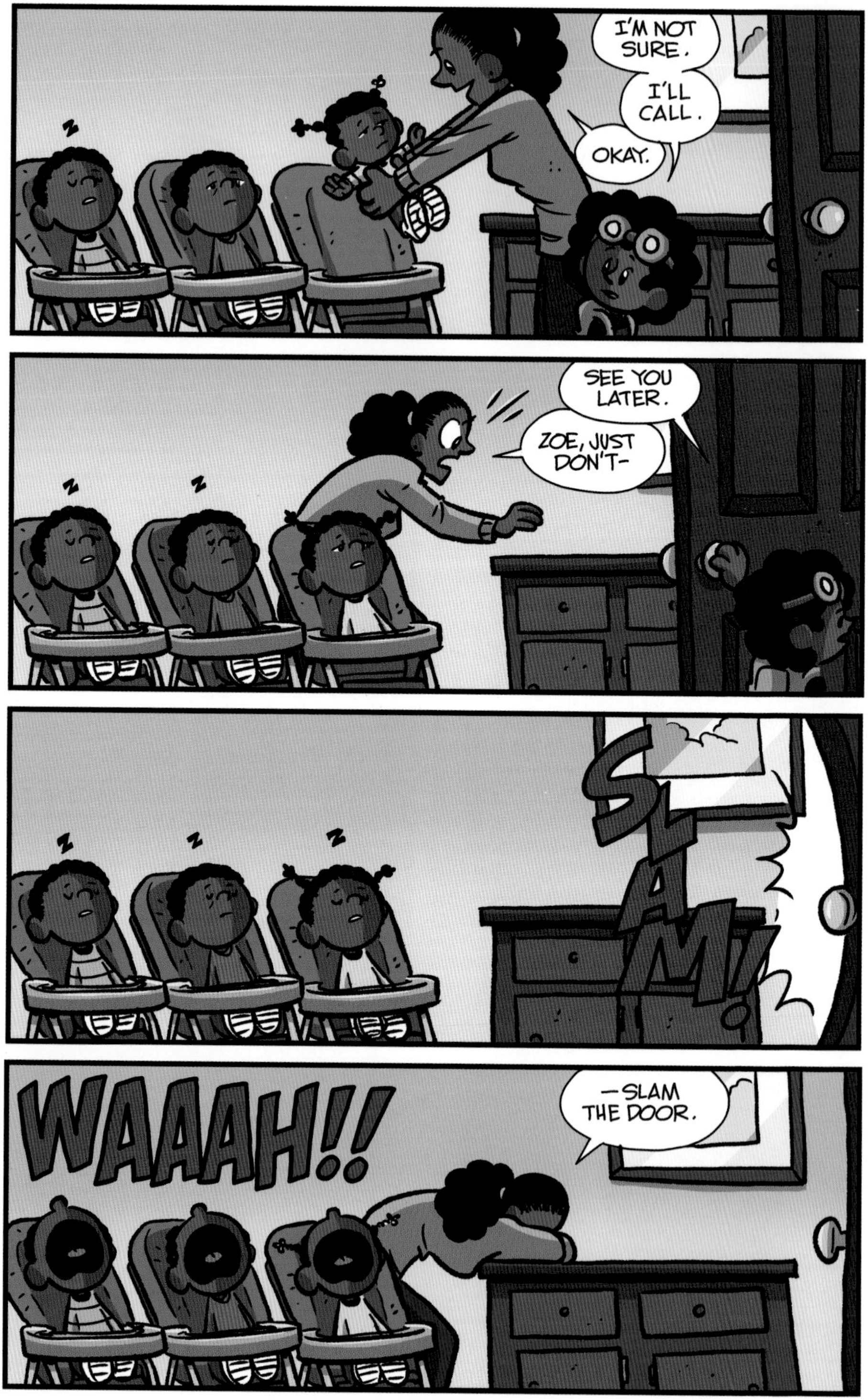
I'M NOT SURE.
I'LL CALL.
OKAY.
SEE YOU LATER.
ZOE, JUST DON'T-
SLAM!
WAAAH!!
—SLAM THE DOOR.

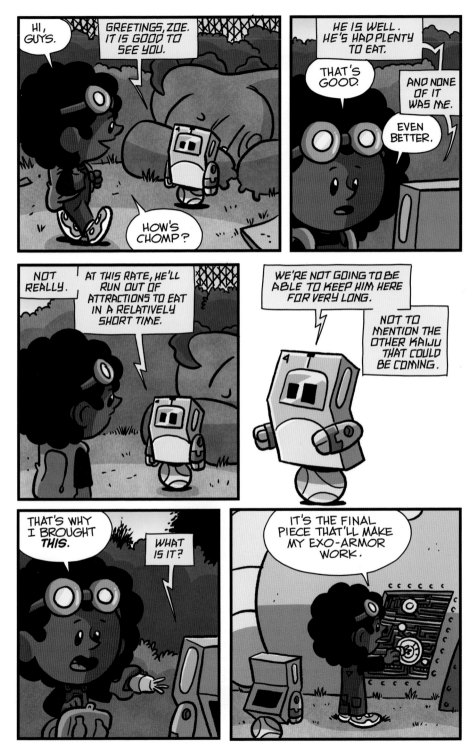

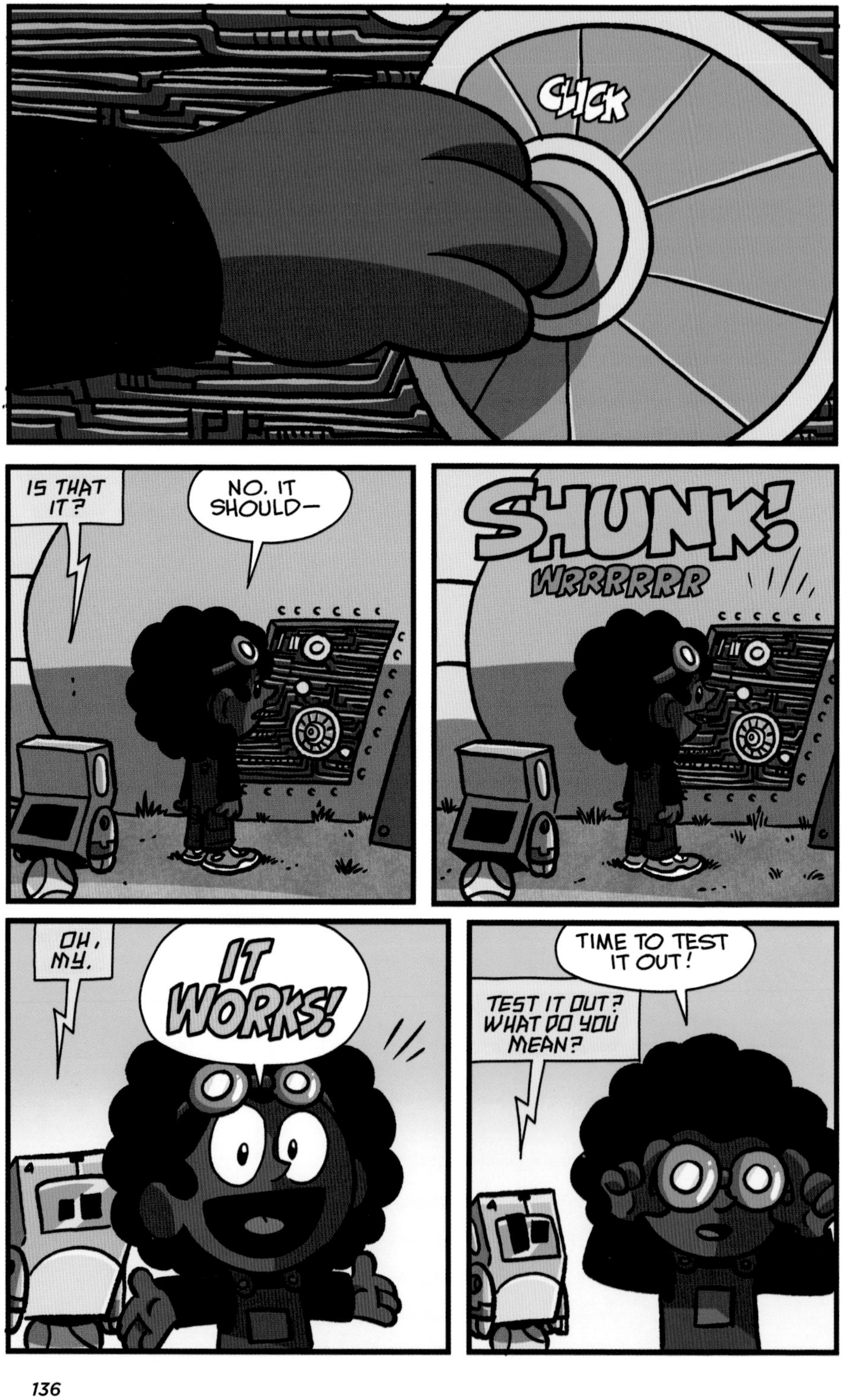
CLICK
IS THAT IT?
NO. IT SHOULD—
SHUNK!
WRRRRRR
OH, MY.
IT WORKS!
TIME TO TEST IT OUT!
TEST IT OUT? WHAT DO YOU MEAN?

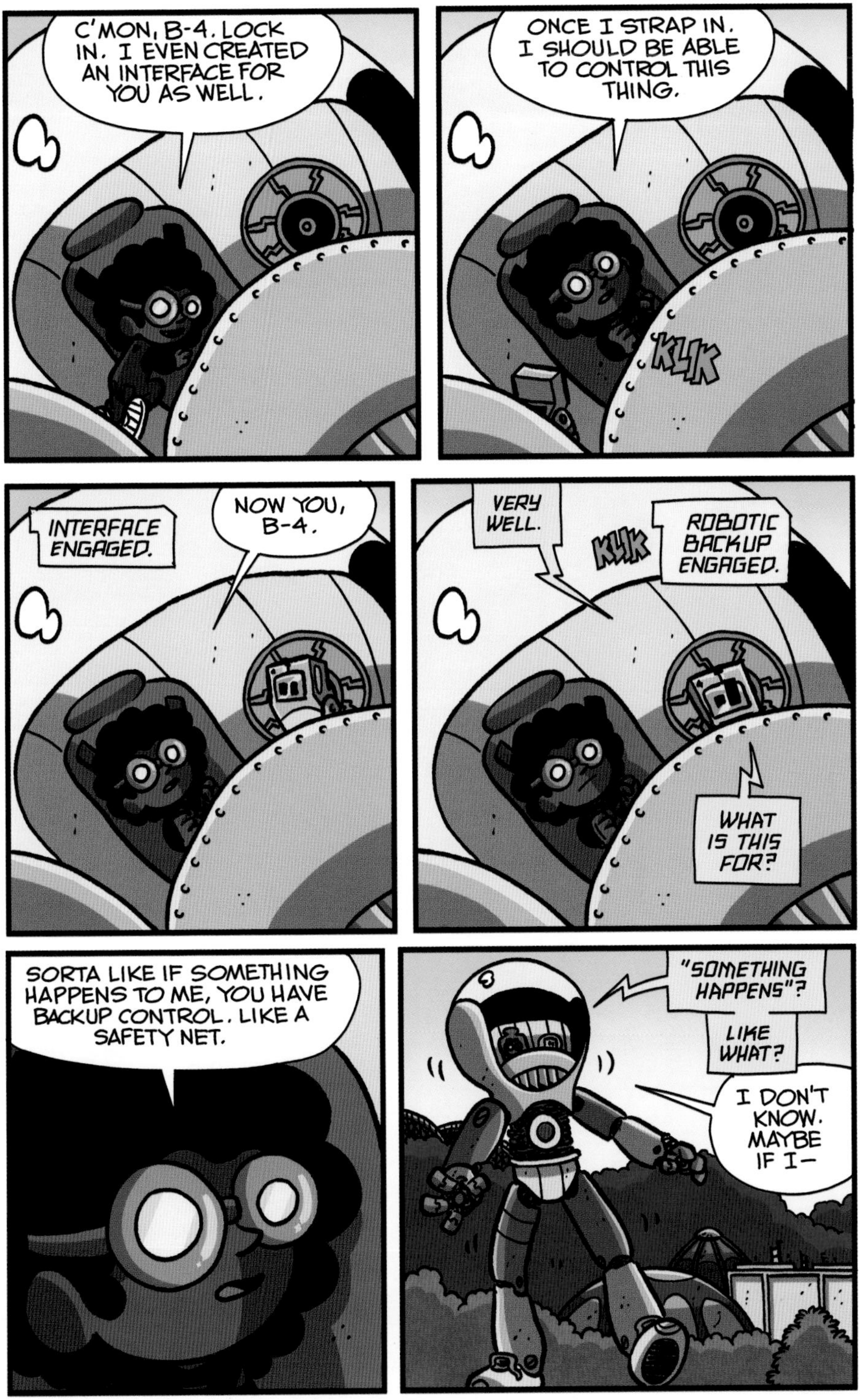
C'MON, B-4. LOCK IN. I EVEN CREATED AN INTERFACE FOR YOU AS WELL.
ONCE I STRAP IN, I SHOULD BE ABLE TO CONTROL THIS THING.
KLIK
INTERFACE ENGAGED.
NOW YOU, B-4.
VERY WELL.
KLIK
ROBOTIC BACKUP ENGAGED.
WHAT IS THIS FOR?
SORTA LIKE IF SOMETHING HAPPENS TO ME, YOU HAVE BACKUP CONTROL. LIKE A SAFETY NET.
"SOMETHING HAPPENS"?
LIKE WHAT?
I DON'T KNOW. MAYBE IF I—

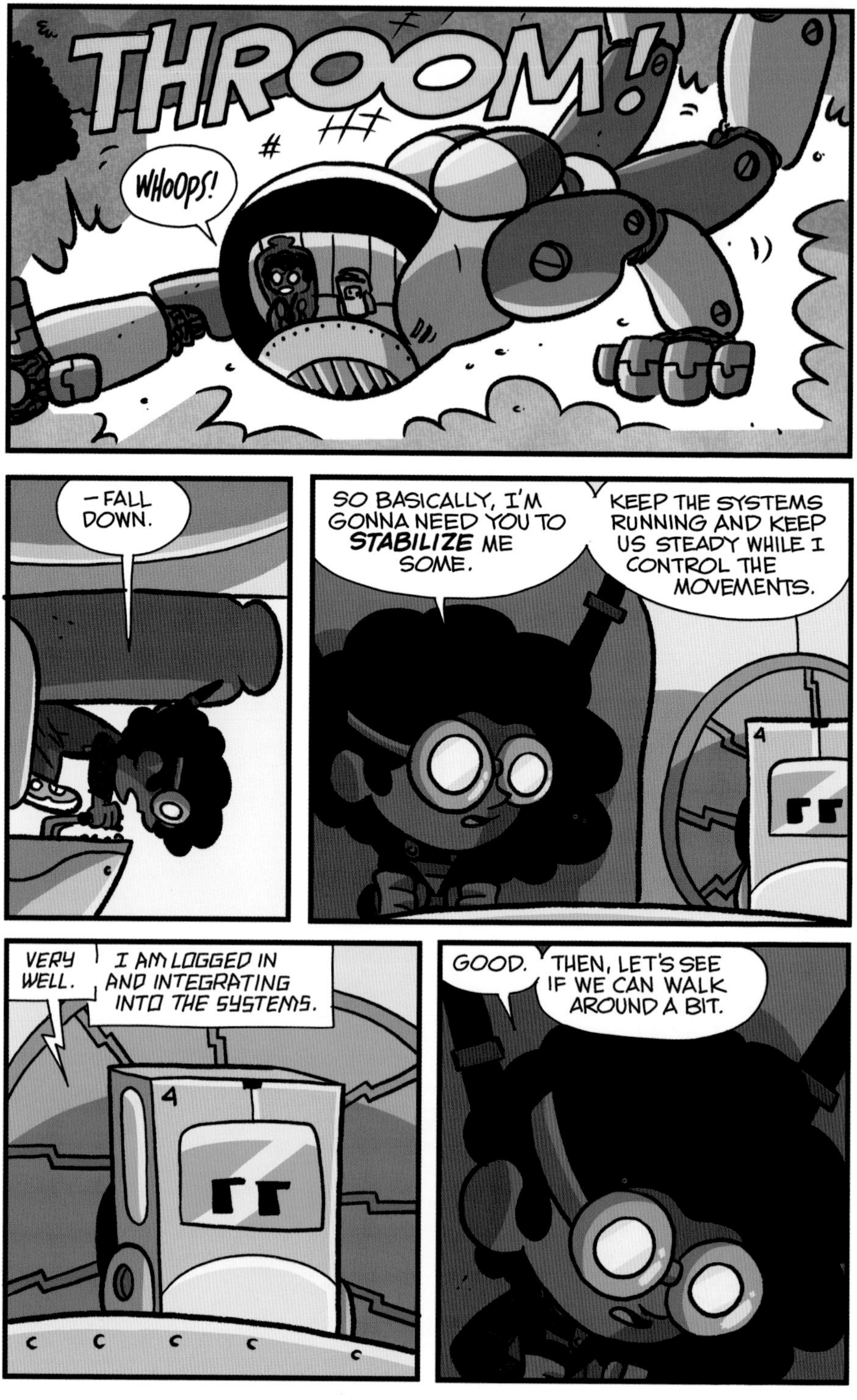
THROOM!
WHOOPS!
—FALL DOWN.
SO BASICALLY, I'M GONNA NEED YOU TO STABILIZE ME SOME.
KEEP THE SYSTEMS RUNNING AND KEEP US STEADY WHILE I CONTROL THE MOVEMENTS.
VERY WELL.
I AM LOGGED IN AND INTEGRATING INTO THE SYSTEMS.
GOOD.
THEN, LET'S SEE IF WE CAN WALK AROUND A BIT.

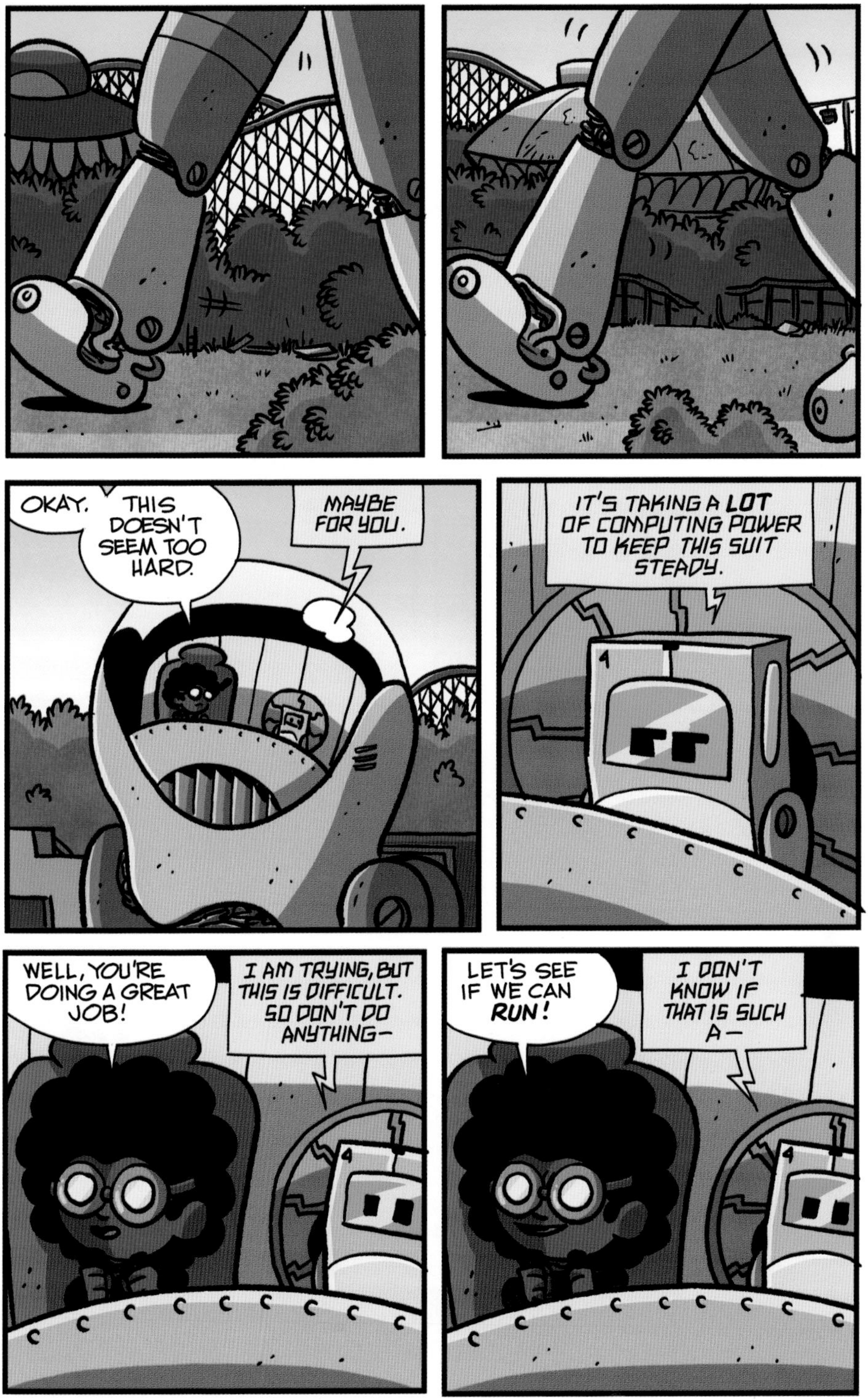
OKAY.
THIS DOESN'T SEEM TOO HARD.
MAYBE FOR YOU.
IT'S TAKING A **LOT** OF COMPUTING POWER TO KEEP THIS SUIT STEADY.
WELL, YOU'RE DOING A GREAT JOB!
I AM TRYING, BUT THIS IS DIFFICULT. SO DON'T DO ANYTHING—
LET'S SEE IF WE CAN **RUN**!
I DON'T KNOW IF THAT IS SUCH A—

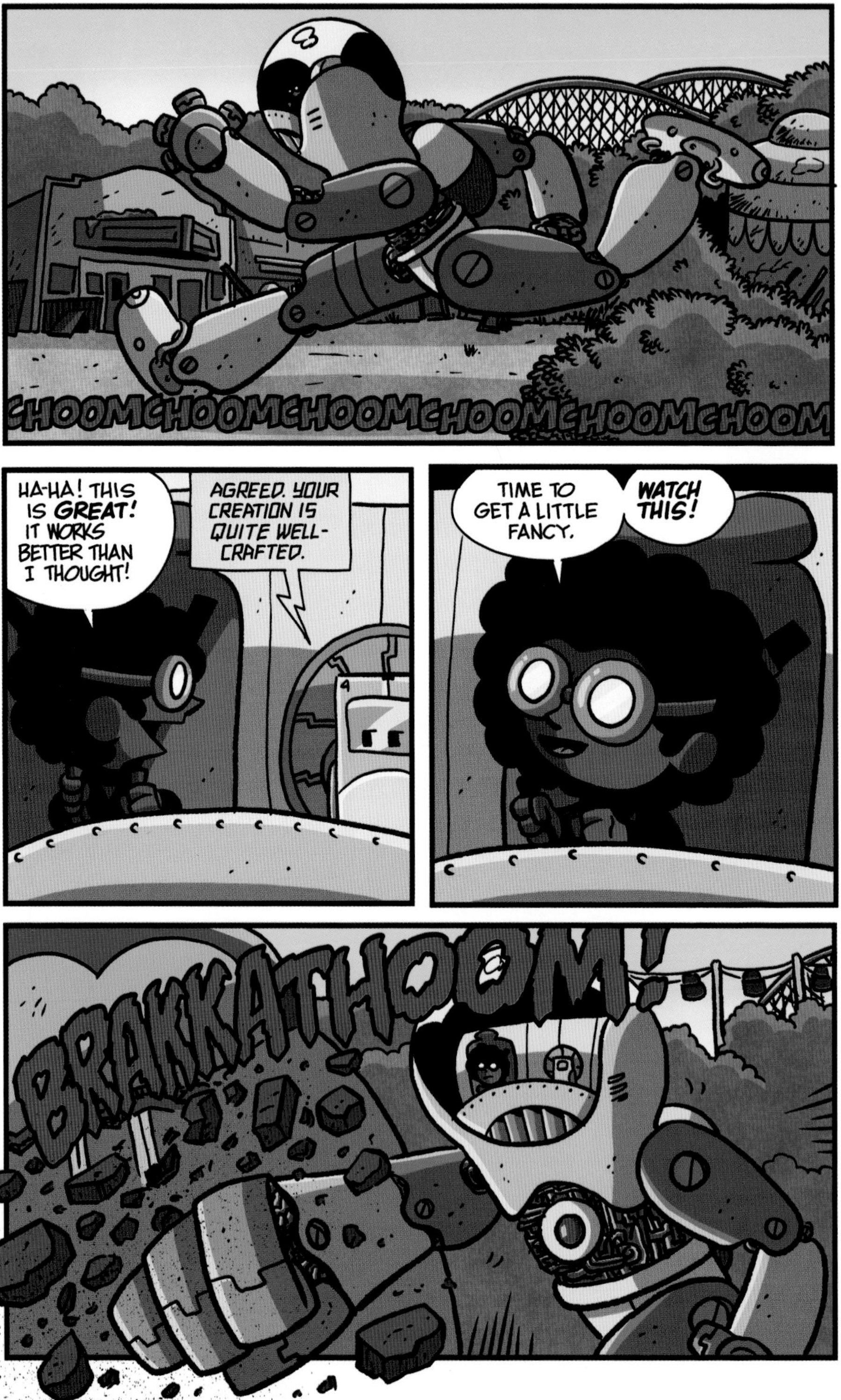
CHOOMCHOOMCHOOMCHOOMCHOOMCHOOM
HA-HA! THIS IS GREAT! IT WORKS BETTER THAN I THOUGHT!
AGREED. YOUR CREATION IS QUITE WELL-CRAFTED.
TIME TO GET A LITTLE FANCY.
WATCH THIS!
BRAKKATHOOM!

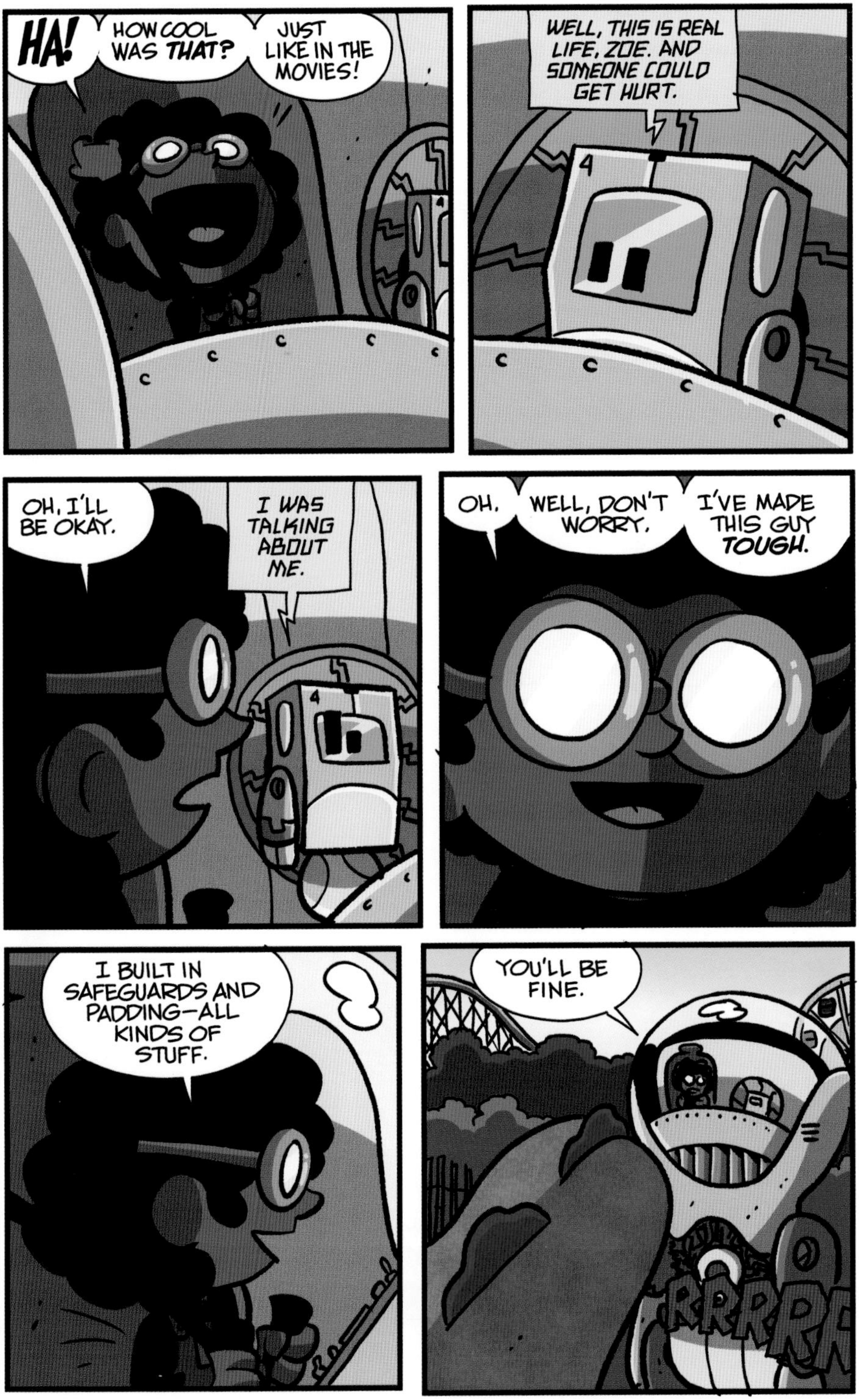
HA!
HOW COOL WAS THAT?
JUST LIKE IN THE MOVIES!
WELL, THIS IS REAL LIFE, ZOE. AND SOMEONE COULD GET HURT.
OH, I'LL BE OKAY.
I WAS TALKING ABOUT ME.
OH.
WELL, DON'T WORRY.
I'VE MADE THIS GUY TOUGH.
I BUILT IN SAFEGUARDS AND PADDING—ALL KINDS OF STUFF.
YOU'LL BE FINE.
RRRR

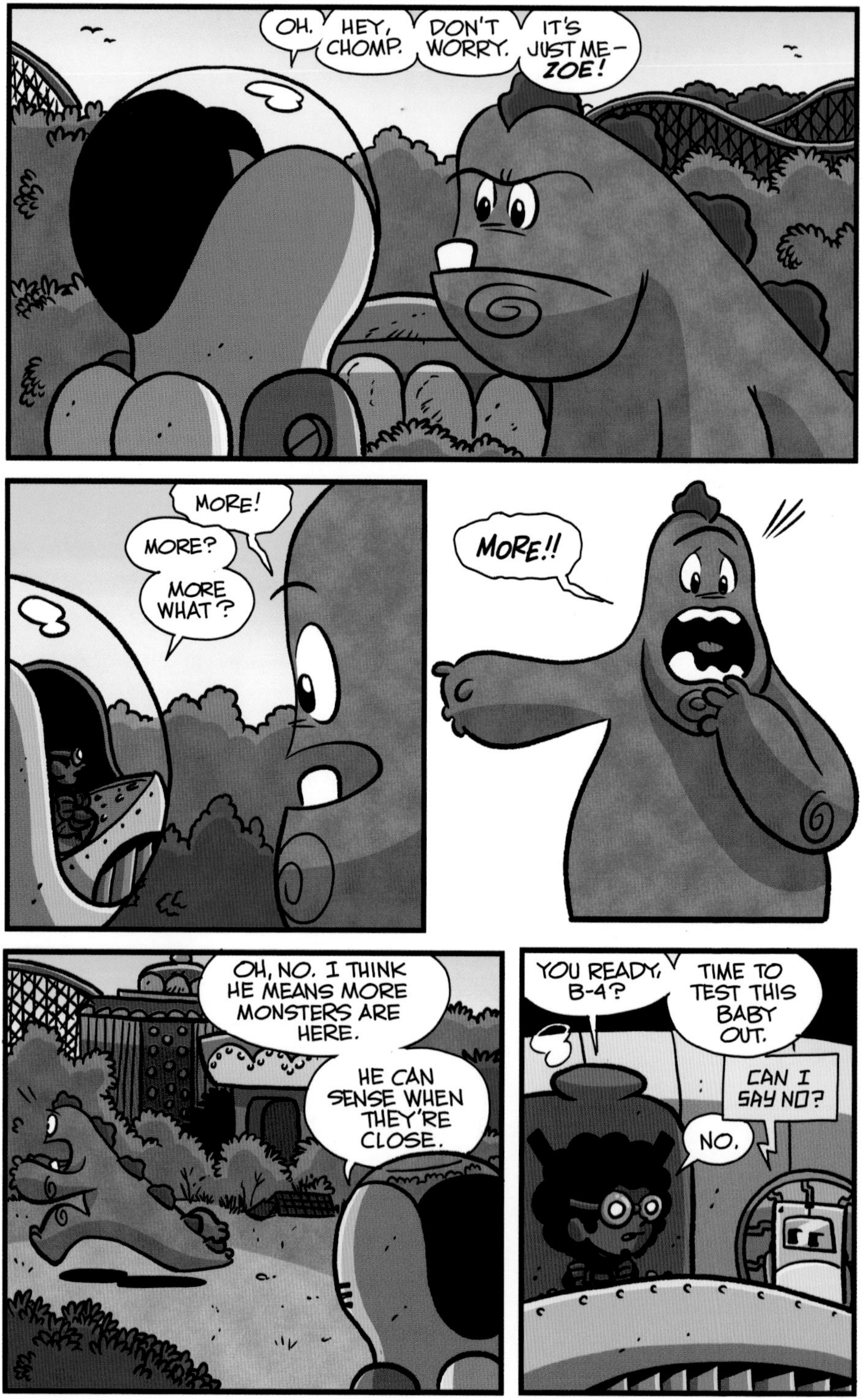
OH.
HEY, CHOMP.
DON'T WORRY.
IT'S JUST ME-ZOE!
MORE!
MORE?
MORE WHAT?
MORE!!
OH, NO. I THINK HE MEANS MORE MONSTERS ARE HERE.
HE CAN SENSE WHEN THEY'RE CLOSE.
YOU READY, B-4?
TIME TO TEST THIS BABY OUT.
CAN I SAY NO?
NO.

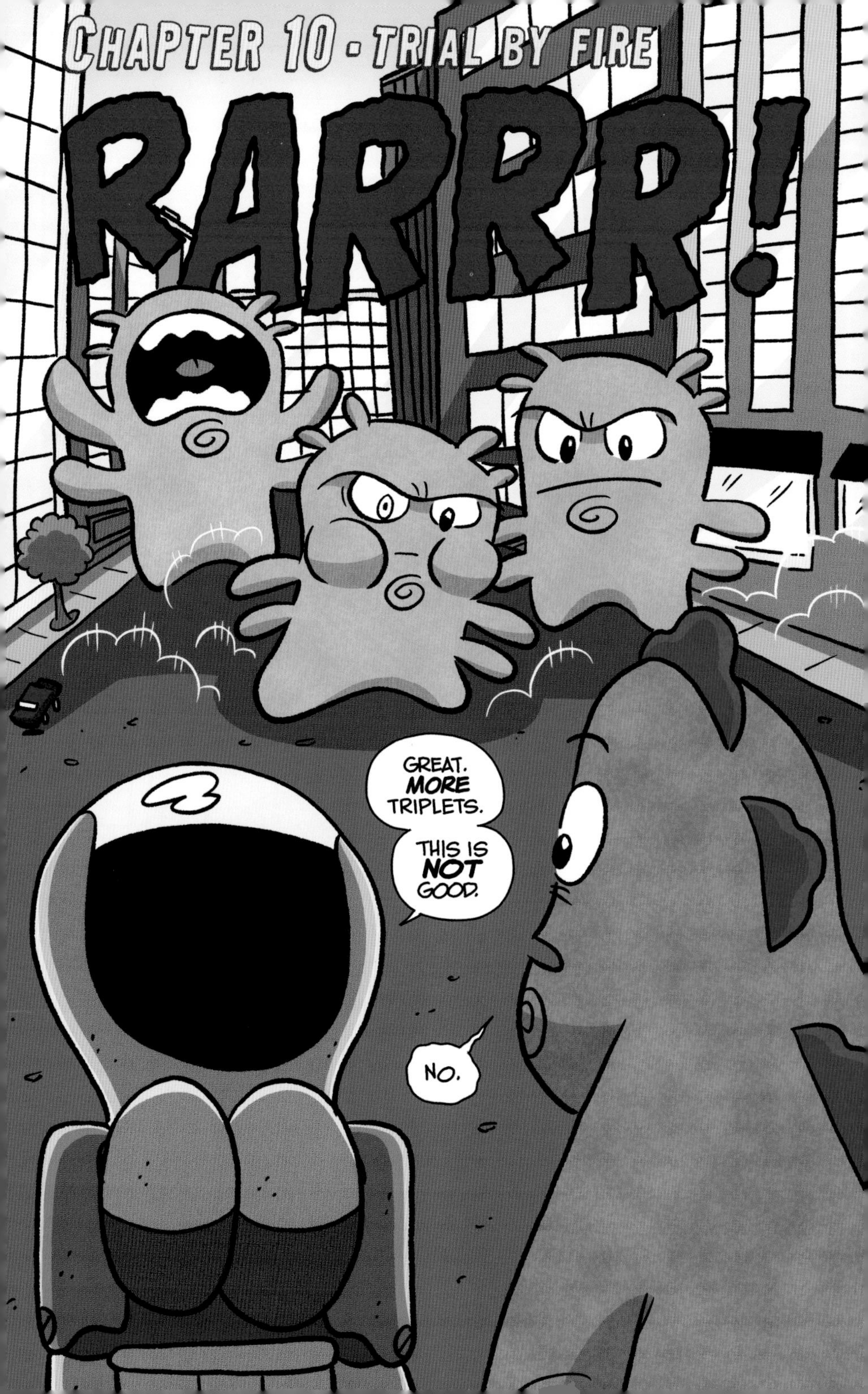
CHAPTER 10 - TRIAL BY FIRE
RARRR!
GREAT. MORE TRIPLETS.
THIS IS NOT GOOD.
NO.

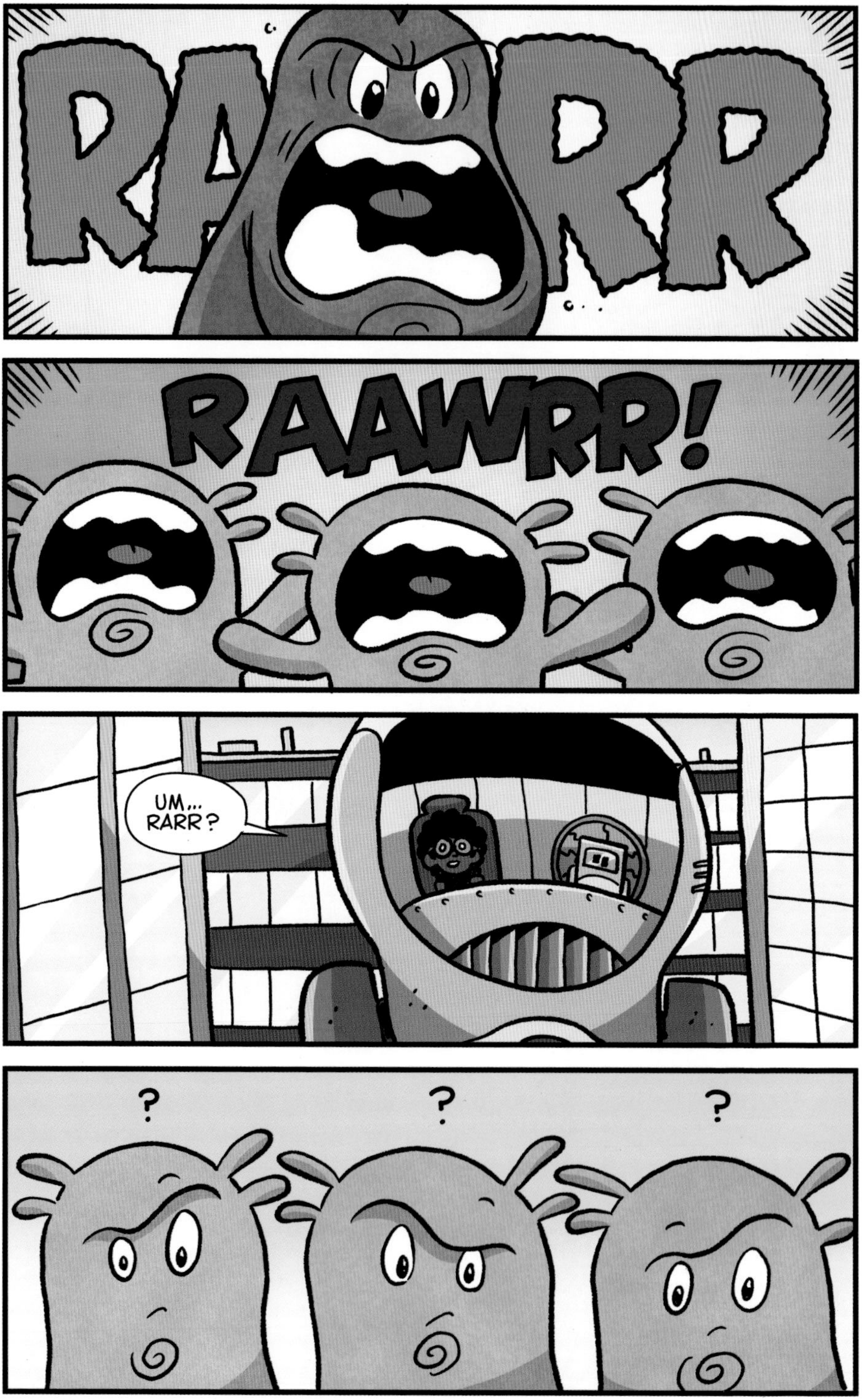
RAWRR
RAAWRR!
UM... RARR?
?
?
?

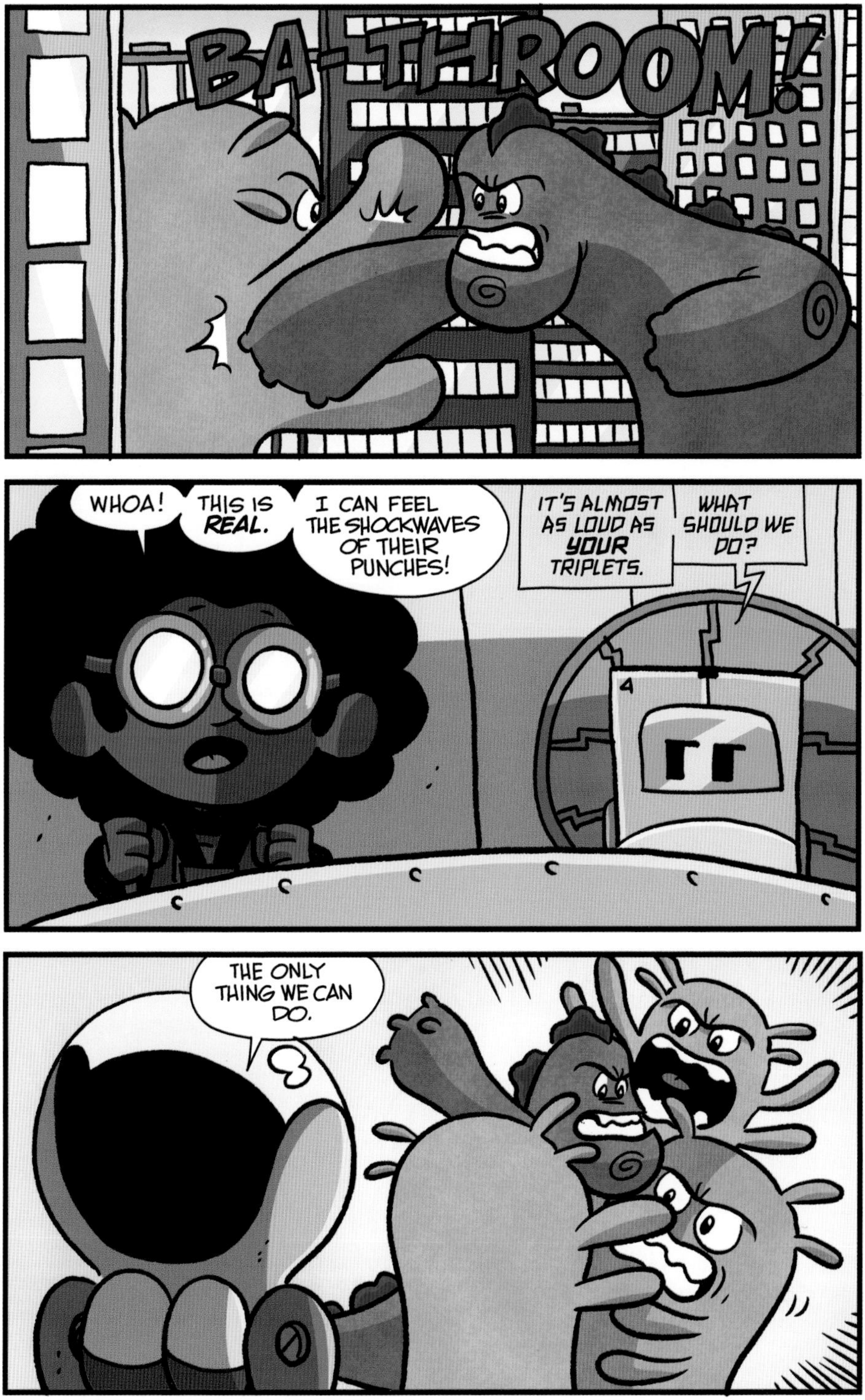
BA-THROOM!
WHOA!
THIS IS **REAL.**
I CAN FEEL THE SHOCKWAVES OF THEIR PUNCHES!
IT'S ALMOST AS LOUD AS ***YOUR*** TRIPLETS.
WHAT SHOULD WE DO?
4
THE ONLY THING WE CAN DO.

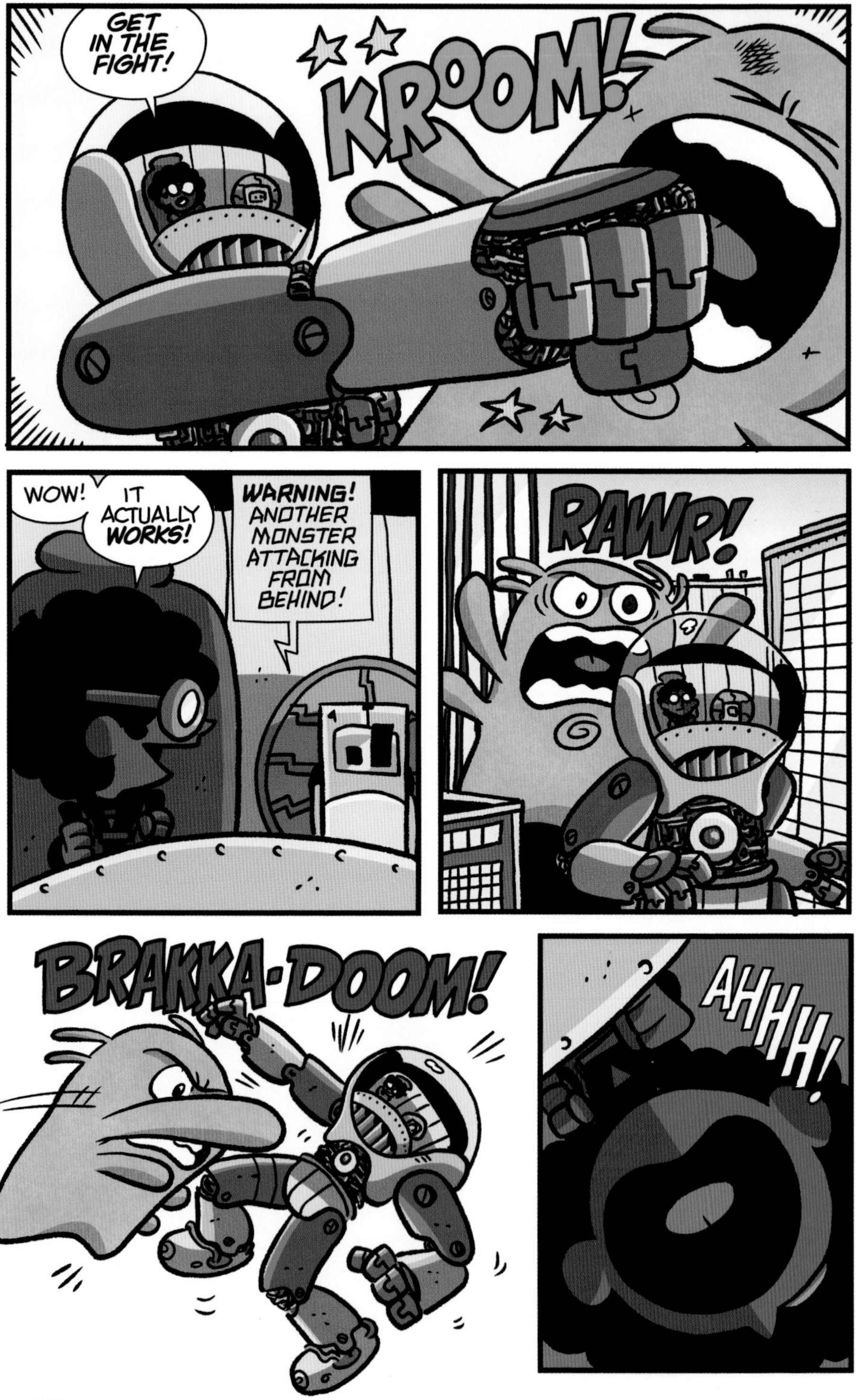
GET IN THE FIGHT!
KROOM!
WOW!
IT ACTUALLY WORKS!
WARNING! ANOTHER MONSTER ATTACKING FROM BEHIND!
RAWR!
BRAKKA-DOOM!
AHHHH!

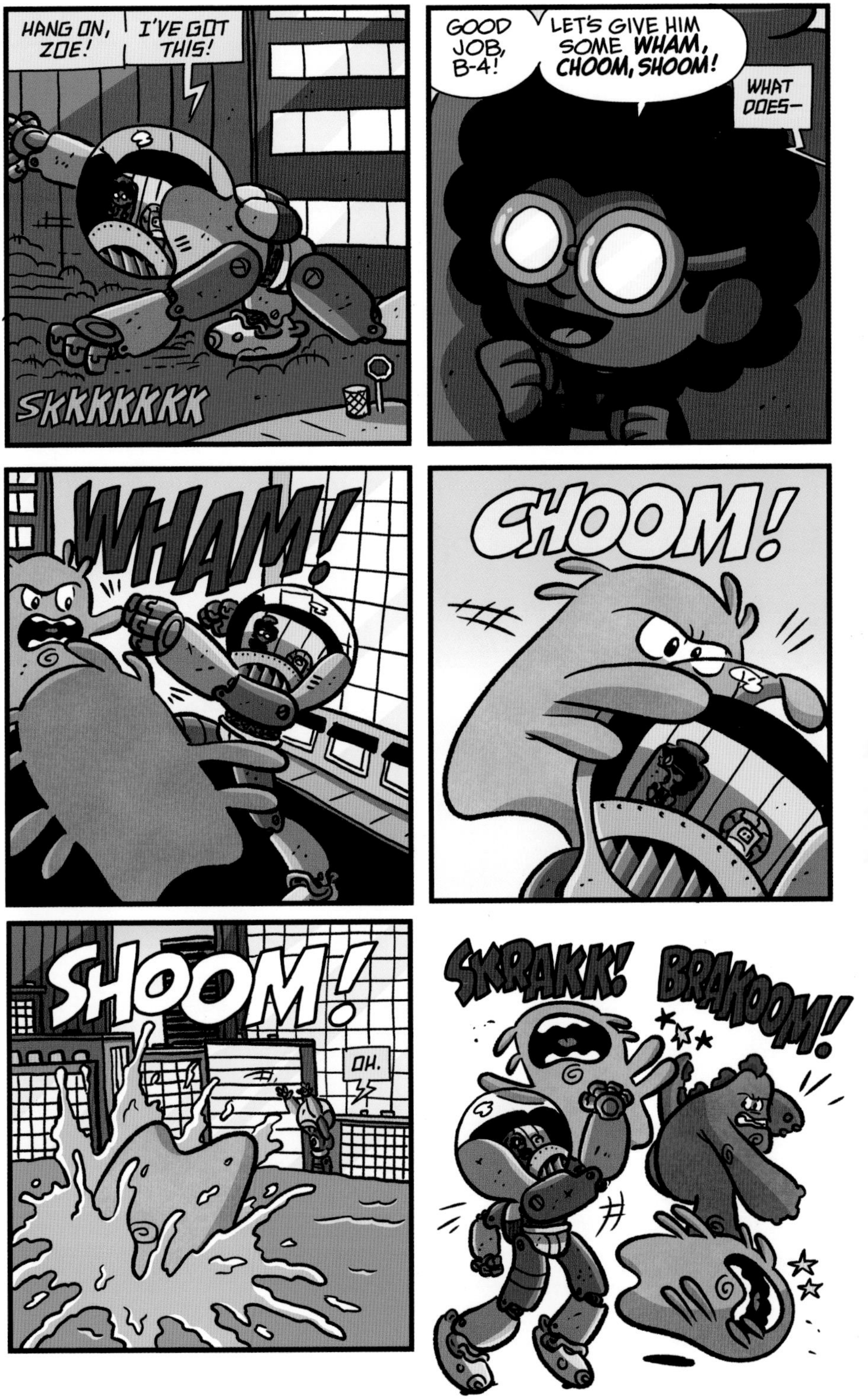
HANG ON, ZOE!
I'VE GOT THIS!
SKKKKKKK
GOOD JOB, B-4!
LET'S GIVE HIM SOME WHAM, CHOOM, SHOOM!
WHAT DOES—
WHAM!
CHOOM!
SHOOM!
OH.
SKRAKK! BRAKOOM!

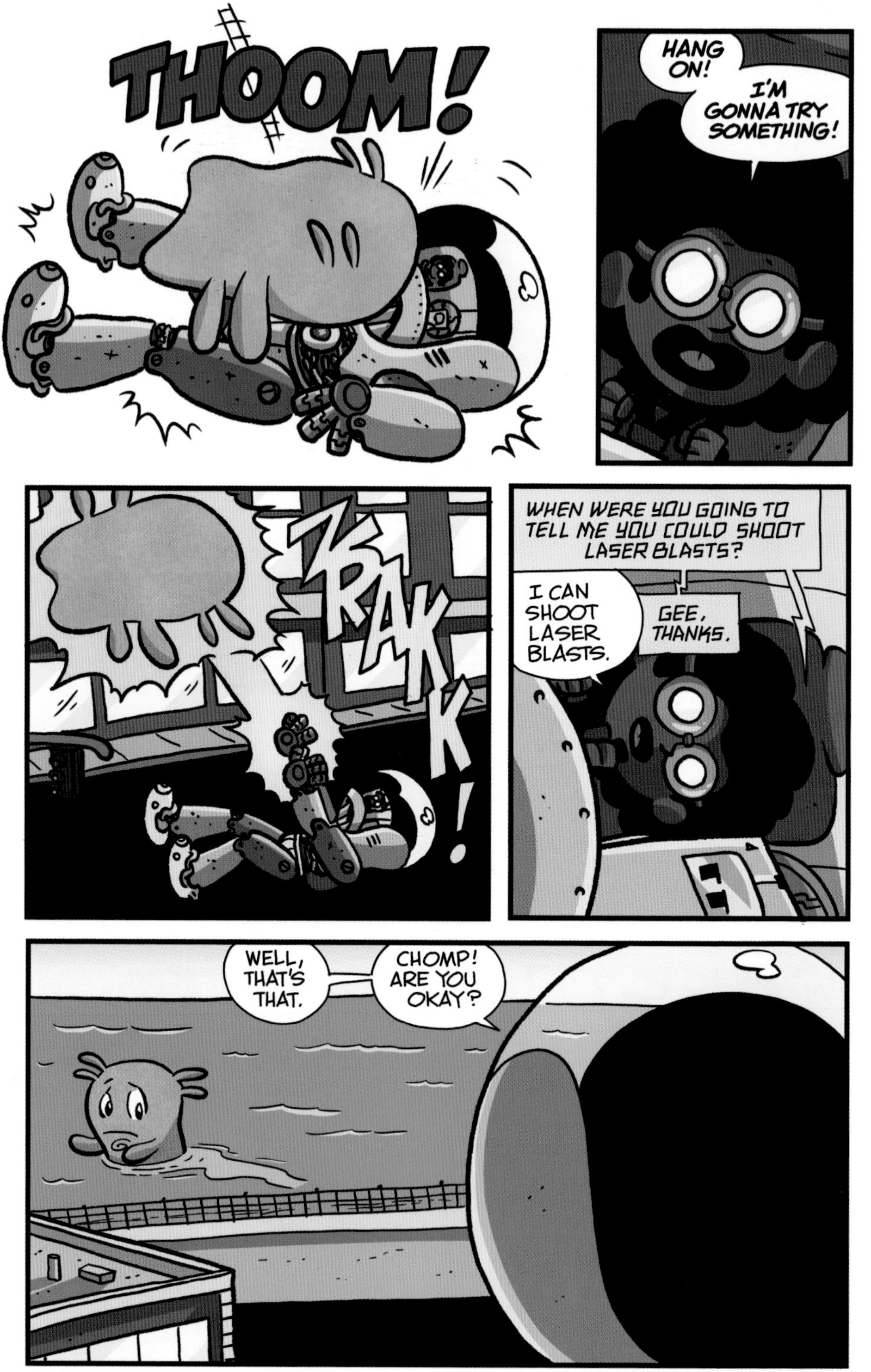
THOOM!
HANG ON!
I'M GONNA TRY SOMETHING!
ZRAKK!
WHEN WERE YOU GOING TO TELL ME YOU COULD SHOOT LASER BLASTS?
I CAN SHOOT LASER BLASTS.
GEE, THANKS.
WELL, THAT'S THAT.
CHOMP! ARE YOU OKAY?

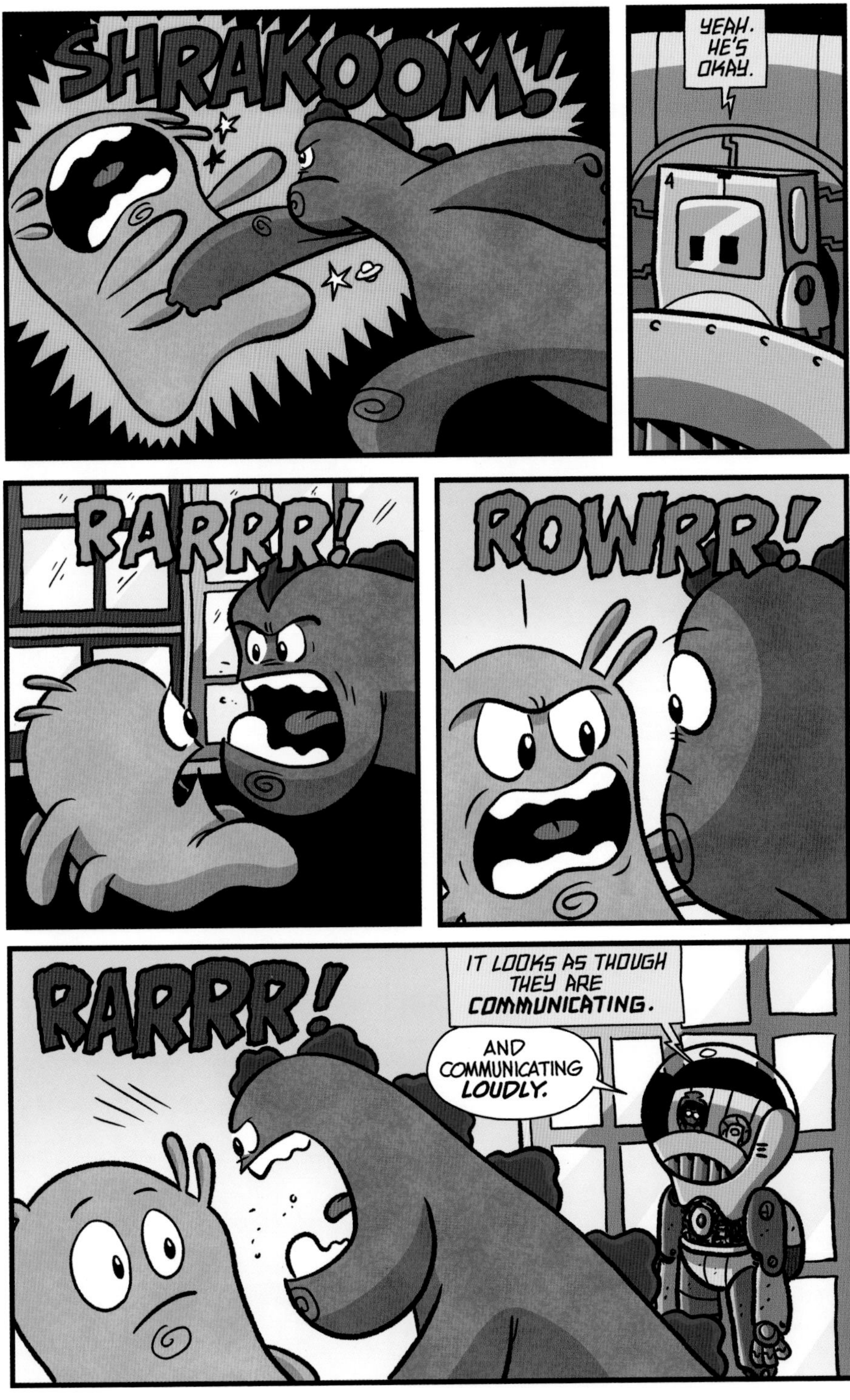
SHRAKOOM!
YEAH. HE'S OKAY.
RARRR!
ROWRR!
RARRR!
IT LOOKS AS THOUGH THEY ARE COMMUNICATING.
AND COMMUNICATING LOUDLY.

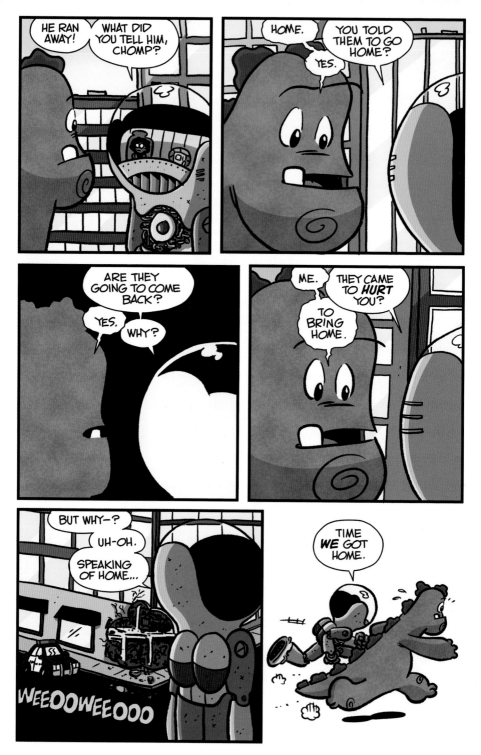

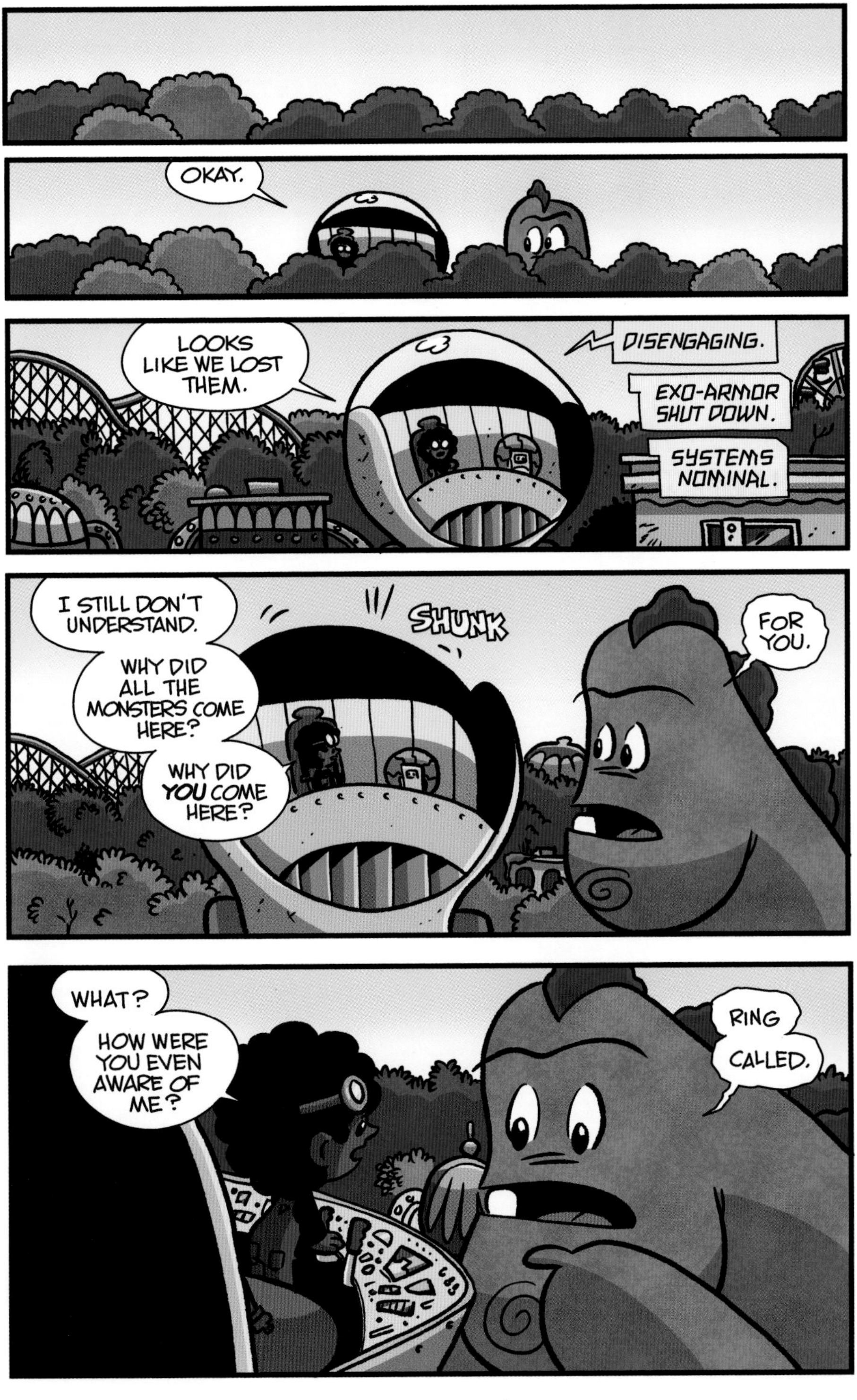
OKAY.
LOOKS LIKE WE LOST THEM.
DISENGAGING.
EXO-ARMOR SHUT DOWN.
SYSTEMS NOMINAL.
I STILL DON'T UNDERSTAND.
WHY DID ALL THE MONSTERS COME HERE?
WHY DID **YOU** COME HERE?
SHUNK
FOR YOU.
WHAT?
HOW WERE YOU EVEN AWARE OF ME?
RING
CALLED.

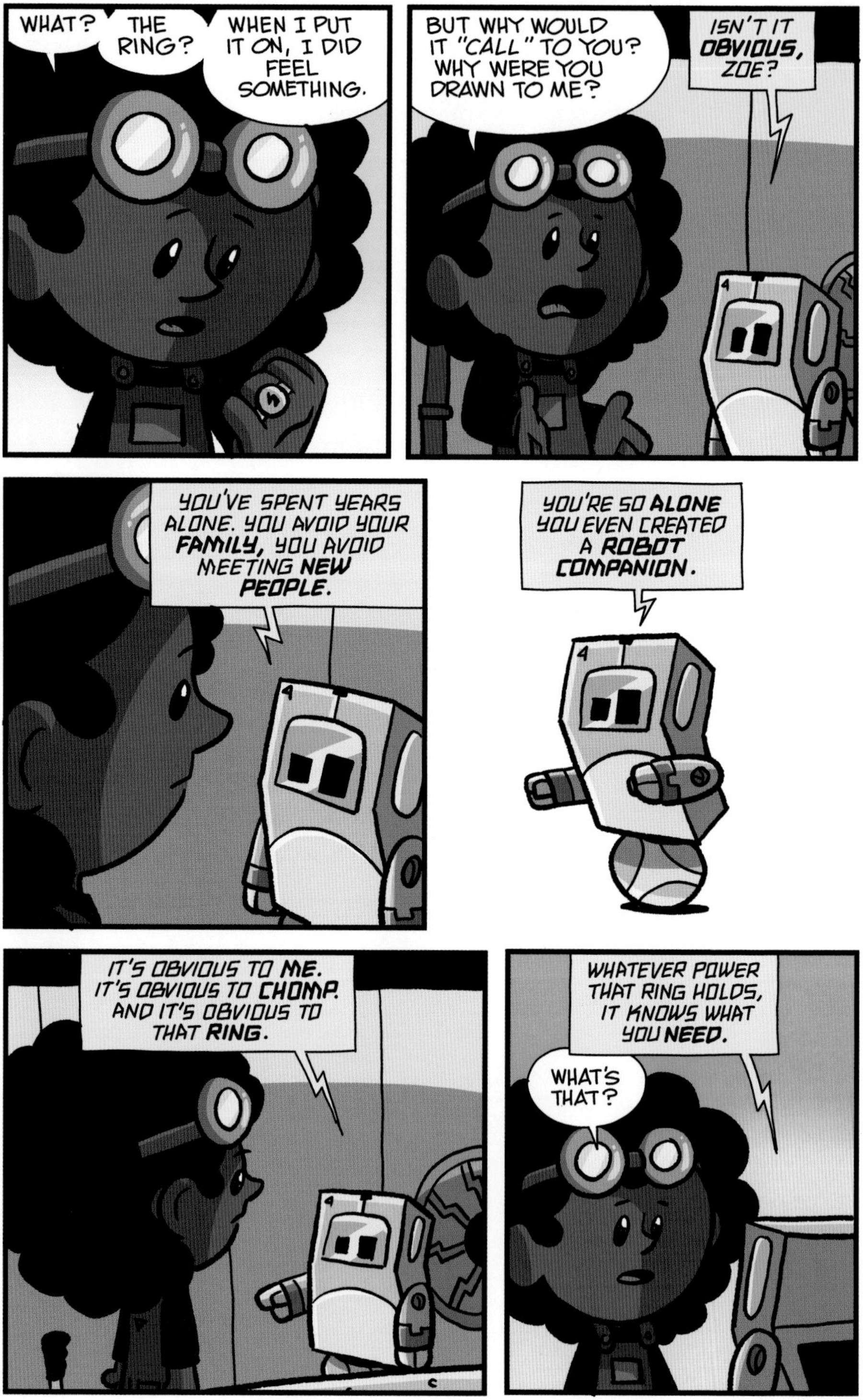
WHAT?
THE RING?
WHEN I PUT IT ON, I DID FEEL SOMETHING.
BUT WHY WOULD IT "CALL" TO YOU? WHY WERE YOU DRAWN TO ME?
ISN'T IT **OBVIOUS,** ZOE?
YOU'VE SPENT YEARS ALONE. YOU AVOID YOUR **FAMILY,** YOU AVOID MEETING **NEW PEOPLE**.
YOU'RE SO **ALONE** YOU EVEN CREATED A **ROBOT COMPANION**.
IT'S OBVIOUS TO **ME**. IT'S OBVIOUS TO **CHOMP**. AND IT'S OBVIOUS TO THAT **RING**.
WHATEVER POWER THAT RING HOLDS, IT KNOWS WHAT YOU **NEED**.
WHAT'S THAT?

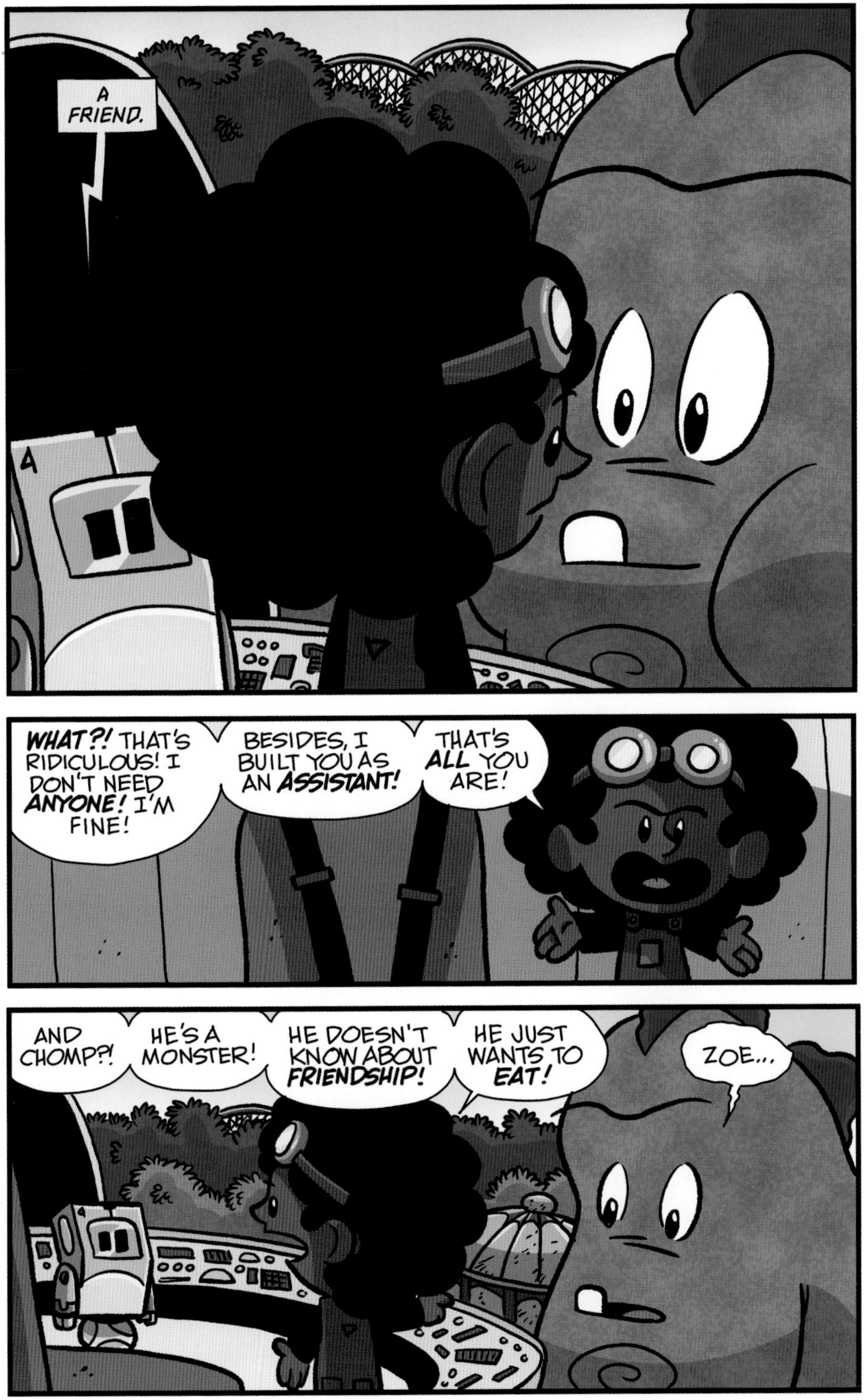
A FRIEND.
WHAT?! THAT'S RIDICULOUS! I DON'T NEED ANYONE! I'M FINE!
BESIDES, I BUILT YOU AS AN ASSISTANT!
THAT'S ALL YOU ARE!
AND CHOMP?!
HE'S A MONSTER!
HE DOESN'T KNOW ABOUT FRIENDSHIP!
HE JUST WANTS TO EAT!
ZOE...

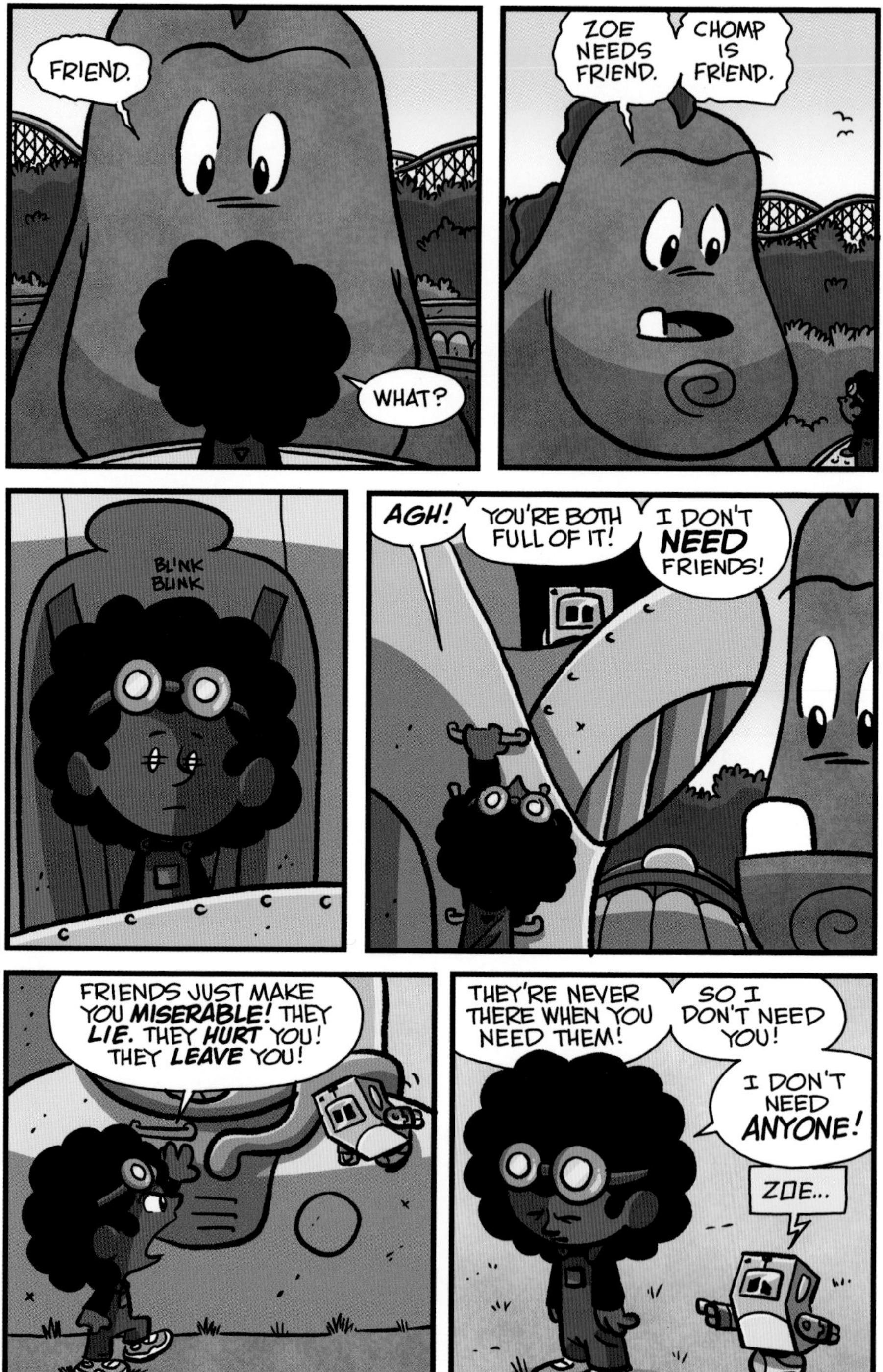
FRIEND.
WHAT?
ZOE NEEDS FRIEND.
CHOMP IS FRIEND.
BLINK BLINK
AGH!
YOU'RE BOTH FULL OF IT!
I DON'T NEED FRIENDS!
FRIENDS JUST MAKE YOU MISERABLE! THEY LIE. THEY HURT YOU! THEY LEAVE YOU!
THEY'RE NEVER THERE WHEN YOU NEED THEM!
SO I DON'T NEED YOU!
I DON'T NEED ANYONE!
ZOE...

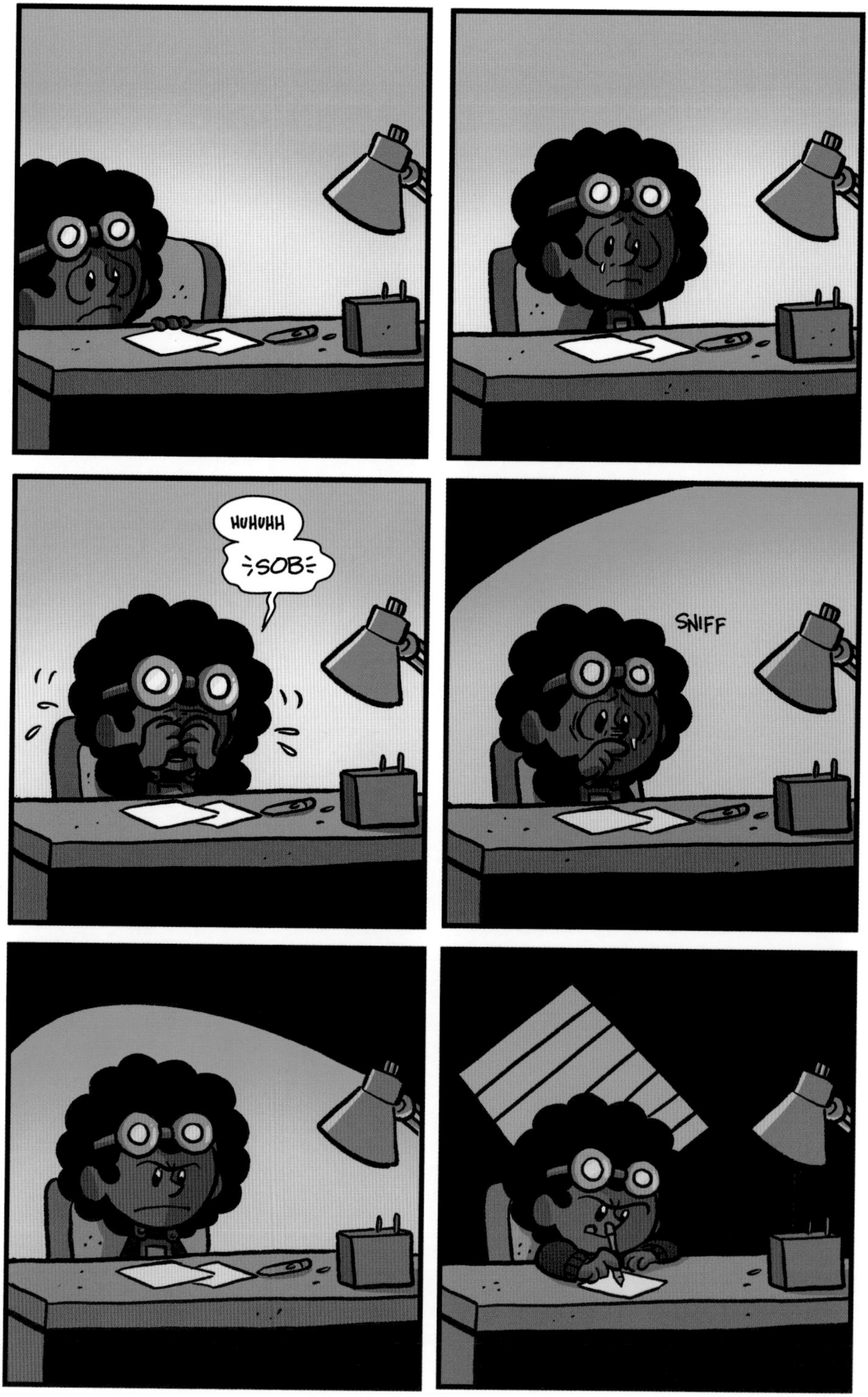
HUHUHH
SOB
SNIFF

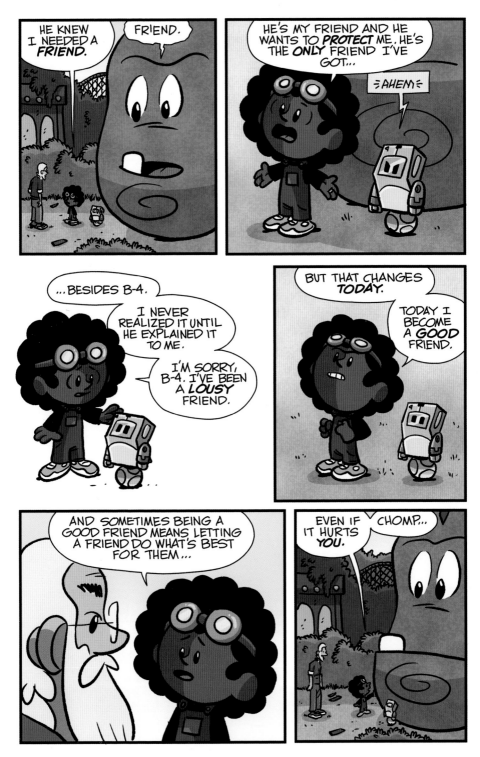

171

CHAPTER 14 - BATTLEFRONT

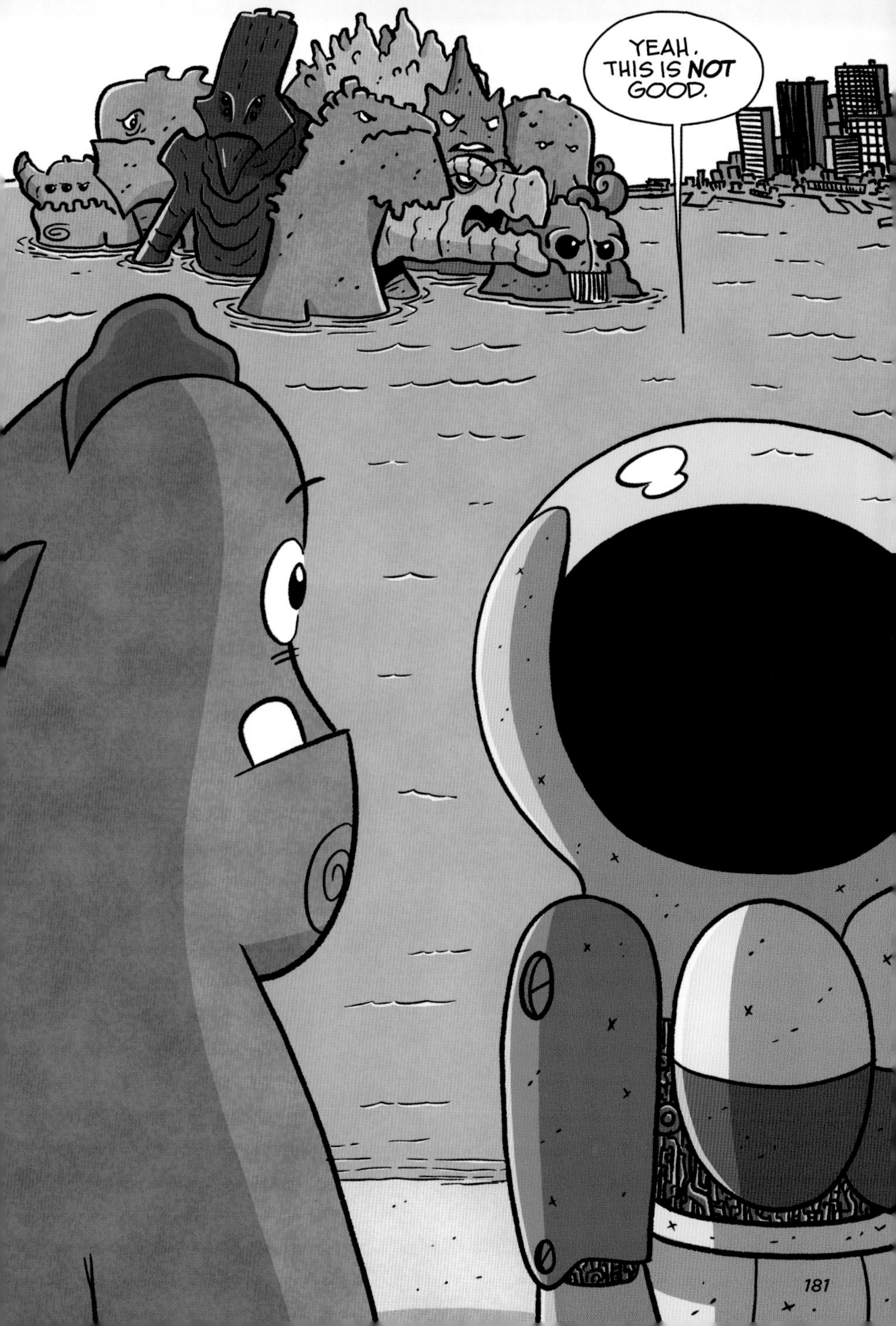
YEAH. THIS IS **NOT** GOOD.

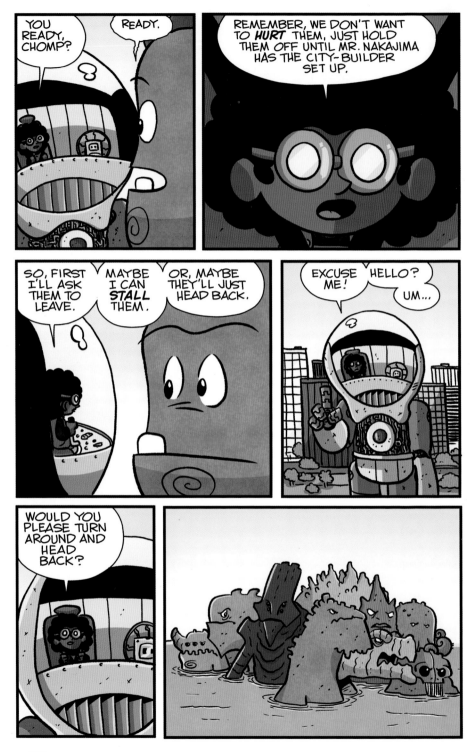

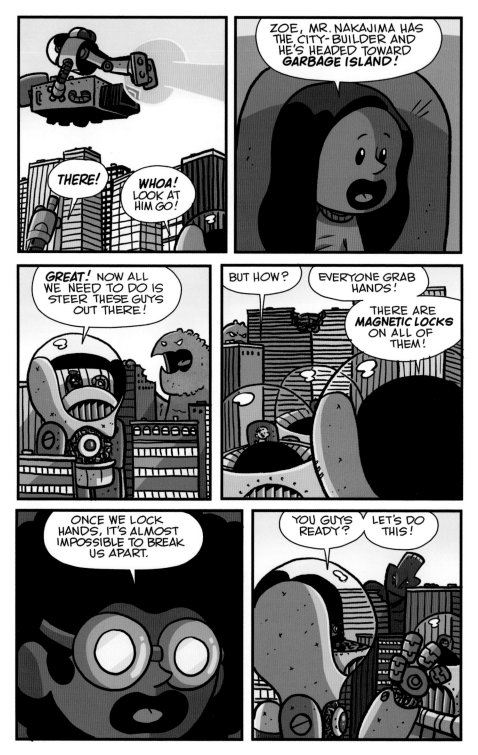

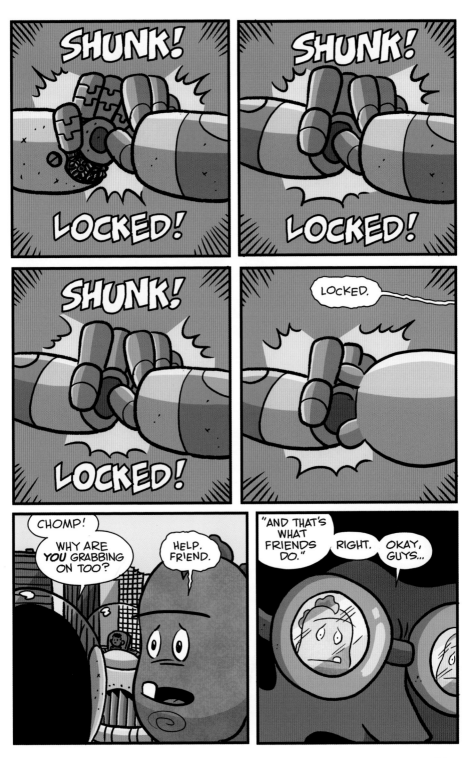

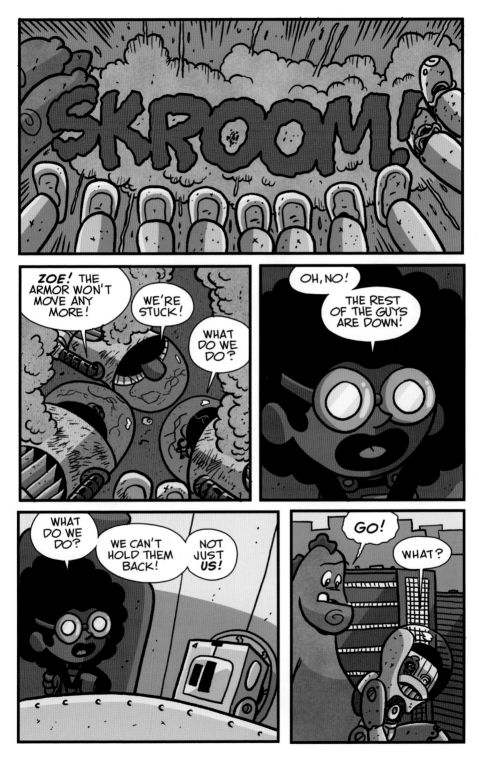

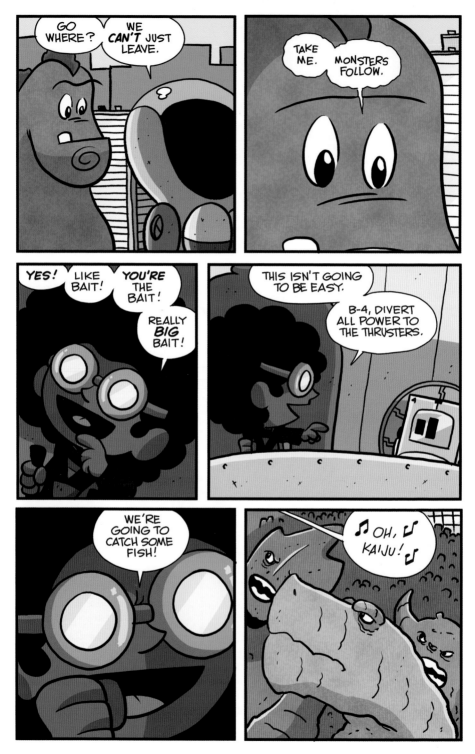

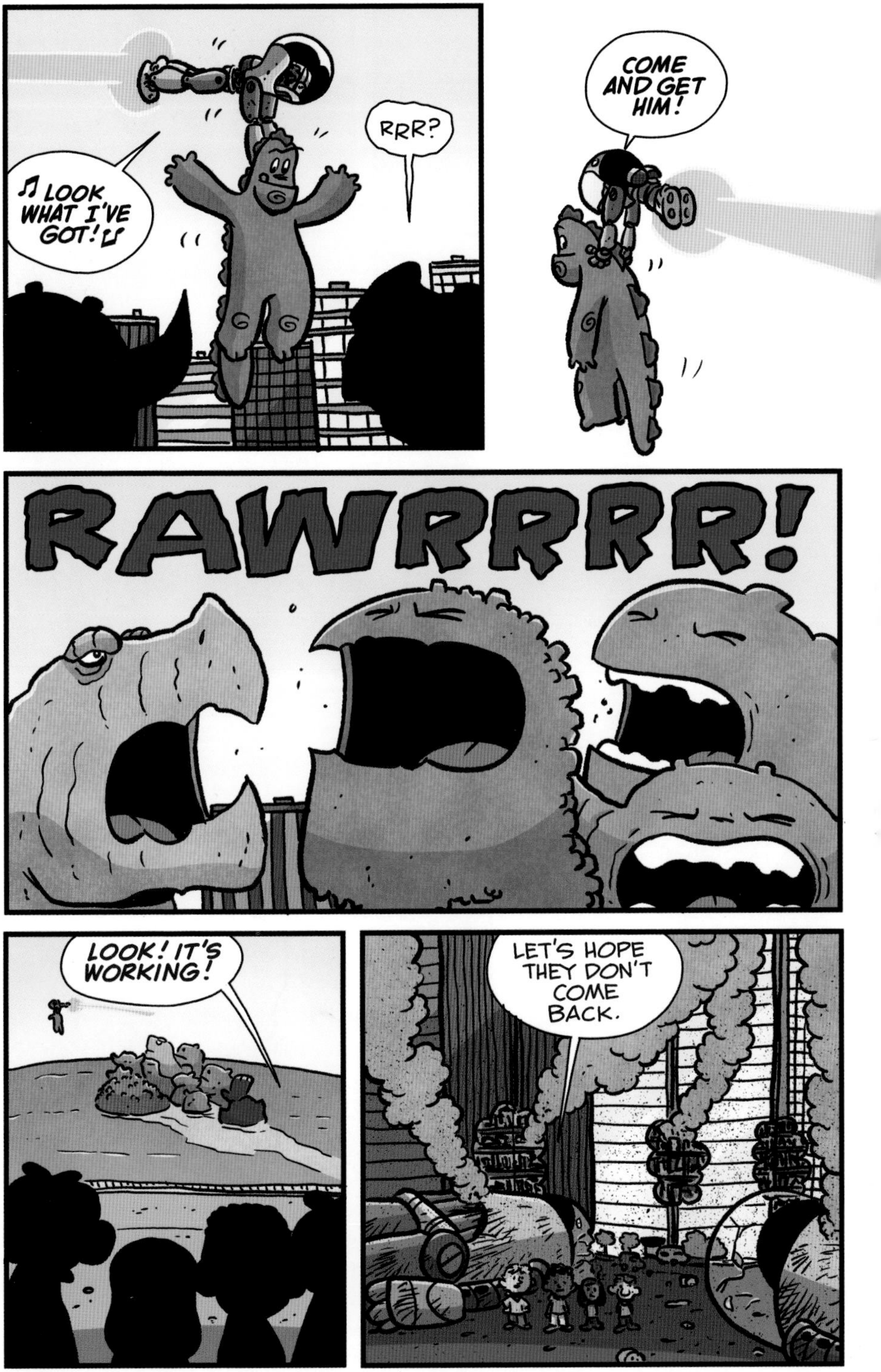
♫ LOOK WHAT I'VE GOT! ♫
RRR?
COME AND GET HIM!
RAWRRRR!
LOOK! IT'S WORKING!
LET'S HOPE THEY DON'T COME BACK.

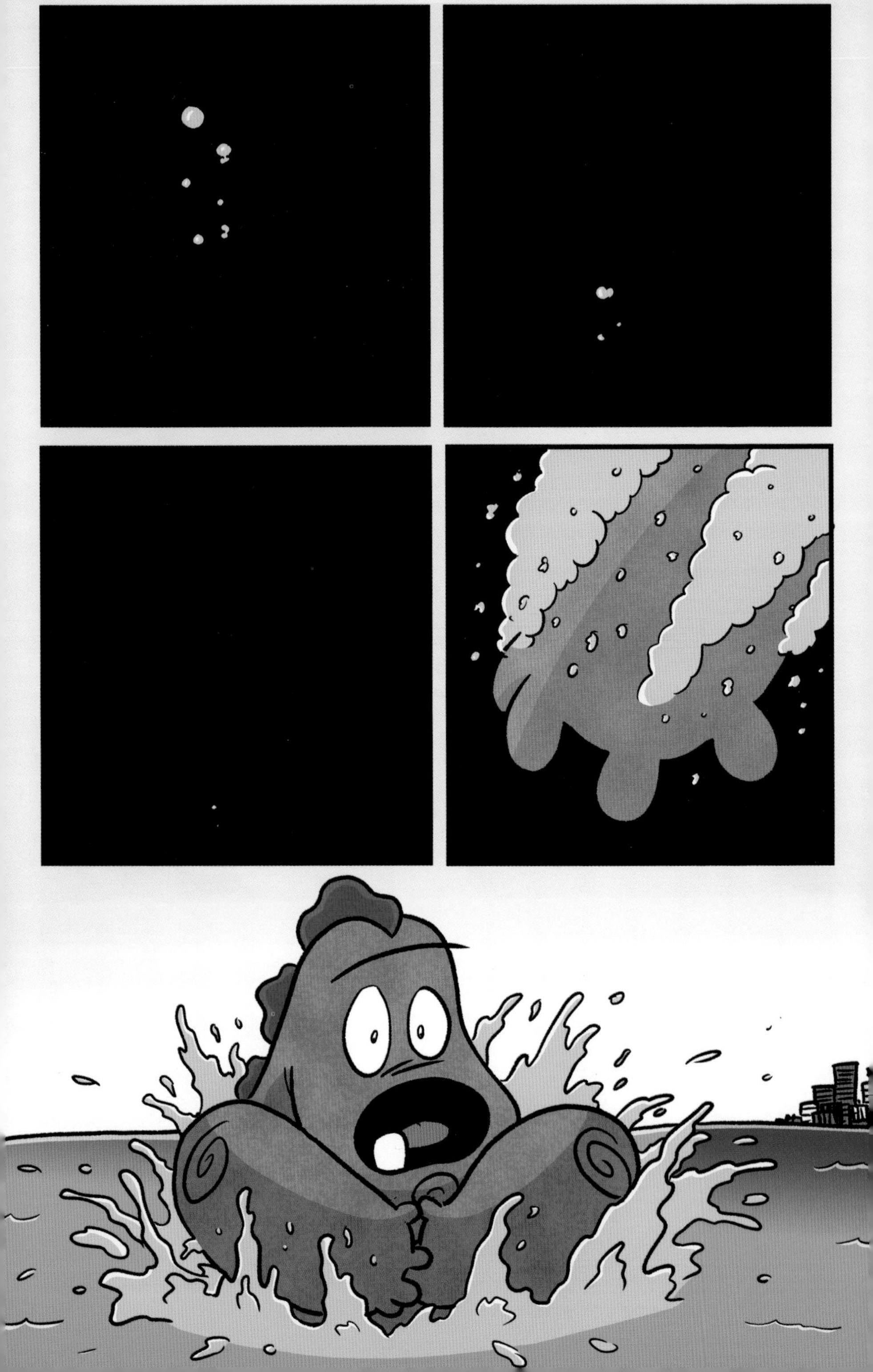

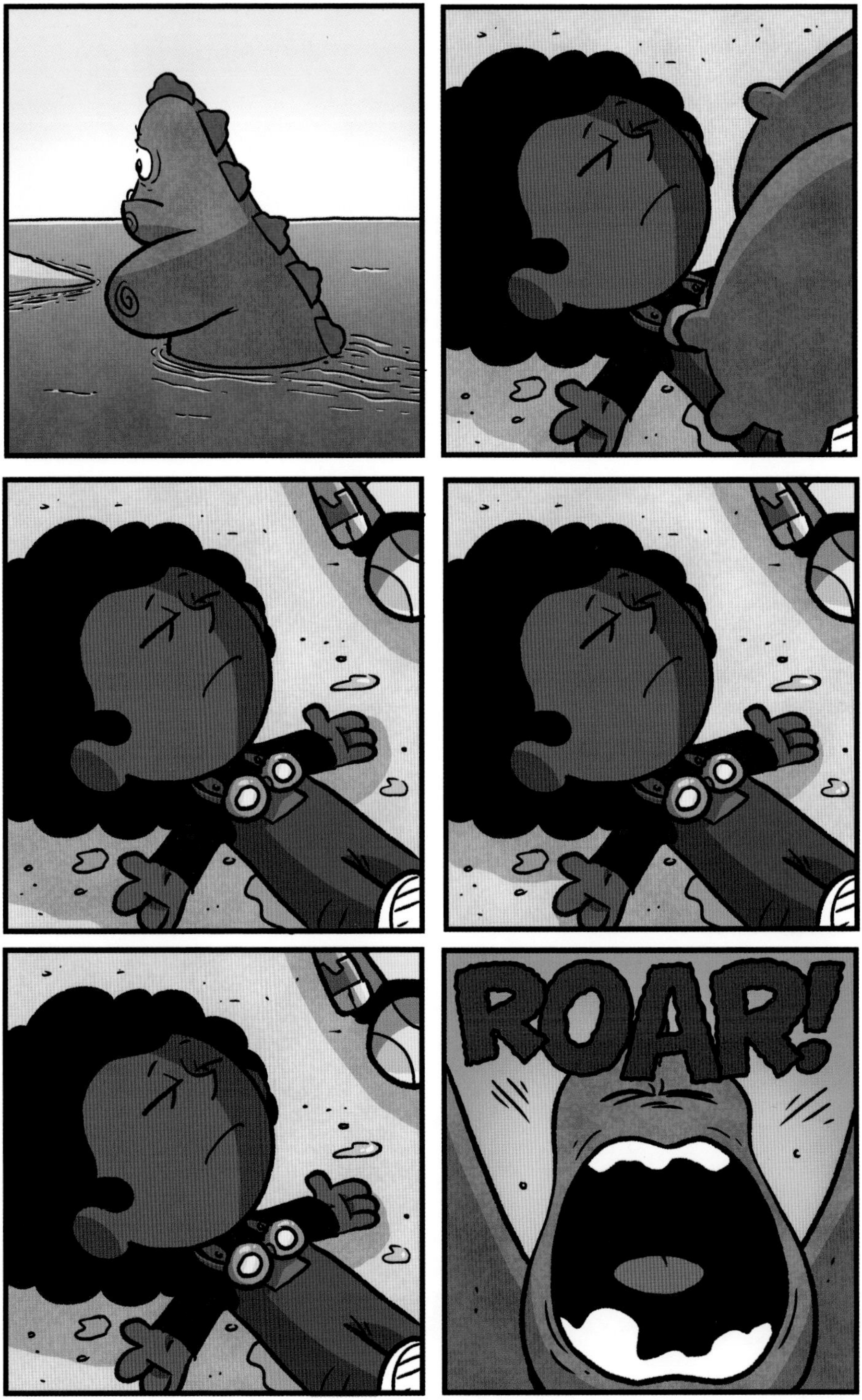
ROAR!

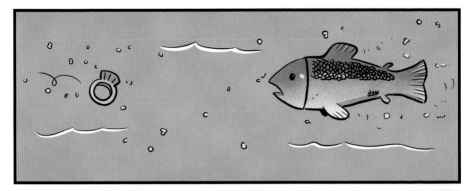

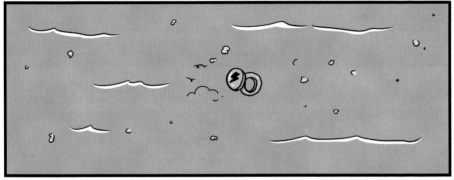

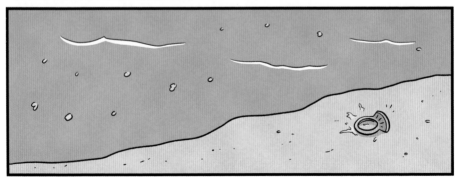

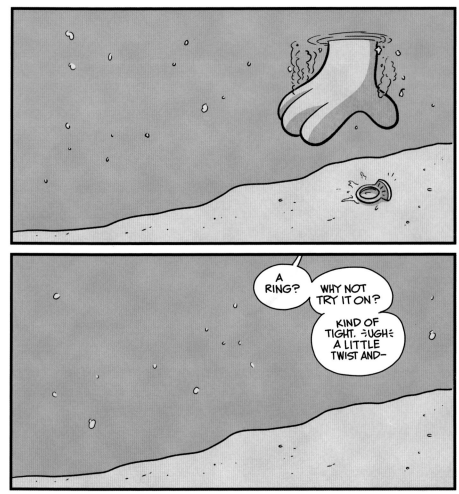

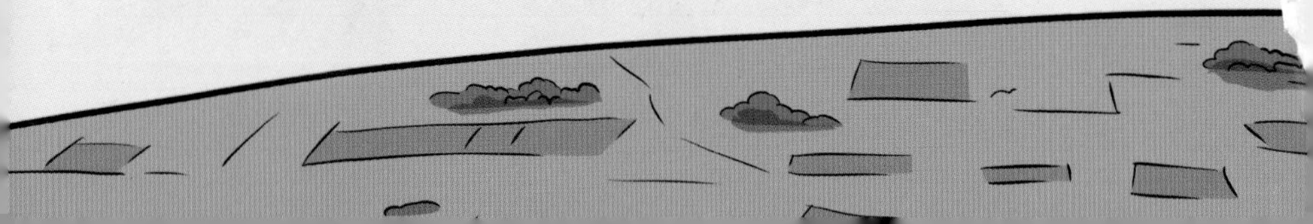